Den~~ise~~ storytelling. Her novels r~~...~~ strives to ~~pen entertaining~~ the ~~heart.~~ She's an ~~RWA~~ English from the Unive~~...~~ isn't writing, she enjoys ~~...~~ ~~...~~ below. chatting with readers. Foll~~ow her on~~ social media.

Instagram: @Denise_Wheatley_Writer
Twitter: @DeniseWheatley
BookBub: @DeniseNWheatley
Goodreads: Denise N. Wheatley

Having written over ninety novels, **Tara Taylor Quinn** is a *USA TODAY* bestselling author with more than seven million copies sold. She is known for delivering intense, emotional fiction. Tara is a past president of Romance Writers of America and a seven-time RITA® Award finalist. She has also appeared on TV across the country, including *CBS Sunday Morning.* She supports the National Domestic Violence Hotline.

Also by Tara Taylor Quinn

Her Detective's Secret Intent
Shielded in the Shadows
Colton's Killer Pursuit
Colton 911: Family Defender
Colton's Lethal Reunion

Discover more at millsandboon.co.uk

COLD CASE
TRUE CRIME

DENISE N. WHEATLEY

FALLING FOR
HIS SUSPECT

TARA TAYLOR QUINN

MILLS & BOON

First Published in Great Britain 2021
by Mills & Boon, an imprint of HarperCollins*Publishers* Ltd
1 London Bridge Street, London, SE1 9GF

www.harpercollins.co.uk

HarperCollins*Publishers*
1st Floor, Watermarque Building,
Ringsend Road, Dublin 4, Ireland

Cold Case True Crime © 2021 Denise N. Wheatley
Falling for His Suspect © 2021 TTQ Books LLC

ISBN: 978-0-263-28343-3

0621

MIX
Paper from
responsible sources
FSC™ C007454

This book is produced from independently certified FSC™ paper to ensure responsible forest management.

For more information visit: www.harpercollins.co.uk/green

Printed and bound in Spain
by CPI, Barcelona

COLD CASE
TRUE CRIME

DENISE N. WHEATLEY

To my mother, who's the most glamorous bookworm
I know. Thank you for introducing me to the wonderful
world of Harlequin all those years ago.

Chapter One

Samantha Vincent flinched when the coffee shop door slammed shut behind her. She stared down the dark, vacant street in search of her car—she hadn't realized she'd parked so far away.

The temperature had dropped severely since she'd arrived at the café. There was now a stinging chill in the night air. She set out toward the sidewalk, tightening her houndstooth-patterned scarf in an effort to block the wind as it whistled eerily past her ears.

Samantha had spent the day working on her popular true crime cold case blog, *Someone Knows Something*, and time had gotten away from her. By now, businesses were closed and most residents of small-town Gattenburg, Illinois, had retired for the evening.

A frigid breeze whipped through her golden-brown bob and blew open Samantha's black wool peacoat, sending unsettling shivers throughout her entire body. But it wasn't just the icy climate that had unnerved her.

She was still rattled by an email she'd received from Ava Jennings, an old high school friend whose family Samantha had grown close to after spending countless days at their home during her teenage years. In her message, Ava pleaded with Samantha to investigate her brother Jacob's mysterious death, which police had just officially stated was cold with no leads.

Tree branches scraped against dim streetlights that barely illuminated the road. Samantha glanced down at the ground, her lone shadow a stark reminder that she was unaccompanied in the unnerving darkness. Moments like these brought on paranoid thoughts of all the unsolved cases she worked so hard to crack. Many of those victims found themselves in her exact same position seconds before their demise—isolated and vulnerable.

Samantha pushed those disturbing thoughts out of her mind and hurried along the pavement. Her feet ached in her high-heeled boots. But in spite of the pain, she clenched her jaw and fought through it, anxious to get off the desolate street and inside her car.

Just when Samantha's convertible appeared in the hazy distance, the sound of screeching tires pierced her eardrums.

She stopped abruptly. The vehicle's engine emitted a menacing roar.

Samantha spun around, almost losing her footing. Bright yellow headlights blinded her squinted chestnut eyes. She inhaled sharply, watching while the black sedan crept toward her.

She curled her hands into tight fists and took a step back, her lean legs quivering in the wind. Remembering the mini stun gun she'd slipped into her back pocket, Samantha pulled it out and contemplated making a run for her car. But she was too afraid to turn her back on the man she presumed was behind the wheel.

Collin Wentworth...

That's the name Ava had mentioned several times throughout her email as she dissected the details of her brother's murder.

Collin and Jacob had been childhood friends who grew

apart during their teenage years once Collin went rogue. The incident that officially ended their friendship occurred one night when Collin convinced Jacob to accompany him on a wild joyride in a stolen vehicle. After being apprehended by the police, Jacob received six months in a juvenile detention center while Collin was given probation. That's when Jacob realized it was time for them to go their separate ways. But the pair remained cordial over the years, and Collin even hired Jacob to work for him at Westman's Automotive Factory, where Jacob served as a team assembler building car engines and Collin acted as the facility's general manager.

The day Jacob's body was found, he'd met with Collin to discuss the whereabouts of three fellow team assemblers who had gone missing. The official police report noted that Jacob had been seen walking out of the factory with Collin while having what appeared to be a heated conversation. After a brief exchange, they went their separate ways. Collin admitted to police that he'd spoken with Jacob the day he went missing. But he refused to disclose the details of their conversation. Ava believed that Collin was the last person to see Jacob alive.

Collin was a narcissist whose temper exploded when he drank. From bar fights to the destruction of property, public intoxication to reckless driving, his foul reputation certainly preceded him. But because Collin's father was Walter Wentworth, Gattenburg's chief of police, he usually got off with light warnings and slaps on the wrist.

Ava was convinced that Collin was withholding information that could help solve the case.

Beep, beep!

Samantha jumped at the sound of the blaring horn. The looming car was getting closer. She couldn't help but wonder whether Collin had seen her latest blog post, where she'd insisted that he could've been a huge help in Jacob's death investigation had he simply cooperated with the police.

News tended to spread quickly throughout Gattenburg, and Collin seemed to have undercover eyes and ears all over town.

Samantha shoved her trembling fingers inside her handbag in search of her key fob. When sharp metal edges grazed her palm, she grabbed it and pounded the remote until her taillights blinked up ahead.

Her calf muscles throbbed as she sprinted into the street. The second she grasped her door handle, screeching brakes brought the menacing car to a halt right next to her. She tightened the grip on her stun gun, watching through the corner of her eye as the tinted passenger window lowered.

"I thought that was you…" a low voice boomed.

Samantha's heart thumped erratically at the thought of coming face-to-face with Collin. She bent down and peered inside the car.

When she locked eyes with Gregory Harris, a handsome police detective who was new to Gattenburg, Samantha inhaled sharply.

"Officer Harris!" she exclaimed, gripping her chest with relief. "Hello. Hi. I, uh—sorry. I thought you were someone else."

He chuckled softly, his full, sexy lips spreading into a crooked grin. "Really? Well, I hope you're not too disappointed that it's just me."

"No," she murmured, reaching back and discreetly slipping her stun gun into her pocket. "Not at all."

A jolt of heat shot up Samantha's spine. The detective had had that effect on her ever since she met him last month at Hannah's Coffee Shop.

He had just moved to Gattenburg from Chicago, where he'd worked on the police force for over ten years. Detective Harris claimed to have left in search of a slower, more peaceful lifestyle. But the bitterness behind his dark brown eyes told a different story when he spoke of his departure.

The detective reached out and turned down the radio, his muscular arm bulging through his navy cashmere sweater. "I'm guessing you just left the coffee shop after working on your blog all day?"

"You guessed right. I usually don't stay this late, but I was on a roll."

"Wow. Your dedication to reporting on all those mysterious cold cases is admirable. That piece you wrote last week about the kidnapped student at the University of Illinois? Impressive."

Samantha's skin tingled under his intense stare. "Why, thank you. I appreciate that."

"You're welcome. So, what's the latest post about?"

She paused, her cheerful expression wilting into one of concern.

"The death of an old high school friend." Samantha's voice quaked. She cleared her throat before continuing. "His name was Jacob Jennings. You may have heard of him. He died mysteriously months ago, and his body was found two blocks away from Westman's Automotive Factory."

"Hmm," the detective sighed, running his large hand over his freshly trimmed goatee. "That name doesn't ring a bell."

Samantha dropped her head in disappointment. "Of course it doesn't. The case went cold less than forty-eight hours into the investigation. The Gattenburg Police Department has done nothing to solve it. That's why I've committed to helping Jacob's sister get to the bottom of it. And I'll be using *Someone Knows Something* to provide the community with updates on my progress. If I can stir up some sort of public outcry, maybe the police department will feel pressured to reopen the case."

She hesitated, waiting to hear Gregory's response. When he shifted in his seat and remained silent, she pressed on.

"Hey, I'd love to get your take on the situation. The fact that you're new to the Gattenburg PD is huge. You'd bring a fresh eye to the investigation. Plus you've got access to the file and critical inside information. If we join forces, I bet you and I could—"

Detective Harris held up his hand. "Hold on, Samantha. First off, let me just say that I am very sorry to hear about the loss of your friend. With that being said, I'm new to this force, and there are certain protocols that I need to follow. I know I haven't been in Gattenburg for very long, but judging from the upstanding reputation and track record of Chief Wentworth, I can't imagine he didn't do all that he could to ensure Jacob's death was thoroughly investigated."

Despite the gust of cold air that swept past Samantha, she felt herself growing hot with frustration. She loosened her scarf and took a deep breath.

"Detective Harris, there is so much more to this case than you know. And if I may be blunt, there are rumors that some of the men in blue working next to you aren't as ethical as they may seem."

An uneasy silence filled the air. Samantha crossed her arms and tapped her foot rapidly against the asphalt. She knew she was being forward, but after hearing that a new detective would be joining the force, she'd hoped there would be renewed interest in the investigation, along with a fresh perspective.

After several tense seconds, the detective finally spoke up.

"Listen. The reason I'm no longer with the Chicago PD is because I refused to abide by the department's shady code of silence. So if I suspected there was any corruption going on within Gattenburg's law enforcement agency, believe me, I'd be the first one to call it out."

Samantha resisted the urge to slam her fist against the hood of his car. "Says the man who joined the force literally a month ago..."

"Wow. Okay," Gregory sighed, running his hand down his thick, closely cropped black hair. "Samantha, I understand that you and your friend are hurting. But please know that this force's only objective is to do the right thing. I may be new, but I've had connections here in Gattenburg for years. And I don't believe there are any cover-ups happening. So, with that being said, maybe we should end this conversation before it goes too far—"

"Fine," Samantha interrupted, taking a step back. "And with all due respect, Officer Harris, I think you're being a bit naive. If nothing else, I do hope you'll continue following my blog. It'll open your eyes to the truth. And with *that* being said, have a good night."

Before the detective could respond, Samantha climbed inside her car and sped off.

GREGORY FELT A pull in his chest as he watched Samantha drive away. Bumping into her had been such a pleasant surprise. He'd barely been able to control the shudders of excitement in his gut during their conversation. But that buzz completely fizzled after their encounter ended in disaster.

He drove somberly down the street before noticing Samantha stopped at a red light up ahead. The detective quickly maneuvered his car alongside hers and rolled down the window.

When he glanced over, he noticed tears trickling down her cheeks.

"Hey! Sam!" he called out, frantically waving his arms.

She stared straight ahead. As soon as the light turned green, she jetted off.

Gregory hit the accelerator and followed her. Before he knew it, he'd trailed her all the way home. When she noticed him parked in front of her house, she stormed over to his car.

"Here we go…" he muttered, opening the door and stepping out.

"What are you doing?" Samantha snapped. "Did you really just follow me home?"

"I did. I, uh… I wanted to apologize for the way I responded to you." He tried to ignore the rush of energy he felt at the sight of her curls blowing seductively across her delicate face.

Focus, he thought, shoving his hands deep inside his pockets.

"I know that losing a friend so tragically can't be easy," he continued, "and I hope I didn't seem insensitive. I'm just very protective of my brothers in blue. But I should've been more sympathetic toward you."

"Humph," Samantha huffed, tilting her head to the side and studying him closely. "Well…thank you for that. I accept your apology."

Gregory felt his taut muscles relax when he sensed that she had dropped her guard a bit.

She shook her head and stared up at the sky. "This all just feels so surreal. I'm not used to covering cases that hit so close to home. And the fact that this one hasn't been solved really hurts. It actually makes me wish I would've followed in my father's footsteps and gone into law enforcement. But that didn't end well."

"What do you mean?" he asked.

"My dad was killed in the line of duty back in Chicago. The fire went out of my desire to join the force after that."

Gregory moved in closer and gently placed his hand on Samantha's arm. "I'm so sorry. I didn't realize your father died on the job."

"That's what brought my mom and me here to Gattenburg. We needed a fresh start in what we thought would be a safe town. And now this. Which is why I can't just stand by and do nothing. I went through that once with my dad's killer. I refuse to go through it again."

"Wait, what do you mean? Your father's murderer wasn't apprehended?"

"No." Samantha sighed, dabbing her fingertips against the corners of her damp eyes. "The offender was a big-time drug dealer who'd been paying off several city officials. Apparently that dirty money meant more to them than justice for my father."

"You certainly have my sympathies, Samantha. But when it comes to Jacob's case, I'd be remiss if I didn't advise you to use caution."

"Why?"

The detective hesitated, struggling to choose his words wisely. "I'll put it this way. Chief Wentworth and Gattenburg's judicial powers that be have a very...*amiable* relationship. They make special efforts to look out for one another. And while I now know that the investigation into Jacob's death concluded somewhat hastily—"

"Somewhat," Samantha interjected.

"—it could in fact be because Collin is Chief Wentworth's son," Gregory continued, purposely ignoring her sarcasm. "And I'm not saying that Collin was involved, because that I don't know. I'm just going off what you're telling me. But what I *do* know is that Chief Wentworth is a trusted leader in this community. As far as the higher-ups are concerned, he can do no wrong. And while I do respect the chief, I'll admit he can be one relentless son of a bitch."

Samantha backed away from him. "I'm not afraid of the chief! He may have a hold on this town, and he's clearly got all of you under his spell. But he's got nothing on me."

"I'm not saying you should be afraid," Gregory lamented. "Just be careful."

When Samantha waved him off, he pressed on.

"Listen to me. Chief Wentworth has a lot of power. And when it comes to his son, he does appear to be jaded. If you even insinuate that Collin's involved some sort of illegal activity, the chief could see to it that Jacob's case is never reopened."

Samantha threw her arms out at her sides. "It shouldn't matter *who's* involved in Jacob's death. The bottom line is he deserves a proper investigation. And that starts with Chief Wentworth putting an end to the nepotism and doing his job. He should want to get Jacob's killer off the street, even if it is his own son. Now, if you're not with me, then you're against me. So thanks for letting me know where you stand. We're done here."

She spun around and stormed up her walkway.

"I'm not against you, Samantha!" Gregory called out. "It's just that…" His voice faded as the sting of remorse burned his throat.

He waited until she was safely inside the house before hopping in his car and speeding off, anxious to get home and check her blog to find out what she'd reported on Jacob's case thus far.

Chapter Two

And that, my dear readers, Samantha typed, is how you color code your calendar in order to remain organized throughout the week.

She saved the document to her *Elevate Women's Journal* file, then glanced around the dining area of Danica's Deli.

The afternoon crowd had already cleared out of the quaint 1950s-style eatery. Most of the red vinyl booths and high-top tables were empty. A few patrons still sat in swivel stools along the counter, chatting up the servers while finishing their meals.

Samantha's head was still buzzing after meeting with Ava for lunch a couple of hours ago. She couldn't wait to post the latest intel she'd just received on Jacob's murder.

Before she was able to get to that, Samantha had to edit her monthly "A Woman's Guide to Practical Living" column for the women's journal, which was what paid the bills.

Just as she began composing an email to her column's editor, Regina, her cell phone buzzed.

"Speaking of the devil," she moaned after glancing down and seeing a text message notification from Regina pop up on the screen.

Samantha rushed to email the article to her, then opened the text.

Hey, Sam! Please be sure to turn your column in to me before 3:00 p.m. I'd like to finalize the layout by tomorrow so that we can go to press before the end of the week. Thanks! Regina

"Two steps ahead of ya, Reggie Reg," Samantha muttered as she replied to the message.

Good afternoon! Have you checked your email recently? I just sent the article to you. Looking forward to hearing your thoughts. Thank you!

As soon as she sent the text, Samantha felt a strong, warm hand grip her shoulder. She gasped and practically jumped out of her seat before grabbing the edge of the table and spinning around.

When she saw Detective Harris standing over her, Samantha closed her eyes and emitted a slow sigh of relief.

"Hey, you," he chuckled, clearly amused by her startled reaction. "I didn't scare you, did I?"

"Um, *yeah*, you did."

In spite of still being irritated with him for refusing to get involved with the investigation of Jacob's death, Samantha felt her demeanor soften at the sight of the detective's seductive smirk.

"You can't just walk up on somebody like that from behind and put your hands on them," she continued, her high-pitched tone filled with sass.

"My apologies. Next time I'll be sure to walk up on you from the front before I put my hands on you…"

Samantha eyed the detective curiously, taken aback by his blatant flirtation.

"So what's up?" he asked, glancing over at her computer screen. "You working on your blog?"

"Not yet. I just wrote an article for the women's journal

I work for called *Elevate*. Now that it's done, I'll be getting back to *Someone Knows Something*."

As Detective Harris's gaze traveled from Samantha's eyes to her lips and lingered there, she felt flickers of heat creep up the back of her neck. She grabbed her glass of iced green tea and took several long sips.

"I checked out your blog when I got home last night. After our—" he paused, staring up at the ceiling as if searching for the right words to say "—rather *spirited* conversation, I decided to look a little deeper into Jacob's death. But I noticed you hadn't posted much information on it."

"That's because I didn't have much information on it up until now. I just had lunch with his sister, Ava, and she shared a ton of info with me."

Samantha paused, peering at the detective as he appeared to hang on her every word.

"Wait." She continued, "What's with the sudden curiosity? I thought you weren't interested in finding out the truth about Jacob's murder."

Detective Harris turned away from her. He shifted his weight from one foot to the other, then shrugged his shoulders.

"I was never *not* interested. You've just managed to capture my attention."

Samantha couldn't tell whether he was referring to her blog, or her, or both. Either way, his suggestive statement caused a tingling sensation to swirl inside her chest.

"Oh, so I've captured your attention, huh?" she quipped.

"Yes. You have. And don't be shocked by what I'm about to say, but I'd actually like to check out the area where Jacob's body was found."

She leaned back in her chair as her eyelids lowered with surprise. "Really? *Wow.* I am shocked to hear that. And what's interesting is that after meeting with Ava today, I was thinking I should go check out the crime scene as well.

Maybe even post some photos of it on *Someone Knows Something*. You never know. Those pics might trigger someone to come forward with information on something they've seen or heard."

The detective glanced down at his watch. The corners of his shapely lips curled into a subtle smile.

Just as thoughts of how his mouth would feel pressed against hers crept into Samantha's mind, he spoke up.

"Well, what do you think of us heading over there together now?" he asked before abruptly holding out his hands. "I mean, unless you're too busy and don't have time."

"No, no. Now is cool, actually. That way I can get those photos taken and include them in my next blog post. Plus this will give me a chance to tell you everything I found out from Ava today. If you want to hear about it, that is," she added quickly.

Samantha folded her hands tightly, anxiously awaiting his response. It was clear that she and the detective were both walking on eggshells with one another as they wondered just how far this investigation would take them. She hoped that this would be the start of his involvement in the cold case.

"Sure," he said, readjusting the shoulder holster that was tucked inside his black leather bomber jacket. "I'm open to hearing more about it. Did you drive here?"

"I did. I'm assuming you did as well?"

"Yes. Why don't you leave your car here and I'll drive?"

The thought of sitting in the car next to Detective Harris caused a wave of nervous flutters in the pit of Samantha's stomach.

Okay, she thought to herself. *Stop acting like a googly-eyed high schooler and pull yourself together.*

"Yes, that does make sense," she said, struggling not to sound as excited as she felt.

Samantha looked down and noticed that her hands were

shaking as she closed her laptop and slid her things inside her tote bag. She peeked over at the detective, hoping he wasn't watching her fumble about. Luckily he was too busy tapping away on his cell phone to notice.

After taking a few discreet, calming breaths, Samantha drained her glass of iced tea, stood up and grabbed her bag.

"Are you ready?" she asked. *"Partner?"*

"Hold on, now, hold on," Detective Harris chuckled. "Don't go getting too excited. Just because I'm accompanying you to the crime scene doesn't mean I'm about to get all wrapped up in this case with you."

"We'll see," she rebutted.

And with that, Samantha spun around on her heels, brushing up against the detective's gym-honed chest before sashaying toward the door with an extra twist in her hips.

GREGORY SWALLOWED HARD, struggling to compose himself. He couldn't take his eyes off Samantha as she breezed past him. Her slim, curvy silhouette, which was perfectly outlined in her cropped moto jacket and dark blue skinny jeans, roused a sensation within him that he hadn't felt in quite some time.

"You coming?" Samantha asked him, her hair swinging over her shoulder when she turned around and peered back at him.

He put a little pep in his step and hurried toward the door.

"Yep, I'm right behind you."

Pull it together, man...

Gregory held the door open for Samantha, then shuffled over to her right side, making sure that she walked on the inside of the sidewalk.

"Such a gentleman," she gushed. "Thank you."

He glanced over at her, wondering whether her flirty demeanor was genuine or if she was putting on a show in an effort to lure him further into her investigation. Either way, he liked it.

"I'm parked right up ahead, on the corner," Gregory told her while pointing at a black Chevy sedan with black tinted windows.

"Nice. This makes me feel like I'm going on a real-life ride along."

"Uh-oh," he chuckled, amused by her excitement as she practically skipped toward the car and grabbed the passenger door handle.

Gregory clicked the key fob. When the doors unlocked, he moved in a bit closer than necessary and gently placed his hand over hers. "Here, let me get that for you."

Samantha looked up at Gregory and emitted a slight gasp. The pair stood so close to one another that he could smell the piece of cinnamon candy rolling around in her mouth.

"Thanks," she said quietly, taking a step back.

Gregory opened the door and once again found his eyes stuck on Samantha, watching while she slipped inside the car. She looked up at him and opened her mouth, as if she were going to say something. But then she turned and looked straight ahead, remaining silent.

The detective would've been confused had it not been for the glimmer in her eyes. He'd seen that twinkle time and time again while on the force, in the gaze of many people he'd encountered over the years. By now he knew that it was an indication of pure gratitude for listening, for taking them seriously.

He jogged around to the driver's side, patting his jacket just to make sure the report he'd copied before leaving the station was still securely tucked away inside his pocket. It was.

Gregory hadn't yet told Samantha that he'd pulled Jacob's file and studied up on his case. He didn't know how deeply involved he wanted to get just yet. The detective figured he'd see how today went, then decide from there.

"So the location where Jacob's body was found isn't too far from here," he told her after climbing inside the car and pulling off.

"Not at all. According to the map app on my phone, the exact address is less than three miles away."

"Right. So Westman's Automotive Factory is on Everhart Avenue, and Jacob's body was recovered in an alleyway off Kenwood Street."

"Correct," Samantha confirmed. "And Kenwood is located two blocks away from Westman's, which you already know is where Jacob worked."

Gregory noticed a change in her demeanor. She was sitting straight up in her seat, her expression stern as she typed away on her cell phone.

Gone was the coy, playful attitude she'd had back at the deli. She was now strictly business. Had he not known any better, Samantha's authoritative attitude would've had him thinking she was a member of law enforcement. But then he remembered that her father had been a police officer, and he assumed she'd acquired some of that commanding bravado from him.

The detective glanced down at her slender left hand, which was perfectly manicured with pale pink nail polish. She wore a silver band on her pinkie finger, but her ring finger was noticeably bare.

What are you doing? he asked himself.

Gregory never paid attention to those types of minor details, especially when it came to a woman's marital status.

Stay focused...

"So according to Ava," Samantha continued, "the alleyway where Jacob was found is on the eight hundred block of Kenwood."

"Yes. Near housing numbers eight fifteen and eight seventeen, to be exact. I saw that his body was discovered in between two large metal dumpsters. And honestly, after seeing the crime scene photos, it looked to me as though his body had been forced into that small space. There's no way he could've ended up there on his own, especially if he was high on drugs like the police report suggested, and…"

Gregory's voice trailed off when he noticed Samantha gripping her chest while scrutinizing him intently.

"After seeing the crime scene photos?" she repeated. "And like the police report suggested? Umph. Sounds to me like you've done your homework on this case. I thought you weren't interested in getting involved. What's with the sudden change of heart?"

There's a beautiful, intelligent, inquisitive woman who cares about this deceased individual and who's captured my attention, he wanted to blurt out. But instead, the detective kept his cool and racked his brain for a more appropriate answer.

"Well," he began right before stopping at a red light and turning to her, "after that heated exchange we had in front of your house, you sparked my curiosity. Your pain over Jacob's death and desire to see him get the proper justice pushed me to take a look at the police report and find out what took place during the investigation."

"I appreciate that," Samantha uttered, crossing her arms and staring out the window. She eyed the quaint Tudor-style homes and their perfectly manicured lawns lining the narrow street, while struggling to keep her cool. "I'm sure it didn't take long for you to realize just how botched, rushed and inadequate that investigation was. I mean, seriously, it was a complete sham. I'd love to see that police report. It's probably one tiny little paragraph long. Tops."

Gregory once again held his hand to his pocket and discreetly tucked the police report farther inside. No matter how involved he got with Samantha and this case, he had no plans of going against department policy and disclosing any of the investigation's confidential details. At least that was his intention…

"So tell me more about your meeting with Ava," the detective said as he made a right turn onto Everhart Avenue. The bleak, desolate street, which was where Westman's Automotive Factory was located, was a drastic switch from the charming areas surrounding it. "You said you found out a lot more about Jacob's death than you knew before. What'd you learn?"

"Well, we already knew this but, we talked about the medical examiner's ruling that Jacob's death was an accidental drug overdose. That's a huge red flag in the case."

"Okay, and why is that a red flag?"

Gregory noticed Samantha slump down in her seat as they drove past Westman's, which took up half the block. Her eyes filled with tears as she peered out at the industrial building's drab gray cement exterior. It was clear that the owners hadn't done much to maintain the factory's appearance since it had been built in the 1960s. Its few dark windows were covered in thick layers of dust. Old, rusted auto parts had been carelessly tossed along the side of the discolored outer wall. Overgrown patches of grass blew against the crumbling facade.

"Wow," she sighed. "This place just reeks of depression. There's something sinister about it." She shook her head and turned away. "Anyway, the idea of Jacob overdosing on drugs is asinine. He's never done drugs a day in his life. And trust me, he liked to party back in the day. He could drink anybody in this town under the table. But drugs? That's never been Jacob's thing."

"Hmm," the detective breathed thoughtfully while making a left turn down Kenwood Street. "That's interesting. I did a little research on Westman's and saw that they have a pretty strong support system for former drug addicts."

"Yeah. Ava mentioned that, too. Before Jacob died, he talked up the company's bid to help recovering addicts get back on their feet by giving employment opportunities to people with felony drug convictions."

Gregory pulled his car into the alleyway where Jacob's body had been found and let up on the accelerator. "True. But before the employees could gain permanent employment, they had to complete a one-week second-chance program. If they didn't get through that and pass random drug tests during their three-month probationary period, then they weren't officially hired."

"Please." Samantha snorted as the detective crept toward a pair of rusted-out green metal dumpsters. "Do you really believe that?"

"Yes. I do. Westman's has been applauded by the entire community of Gattenburg for their efforts to help recovering addicts stay clean and obtain job opportunities. The mayor even honored the factory's efforts last month with a community impact award."

Samantha slid toward the edge of her seat and pointed up ahead. "It looks like those dumpsters are the only two in the alley. This must be the crime scene."

Gregory craned his neck and eyed the entire length of the passage. "I think you're right." He parked the car off to the side near a garage door. "Let's hop out and take a closer look."

A chill swept through Samantha as she opened the camera app on her cell phone. She stepped out of the car and took several pictures of the waste containers, moving back and forth in an effort to capture every angle.

"So wait a minute," she said, bending down and shuffling in closer. "Jacob's body was found in this tight little space in between these two dumpsters?"

"From the looks of the crime scene photos, yes."

While Samantha examined the cement walls located on

either side of the bins, Gregory found himself once again unable to tear his gaze away from her long, lean legs.

She placed her hand on her curvy hip and tilted her head to the side.

"Judging from the snug proximity of the dumpsters to these walls," Samantha continued, "there's no room for them to be moved farther apart. So I agree with you in that Jacob had to have been shoved in between this space by somebody else. There's no way he could've ended up here on his own. Especially if he was high on drugs, as law enforcement would like for us to believe."

Just as Samantha began taking close-up photographs of the area, a loud engine roared down at the end of the alleyway. She and Gregory simultaneously jerked their heads toward the thunderous rumble.

"What the…" the detective uttered.

He stood up and tried to get a better look at the vehicle. But before he could catch a real glimpse, its tires screeched and skidded down the block.

"Got it," Samantha said while staring down at her cell phone.

"Got what?"

"A few pics of that vehicle. Looks like it was a white van with some sort of blue and orange signage along the side."

"Hmm," Gregory grunted. "Interesting. Sounds like it may have been some sort of business vehicle, then?"

Samantha stared up at him, nodding her head knowingly while holding up her phone. "The photos are a bit blurry. But if I'm not mistaken, I spy an orange letter *R* and a blue letter *Y*. Wanna take a wild guess as to what company in Gattenburg has blue and orange signage on their white vans, with that lettering in their name?"

Gregory took the phone and scrolled through the fuzzy images.

"Westman's Automotive Factory," Samantha blurted out

before giving him a chance to respond. "Do you see it?" she asked, frantically tapping her fingertip against the phone screen. "Right there. Can you make it out? Because I can."

"Yeah, you're right," Gregory replied smoothly in an effort to keep her calm. He could tell by the shrill tone of her voice that she was getting worked up.

Samantha threw her arms out to her sides and kicked up a few rocks with her black ankle boot. "Good to know that it's not just me. You see what I see."

"No, it's not just you." The detective scrolled back to the clearest photo and enlarged it. "I definitely see the end of Westman's company name here." An uneasy twinge pulled inside his chest. "Hey, would you mind texting those photos to me?"

"Of course not." Samantha took the phone and pulled up his name in her list of contacts. "It looks like the only number I have saved for you is your work phone down at the station."

"Really? I could've sworn I'd given you my personal cell the night we ran into one another at the community center fundraiser."

"Nope," she chirped. "You didn't."

He held out his hand. "Here, let me program it in for you. I'll give you my personal email address, too."

Samantha handed him the phone, her eyebrows rising curiously.

"You know," Gregory quickly added, "in the event that you ever need to send me something."

"Mmm-hmm," she muttered, her tone filled with skepticism. It seemed clear to her that the detective was slowly getting more involved in Jacob's case than he'd initially intended. "Well, I appreciate that. From the looks of things," she continued, pointing toward the alleyway entrance where the Westman's van had appeared, "I just may be needing you."

Gregory stopped typing his email address into the phone and glanced up at her, wondering whether she was referring to more than just the investigation. He couldn't quite tell from the tense, faraway look in her eyes.

"So," Samantha continued, "don't you find it odd that the factory's vehicle was creeping past the crime scene like that? Then the driver revved its engine like a complete maniac once he saw us?"

"I don't know," he said, not wanting to make her fearful. "The factory is located a couple of blocks away from here. So the drive-by could've simply been a coincidence."

Samantha crossed her arms tightly in front of her. "Nah, I'm not going for that. I think there's more to it. And you know what they say—criminals love returning to the scene of the crime."

Gregory saved his information in Samantha's phone and handed it back to her. "That is what they say. But when it comes to this case, I don't want to jump to any unsubstantiated conclusions."

She twisted her lips warily. "Come on. Seriously? That was no coincidence. But anyway, I'm texting the photos to you now. I can't wait to show these to Ava and tell her about how you and I came out here and—"

"Hey," Gregory interrupted, holding out his hand. "Let me say this. I'm not trying to control whom you discuss your personal investigation into this case with or anything. But I'd like for you to refrain from telling anyone you've been talking about it with me. You know I'm new on the force, and I'm all about following the proper code of police conduct."

"Okay," Samantha replied coolly, shrugging her shoulders as if the request didn't bother her.

But when the detective noticed her pink-glossed lips turn downward, he knew that it had.

"Look, I hope you can understand why I don't want you to—"

"I do," she interjected before he could finish. "So no worries. I get it."

Gregory turned around and eyed the alleyway entrance again. "Well, now that we've both gotten a look at the crime scene and you've taken your photos, we should probably get out of here."

"Good idea. I don't want to be here if that van comes back around. Thanks for bringing me along to check it out. Between my meeting with Ava and these pics, I've got some great new leads to post on *Someone Knows Something*."

"No problem. Glad you were able to join me."

The pair climbed inside the car. As Gregory headed back to the deli, Samantha began cropping and brightening the photos she'd taken at the crime scene.

Just when the detective began to wonder whether he needed to tone down his involvement with her and Jacob's case, he heard Samantha's cell phone ping.

She stared down at the screen for several moments before squealing loudly.

"What's going on over there?" Gregory asked.

"I just got a text message from Ava. She worked her magic and landed me a meeting with a woman named Kenzie Stevenson, who works at Westman's. Kenzie was really good friends with Jacob, and Ava thinks she's got some insight into the shady dealings happening inside the factory."

"Really? That's great. But I'm surprised to hear a current employee is willing to talk to you."

"Well, she's only doing so under one condition. I have to keep her identity anonymous. Kenzie's actually terrified of Collin. And like Ava and me, she's convinced he had something to do with Jacob's murder. We all agree that his enabling father, Chief Wentworth, helped him cover it up, too."

In spite of the chilly breeze blowing through the cracked window, Gregory felt beads of sweat forming along his hairline. He swiped his hand across his forehead and turned down Madison Street.

"Don't worry," Samantha continued as she slipped her cell phone inside her handbag, "I know the chief is your boss. So I don't expect you to agree with me on that."

"My views on this case aren't based on the fact that I report to Chief Wentworth. I know I'm a by-the-book kind of guy, but I do have a mind of my own," he told her before pointing up ahead. "Is that your convertible parked on the right?"

"It is. So, um…listen. Ava has arranged for me to meet with Kenzie tomorrow night after her shift at Westman's. We're getting together at seven. She wants to meet at Barron's Bar and Grill. I'm not sure if you've heard of it, but it's located on the outskirts of town, near Peoria."

Gregory pulled his car over and parked behind Samantha's. "Barron's, Barron's… Oh yeah, I'm familiar with it. Why are you all meeting all the way out there?"

"Because Kenzie doesn't want to risk running into someone from Westman's. There are a good number of people in this town who know that I'm reporting on Jacob's case. So to put it bluntly, she doesn't wanna be seen with me."

"Okay, well, all things considered, I guess I can understand that."

The detective watched as Samantha zipped her handbag and grabbed the door handle. He was surprised at the buzz of disappointment that fizzled in his head, knowing their time together was coming to an end.

"Thank you again for taking me to the crime scene," she said. "I really appreciate it. I'm feeling good about the headway that I'm making in this case."

"You're welcome. Thanks for riding along with me. I

look forward to keeping up with your progress. I'll definitely be keeping an eye out for your updated blog post."

"Do you have your new-post notifications turned on?" Samantha asked, pointing over at him playfully.

"I don't," Gregory chuckled, "but I'll be sure to turn them on the first chance I get."

"Good." She opened the door, then suddenly turned to the detective. "Hey, why don't you come out to Barron's tomorrow night and meet with Kenzie and me? I'd love for you to be there to hear what she has to say and get your take on everything from a detective's point of view."

Gregory put the car in Park and stared straight ahead, gripping the steering wheel a little tighter. While he did want to see Samantha again, he didn't want to do so during another investigative outing.

"I'm sorry, Samantha, but I can't. I—I just…"

"I understand," she sighed after his voice trailed off. "You don't want to get pulled into this case any further. But if you change your mind, you know where we'll be. And you have my cell phone number now, too."

"I do," he told her right before a surge of temptation came over him. But the detective resisted the urge to give in to it.

"I guess I'll see you around then," Samantha responded quietly. "Thanks again for this afternoon."

Gregory cringed when Samantha slammed the door. He cracked his knuckles while watching her strut in front of his car and climb inside hers. He longed to jump out and embrace her. Tell her how sorry he was that he couldn't get more involved.

For a brief moment, Gregory considered showing up at Barron's simply to protect Samantha. The meeting with Kenzie could be some sort of setup.

But he quickly pushed that thought out of his mind and forced himself to stay put, knowing he was doing the right thing. His instincts were telling him Kenzie could be trusted. Plus, the last thing he needed was a repeat of what had happened back in Chicago, where he'd made the mistake of getting heavily involved in a case that put both his livelihood and heart on the line. He'd wound up getting burned, *badly*, after the situation ended in disaster.

No good deed goes unpunished, his mother always told him. In that instance she was absolutely right. But not only had Gregory been punished, he was practically destroyed.

That experience was a part of his past he seldom discussed. It was too painful. Maybe one day he'd explain it to Samantha so she would understand why he'd chosen to keep his distance.

Chapter Three

Samantha glanced down at her cell phone. No new text messages or missed calls. She sighed heavily and took another sip of her merlot.

Samantha looked around Barron's Bar and Grill. The place wasn't too packed. A few groups of college students dressed in their sorority and fraternity paraphernalia were scattered around the bar area. Several jocks hovered over a pool table while a cluster of rowdy construction workers stood nearby, guzzling beers and waiting on them to finish their game.

She and Kenzie had been there for over an hour. While Kenzie stepped away to take a phone call, Samantha scanned the notes she'd been taking. She tried not to appear as appalled as she felt when Kenzie shared one wild Westman's story after another.

Samantha practically jumped out of her chair when her phone buzzed. She grabbed it and peered down at the screen. Her chest thumped with disappointment when she saw it was an email from her editor.

"Ugh," she grumbled, opening the message to find out whether her calendar organization article had been approved.

Samantha couldn't deny how disappointed she'd felt when Detective Harris shut down her offer to meet with

Kenzie. She was hoping he'd be an ally in helping get to the bottom of Jacob's murder. But Samantha now realized that she and Ava were in this fight alone.

"Oh well," she whispered before reading her email from Regina.

Hey Sam! Great job on your latest piece. I only have a couple of suggestions that I'd like you to include. Do you think you could break down potential differences between a working mom's schedule versus a stay-at-home mom's? I'm thinking that could affect how their calendars are organized.

Also, please include a paragraph or two on how a family could work together to maintain one large calendar that they can hang in a designated area in the home. Once you send those additions to me, I'll approve the article. Thanks! Reg

"I don't have time for this, Regina," Samantha mumbled before hitting the reply button. She knew she had a lot of nerve giving her editor attitude considering her writing job with *Elevate* helped to maintain her lifestyle. But all Samantha could think about was Jacob's cold case, especially now that she'd received a slew of intriguing new intel from Kenzie.

Sure, Reg, Samantha typed. I'll work on those changes and get them back to you tomorrow. Have a great evening. Samantha.

She sent the message, then glanced outside, wondering what was taking Kenzie so long to come back. Samantha caught a glimpse of her pacing the parking lot, her tight jet-black curls whipping around her face as she appeared to be yelling into the phone. Judging from her crumpled expression and wild hand gestures, it was not a pleasant conversation.

Samantha closed her notebook and slid it inside her handbag. From the looks of things, it appeared as though she and Kenzie were done.

Just as she scooted her chair away from the table and stood up, Samantha noticed a black Chevy with black-tinted windows pulling into Barron's parking lot.

She froze. Her heart suddenly thumped so hard in her chest that she trembled, causing the pearlized buttons on her cream silk blouse to rattle.

It can't be, she thought.

But when Detective Harris stepped out of the car and strutted toward the bar's entrance, Samantha realized that, indeed, it was.

After he swaggered through the door, she raised her hand in the air and waved, immediately catching his attention. The detective nodded his head and flashed a smile that caused a wave of lust to roll through her stomach.

Calm down, girl, Samantha told herself, taking a deep breath and straightening her shoulders. The last thing she wanted was for Detective Harris to know just how thrilled she was to see him. But as he slowly approached her with outstretched arms and an even broader grin, it appeared as though he was just as excited to see her.

"I bet I'm the last person you thought would walk through that door tonight," he said, running his hands along her waistline, then clenching them against the small of her back.

"To say that is an understatement would be putting it lightly," Samantha murmured. She wrapped her arms around him, inhaling the sandalwood cologne pulsating off his neck. The pair embraced for several seconds before simultaneously pulling away from each other, as if on cue.

"Well, before we get into just how surprised you are to see me, I'm gonna go grab a beer from the bar." He pointed at the empty chair next to Samantha. "Hey, where's Kenzie? She didn't leave already, did she?"

"No, she's still here. She's out in the parking lot on a phone call."

"Okay, cool. What are you drinking?"

"Merlot."

"I'll grab you another one. Be right back."

Gregory took a few steps away from the table without taking his eyes off Samantha. She had to admit, she liked the detective after dark. He was much more relaxed and even flirtier than he'd been yesterday afternoon.

Detective Harris turned around coolly and flagged down the bartender. Samantha observed his smooth demeanor, watching as he pulled off his black leather biker jacket. Well-defined biceps bulged from underneath his fitted white T-shirt. When he leaned into the bar, his flexing deltoids caused palpitations to stutter inside her chest.

"Hey!" she heard Kenzie exclaim.

Samantha practically jumped out of her nude patent pumps when Kenzie bum-rushed the table. She'd been so enthralled with the detective that she hadn't even noticed the other woman walking back into the bar.

"I am *so* sorry about that," Kenzie continued. "My boyfriend is going crazy because I wasn't home when he got off work. I told him over a hundred times that I had a meeting tonight. I guess he forgot. *He is so controlling,*" she muttered, more to herself than Samantha.

"No worries. I really appreciate your coming out to talk with me tonight. If you need to leave, I completely understand."

Kenzie grabbed her backpack and tossed it over her shoulder. "I think I should. I don't want any trouble out of Alex tonight."

"Wait. Before you go, I want you to meet that detective I was telling you about who's new to Gattenburg's police force."

"He actually showed up?" Kenzie asked, her eyes wide with surprise.

"Yep. He did."

Kenzie turned her head to the side and eyed Samantha suspiciously. "Uh-uh, I know that look when I see it. You aren't crushing on this detective, are you?"

Before Samantha could answer the question, Gregory walked back over to the table holding a mug of beer and Samantha's wine. He handed her the glass, then turned to Kenzie.

"Hello," he said, extending his hand. "I'm Detective Gregory Harris. You must be Kenzie."

"I am," she replied quietly, placing her limp hand in his.

Samantha noticed Kenzie's body stiffen, and she suddenly appeared reserved and a bit timid.

Earlier in the evening, Kenzie had mentioned not being too keen on talking to law enforcement, especially someone who reported directly to Chief Wentworth. Samantha had tried to convince her that Detective Harris was cool and on the right side of the law. But Kenzie never seemed to warm up to the idea of talking to him.

"It's nice to meet you, Kenzie. Thanks for coming out tonight and talking to us about Jacob's case. I know that couldn't have been easy, especially considering you two were friends. You have my condolences."

"Thank you," Kenzie mumbled before running her trembling hands down the front of her khakis. "I, uh… I need to get going. I'm sure Samantha will bring you up to speed on everything we talked about."

"I hope I'm not chasing you away," Gregory told her. "I don't bite. I promise."

Kenzie let out a forced, uncomfortable laugh. "I'm sure you don't. I just have to get home." She turned to Samantha. "Thanks again for meeting with me. I hope that info I shared with you will help bring justice to Jacob."

Samantha reached out and gave her a hug. "I hope so, too. Thank you so much. I really appreciate your willingness to confide in me. I'll keep you posted as things progress."

"And I'll stay tuned to your blog. I just love *Someone Knows Something*. I kinda feel like I met with a famous journalist tonight."

"You did," Detective Harris chimed in, throwing Samantha a wink. "I often feel the same way when I'm in her presence."

"Yeah, right," Samantha said, blushing while waving them both off. "You two better stop it before I get all bigheaded and whatnot."

"I doubt that," Kenzie told her. "You're way too humble and down-to-earth for that. But anyway, I'm gonna go. Feel free to call me if you have any questions. And it was nice meeting you, Detective."

"Same here," Gregory said. "Take care."

Before Samantha could say her goodbyes, Kenzie scrambled toward the exit.

"Wow," Detective Harris chuckled, "she really is in a hurry, isn't she? Was it something I said?"

"I think she's just a little spooked by the idea of you working for Collin's father. You know Collin is her boss. Kenzie's terrified of what may happen to her if word gets out that she's been talking to us."

"Well, I hope you have time to stay a little longer and fill me in on your conversation with her."

Samantha nodded her head and sat back down, unable to control the tingling feeling buzzing through her legs. She couldn't remember the last time she'd felt such an intense attraction toward a man. Even though she and the detective were technically out on business, tonight certainly felt more like pleasure.

"I do have time," she told him.

"Good," he said, sitting down in the chair across from her. "So let's hear it."

Samantha hesitated. She took a long sip of wine, gazing over at the detective. He parted his lips and curled them around the rim of his mug, then took a leisurely swallow. She shifted in her seat and cleared her throat.

Focus, Sam.

She diverted her eyes down toward her glass, setting it on the table and twirling the stem between her fingertips.

"Before we get into my conversation with Kenzie, let me ask you this. What made you come out tonight? You seemed pretty adamant about not getting involved in Jacob's case."

Detective Harris took a couple more sips of beer, then peered across the table at Samantha. "I guess you struck a chord while we were out at the crime scene. I saw the passion behind your mission to try and help Ava get justice for her brother."

"Hmm, interesting," Samantha said, trying to concentrate on the detective's words rather than the way his triceps tightened as he clasped his hands together.

"But I have to be honest with you," he continued. "I can't promise that I'm going to delve too deep into your investigation. I am still obligated to the Gattenburg Police Department. My loyalty lies with them. But you asked me to come out and meet Kenzie, and after giving it a second thought, I didn't see the harm in that."

"Understood. Now if I may be honest with *you*, it seems as if there's more to you not wanting to get involved in this than just the Gattenburg PD. You've said you're a by-the-book man, that you respect the chief. I get that you don't want to make waves. But I sense there's something else keeping you from getting in too deep. Am I wrong?"

The detective propped his elbows on the table and rested his chin on his folded hands.

"No. You're not wrong," he admitted. "Let's just say that I got burned back when I was working for the Chicago PD. I got a little too wrapped up in a case, and before I knew it, *bam*. I was in way over my head."

Samantha observed how the detective's eyes darted anxiously around the bar. He appeared to be in his head again, reliving whatever it was he'd gone through.

"I'm really sorry to hear that, Detective. But obviously you came out of it unscathed, right?"

"Barely," he mumbled, finally making eye contact with her. "I'm telling you, that time in my life was crazy. It all went down right before I moved to Gattenburg. Actually, that experience was the primary reason why I moved the Gattenburg."

"Really? It was so bad that you had to leave town?"

Detective Harris drained his mug of beer, then swiped a napkin roughly across his mouth. "Yep. It was. But enough of all that. Let's get back to Kenzie. What did you find out?"

The mood between the pair suddenly shifted. Their warm, flirtatious energy had been replaced by an air of cool standoffishness. Samantha couldn't help but wonder whether the situation in Chicago involved a woman.

She was dying to press the detective for more information. But judging from his expression, which was now twisted in frustration, she decided to leave it alone.

"Well, first of all," Samantha began, "I have to tell you that Ava gave me the names of several Westman's Automotive workers she thought I should talk to. I reached out to all of them. Kenzie was the only person who agreed to speak with me. I found that interesting."

"That is interesting. But it could just be that they don't want to get involved in Jacob's case for fear of losing their jobs."

"Or they have something to hide," Samantha rebutted. "But anyway, Kenzie shared with me that she and Jacob worked side by side on the production line, so that's how they'd become such good friends. But check this out. Kenzie is also Collin's ex-girlfriend."

Detective Harris cocked his head to the side. "Is she? Now that puts a different perspective on things."

"Yes, it does."

Gregory sat back in his chair and straightened his hunched shoulders. Samantha could sense that he was coming out of the funk he'd fallen into after talking about Chicago.

"Would you like another beer before we really get into this?" she asked him.

"No, thanks. I'm good for now. Let's keep going. I really wanna hear this."

"Cool," Samantha said, encouraged by his enthusiasm. "So Kenzie and I discussed Westman's second-chance drug rehabilitation program. She told me that most of the employment opportunities go to people with felony drug convictions, especially those who've recently been released from prison. But the thing is, three of the former addicts who were hired went missing shortly after they completed the program."

Detective Harris's mouth fell open. He leaned into the table and squinted his eyes curiously. "Wait, what do you mean, *went missing*?"

"Exactly what I said. These workers just disappeared without a trace. *Months* ago."

"Well, does Kenzie know anything about what came of the investigations into their disappearances?"

"When I asked her that question, she replied with a resounding *nothing*. Apparently, the missing men had been ravaged by drug addiction and all the trouble that comes along with it. So their families and friends had written them off and no one was keeping tabs on them. These men were hoping to turn their lives around through Westman's program. But before they really had the opportunity to do so, they just up and vanished."

Gregory reached into his jacket and pulled out a small notebook and pen. Samantha was pleasantly surprised when he opened it up and began taking notes.

"Old-school, huh," she joked. "Most of us living in the modern world take notes on our cell phone apps. But don't mind me. Do your thing."

"I will," he quipped before quickly turning serious again. "So did Kenzie mention how the other employees at Westman's reacted after the employees went missing?"

"She did. The crazy thing is, they really didn't even have a reaction. According to Kenzie, none of her coworkers gave the disappearances a second thought because of the employees' backgrounds. Everyone just assumed that they'd reverted back to their old ways and didn't want to work anymore."

"Wow. That's pretty sad."

"It is, isn't it? But there is one person who was extremely concerned about the missing men and willing to speak up about it. I'll give you one guess as to who it was."

"Jacob?"

"Bingo."

"Oh boy," Detective Harris sighed as he rigorously wrote in his notebook.

Despite the unfortunate circumstances they were meeting under, Samantha couldn't help but feel an exhilarating thrill at the idea of the detective's involvement in Jacob's case. He may have gotten burned in Chicago, but it certainly appeared as though he was rising from the ashes now that he was in Gattenburg.

"But here's where the story really gets deep," she continued. "Right before Jacob was found dead, he'd decided to talk to Collin about the missing employees. A few of them worked on Jacob's assembly team, and he'd gotten to know them pretty well. So he was happy to see them turning their lives around and getting back on their feet."

"You know, the more I hear about Jacob, the more I realize how decent a guy he was."

"He really was a good man. And what's sad is that Kenzie tried to warn him against confronting Collin. But Jacob did anyway, thinking that Collin would talk his father into opening a serious investigation into the disappearances."

"Clearly that didn't go over too well," Gregory retorted.

"Not at all. The day that Jacob was scheduled to meet with Collin was the last time Kenzie saw him alive."

"Whoa," Detective Harris uttered, tapping his pen against the notebook. "Did Kenzie happen to give you the names of the men who went missing?"

"No, she didn't." Samantha grabbed her cell phone. "I'll shoot her a text message right now and ask if she can send them to me."

"Good. I'd like to run them through the missing-persons databases and see what comes up. I can also casually ask around the station and see if any of the other detectives have looked into their cases."

Once her text message was delivered, Samantha grabbed her glass and held it to her lips, hoping it would hide the look of elation spread across her face. As much as the detective tried to fight it, he just couldn't seem to stop himself from delving deeper into the investigation with her.

Samantha glanced down at her watch. It was already after nine o'clock. She didn't want the night with Detective Harris to end. But she was eager to get home and knock out the edits on her article for *Elevate*, then update her blog with all the explosive new information she'd received.

The detective reached across the table and nudged her

hand playfully. "You're already writing out your latest blog post in your head, aren't you?"

"Oh, so you're a psychic now?" Samantha laughed, grabbing her handbag and slipping her phone inside.

"I wouldn't say all that. It's just written all over that determined, impassioned look on your face."

His intense gaze caused her cheeks to burn self-consciously. Samantha drained her wineglass and swallowed hard. "Well, you're actually right, because yes, that's exactly what I was doing."

"I can understand that. I'm not gonna lie, this case has piqued my interest. Especially now that you've told me about those missing employees. Make sure you send me their names as soon as you get them."

Samantha was once again hit with a heady feeling of excitement knowing that Detective Harris was getting more involved in the case.

"I won't forget. Trust me."

"And hey, can you do something for me?"

"Of course. What do you need?" Samantha asked.

"I need you to stop calling me Detective Harris and start calling me Gregory."

She gazed at him. She could feel a shift in their rapport. It was taking on a much more personal tone, and she was savoring every second of it.

"I think I can do that for you, *Gregory.*"

"Good. Now, may I walk you out to your car?"

"Yes, you may. Thank you."

The detective stood up and threw on his leather jacket. Samantha diverted her eyes, struggling not to gawk at his athletic physique. When they strolled through the bar and outside to the parking lot, she found herself resisting the urge to slide her hand into his.

Just as they reached her car, Samantha's cell phone buzzed. "Oh, good!" she exclaimed after checking her text messages. "Kenzie just sent me the names of the missing West-man's employees. I'll forward them to you now."

"Great. I'll look into those as soon as I'm in front of my computer. And once you go public with that information on your blog, I'll have a good reason to be searching for them."

"Thank you again for doing that. And for coming out tonight. I hope you know how much I appreciate it."

"I do. And you're welcome."

The pair stared at one another silently for several sec-onds before Samantha interrupted the intimate moment.

"I guess I'd better get going."

"Yeah, me too. I'll be in touch soon with whatever info I'm able to find on those missing employees."

"Sounds good, Detecti—I mean, *Gregory*."

"All right then, *Samantha*." He smirked. "Talk to you soon."

He waited as she climbed inside her car and pulled away. Samantha glanced in the rearview mirror, waving before turning out of the parking lot and speeding off into the night.

Chapter Four

Samantha's eyes shot open. The sound of shattering glass jolted her out of sleep. She blinked her eyes to clear her blurry vision as she stared into the darkness of her bedroom.

But now, as she raised her head and peeled back the comforter, complete silence filled the air.

Maybe I was dreaming, she thought, slowly sinking back into the pillow. She glanced over at the clock. It was almost three in the morning.

"Ugh," she moaned, patting her chest in an effort to ease her pounding heartbeat. She listened. Nothing. It had to be a dream. She took a deep breath and closed her eyes, willing herself to fall back asleep.

Just as she felt herself drifting off, the crackling sound of shattering glass once again invaded her consciousness.

She gasped, sat straight up, gripped her comforter and pulled it farther up her body. Her watery eyes widened with fear. When silence once again filled the air, she reached for her cell phone and crept out of bed.

Her bedroom door was cracked open. She didn't know whether to go out into the living room of her two-story bungalow and see what was going on or hide out and call the police.

Boom!

Samantha screamed as she heard her lamps crash to the floor out in the living room. She ran inside her bathroom and locked the door, her hands trembling as she dialed 9-1-1.

"Nine-one-one, what is your emergency?"

"Yes, my name is Samantha Vincent, and someone's trying to break into my house!" she hissed into the phone.

"What is the address, ma'am?"

"Thirty-five fifty-one East Evergreen Street. Please send someone out as fast as you can."

"I'm alerting the police officers now, ma'am. Are you still inside the house?"

"Yes, I am," Samantha said, crouching down against the back of the door and wrapping her arms around her legs tightly. "I've locked myself in the bathroom."

"Okay, Miss Vincent. Stay in there. I'm going to wait on the line with you until the officers arrive. A squad car is on the way. I'll let you know as soon as they get there so that you can let them in."

"Thank you."

Samantha pressed her ear against the door. There was no sound coming from the other side.

"I don't hear any more noise," she whispered.

"Good. But please, just stay put. While you wait on the authorities to arrive, can you tell me what happened?"

"Yes. I was awakened by the sound of shattering glass. I think my living room windows were busted out. And I don't know whether someone has entered the house, but I'm pretty sure some of my possessions have been destroyed."

Samantha felt her entire body shake with fear. She thought about calling Gregory but didn't want to hang up with the dispatcher.

"Okay, Miss Vincent. I'm making note of that. The police officers just informed me that they're turning down your block now. They'll let me know when they're at the front door. Did you see anyone inside the house?"

"No, I didn't."

"Do you believe that someone entered the house at some point?"

The thought of an intruder breaking into her home caused Samantha to release a chest-rattling sob. "I don't know. I haven't been out of my bedroom."

When the doorbell chime rang out, she jumped away from the door.

"Ma'am, the police officers are outside your home. Do you feel safe leaving the bathroom and going to let them in?"

Samantha grabbed her emerald silk robe that was hanging on the back of the door and slipped it on over her matching floor-length gown.

"I do," she told the operator.

"Okay. I'll let them know you're on the way out."

"Thank you." Samantha unlocked the door and gradually opened it. She peeked out into the darkness.

"Are you still there?" she asked the dispatcher.

"Yes, ma'am. I'm still here. I won't disconnect the call until you're with the police officers."

Samantha found comfort in the operator's presence, despite it being over the phone. "Good. Thanks."

She tiptoed out of the bathroom and slid her feet into a pair of furry silver slippers, then shuffled toward the bedroom door.

"I'm going out into the living room now."

"Okay, Miss Vincent. Just keep your eyes open and be careful."

"I will."

Samantha squeezed the door handle and pulled it open, then crept down the hall. When she turned on a light and laid eyes on the living room, she almost fell to her knees.

"Oh *no*," she cried, collapsing against the wall.

Her windows had been shattered, and several bricks

were strewn across the floor. Just as she'd suspected, her crystal lamps had been destroyed along with her hand-crafted indigo art glass vases. The mirrored end tables on either side of her sofa were covered in cracks.

"Miss Vincent, are you still there?"

"Yes. I'm here. I just came out into the living room, and it's been destroyed. The windows are busted out and there's glass everywhere. My lamps and vases are ruined. There're bricks all over on the floor. And now I'm seeing that bottles were thrown through the windows, too."

Samantha dropped her head in her hands. She felt so vulnerable and violated. It didn't take a rocket scientist to figure out who was behind the attack. It had Collin Went-worth's name written all over it.

She had uploaded the latest post about Jacob's murder to her blog earlier that night. Word was getting around town that she was covering the case and looking for leads. She'd been stopped several times in the grocery store, coffee shop and deli by her readers, who would inundate her with questions. They all had various theories—some wild, some re-alistic. But one thing was for certain. Everyone suspected that Collin had had something to do with Jacob's death and felt that he should have cooperated with the investigation.

Samantha was jolted out of her thoughts when the door-bell rang again.

"Ma'am, the police officers are waiting on you to answer the door," the dispatcher said. "Are you able to let them in?"

"Yes, I am."

Samantha slunk through the living room, struggling to avoid stepping on the shards of glass. But she soon deemed her efforts impossible considering there were fragments everywhere.

"Forget it," she muttered, hoping her slippers' rubber soles could withstand the myriad fragments as she made her way to the front door.

When Samantha opened it, two police officers she didn't recognize were standing on the other side. Judging from the looks on their scowling faces, they weren't happy to be there.

"Operator," she said, "thank you for staying on the line with me. I'm letting the officers in now."

"You're welcome, Miss Vincent. I hope you're able to get everything resolved."

"Thank you. I appreciate it."

She disconnected the call and opened the door wider, her legs trembling as she stepped to the side. "Hello, Officers. Please, come in."

A short, stubby policeman with slick dark hair sauntered inside first without bothering to greet her. His long-faced, lanky partner followed him. He was carrying a cup of coffee and greeted Samantha with a nod of the head before tipping his hat.

"Good evening," he said through his thin-lipped mouth. "Or morning, I should say."

"Wow," the stubby officer uttered. "What happened here?"

"I was awakened by the sound of shattering glass. So I hid in the bathroom and called nine-one-one. When you all arrived, I came out to the living room and saw all this damage that was done."

"Yeah, this is pretty messed up," the officer said nonchalantly. He walked over to the couch and bent down, taking a closer look at the broken lamps.

The sound of glass crunching underneath his shoes, along with his lackluster demeanor, sent a streak of anger through Samantha.

"So, I'm sorry, what's your name?" she asked the stubby one.

"Officer Baxter. That's Officer Miller," he mumbled.

Samantha opened the notes app on her phone and typed

in both of their names. "Okay, Officer Baxter, you're asking me what happened, but neither you nor Officer Miller are recording my statement."

"I am so sorry, Miss Vincent," Officer Miller said, quickly whipping a notepad out of his back pocket. "I'm just shocked by all this damage. Can you tell us what happened here?"

Samantha watched as he walked around the room eyeing the wreckage while Officer Baxter stood in one spot, glaring at his partner angrily. She resisted the urge to shake her head and instead focused on Officer Miller.

"I heard the sound of broken glass," she began, "hid inside the bathroom and called nine-one-one. When you all arrived, I came out here and saw all this damage that had been done."

"Any idea why someone would vandalize your property to this extent?" Officer Miller asked.

"Well, I run a true crime cold case blog called *Someone Knows Something*, and I'm currently covering Jacob Jennings's murder investigation—"

"Murder." Officer Baxter snorted. "Jacob wasn't murdered. Everybody knows he overdosed on—"

"Come on, Baxter," Officer Miller interrupted before turning back to Samantha. "I'm sorry, Miss Vincent. Please, continue."

"Thank you," she murmured, tightening the belt on her robe and folding her arms in front of her. "I was saying that I'm covering Jacob Jennings's murder investigation on my blog. And I find it awfully coincidental that this happened after I posted a pretty controversial update today where I called out the general manager of Westman's Automotive Factory, Collin Wentworth. I'm sure you two have heard of him."

"Of course we've heard of Collin," Officer Baxter

barked. "He's Chief Wentworth's son. Why would you be calling him out in an article about Jacob OD'ing on drugs?"

As he waited for Samantha to respond, the policeman poked out his chest and gripped his holster. His hostile behavior told her everything she needed to know about his thoughts on Collin's involvement in Jacob's death.

While Samantha wanted to open up to Officer Miller, she questioned just how much she should share in the presence of Officer Baxter. It was becoming clearer by the second that he was not on her side.

"I just wondered whether the blog post hit a nerve," she continued carefully, "and someone did this as a warning. Maybe to try and convince me to stop reporting on the case."

Officer Baxter bent down and picked up one of the bricks off the floor. Samantha was surprised to see that he'd done so without wearing a glove. Now his fingerprints would be on it as well as the perpetrator's. She glanced over at Officer Miller, hoping he'd reprimand Officer Baxter for tainting the crime scene. But he was so busy staring down at his notepad that he hadn't even noticed.

"Welp, first of all," Officer Baxter began, "I think I'd be pissed off, too, if I was being accused of something I didn't do on some random blog. So, Samantha, is it?"

"Yes," she snapped.

"You have to be careful going around blaming folks for crimes they didn't commit," he continued. "The medical examiner ruled that Jacob's cause of death was an accidental drug overdose."

"You mean the same medical examiner who has a very close relationship with Chief Wentworth as well as every important official in Gattenburg?"

"Look, I'm not going there with you. Now I know word around town is that Jacob *may* have been murdered. But you're not gonna help solve anything by inserting your uneducated, uninformed opinion. You don't have the authority or the expertise to even be speaking on the matter."

Samantha opened her mouth in an attempt to fire back at him, but Officer Baxter continued his verbal ambush without taking a breath.

"And before you go accusing Collin of being behind this attack on your house, keep in mind anybody could've done it. We gets calls every week about some high school kids vandalizing property all over town."

"Have any arrests been made?" Samantha asked as she glared back at him. A sick feeling seeped into her stomach. It was obvious that he was team Collin all the way.

"Unfortunately, no." Officer Baxter sighed nonchalantly. "But we're workin' on it." He tossed the brick he'd been holding down onto the couch and turned to Officer Miller. "You got everything you need?"

Samantha looked over at Officer Miller, confident that he would step up and be of more assistance than his defiant partner. But when he avoided her gaze and nodded his head at his partner, her expectations quickly faded.

"Yeah, I think I've got enough," Officer Miller replied, closing his notepad and sliding it inside his back pocket. "Miss Vincent, I'm really sorry that this happened to you. I'll be sure to—"

"All right, then," Officer Baxter interrupted, practically pushing his partner toward the door. "Let's get outta here."

"So wait, that's it?" Samantha asked, watching in complete shock as the officers stepped out onto the porch. "You're not going to thoroughly process the crime scene, take photos, *nothing*?"

"Like we said, we've got everything we need," Officer Baxter told her. When Officer Miller opened his mouth to speak, Baxter quickly continued. "We'll file the report down at the station and follow up with you if we have any questions."

And with that, the policemen bounced down the stairs and headed to their patrol car.

Samantha slammed the door behind them. Her chest heaved in anger. She eyed the busted windows and fought off tears while storming down into the basement to search for sheets of plywood.

On the way there, she called Detective Harris. At this point she didn't care what time it was. She was disgusted by the way Officer Baxter had treated her and floored after they'd both neglected the crime scene. But more importantly, she couldn't cope with the trauma of what she'd just experienced alone.

"Hello?" the detective said after answering on the first ring. Samantha was surprised to hear that he sounded wide-awake.

"Detective Har—I mean, Gregory?"

"Yeah, hey. How ironic that you'd be calling me at this ungodly hour. I was actually just thinking about you."

"Were you?" Samantha asked, momentarily forgetting all about her home being vandalized. "What were you thinking about?"

"I just finished reading your latest blog post about Jacob. This is great stuff, Sam. I mean, you did go in on Collin pretty hard, but you presented some solid evidence that backs up your claims. And I love the way you concluded the post. 'Come on, people,'" he read. "'Do the right thing. Come forward. Speak up. Be heard. Help bring justice to Jacob Jennings and his family. Because as we all know, someone knows something...' That's really awesome, the way you worded that ending."

"Thanks, Gregory. Unfortunately, the post really struck a nerve with a certain someone here in Gattenburg."

"What, did you receive some negative feedback on it?"

"Worse. My house was just vandalized."

"Wait, *what*?" the detective shouted so loudly that Samantha had to pull the phone away from her ear.

"Somebody just drove by my house and threw bricks and bottles through my living room windows. They're all busted out, my lamps and vases are shattered, there's glass everywhere…it's a mess."

She could hear the detective rummaging around as he breathed heavily into the phone.

"I'm getting dressed now," he huffed. "I'll be there shortly. Did you call the police?"

"I did. They've already been out here, and one of them in particular was absolutely terrible."

"Really? What happened?"

"Well, one of the officers tried to sympathize with me, but the other guy was so abrupt and rude," she insisted, waving her arm in the air. "And they didn't even process the crime scene. When they asked who I thought may have done this, I of course told them Collin. After that? The alpha officer grabbed the beta officer and practically ran out the door. But not before telling me he doesn't think Collin had anything to do with Jacob's death, and that I need to stop with the accusatory blog posts."

"Well, without processing the scene, how would he even know whether it was Collin or not?"

"My point exactly! He tried to convince me that it could've been some high school kids. I honestly think he was saying anything just to take the attention away from Collin. But you already know I'm not going for that. It's no coincidence this happened right after I posted that update on Jacob's murder."

"I think you're right. Did you happen to get the police officers' names?"

"I sure did."

"Good. I'll see to it that the situation is dealt with. But in the meantime, I wanna make sure you're okay. I'm so sorry this happened to you, Samantha. I wish you'd called me sooner."

Just hearing those words of support caused her anger level to go down several notches. "I didn't want to wake you."

"Listen. First off, I barely ever sleep. Secondly, I don't care what time of day or night it is. If you need me, call me."

"Thank you, Gregory. I will."

"Do you have the supplies I'll need to board up your windows? Or should I stop by the store and pick up some plywood?"

Marry me, Samantha wanted to blurt out. But instead she checked her basement closet and saw that she had several plywood panels left over from last year's flooring project.

"I do have the supplies here. And Gregory? Thank you so much for this. I really—"

"No need to thank me," he interrupted. "I'm glad to help. You're doing great work for the community of Gattenburg while trying to get justice for your friend. I really admire that. This is the least I can do."

"Well, just know that you're greatly appreciated," she said right before hearing his car door slam. "Are you already on your way here?"

"I am. I should be there in about ten minutes."

Samantha exhaled with relief. "Great. I'll put on a pot of coffee."

"That sounds good. And by the way, make sure you don't disturb the crime scene. You should contact your insurance company first thing in the morning and file a claim, too."

"Oh yeah. Thanks for reminding me of that. And I'll be sure to leave the scene as is."

"See you soon." As Samantha climbed the stairs and headed into the kitchen, she felt the heaviness of the attack lift a bit. Gregory's reassurance had given her a deep sense of protection, even in the midst of clear and present danger.

Chapter Five

Gregory parked his car in front of Samantha's house. He grabbed his brown leather messenger bag, hopped out and ran to the front door. On the way there, he checked the lawn and pathway for footprints and assessed the damage that had been done to her windows.

"Wow," he breathed, shocked by the extent of the destruction.

His chest ached at the sight of huge holes in the windows and shattered, jagged glass surrounding them. It was obvious that the act of violence had been committed by someone with malice in his heart who had something to hide as well as something to lose if he were to be found out.

The attack was a warning shot that rang out loud and clear. And for Gregory, it sent a message that there was more, and probably worse, where this came from.

Just when he reached out to ring the bell, Samantha flung open the door. He'd expected her to have a distressed, just-rolled-out-of-bed look going on. But instead, Samantha was dressed in gray yoga pants and a matching tank. Her hair was pulled up into a messy, sexy bun, and her skin had a freshly washed glow.

"Hey," he said, unable to wipe the slight grin off his face. He knew a subdued greeting would be more appropriate considering what she'd just been through. But the sight of Samantha made it impossible to appear somber.

"Hi," she replied softly, stepping to the side as he walked through the door. "I know you said no more thank-yous. But I'm my own woman and you can't tell me what to do. So, with that being said, thank you again for coming over. You really have no idea how much this means to me."

"You're welcome. I'm happy to be here and happy to help."

Gregory walked farther into the living room and assessed the damage. "This is unreal," he said, looking around the room in complete awe.

"It really is. But I'm more concerned about my safety than any of this damage that was done."

"Of course. So am I." Gregory walked over toward the couch. "You haven't touched any of the bricks or bottles that were thrown through the windows, have you?"

"*I* haven't. But Officer Baxter picked a brick up off the floor and just cavalierly tossed it onto the couch. Without gloves, might I add."

"Huh? Why would he do that?"

"I have no idea. My guess is that he just wanted to be an ass."

"Yeah, I've observed quite a bit of his frat boy behavior around the station. So hearing that doesn't surprise me." Gregory stepped carefully over the piles of glass that Samantha had swept up and approached the windows. "So who came out with Officer Baxter?"

"Officer Miller. He's the one who recorded my statement. He tried to be decent, but Officer Baxter completely overpowered him."

"Oh yeah. Miller seems to be a pretty decent policeman. But he hasn't been on the force for long, and I think he's easily intimidated by officers with more seniority. And as for Baxter, he's already skating on thin ice for giving out bogus parking tickets around town in order to meet his quota."

"Figures. I just hope Baxter is reprimanded after the way he treated me. And they both need to be dealt with over the mishandling of this crime scene."

Detective Harris reached inside his bag and pulled out a pair of gloves, along with several evidence bags. "Don't even worry yourself with that. I'll be sure to make that happen. In the meantime, I'll process everything here thoroughly, and take these bricks and bottles in for DNA testing."

"You are such a lifesaver. If I weren't so sweaty, I'd come over there and hug you."

Gregory stopped midmotion while bending down to pick up a bottle as the thought of Samantha wrapping her arms around him crossed his mind.

Focus on the crime scene, he told himself, forcing his eyes to divert from her curvy, svelte frame, which was perfectly outlined in her skintight spandex outfit.

"So how do you like your coffee?" Samantha asked.

"Black."

"I figured as much. You're too tough to have it any other way."

"Don't be fooled by my hard demeanor," he joked. "Underneath it all I'm just a soft teddy bear. How do you take your coffee?"

"With a dash of oat milk and a touch of raw sugar."

"Child's play. That's how I drank it back in the day when I was a kid. My mother would indulge me every Saturday morning. But we weren't all bougie and gourmet like you. We used whole milk and white sugar."

Samantha threw her head back and laughed. "*Please.* I am far from bougie. I'm just trying to keep it healthy."

Gregory eyed her figure a little more lustfully than he'd intended. "Yeah, I can see that…"

She quickly turned away and swept a pile of shattered glass into a dustpan.

You're doing too much, the detective thought, wishing he had kept that last comment to himself. He turned away from her and picked a brick up off the floor.

"Once I collect all this evidence, I'll start boarding up the windows," he said in an attempt to deflect from his provocative remark.

He glanced over at Samantha, anxious to hear her response. When she flashed him a soft smile, his head bowed with relief.

"That sounds good," she said. "Thank you. And while you do that, I'll go grab the coffee."

"Can I give you a hand?"

"No, no. I've got it. I'll be right back."

Gregory felt hypnotized by the sight of Samantha's swaying hips as she sauntered into the kitchen. Her open floor plan allowed him to watch as she pulled mugs down from a shelf and placed them on the counter.

"So since those two officers decided that taking photos of all this damage wasn't important," she called out, "I made sure to take plenty of pictures before I started cleaning up."

"Oh good. Smart thinking. I took some, too, but make sure you email yours to me." Gregory picked up the rest of the bricks and placed them in evidence bags. "By the way, I ran those names of the missing Westman's employees through the system. It took some digging because, strangely, none of their names were spelled correctly. But I was able to access their police reports."

"Their names were spelled incorrectly? How convenient. I'm guessing that the reports were completely bogus, too."

"Unfortunately, your guess is correct. The first thing I noticed is that there was no exact date or even time frame listed for when the men went missing. The only date recorded was the day the reports were filed. And ironically, all the reports were filed on the same day."

Samantha carried their coffee back into the living room and handed Gregory a cup. "And we both know those men didn't all disappear on the same day. I bet someone from Westman's filed the report once they realized that the men had just up and vanished without a trace, and no one was doing anything about it."

"I agree. Which is sad. Because it just further proves that those men didn't have any family or friends keeping up with them."

"Yeah, it's definitely sad. But it's also not surprising. Oftentimes there's only so much the supporters can take before they give up on an addict."

"True indeed," Gregory replied quietly as he sipped from his mug.

"I just hate the fact that those missing men's cases were left unresolved. It's as if they were completely forgotten. I've dealt with so many cold cases throughout my career, and it's painful when the families have to live with no answers as to what happened to their loved ones. Maybe that's how you managed to suck me into this investigation of yours," he said before nudging her playfully in an attempt to lighten the mood.

"Hey, if that's what it took, then so be it," she giggled. "Seriously, I'm sure you already thought of this, but Jacob may very well be the person who reported the Westman's workers as missing. That could've been the motive behind his murder."

"I did think of that. And it very well could be." Gregory took another sip of coffee. "Mmm, this is really good."

"Thanks, glad you like it. I buy the grounds at Hannah's Coffee Shop. She actually roasts her own coffee beans. Her secret is that she blends both arabica and robusta beans to give it that nice mix of fruity and nutty flavors."

"Good to know. I'll have to pick some up next time I'm there," the detective said before taking a few more sips. "Listen to you, sounding like a full-blown coffee expert."

Samantha set her mug down on the table and continued sweeping up glass. "I'm far from an expert. I just know the good stuff when I taste it."

She turned and locked eyes with the detective. Just then the intensity of her gaze made him feel as if time had stopped and they were frozen in the moment.

"Anyway," she continued abruptly before turning away from him, "back to those missing-persons cases. The question of who reported them to authorities could possibly be answered by Kenzie, since the calls were placed anonymously."

"I agree. Because my guess is that if it wasn't Jacob, it was her. Do you feel comfortable reaching out to her and asking?"

"I do. I'm pretty sure I earned her trust after we met up at Barron's. At this point I'm willing to do whatever it takes to help apprehend Jacob's killer."

Gregory dropped the last bottle into an evidence bag, then glanced over at Samantha. He couldn't deny the fact that he was taken by her beauty. But his attraction toward her fiery intellect and passion for justice was growing stronger by the minute.

Reel it in, Harris, he told himself. *You cannot endure a repeat of what went down in Chicago…*

"So was there *any* useful information on the men's disappearances in the police reports?"

"Not really," he replied, placing the evidence bags near the front door. "Just a bunch of filler. And a major focus on their prior drug addiction."

"Of course."

Gregory walked over to the sheets of plywood leaning

against the wall and grabbed a board. "Do you have nails and a hammer?"

"I do. They're on the kitchen counter. I'll go grab them."

"Thanks," he said, once again finding himself unable to take his eyes off her as she walked across the room.

"So I, uh…" he began, struggling to find his words, "what I also found interesting is that none of the men's names had been entered into any missing-persons databases. At least not the major ones. And I checked several, including Illinois's clearinghouse and the four federal databases. I even checked NamUs, which you know is the National Missing and Unidentified Persons System. Nothing there, either. That's pretty bad considering their family members or friends could've entered their names in that system themselves."

"It's terrible. On their part as well as Gattenburg PD's."

Samantha strolled over to the window and handed Gregory a nail. When he reached for it, his fingertips brushed up against hers. He jumped back a bit as the feeling of her supple skin sent tremors up his arm.

"You all right?" she asked, eyeing him curiously.

"Yep, I'm good," he lied, knowing full well Samantha had practically knocked him off his feet.

She handed him the hammer, and Gregory made sure to grab the head so not to make contact with her skin again.

He turned around and placed a sheet of plywood over a window. Samantha came behind him, brushing up against his back before reaching out and helping to hold the sheet in place.

Gregory felt a fervent stirring emerge from deep within. His limbs went numb, and he almost dropped the hammer.

"Go ahead and pound the nails in," Samantha said, her lips so close to his ear that he could feel her breath on his lobe. "I've got the board."

He closed his eyes, mentally reprimanding himself for allowing his mind to drift off to taboo places.

"So, um…back to the missing men," he said as he hammered the nail through the plywood. "At this point, since the disappearances occurred months ago, the FBI should've been brought in. But according to the police reports, they were never contacted. So I took it upon myself to enter the names into the NamUs database. I also submitted them to the criminal justice agencies that manage the federal clearinghouses. Hopefully we'll get some leads from that."

"You're so awesome," Samantha gushed. "Thank you for doing that."

"Of course. It's my job."

"You do realize that those names not being submitted is a sign of a cover-up, don't you? Because think about it. Any sort of questionable activity coming out of Westman's is being completely ignored by Gattenburg's law enforcement. That includes this attack on my house. Somebody at Westman's is up to no good. And by somebody, I mean Collin. I believe his shady father and the entire police force have turned a blind eye to his crimes."

Gregory secured the board, then moved on to the next window. "I agree that at least some of the police force is looking out for Collin. And there's obviously something way deeper to those men going missing as well as Jacob's death, which just so happened to occur right after he confronted Collin about the disappearances."

"We've got to get to the bottom of all this. I should check my blog and see if anyone has messaged me with new leads. I bet the comment section is blowing up now that I've name-checked Collin."

"I'm sure it is. The people in this town may be afraid to speak out against Collin publicly, but they're probably willing to say their piece anonymously. From what I've gathered, he certainly isn't loved, but he is definitely feared.

And with that being said, you need to be careful, Samantha. I don't want something like this to happen to you again."

Her eyes narrowed defiantly. "If you think I'm about to let up over this amateur, punk move, you're wrong. This little incident just motivated me to go in even harder."

"*Little* incident? Samantha, I don't think you should diminish what happened here tonight. This was a serious act of violence. What if you had been sitting in your living room when those bricks and bottles came flying through the windows? You could have been seriously injured."

"But I wasn't," she rebutted, her stern tone laced with defensiveness as she backed away from him. "You know Collin did this to try and silence me. Unfortunately for him, that's not about to happen."

Gregory realized he'd hit a nerve. Instead of responding, he grabbed his coffee and took a few gulps.

"Would you like a refill?" Samantha asked, her voice softening a bit.

"No, thanks. One cup was perfect." He emptied his mug then studied the boards. "Looks like these should do the trick until you get someone in here to replace the windows."

"Great. I'll call an installer first thing in the morning."

He looked around the living room and nodded his head. "Looks like you've got everything cleaned up. Don't forgot to email the photos you took to me. I'll add them to mine on the police report and include all the details that were left out."

"So in other words, you'll be filling out the report from scratch. Because my guess is that Officer Baxter is going to force Officer Miller to destroy whatever information he recorded."

"Don't worry. I'll take care of it."

Gregory noticed Samantha's rigid posture slacken at the sound of those words. He felt himself wanting to wrap his arms around her and hold her reassuringly. As soon as that visual popped into his head, he shook it off.

"It's, uh…it's pretty late," he continued, "and I have to be at the station early. So I'd better get going."

"Ooh," Samantha moaned. "That means you're not gonna get any sleep."

"That's okay. I usually don't. Too many thoughts constantly flying through my head for me to ever fully unwind."

"Sounds like you need a vacation."

"What is a vacation?" Gregory asked before the pair broke out into laughter. He grabbed the bags of trash that were filled with broken glass. "I'll take these out. Anything else I can do before I go?"

He watched as Samantha hesitated, biting her ample bottom lip while clasping her hands behind her back. She glanced up at the ceiling, then back down at him.

"No. But I'd like to do something for you," she told him. "As a thank-you for—"

"No, no," Gregory interrupted, adamantly shaking his head. "You do not have to do anything for me. I'm just doing my job, and—"

He stopped speaking when Samantha held her hand in the air. As she sauntered toward him, Gregory felt himself once again becoming both hypnotized and aroused by the sight of her sensual gait.

"That wasn't a question," she murmured. "And it wasn't your job to come over here in the middle of the night to check on me and board up my windows. Not only that, but you collected the evidence that those sorry police officers left behind, then volunteered to update my police report. Don't even get me started on how you've gotten involved in Jacob's case, which you originally had no intention of doing, and—"

"Okay, okay," he interjected, throwing his arms out at

his sides. "You got me. I'll let you do something for me. What did you have in mind?"

"I was thinking I could treat you to dinner. Better yet, I'll cook dinner for you. How does that sound?"

Gregory was taken aback by the offer. "That sounds really nice, actually. I haven't had a home-cooked meal in…" He paused, running his hand over his goatee. "I don't even remember the last time I had a home-cooked meal."

"Well, you're going to have one this weekend. Does Saturday night work for you?"

"Yes. It does."

"Good. Any allergies?"

"Nope."

"Excellent," Samantha said while walking him to the door. "I'm already looking forward to it."

"Same here. Hey, are you sure you feel safe staying here tonight?"

"I do. I'm not about to let Collin run me out of my own home."

"You know you're more than welcome to stay at my place if you want."

Samantha paused. Her mouth fell open as she stared into the detective's eyes. "I really appreciate that. But I'll be fine."

He cocked his head to the side and threw her a look of uncertainty. "You sure?"

"I'm positive. Now go home so you can at least get a few hours of rest."

"Okay. If you change your mind, you know how to reach me."

Samantha slowly opened the door. "I do. And for the thousandth time, thank you."

"For the thousandth time, you're welcome."

She leaned in and embraced him tightly, then planted

a soft kiss on his cheek. Gregory closed his eyes, reveling in the comfort of her affection.

"Why don't you give me a call when you wake up?" he asked. "Let me know how you're doing."

"I will."

"Be safe."

As Gregory walked out the door, he realized just how hard it was to leave Samantha. And it wasn't just because of his desire to look after her.

"You're slipping, man," he told himself after dumping the garbage in a trash can, then heading to his car.

But as he glanced back at Samantha, who was standing in the doorway watching him leave, he couldn't help but question whether he'd already fallen.

Chapter Six

Samantha walked into Hannah's Coffee Shop and approached the counter.

"Hey, good morning, Sam!" Hannah called out over the loud hissing of the espresso machine. "What can I get for you?"

"Good morning. I'll have a medium caramel mocha, please."

"Coming right up."

Samantha eyed the shelves behind the cash register, which were filled with bags of coffee grounds.

"You know what? I'll also take two bags of your medium-roast house-ground coffee, too."

"You got it."

Samantha smiled as she reached inside her handbag and pulled out her wallet. Detective Harris would be pleasantly surprised to see that she'd picked up a bag of coffee for him when he came to her place for dinner.

After several moments, a beaming Hannah slid her coffee across the counter.

"Here's your caramel mocha, and here're your two packs of medium-roast house grounds."

"Thank you so much. What do I owe you?"

"Nothing."

"What do you mean, *nothing*?"

"Just what I said. Nothing," Hannah reiterated, her wide-set eyes narrowing mischievously as a deep shade of red crept across her chubby cheeks.

Samantha tilted her head to the side curiously. "Hannah, what in the world are you up to?"

"Oh, nothing. Just showing a little appreciation toward my hometown hero."

"*Hometown hero...* Are you actually referring to me?" Samantha asked, pointing at her chest.

"Yes. *You.* I've been keeping up with *Someone Knows Something.* And let's just say I am absolutely loving the work you're doing on Jacob's cold case. Sam, that man was one of my best customers. I knew him better than anyone and cared for him like a son. There's no way he overdosed on drugs. *No* way. He just wasn't that type of person."

"I know, Hannah. That's why I'm doing all that I can to shed some light on his case in hopes that Gattenburg's law enforcement will reopen it. But I'm sure you can imagine how hard that would be. Because, you know..."

Hannah snatched a towel from underneath the counter and began rigorously wiping it down. "Yeah, I do know," she spewed. "But the people of this town aren't stupid. We all know that Collin had something to do with Jacob's death. We just don't know the reasoning behind it. And hey," she said, lowering her voice, "you may not realize this, but practically the entire town is following that blog of yours."

"Really?"

"Yes. Really. Most of us are remaining pretty quiet about it, though, because as you already know, the Wentworth family is pretty powerful around here."

"I do know that." Samantha sighed. "All too well."

"Just keep fighting the good fight, though, sis. You've got our support, even if it doesn't seem obvious."

"I appreciate you saying that, Hannah," Samantha said,

reaching across the counter and squeezing her hand. "And thank you for the coffee."

"Don't mention it. Oh, and I hope that new friend of yours is helping you out with your investigation. What's his name? Detective Howard? Hardwick? Henderson?" she asked with a sly wink.

"Harris," Samantha giggled. "And stop trying to be slick. You know exactly who Detective Harris is. He comes in here for coffee almost every day."

"Yeah, and looking for you..."

"What do you mean—" Samantha began just as someone call out her name. She turned toward the door and saw Ava walk in.

"Hey, girl! How are you?"

"Oh, I'm hanging in there," Ava said. "How are you?"

"Same. Hanging in there. Do you have a minute to chat?"

"I do. I don't have to be at work for another twenty minutes," she replied, running her perfectly manicured hand through her spiked pixie haircut.

"Cool. I'll go grab us a table in the back."

"All right. I'll be there as soon as I order my—"

"Large Americano with a dash of almond milk steamed in?" Hannah asked.

"Yes, ma'am," Ava said.

"I'll get that started for you right now. Go ahead and have a seat. I'll bring it over to the table."

"You're the best, Hannah. Thank you."

"Don't mention it."

Samantha led the way as she and Ava walked toward the back of the quaint, rustic coffee shop and took seats at an empty table near the window.

"I'm so glad I ran into you," Ava said. "I've been meaning to call you, but things have been so busy at the advertising firm. Plus my husband threw his back out last week after insisting he could install our new refrigerator by himself."

"Oh no! Why are men so insistent on doing things they know they can't accomplish?"

"Girl, I don't know. But when you find out, please inform me," Ava quipped before she and Samantha broke out into a fit of giggles. "But anyway, on top of all that, the kids are running me ragged with their football practices and dance lessons and tutoring sessions. I can barely keep up!"

"I can only imagine," Samantha muttered, unable to stave off the twinge of jealousy stabbing at her chest. The hope for a family was never too far from her mind. And while she was able to find satisfaction in other areas of her life, nothing could fulfill her desire to have a family of her own.

"But one thing I *have* been doing," Ava continued, "is keeping up with *Someone Knows Something*. And Sam, let me tell you, you are doing an excellent job with Jacob's case. I am so glad I reached out and asked you to cover it. My phone and email inbox have been blowing up with people celebrating the fact that new light is being shed on his murder."

"That's so great to hear. And I'm happy to help. Hannah was just telling me how everyone in town is excited about the possibility of the case being reopened. But of course they're not going to say much about it publicly."

"Of course not."

Samantha took a long sip of her coffee. She glanced out the window at all the happy people strolling down the street, appearing as though they didn't have a care in the world.

"I haven't told you the latest about what's happened to me," she said in a hushed tone.

Samantha was interrupted when Hannah walked over.

"Here you go, hon," she said, placing Ava's coffee in front of her.

"Thanks, Hannah."

As soon as she was out of earshot, Ava focused her attention back on Samantha.

"So what's going on?"

"My house was vandalized last night."

"Are you *serious*?" Ava shrieked before looking around the coffee shop self-consciously. "Sorry," she uttered to a nearby couple who were staring at her through bulging eyes. She turned back to Samantha and leaned into the table. "What happened?"

"Someone busted out my living room windows. I woke up to glass everywhere, broken lamps, shattered vases... It was a complete mess."

"Oh, Sam, I am so sorry."

"You know what this means, don't you? I've struck a nerve in someone. I'm getting closer to the truth, and somebody out there doesn't like it. So they're trying to shut me up. But that's not gonna happen."

"Listen, Sam. I appreciate your passion. But I don't want you to get hurt. We're obviously dealing with a killer here. We see the lengths this criminal will go to in order to get away with his crimes." Ava paused, propping her hand underneath her chin while staring at Samantha through teary eyes. "I miss Jacob," she continued quietly.

"I know, hon. I do, too."

"Remember all those nights the three of us would spend hanging out in our basement, singing and dancing and rapping our hearts out?"

"How could I forget?" Samantha laughed. "When I think back on our high school years, those memories immediately come to mind. We were a mess. We just *knew* we were gonna get signed by somebody's record label."

"Yeah we did. With our talentless selves."

"Hey, speak for yourself! I was definitely the star of the group. But no, seriously, Jacob was the one. He could sing, dance, act… I thought he'd pack up and move to Hollywood one day to try and make it out there."

"I did, too," Ava said. "But instead he got caught up in Gattenburg's mayhem. And look where it got him." She picked up her spoon and slowly stirred her coffee. "Do you think you should back off the investigation? At least for the time being?"

"I'm positive I shouldn't back down. Jacob deserves better than that. I have the platform to help bring his killer to justice, and just like I told Detective Harris, I intend on doing just that."

"Wait, did you just say Detective Harris?" Ava asked, her tone filled with skepticism. "Meaning the law enforcement officer who reports directly to Chief Wentworth?"

"Yes. He's actually been helping me out a lot."

Ava rolled her eyes and dropped her head in her hand. "Sam, why would you pull him into this?"

"Why wouldn't I? If he's willing to help us, then I'm going to take him up on it. Think about it. We have someone on the inside assisting in this investigation. That's huge."

"But how do you know his intentions are good? That man's loyalty is to his brothers in blue, not some woman he barely knows who's incriminating the chief's son!"

Samantha leaned back and tapped her fingernails against the table. "You're wrong, Ava. Detective Harris is one of the good guys. I can admit that he was a bit hesitant to get involved in this case in the beginning. But over time, he's realized that we're on to something here. And he's legitimately trying to help me."

"Oh *really*," Ava snarked, propping her hand underneath her chin. "How so?"

"Well, for starters, he and I went to the crime scene together. He agreed that Jacob probably wasn't high on drugs and didn't collapse into that tiny little space in between the two dumpsters alone. He also came to my house at three in the morning and boarded up the windows after the attack, processed the crime scene and promised to handle the investigation properly since the officers who showed up didn't do so."

"Humph," Ava huffed, her eyes shifting around the coffee shop sheepishly. "That, uh…that was nice of him."

"Yes, it was."

The twosome sat silently for several seconds before Ava spoke up.

"Well, if you think Detective Harris is on our side and legitimately trying to help with this investigation, then I'm cool with it. And I apologize for what I said about him. I shouldn't have made that assumption. He does sound like a good guy."

"No worries. I understand your concern. But trust me, he's definitely on our side."

"Good. We need all the allies we can get." Ava glanced down at her watch, then grabbed her coffee and briefcase. "And on that note, I need to get to the office. I've got an important meeting with a client this morning, and I wanna make sure my assistant has everything set to go."

"Okay. Thanks for the impromptu chat. I'll keep you posted as things continue to progress."

"Please do. Oh, and by the way, have you heard from Kenzie? I tried reaching out to her earlier this week to ask how things went after you two met, but I never heard back."

Samantha grabbed her cell phone and pulled up the latest text message exchange between her and Kenzie.

"You know, it's funny you mention that," she said. "I texted Kenzie a few days ago asking for more information on the Westman's employees who went missing. Detective Harris and I are trying to figure out who reported their disappearances to law enforcement. We're thinking it was either her or Jacob. But she never responded."

"Hmm, interesting…" Ava shrugged her shoulders and scooted away from the table. "Oh well. Maybe she's caught up with that crazy boyfriend of hers. I'm sure she'll get back to us soon."

"I hope so. Because that information could be vital."

"It sure could. Samantha, thanks again for everything you're doing."

"You're welcome. I'll be in touch."

"Sounds good. Talk to you soon."

After Ava left, Samantha pulled out her laptop. Just as she opened it, she caught a glimpse of an unmarked white van creeping past the coffee shop.

As the van came to a complete stop right in front of the window, the driver, who was wearing a baseball cap and dark aviator sunglasses, revved the engine. Samantha's breath caught in her throat. A chill overcame her.

"What is all that commotion?" Hannah called out from behind the counter, and then headed to the door.

"Hey!" Hannah yelled from the doorway. "Stop revving that engine! You're disturbing my customers!"

As she turned away, the driver reached inside his jacket and pulled out a gun. He pointed it at Samantha, a sinister grin spreading across his skeletal face.

Samantha jumped out of her chair and crouched down behind the table as her stomach fell and she recoiled in horror.

"Get down!" she yelled at Hannah, who stared at her, openmouthed, then turned back to the front door.

The driver laughed and gave Hannah the finger, his gun now gone.

"Up yours! I *will* call the police on you, jerk!" she yelled right before the driver revved the engine once again, then sped off.

"Are you all right?" Hannah asked Samantha, going over to her and helping her up. "Looks like that clown was here to send a message."

"Yes. To me," Samantha said, half to herself.

"Should I call the police?"

"Oh, no. Please don't. I guarantee you they will be of no assistance. I'll reach out to Detective Harris."

"Good. I'm so glad you've got him by your side, looking out for you."

Samantha held her hand over her heaving chest. "Yeah. Me too." She waited several seconds before her trembling legs steadied, and then grabbed her cell phone. Her hands shook with fear as she dialed Gregory's number. When the call went straight to voice mail, she hung up and sent him a text message.

Can you meet me? I'm at Hannah's and just had a terrifying incident with some maniac driving an unmarked white van.

While she waited for him to respond, Samantha gathered her things.

Seconds later, her phone buzzed with a response from Gregory.

I'm so sorry, Sam. I'm in South Beloit for an all-day search and seizure training course. Can you stay put at Hannah's until I'm able to get there? I can send a patrol car out to keep an eye on the shop in the meantime.

"Ugh," Samantha groaned before turning to Hannah. "Gregory's all the way out in South Beloit, and he's going to be there all day. He suggested I stay here until he gets back to town."

"I think that's a good idea. You can hide out in my office and lock the door. Stay as long as you want."

"Are you sure? I don't want to impose."

"Are you kidding me? Of course I'm sure. Your well-being is my number one concern. I'll do whatever I can to help protect you. We've got a fugitive running around town, and we're all depending on *you* to help bring him to justice."

A seething flash of anger burned behind Samantha's eyes. "And I will. That much I can promise you."

"My girl," Hannah shot back. She raised her hand in the air and gave Samantha a high five. "Follow me. I'll show you to my office. I'll also bring you a fresh cup of coffee and a bacon, egg and cheese wrap."

"I don't have much of an appetite after what just happened, but maybe that'll change once I settle down. Thank you."

"No problem."

Samantha walked behind the counter and trailed Hannah as she led her through a door and down a short hallway.

"By the way, Detective Harris mentioned that he'd have a patrol car come out and keep an eye on the shop just in case whoever was driving that van decides to come back."

"Oh, good. Please thank him for me."

She opened a door and showed Samantha inside a small, cluttered office.

"Sorry it's nothing fancy," Hannah continued, pushing stacks of paper toward the corners of the desk. "But the Wi-Fi works, my chair is comfy and no one will ever know you're in here."

"Please. This is more than enough. Plus, you had me at *the Wi-Fi works*."

Samantha gave Hannah a playful wink in an attempt to lighten the mood. She felt guilty dragging her into the mess being caused by her investigation into Jacob's murder.

"Well, if you're okay, I'll leave you to it. Be back soon with that coffee and breakfast wrap. And if you think of anything else you need, just shoot me a text message. Otherwise I'll jet back here and check on you periodically."

"You're the best, Hannah. Thank you."

As soon as she left the office, Samantha locked the door behind her, then settled in behind the desk.

You will not let Collin deter you, she affirmed in her head.

She pulled out her laptop and opened the most recent *Someone Knows Something* blog post, where she'd discussed the missing Westman's employees and act of vandalism on her house. It had over two hundred comments.

"Awesome…"

Right before she opened the comment section, Samantha noticed a new message notification flash across the bottom of the screen. She clicked on it.

QUIT WHILE YOU'RE AHEAD, UNLESS YOU WANNA BE NEXT. CONSIDER THIS YOUR LAST WARNING.

Samantha abruptly pushed away from the desk. Her eyes blurred with tears as she reread the message over and over again.

Think of Jacob, she said to herself as her body began to shake. *Think of Jacob, Ava and rest of the Jennings family. Think of the men who went missing from Westman's. And keep going.*

That was all Samantha needed to remind herself of why she was doing this. She slid her chair closer to the desk and tapped the New Post button, then proceeded to update her readers on the latest developments involving Jacob's investigation, including the most recent threats made against her.

Chapter Seven

Samantha jumped when she heard a knock at the door.

She'd been tucked away in Hannah's office for hours. After facing the horror of having a gun pointed at her, then receiving the threatening message on her blog, Samantha had been overcome by the need to take action. She'd turned to *Someone Knows Something* for solace and before long had uploaded two new posts and filmed a video answering readers' questions about Jacob's case.

"Coming!" she called out, opening the door slowly and peeking through the crack. Hannah was standing on the other side, her eyebrows furrowed and hands folded tightly in front of her.

"Hey," Hannah said softly, "I just wanted to check on you. Everything going okay back here?"

"As okay as it can be, I guess." Samantha shrugged. "I'm kind of struggling to hold it together emotionally, quite honestly. But the good news is I've gotten so much done. I don't know, Hannah. I may have to start working out of your office every day. How much would you charge me for rent?"

"Girl, please. You don't wanna be stuck back here in this cramped little space. Plus, your home office is gorgeous. I'd never leave it if I were you."

Samantha walked back over to the desk and closed and slid her laptop inside her tote bag. "Thanks, but that would mean missing out on all your good coffee and edibles. Plus, working out of my home office can sometimes get lonely. There's not enough human interaction. I love being here at the shop, socializing with you and the patrons. Except..."

"I know. Except for days like this."

Hannah glanced down at her watch, then looked back up at Samantha wearily. "Listen, hon, it's a little after six, and I've already closed up the shop. I need to get home and start dinner for my husband. For some strange reason, he forgets how to use the stove when it's time to prepare something besides hot dogs and instant macaroni and cheese."

"It is already after six?" Samantha asked, shocked at how quickly time had passed. She slung her bag over her shoulder and followed Hannah out of the office.

"It is. Time flies when you're working on a passion project. Oh, and just to let you know, that patrol car Detective Harris said he would send out never showed up." Hannah pursed her lips and tilted her head, peering at Samantha over the top of her rimless eyeglasses. "Are you thinking what I'm thinking?"

"That Gattenburg's entire police department is covering for Collin at the directive of Chief Daddy Wentworth?"

"You got it," Hannah said before hesitating, then grabbing Samantha's arm. "Hey, why don't you come over to my house for dinner?"

"I couldn't. I've imposed on you enough for one day. Plus, I've got a vast array of delightful frozen dinners in my freezer just waiting to be eaten."

"In no way would your presence be an imposition. Are you sure?"

"I'm positive."

"Okay." Hannah sighed apprehensively as she held open the door.

When Samantha stepped outside, a heavy feeling of dread crept through her body.

Dusk had settled over the block. She glanced down the street warily, imagining that white van zooming toward her out of nowhere.

Pull it together, she told herself, tightening the belt on her coat.

Samantha turned around to say goodbye to Hannah, who was still standing in the doorway. Her tense expression was creased with worry.

"I don't feel comfortable with the idea of you going home alone," Hannah told her. "Not after what happened this morning."

"Come on," Samantha replied, her tone more confident than her feelings. "Don't worry about me. I'll be fine." She grabbed Hannah's hand and pulled her out of the doorway, then took the key and locked the door herself.

"Well, I would probably feel a whole lot better if I knew Detective Harris was around. Have you heard from him lately? I was hoping he'd be back in Gattenburg by now."

"I actually sent him a text about an hour ago, but I haven't heard back just yet—"

Samantha was interrupted by the buzzing of her cell phone. A message notification from Gregory popped up on the screen.

"Seems I just needed to mention him to have him reply. This is him texting now."

"Oh, good," Hannah sighed, pressing her hands against her cheeks. "What'd he say?"

Samantha swiped her security code across the screen and opened the message.

"'Hey, Sam,'" she read aloud, "'sorry for the late response. I just got out of the training. They tacked on an impromptu use of force segment at the very end. I should be back in Gattenburg in about an hour or so. Do you want me to meet you at the coffee shop?'"

"Tell him yes!" Hannah exclaimed. She grabbed the key

out of Samantha's hand and unlocked the door. "Let Detective Harris know that he can absolutely meet you here. I'll call my husband and tell him that he needs to find a snack to munch on until I get home—"

"You will do no such thing," Samantha interrupted. "You've been here since five o'clock this morning. I refuse to make you stay any longer."

Hannah opened the door. "Do not concern yourself with me. I'm thinking about you and that van incident. Now come on. Let's go inside and wait until Detective Harris gets here."

"I'm not doing this with you, Hannah. That incident happened hours ago. I will be fine. Now go home and enjoy dinner with your husband. I'll just have Detective Harris meet me at my house."

"Are you *sure*, Samantha?"

"Yes. I'm positive."

Hannah shook her head and relocked the door. As the pair headed toward the curb, Samantha grabbed her hand.

"I appreciate you. Have a good night."

"You, too."

Samantha climbed inside her car and composed a text message to Gregory.

The coffee shop is closed, so I'm heading home. Can you meet me there instead? Thanks again for this…

She sent the message, then started her engine and glanced uneasily in the rearview mirror.

Dusk had quickly turned to darkness. The road was empty, and the block appeared bleak.

She clenched her jaw and waited until Hannah was safely inside her car before pulling off. She didn't feel nearly as self-assured as she had at the coffee shop. Now that she was alone and on her way home, pangs of vulnerability throbbed in the pit of her stomach.

Samantha stopped at a red light. Her eyes shifted cautiously around the intersection. Visions of that van speeding out of nowhere and crashing into her came to mind.

Stop terrifying yourself. You are fine.

But as her knees quivered uncontrollably, Samantha knew that she was far from fine. She gripped the steering wheel and let up on the brake, ready to punch the accelerator as soon as the light turned green. The second it did, she sped through the intersection.

Stay calm. You're good. Just breathe.

Samantha pulled a deep breath in through her nose and blew it out of her mouth. She contemplated calling Gregory or Ava, just to help calm her nerves. But as she got closer to her house, Samantha decided against it. The last thing she wanted was to appear as though she was starting to unravel.

When she turned down her block, Samantha let up on the accelerator and surveyed the street. There were no unfamiliar cars parked along the curb. No strange vehicles were lurking near her house.

"Good," she whispered, sitting up straighter in her seat and squaring her shoulders.

She loosened her vise grip on the steering wheel while maneuvering her car into the driveway.

Just when she finally felt her rigid muscles relax, Samantha noticed a huge dent in the middle of the garage door. Splatters of red spray paint were splayed across the top.

"What the…"

She slammed on the brakes and threw the car into Park before jumping out. Her feet felt like cement blocks as she walked in slow motion toward the garage.

Samantha squinted her eyes, struggling to make out the message that had been scrawled across the stark white door.

STOP WHILE YOU'RE AHEAD BITCH!

"Oh no," she moaned, fighting to steady herself as she stumbled backward.

Fear burned her chest. She peered down the street. No one was in sight.

Bushes rustled against the side of her house. She spun around.

"Hey!" she called out. "Who's there?"

The only response she got was the sound of shoe soles thumping rapidly against the concrete. She froze, listening as the footsteps scurried away from her.

Anger overpowered fear as Samantha darted toward the pathway leading to her backyard. She flipped on her phone's flashlight and caught a glimpse of a husky figure dressed in all black. He hopped the fence and landed in the alleyway behind her house. She ran after him, willing her boots to carry her faster so that she could get a good look at the perpetrator. She wouldn't let him get away this time.

Samantha sprinted through the backyard and slammed into the gate, opening it. She thrust her body forward, watching as the man ran down the alleyway. He dived inside the back seat of a dark sedan waiting at the end of the passage. Before he could close the door, the car peeled off, its screeching tires leaving a trail of smoke in its wake.

"You mother—"

Samantha turned and raced back toward the front of the house. She jumped inside her car, her trembling hands fumbling while trying to slide the key in the ignition.

"Come on, come on!" she shouted before finally shoving it inside.

She turned the engine on, put the car in Reverse and floored the accelerator. The car flew out of the driveway. Samantha's head almost slammed against the window when she hit the curb. She ignored the jolt and sped down the street.

"Where did you go? Where did you *go*?"

Her fury pushed her forward as she swerved into the alley behind her house. Empty. When she reached the end of it, Samantha slammed on the brakes. Her head swiveled frantically from right to left. Nothing. No cars on the street.

"Dammit!" she yelled, slamming her hands against the steering wheel.

Tears trickled from the corners of her eyes and slid down her cheeks. The seething rage she'd felt after seeing her vandalized garage door suddenly dissolved, replaced by terror.

Samantha looked around the dark, deserted block, realizing just how vulnerable she was in that moment. She nixed the idea of trying to find the vandals and quickly sped off.

Her heart pounded now with fear, not anger. Samantha pressed the talk button on her touch screen and used the voice command to dial Hannah's number. When the call went straight to voice mail, a lump of anxiety formed in her throat.

"Hannah," she choked, "it's Sam. I'm on my way to your house. Someone crashed into my garage door and wrote a hideous message on it. I'll be there soon."

She disconnected the call. "Dial Detective Harris." When his phone went straight to voice mail, too, her chest constricted as if she were in the throes of a full-blown panic attack.

"Gregory, it's Samantha. My home was vandalized again. This time it was the garage. I'm on my way to Hannah's house now. Meet me there instead of my place. I'll text you the address. Please call me as soon as you get this."

Samantha hung up and sped off into the night, anxious to get to safety as soon as possible.

Chapter Eight

"This is not how our home-cooked dinner was supposed to go down," Samantha said to Gregory as she propped her legs up on the tan leather couch in his spacious living room. "I was planning on doing the cooking, and you should have been my guest. Not the other way around."

"Yeah, well, plans change, right?"

Gregory stood at the stove and flipped over two pieces of salmon, then turned around and looked out at Samantha. Moonlight drifted through his bay windows, shining silver beams of light on her. Despite appearing a bit shaken, she still somehow managed to look beautiful.

"Are you sure I can't help with anything?" she asked, glancing around his modern two-bedroom town house.

"I am absolutely positive you can't help with anything." He grabbed a container of romaine lettuce out of the refrigerator and tossed it into a strainer. "But thank you for offering."

Gregory couldn't seem to shake the guilt he'd been harboring ever since Samantha told him about the damage that was done to her garage. He regretted not being there for her, even if the situation was out of his control.

"Hey, by the way," she said, pulling a gray afghan off the back of the couch and wrapping it around her shoulders, "how did you get to Hannah's house so fast? After I texted you her address, it seemed like you were there within twenty minutes or so."

"I may or may not have done a hundred-plus miles per hour after I heard your voice mail message."

"Aww, really? You make me feel so special."

"That's because you are special."

Gregory's heart thumped at the sight of Samantha's bashful smile.

"You're also very tough," he continued. "Considering everything you've been through since you started covering Jacob's case, you're holding up really well."

Samantha climbed off the couch and approached the kitchen counter. "Why, thank you. But I have no other choice. I'm on a mission."

Gregory felt his mouth go dry when she slid onto a stool and crossed her long, slender legs. He turned away and gripped the edge of the sink while running water over the lettuce.

"Would you like a glass of wine?" he asked. "I've got pinot noir and chardonnay."

"A glass of pinot noir would be great."

He poured two glasses and handed one to Samantha. He took a huge gulp of his before clearing his throat.

"So I was thinking, you probably shouldn't stay at your house again until I can get a patrolman out there to keep an eye on it. And you."

"Please," Samantha retorted. "The patrol car you called to watch over Hannah's Coffee Shop today never even bothered to show up."

"Wait, it didn't?"

"Nope. So what would make you think a cop would show up for me? I'm public enemy number one down at the police station."

Gregory walked back over to the stove and stirred the

mushroom rice pilaf, then took two plates out of the cabinet. "Actually, you're far from that."

"Oh? And what would make you think that after the way I've been treated?"

"Well, for starters, when I filed complaints against Officers Baxter and Miller over the way they mishandled the vandalism incident at your house, Chief Wentworth promised to personally look into it. He also wrote up both of them."

Samantha sat up so abruptly that she almost fell off the bar stool. "Hold on. Did the mayor of Gattenburg hire a new Chief Wentworth? Because you can't possibly be referring to Collin's father, *Walter* Wentworth."

"As a matter of fact, I am. Chief Walter Wentworth is coming through for you."

"*Wow.* I am speechless."

"And of course we'll be filing another report over the damage that was done to your garage. I'll stop by your place in the morning and take pictures."

"I need to find a stronger way to say thank you. Because at this point those two little words just aren't enough."

Samantha's deep gratitude caused a burning sensation to shoot up the back of his neck. "Those two little words are plenty. Because I know you truly mean it. And you're welcome," he uttered, his low tone barely audible. "Like I always tell you, I'm happy to help in whatever way I can."

Gregory dried and tossed the lettuce into a salad bowl and added sliced cucumbers, green bell peppers and cherry tomatoes. He drizzled Italian dressing over it, then prepared their plates. "Shall we eat?"

"Yes, we shall." Samantha grabbed their glasses of wine and followed him into the dining room. "Mmm, this looks delicious. The pressure is officially on once I'm able to have you over for dinner."

"Come on, now. This isn't a competition. It's a win for me

any time I get to sit down and share a meal with you. You could serve up peanut butter and jelly sandwiches, frozen pizza… Whatever you'd prepare, I would be happy with it."

"Humble *and* modest? Those are two qualities I never thought I'd find in a detective." Samantha laughed.

"Yeah, well, I guess I'm not like all the rest."

The pair fell silent as they began eating. After several moments of sneaking quick glances at each other, Samantha spoke up.

"Everything tastes just as good as it looks."

"Thank you. I owe it all to the teachings of Grandma Harris."

Gregory paused, pushing his rice around the plate with his fork before continuing.

"So, um…not to somber up the mood or anything, but did you get a look at the guy who vandalized your garage?"

"No, unfortunately. I didn't. I just saw that he was on the shorter side. I'd say about five eight or so. And husky. Dressed in all black, in what almost looked like riot gear."

"Short and husky. Well, that certainly doesn't fit Collin's physical description."

Samantha sat back in her chair and dabbed the corners of her mouth with a napkin. "I thought about that. Collin is definitely over six feet tall. And he's pretty slim. So this guy must've been one of his flunkies. The skeletal-looking man who drove past Hannah's and pointed the gun at me didn't look like Collin, either."

"Wait, *what*?" Gregory gasped, dropping his fork so abruptly that it crashed loudly against his plate. "The driver of the van pointed a *gun* at you?"

Samantha slammed her hands down onto the table and gripped the edge. "Yes! I cannot believe I forgot to tell you that. There's just been so much going on, with my garage being vandalized and the threatening message I received on my blog today."

"Hold on," Gregory uttered, holding his head in his hands. "This is too much, Samantha. What did the message say?"

"It said, and I quote, 'Quit while you're ahead, unless you wanna be next. Consider this your last warning.'"

Gregory picked up his glass and took a long sip of wine. "Yeah, I definitely need to get that patrol car out to your house. ASAP."

He hoped Samantha hadn't heard the uneasy strain in his voice. But his concern over the escalating threats and acts of vandalism was growing.

Samantha stabbed her fork into a cherry tomato, then peered across the table. "You know what? I'm tired of being passive and trying to fight Collin from behind my computer. The way I'm being attacked is proof that it's just not enough."

"So what more do you wanna do?"

Gregory watched as Samantha parted her lips and slid the tomato into her mouth.

He shifted in his seat and stared down at his plate, determined to remain focused on the conversation as opposed to thoughts of kissing her.

When she neglected to answer his question, he looked up and saw a devilish grin spread across her face.

"Uh-oh," the detective muttered. "Nothing good ever comes from a smile that mischievous. Talk to me. What are you thinking?"

Samantha dropped her fork onto her plate and sat up straighter. "I'm hesitant to even tell you, because I know how by-the-book you are. So just keep an open mind and hear me out before saying yes or no."

"Now I'm really leery," he chuckled, rubbing his hands together.

"Don't be leery. Just be…*adventurous*."

Gregory drained his glass then poured himself a refill. "All right. I'm ready. Hit me with it."

She took a deep breath, then blurted out, "I think we should break into Collin's house."

Gregory froze midsip. "Wait, I must've misheard you. Run that by me again?"

"I said, I think we should break into Collin's house."

Detective Harris bowed his head and released a laugh so boisterous that his shoulders shook. "Sam, I am a detective with the Gattenburg Police Department. What would ever possess you to think that I'd be willing to break into someone's house?"

"Because you're on my side, and you're working to help me prove that Collin killed Jacob."

"And exactly how would breaking into the man's house prove that?"

"You never know. We may stumble upon a treasure trove of evidence. There could be bloody clothes or shoes tucked away somewhere. Or a laptop filled with clues. Or even a murder weapon."

Gregory covered his mouth in an attempt to conceal his amused expression.

"You'd better stop laughing at me! I'm being serious right now. If Collin and his coconspirators have the guts to attack my home and threaten me, then I have a right to fight back. Obviously law enforcement isn't taking me seriously. So I'm ready to take matters into my own hands."

"Listen, Samantha. This isn't an episode of some television crime show. This is real life. You can't just break into people's houses. Plus, the chances of you finding the type of evidence you're looking for just lying around is slim to none. Keep in mind Jacob died months ago. Even if Collin did have incriminating evidence in his possession at some point, I'm sure he's gotten rid of it by now."

"But you never know. Collin isn't that bright. We might go inside that house and hit the jackpot."

When Gregory remained silent, Samantha threw her arms out at her sides.

"So basically what you're saying is that I'm in this alone."

"That's not at all what I'm saying. We just need to do things the right way. The *legal* way. Now that Chief Wentworth is in the loop, I think we can get to the bottom of this. Because in all honesty, I'm still not fully convinced that he's in cahoots with Collin."

"Yeah, well, I'm fully convinced that he is. And did it occur to you that the chief might be on his best behavior to get you—and me—off the trail of his corruption?"

Gregory ignored her question and took a bite of his salmon, then wiggled his fork in the air. "Instead of breaking into Collin's house, why don't you reach out to Kenzie again and find out the latest on what's happening around Westman's? I'm sure the employees have been keeping up with your blog. Maybe she's got some new leads."

"I've actually reached out to Kenzie a few times since our initial meeting and haven't heard back from her. Ava hasn't, either."

"Really? Do you think she got scared off after I showed up at Barron's and decided not to discuss the case with you anymore?" He hoped that was the reason, and Kenzie's silence wasn't due to something sinister.

"She could have." Samantha shrugged. "I'll give it one more try before I give up."

"Good. Now promise me you won't give any more thought to that ridiculous idea of breaking into Collin's house."

Samantha twisted her lips and pushed away from the table. "We'll see…"

As she raised her arms over her head in a sensual stretch,

Gregory found himself unable to take his eyes off her. From her long, slender neck to the outline of her curves, she completely mesmerized him.

"I am exhausted," she continued. "It has been a long, crazy day."

Gregory stood up and took their plates. "Yes, it has. I was thinking about brewing a pot of that Hannah's coffee you were kind enough to get for me. Would you like a cup?"

"I'd love one. Thank you."

He carried their dishes into the kitchen while Samantha followed him with the empty wine bottle and glasses.

"Now, I don't have oat milk and raw sugar," Gregory told her. "But I do have soy milk and stevia. Will that work for you?"

"Aww, how sweet. You remembered how I like my coffee. Yes, that'll definitely work for me."

Samantha approached him from behind and set their glasses on the counter. As he filled the coffeepot with water, her bosom lightly brushed against his back, causing a series of tremors to creep up his spine. He lost his focus momentarily, catching himself when the carafe began to overflow. He quickly poured out some of the water, filled the reservoir and set the machine to brew.

"So, Detective Harris, when are you going to tell me the real reason why you left Chicago?"

"Whoa," he uttered, completely caught off guard. "Where'd that come from?"

"Well, I've been curious about it ever since you arrived in Gattenburg. But I didn't want to pry. Until now, of course."

"Now that I've taken down my guard, huh," he chuckled.

"Exactly."

Gregory stalled for time by turning away from Samantha and taking two coffee mugs down off the shelf. He hadn't discussed his reasons for leaving the Chicago

PD with many people and certainly hadn't expected to do so tonight.

"Where do you keep your detergent?" Samantha asked as she began loading the dishwasher. Her tone was soft, as if she may have known that she'd hit a nerve.

When Gregory pulled the pods from underneath the sink and handed them to her, he noticed a compassionate glint in her eyes. It immediately put him at ease.

"So, Chi-town," he said. "Where do I even begin?"

"How about at the beginning?" she rebutted.

"Cute," he snarked, focusing on the coffeepot as the trickling water brewed.

He was suddenly hit by a jolt of nervous energy. Gregory hoped that Samantha wouldn't think differently of him after finding out why he'd left the CPD behind.

"Would you mind grabbing the soy milk out of the fridge?" he asked in an attempt to stall for time.

"Sure."

He pulled the box of stevia from the cabinet just as the coffeepot pinged. After preparing their drinks, he handed Samantha her cup.

"Why don't we go hang out on the couch?" Gregory suggested. "It'll be more comfortable."

"Sounds good to me," she said, leading the way into the living room.

The detective struggled to stare straight ahead rather than down toward her backside as it swayed in front of him.

The pair took a seat, and Gregory couldn't help but stare as Samantha puckered her lips and blew into her mug.

"Mmm, this is really good," she said after taking a sip. "I can't really even tell the difference between yours and mine."

"So my substitutions are on point?"

"They sure are."

"Good to know."

"Can we be done with all the small talk now? Stop stalling and spill the tea on why you left Chicago."

Gregory stared down at his wringing hands apprehensively. "Before I get into all that, you have to promise me that this conversation will stay between us. Deal?"

"Deal. I would never betray your trust. Please know that."

Hearing those words warmed the detective's heart, making him feel as though they were developing a bond. He slid toward the edge of the couch and turned toward Samantha.

"Just so you know, this situation brings back some pretty painful memories. So bear with me if I seem a little somber."

She covered his hand with hers. "Hey, you don't have to do this. If you don't wanna talk about it, we can change the subject. The last thing I want to do is make you feel uncomfortable, or—"

"No, no," he interrupted, tightening his grip on her hand. "This is good for me. I need to talk about it. Maybe once I do, I'll get rid of the last remnants of pain I can't seem to shake."

"Okay," Samantha whispered.

"So," he began, "I was working on a case involving a married couple who'd recently filed for divorce. Right after they submitted the papers, the wife discovered that her soon-to-be ex-husband had put a hit out on her."

"*What?* That is terrible."

"Yeah, she was devastated. Once we got the husband in custody, I was assigned to keep watch over the wife while we worked to identify the hit man. The husband swore he had no clue as to what was going on. But the recorded phone conversations his wife turned over to us told a different story."

"Wait, so she actually heard her husband making arrangements with someone to have her killed?"

"Yep. She'd had her suspicions, so she secretly installed a spyware smart-card device inside his cell phone. We all heard the man plotting her demise."

"*Wow.* So did you all ever find the hit man?"

"We did. But before I get into that, let me tell you this. During the time that I was protecting the wife, she and I got pretty close. We were spending a lot of time together and developed what I thought was a genuine friendship."

"Uh-oh," Samantha interjected, covering her eyes with her hand. "Please don't tell me you had an affair with this woman."

"No, no…nothing like that. We were just friends. Or so I thought. Long story short, during the investigation, I discovered that the woman's husband was a bookie. He and his business partner had been running an illegal sports betting business for years, and they'd made a killing. The business partner and the wife started having an affair, and they framed the husband. He'd never actually put a hit out on her."

"Okay, so wait," Samantha said, rubbing her temples while falling against the back of the couch. "If the husband didn't arrange to have her murdered, then what about the phone recordings?"

"They were fake. They'd been spliced together and doctored up by a professional who took certain words that the husband actually did say, then edited them together so that they'd blend into a stream of manipulated sentences."

"Oh my word…" Samantha uttered while fanning her face. "That is unbelievable. I mean, it sounds like something straight out of a movie!"

Gregory paused, taking a long sip of coffee in hopes that it would wash down the stinging in the back of his throat. Reliving the experience was more painful than he'd expected.

"So let me get this straight," Samantha said. "The wife

was having an affair with the business partner, all while her innocent soon-to-be ex-husband sat in jail, who she led you to believe was trying to have her killed?"

"You got it. She was just using me in hopes that our friendship would cloud my judgment and block me from conducting a proper investigation. Obviously, she didn't know me as well as she thought she did. There's no way I wouldn't have brought in a forensic audio analyst to review those recordings."

Samantha threw the detective a knowing look. "She should've known the minute you two met that you're not the type to let anything slide."

"You would think. I'm just glad that I was able to get the business partner to confess once he found out we'd made that discovery. The wife, however, continued to deny her involvement."

"Of course she did. Man, Gregory! That was quite a salacious story."

Gregory ran his sweaty palms down the front of his jeans. "Believe it or not, you *still* haven't heard the worst of it."

"Come on now. I refuse to believe this story can get any worse."

"Oh, but it can. When I reported my findings to the police chief, he just blew it off and told me to leave the case alone, then took me off it completely."

"Why would he do that?"

"Because he and several members of the Chicago PD were being paid off by the business partner. They'd gambled with him, taken bribes from him…plus, he allegedly had ties to the mob. The chief thought that if we pursued the case any further, we'd cause too much chaos throughout the city. So he swept everything under the rug as if it never happened. That's why you didn't see anything about it in the news."

"I'm starting to think you're making all this up. Because it's just too insane to be true."

"Like they say, the truth is sometimes stranger than fiction." Gregory stood up and stretched his legs. "And in closing, that's why I left Chicago."

Samantha held her hand to her head. "My mind is spinning from all this. So what ended up happening to the husband, wife and business partner?"

"The husband was released from police custody after we deemed the tapes inauthentic. We never shared our findings with him, and he didn't ask any questions. He was just glad to be out. I figured he'd try and get to the bottom of things on his own. The business partner received six months probation, which was a complete joke. And no charges were ever brought against the wife."

"So was the wife able to collect anything in the divorce?"

"What divorce? The wife ended up dumping the business partner after finding out he'd confessed, then reconciled with her husband."

Samantha jumped up from the couch and once again paced the floor. "Detective Gregory Harris. I refuse to believe that man took his wife back."

"I promise you he did. Not only that, but the husband and business partner are still running their gambling operation together to this day!"

"*Damn.* Well, I certainly can't blame you for leaving Chicago behind." Samantha gazed up at him, her eyes softening sympathetically. "Now I understand why you were so hesitant to get involved in Jacob's case with me. But I can assure you that my intentions are pure, and—"

"Samantha, please," he interrupted. "You don't even have to go there with me. I know you just want justice for Jacob and his family. And while it did take me a minute to come around after everything I've been through, once I realized who you are, I knew I had to help you."

She reached over and gently placed her hand on his shoulder. "I'm glad you're here in Gattenburg now. This town needs you. *I* need you."

"Thank you," he whispered.

Gregory took a step closer to her. The pair studied one another, as if waiting to see what the other would do next.

Just as the detective leaned in toward her, Samantha dropped her head and turned to the couch.

"I'm exhausted," she said, grabbing the throw blanket and folding it neatly. "I'd better get to bed. I really appreciate you letting me stay here tonight."

Gregory felt a thud of disappointment drop in his chest. "Of course. I've already got everything set up in the guest bedroom and bathroom for you. If you need anything else, just let me know."

"I will. Thanks."

As Samantha sauntered off toward the bedroom, the detective eyed her longingly. He wondered how in the hell he would get through the night, knowing she was sleeping in the room right next to his.

Chapter Nine

Samantha pulled out her cell phone and checked it one more time. She was shocked to see a missed call from Kenzie.

"Dammit!" she shrieked after realizing her ringer had been turned off.

When a car horn blasted behind her, Samantha jumped and looked up at the light that had just turned green. She glanced in her rearview mirror. An old man was pointing his finger at her, his wrinkled face snarled in disdain. She waved at him apologetically and hit the accelerator, then pulled over and quickly dialed Kenzie back.

"Hello?" Kenzie breathed into the phone.

"Hey! It's Samantha. I'm so sorry I missed your call. Ava and I have been worried sick about you. Why'd you disappear on us?"

"I—I'm not going to be able to discuss Jacob's case with you anymore."

Samantha felt a twinge of disappointment tighten inside her chest. "Really? Why not? What's going on?"

"Listen, I can't talk for long," Kenzie whispered nervously. "Alex is in the other room. But I'm hearing rumors that Collin is in the drug business and Jacob was somehow tangled up in it."

Samantha closed her eyes and leaned her head back

against the seat. "Oh no," she moaned. "What makes you say that?"

"I don't have any solid proof, but that's been the buzz around Westman's. And with Jacob turning up dead and those other guys going missing, this is all getting too dangerous for me, Sam. I really wanna help you and Ava, but… I'm sorry. This is gonna have to be our last conversation."

"But wait, can't you just—"

Before Samantha could finish, Kenzie disconnected the call.

Samantha pulled the phone away from her ear and stared at it in disbelief. A streak of fiery anger shot through her. She tore away from the curb and sped down the street.

"What in the hell are you doing?" she asked herself. But as she turned down Everhart Avenue and eyed Westman's Automotive Factory, Samantha knew exactly what she was *planning* to do. Now it was just a matter of whether or not she would actually go through with it.

Gregory is gonna be livid, she thought while slowly creeping down the street.

She stopped the car right before she reached the factory's parking lot and scanned the rows of vehicles. There, in front of the Reserved for General Manager sign, was Collin's obnoxious silver pickup truck. Its enormous wheels and bright red flames lining the doors could be spotted from a mile away.

"So he's here," Samantha muttered. "Good."

She hit the accelerator and sped down the street. Guilt stabbed the pit of her stomach as she thought back on the conversation she'd had with Gregory that morning.

Right before he left for work, the detective made her promise that she would go straight to Hannah's Coffee Shop and hang out there until he could get a patrol car to watch over her house.

Well, at least I'm not going home, Samantha thought to herself.

The fact that she was heading to Collin's house was an even more dangerous idea. But now that Kenzie was no longer willing to assist in the investigation of Jacob's death, Samantha had to find another way to get answers.

Her heart pounded uncontrollably as she made a left turn down Canyon Avenue and drove toward Birchway Hills.

"You don't have to do this," she said aloud. "You do not have to do this…"

But as soon as the words were out of her mouth, Samantha knew she was going to follow through with her plan.

She'd tossed and turned all night at Gregory's house. Between the intimate dinner they'd shared, the details he'd divulged on why he had left Chicago and the fiery attraction she felt toward him, Samantha had barely gotten any sleep. But in spite of all that, she was now wide-awake and completely wired.

Since she'd begun covering Jacob's case, Samantha had tried to play by the rules. She'd hoped that her investigative blog posts would generate clues rather than the threats she had been getting. But at this point she'd had it. Being run out of her own home was the last straw. She refused to sit back and wait for Collin to execute another attack. Samantha was ready to take action and start fighting fire with fire.

She made a right turn down Sixteenth Street. An intense wave of heat stung her skin when Collin's block appeared up ahead.

Samantha rolled down the window and inhaled deeply, allowing the chilly air to calm her frazzled nerves. Despite the words of doubt flying through her head, she knew that she'd come too far to turn back now.

She made a sharp left onto Birchway Avenue and let up on the accelerator. Her breathing quickened when Collin's three-story brick townhome came into view.

Samantha suddenly felt herself beginning to panic. Her muscles tensed up as she pressed down on the brake. She swiveled her head from side to side, searching the street for neighbors or passersby.

No one was around.

Stay calm. You can do this...

But in that moment, Samantha couldn't do it. She floored the gas pedal and sped down the street, flying past Collin's house and exiting Birchway Hills.

As she slammed on her brakes at a stop sign, the memory of her shattered living room windows flashed through her mind. Thoughts of bricks and glass bottles lying in the midst of her broken lamps and vases came rushing back.

Samantha thought about the threatening messages left on her blog, the man in the van pointing a gun at her and the devastating sight of her damaged garage door. That, along with Jacob's unsolved murder, his family's grief and the missing Westman's workers, was all it took for her to make an abrupt U-turn.

"Sorry, Gregory, but I have to do this," she muttered aloud, speeding down the street toward Collin's town house.

Samantha parked her car a few houses away from his. She slowly stepped out of the car and tried to walk as casually as she could despite her trembling calves.

She cautiously approached his home, eyeing the cherrywood front door and surrounding windows while wondering exactly how she was going to make her way inside.

Guess I didn't think this all the way through...

The likelihood of there being an open window was slim to none considering it was almost wintertime. Samantha highly doubted she'd be lucky enough for the door to be unlocked. And she hadn't even considered the fact that Collin might have an alarm system installed.

Girl, what are you doing?

"This," Samantha grunted under her breath as she approached the side of Collin's house. "This is what I'm doing."

Her eyes darted along his perfectly manicured lawn and miniature evergreens. She scanned the doorway and windows for security cameras. There were none.

Samantha tiptoed down the concrete driveway toward the backyard. It was guarded by a tall wooden fence. She pressed the lever on the black iron handle and gently opened the gate.

She was surprised to see lush green bergenia plants and vibrant red twig dogwood shrubs planted among more evergreens. Samantha didn't take Collin to be the nurturing gardener type, considering his ruthless nature. But looking around at the birdhouse he'd hung from a lacebark elm tree and leafy greens he'd planted near the back fence, she was clearly mistaken.

She pulled her black leather gloves out of her pocket and slipped them on. After glancing over in the neighbors' backyards to make sure no one was looking, she approached the large double-hung windows along the back of the house.

Samantha gripped the bottoms of the frames, struggling to pull them up on the off chance that one of them might be unlocked.

"Dammit," she mumbled after none of them budged.

She set out toward the other side of the house. On the way there, Samantha passed a pair of glass French doors. The blinds were open. She shielded her eyes with her hands and peered inside.

Her mouth fell open at the sight of Collin's sparkling, modern white kitchen, elegant glass dining room table and white leather chairs. The interior of his home appeared to be just as flawless as the exterior.

Samantha was convinced that either Collin's mother or

some other woman had decorated the house. There was no way a man that wild could maintain such tasteful order.

"But he is a sociopath, so there's that…" she reminded herself as an image of Christian Bale's character in *American Psycho* came to mind.

Samantha paused. She thought about Gregory. He'd been so against her doing this, and for good reason. She threw her hands in her air, wondering what the hell she was doing.

When Samantha dropped her arms down by her sides, her coat's wrist strap looped around the door handle. Just as she pulled her arm away in an attempt to free her sleeve, the handle twisted, and the door popped open.

She froze. Her jaw tightened as she turned and quickly looked around her.

This is a sign, she thought, stumbling backward when a gust of wind blew the door farther open.

There's something here I'm meant to find…

Samantha shuffled her feet, contemplating her next move. There was still no one in sight.

You have more to gain than you have to lose, she thought before slipping inside the house and closing the door behind her.

"Okay, where to start," she said, her eyes darting around the room. She rubbed her hands together vigorously, then loosened the belt on her coat after growing warm with anxiety.

Just get in and get out…

Samantha stepped carefully across the birch hardwood floors. The dining room area opened into the family room, where a beige suede sectional surrounded a wrought iron coffee table. She peered around, noticing that everything was completely spotless. There wasn't a plate, a glass, a piece of clothing lying around…nothing. The house appeared to be more of a model than lived-in home.

She headed over to the stairs and climbed them two at a

time. A couple of bedrooms were located on the top floor. The first one looked to be for guests, considering the neutral-colored bedding appeared untouched and there were no personal effects or photos in the room.

Samantha checked the dresser drawers. They were empty. She looked underneath the bed. Nothing there. She glanced inside the closet. There were a couple of winter coats and sweaters hanging up. The shelves were completely bare.

"Please don't tell me I went through all this for nothing," Samantha muttered.

She spun around and hurried into the other bedroom. It was the master and looked a bit more lived in. Samantha was shocked to see that the bed wasn't made. This was the first sign that Collin may not have been as obsessive-compulsive as she'd thought from viewing the other spaces.

She searched the room, looking for a laptop, drug paraphernalia or anything else that could incriminate Collin. She checked dresser drawers, shuffled through a stack of papers on his nightstand and examined the closet. There was nothing but clothes, bills, shoes and other random accessories.

Just as Samantha got down on her knees to check underneath the bed, her cell phone rang. The startling ringtone almost knocked her onto her back.

She snatched the phone out of her back pocket.

"Telemarketer," she spat. "Of course…"

Samantha shoved the phone back in her pocket and glanced underneath the bed. It was completely bare. There wasn't even a dust bunny rolling across the floor.

"This man must have another house somewhere," Samantha mumbled, "because this can't be it."

She slammed her hand against the floor out of frustration and stood back up. She opened and closed drawers that she'd already searched and rustled through the closet once again, convinced that she must've missed something. This time, she looked inside several shoeboxes, then held her breath while rummaging through a pile of dirty clothes inside the laundry basket. Still nothing.

Samantha slumped out of Collin's bedroom and headed back downstairs, deciding that the best way out would be the exact same way she'd come in.

As she shuffled through the dining room, a door off in the corner of the family room caught her eye. She initially mentally waved it off, thinking that like the rest of the house, it would turn up nothing.

Leave no stone unturned, she told herself in spite of being filled with doubt.

Samantha gradually opened the door, expecting to see a pantry or broom closet. She was surprised when a set of wooden stairs leading down to a dark basement appeared.

Her eyebrows furrowed with curiosity. She palmed the wall until her hand landed on a light switch and flipped it, then slowly descended the steep stairway.

When she reached the bottom, Samantha laid eyes on what looked to be a high-tech man cave. A pool table sat in the middle of the floor. A gigantic flat-screen television hung from the wall, surrounded by framed sports jerseys. Putting green turf covered one side of the floor, while rocker gaming chairs were propped in the other. An oversize chocolate-brown leather couch sat against the wall behind a wooden trunk that doubled as a coffee table.

Like the rest of the house, the basement was immaculate. There was a bar in the back, and the shelves were packed with liquor. Samantha walked behind it and saw nothing but glasses, a mini refrigerator and a sink.

A laundry room area was hidden around the corner from the bar. Aside from the washer and dryer, it contained only an empty countertop and a couple of shelves that held detergent, bleach and fabric softener.

"You have *got* to be kidding me!" Samantha griped, frustrated. She dug her fingernails into her palms and walked back into the middle of the basement. "What am I missing? What am I missing…" she rambled.

As soon as the words were out of her mouth, Samantha's eyes landed on the wooden trunk. She studied the brass draw-bolt lock on its front. A keyhole gave her the impression that the trunk was locked. She felt compelled to try and open it anyway.

Samantha bent down, flipped the latch and gave the lid a pull. She almost fell backward when it popped open.

"Oh sh…" she uttered.

She peered inside the trunk. A Chicago Bears blanket sat on top. Samantha pushed it to the side and saw a glass bong, vaporizer and cigar box underneath. She grabbed the box and opened it, digging through several small bags of marijuana, dry herbs, e-liquids and unmarked bottles of prescription pills.

Just as Samantha placed the box back inside the trunk, she noticed a tattered marble notebook sitting at the very bottom. She grabbed it and thumbed through the pages. They were filled with a slew of numbers, percentages, random addresses and what appeared to be a bunch of gibberish, all written in bright blue ink.

"What the—"

She stopped abruptly when she heard the sound of a roaring engine followed by screeching tires. She immediately recognized the thunderous rumble. It was Collin's pickup truck.

Samantha's entire body stiffened as a numbing chill swept over her. She'd known this could happen. Why hadn't she moved faster?

She folded his notebook in half and shoved it inside her coat pocket, then stumbled away from the trunk and spun around in a circle, struggling to decide whether she should make a run for it or find somewhere to hide.

After a few seconds, she slammed the lid back down on the trunk and darted up the stairs, climbing them two at a time. She could do this. She could get out as he was coming in. Simple. Her right foot got caught underneath one of the steps, and she tumbled forward, cracking her shin on its sharp edge.

Searing pain ripped up her leg. Samantha closed her eyes and tightened her lips, stifling a scream as it crept up her throat.

Get up! her inner voice shouted inside her head. *Keep moving!*

She grabbed the handrail and limped up the last few steps. When she reached the top of the stairwell, Samantha cracked open the door and saw Collin walking through the backyard. That escape route was out. He was waving his arm in the air wildly while talking on his cell phone.

"Oh *no!*" she whimpered.

She thought of the front door. Did she have time? Would it be secured by a special lock needing a key? What if he came in as she was trying to get out?

Samantha quickly closed the door and tiptoed back down into basement. Her thighs quivered so much that her knees buckled, causing her to almost tumble onto the floor. Her injured shin was throbbing. She felt something drip down her leg and looked down, realizing that blood had seeped through her jeans where she'd cracked her shin.

"Dammit!"

Samantha covered her mouth with her hand as tears of panic streamed down her fingers. She limped over to the laundry room area and hid behind the washing machine.

"Dude, you have *got* to be kidding me!" she heard Collin

say. He was in the house now. Good thing she hadn't tried the front door. She'd have run right into him.

She looked up toward the ceiling and saw a vent that led upstairs to the kitchen area.

"I'm already at the crib," he continued. "Dude, I know! I'm so sick of having to hide my weed, man. No, not from my girl. From my maid!"

Samantha held her breath, straining to catch every word Collin was saying.

"You know my aunt doubles as my maid," he continued. "She runs back and tells my parents *everything* she finds in here. Of course I wanna fire her. But how can I? She's my mother's sister!"

Footsteps pounded against the floor right above Samantha's head. Her stomach turned as she crouched down farther against the wall.

Please get out. Please get out. Please get out, she repeated in her head over and over again, wishing her words could telepathically move Collin out of the house.

"Yeah, man. I already picked up the food. I'm just gonna grab the weed, then I'll be back at the factory. And before you even ask, *yes*, I remembered to get your Italian sub sandwich!"

Samantha thought about the marijuana she'd seen in the trunk.

"Nah!" she heard Collin yell. "You know I'm bringing the good stuff. Listen, that's the midgrade weed I keep down in the man cave. It's for the randoms who come through just to hang out and chill. Watch the game and gamble and whatnot. The top-shelf dank is up in the trap spot. Right next to the nine milli."

Samantha's eyes widened with fear at the mention of a gun. But hearing that Collin wasn't coming down to the basement was a relief.

She leaned back against the wall and patted her damp forehead with the sleeve of her coat.

"Please just get the weed and leave so I can get the hell outta here," she mumbled, fanning her face with Collin's notebook.

Samantha felt her pant leg sticking to her skin. Just as she bent down to check and see if it was still bleeding, her cell phone rang.

She jumped up and grabbed the phone out of her back pocket. Her hands shook so violently that it fell from her grip and crashed loudly onto the floor.

"Ahh!" she gasped before biting down on her tongue while fumbling around trying to pick it up and silence the ringer. Why hadn't she done that earlier? Stupid mistake.

"Wait, hold on, dude," she heard Collin say. "I don't know. I just heard some weird noise coming from my basement."

By the time she snatched up the phone and muted the ringer, the call had gone to voice mail.

"Hell yeah, I'm about to go see what's up," Collin exclaimed, "but not without my piece!"

Samantha ducked back down behind the washing machine. She wrapped her arms around her knees and gripped them tightly, cringing at the sound of Collin's feet pounding up the stairs.

Think. Think!

She considered charging up to the dining room and slipping out the door while Collin went upstairs to get his gun. But she knew she probably didn't have enough time. A quick getaway attempt wasn't worth the risk of getting caught.

"I highly doubt that someone would be stupid enough to break into my house, man," she heard Collin holler. "But if somebody *did*? Hell to pay. That's all I gotta say. Hell. To. *Pay!*"

The basement doorknob jiggled, and the creaking door swung open. Samantha winced and recoiled farther into the corner. She could feel the washing machine's cold metal through her jeans, pressing against her throbbing leg.

"Come out, come out, wherever you *aaare*," Collin sang out creepily.

The soles of his shoes thumped slowly down the steps. Samantha's breath caught in her throat when she heard the click of the gun cock.

"You hear that?" Collin barked. "That's the sound of my Glock loading a bullet into the chamber. The next thing you're gonna hear is me pulling the trigger as I unload that bullet into the head of whoever's down here."

Tears streamed down Samantha's face. She closed her eyes and held her breath, afraid to make a sound. Collin had already proven that he wasn't afraid to kill. Samantha knew her name was at the top of his hit list. If he found her in his basement, it would be an automatic death sentence.

"Nah, you don't have to hang up," Collin growled into the phone. "This is what I do. I *want* you to hear me blast the fool that was crazy enough to break into my house!"

His tone grew louder with each word. Samantha realized that she was trapped. If she didn't think of something soon, Collin would undoubtedly find her. And kill her.

As she frantically scanned the laundry room in search of some sort of weapon, the doorbell rang.

"Man, what the f—" Collin griped. His shoes screeched against the floor as the doorbell rang several times. "I'm coming!" he yelled while running back up the stairs. "Uh-uh, it's all good. Whoever's in this basement ain't gettin' out!"

When Samantha heard Collin stomping across the floor above her head, she silently thanked the universe for the gift of more time.

"Oh!" he bellowed, his voice traveling through the vent. "My extra TV screens and poker table are here."

Samantha listened as the front door opened. She once again thought about making a run for it and escaping out the back door. But she didn't think she'd make it without being seen.

"Yep, bring it all in," Collin said. "But just leave it in the living room for now. I'm dealing with a pest control problem in the basement. I'll have my boys help me take this stuff down later."

Samantha hopped up so quickly that she almost tumbled over. Crouching down in the corner had caused her legs to fall asleep. But she couldn't focus on the numbness or the gash in her shin. She had to figure out a way to escape Collin's house.

She held her hands to her face and paced the laundry area.

When she reached the far end of room, Samantha noticed a white folding door that blended into the wall. She slowly opened it. A dark, partially renovated alcove was on the other side.

A bolt of hope shot through Samantha's chest. She slipped inside the nook and pulled the folding door shut, then climbed up on the wooden bench that sat below a frosted arched window.

She carefully pressed her hands against the window, which upon further inspection, appeared to be fixed and unable to open.

"Dammit!" she hissed.

Please don't do this to me, Samantha thought while gripping the handles along each pane. *Please open. Please open...*

"Yep, thanks, guys," Collin called out. "I appreciate you!"

The next thing she heard was the sound of the front door slamming.

She yanked the handles as hard as she could. The window didn't budge.

"Naw, man, I'm telling you, you need to stay on the phone and hear this!" Collin laughed. "I'm about to go back down into the basement and exterminate the rodent that invaded my space!"

Just as Collin bounced down the stairs, Samantha gave the window one last yank. She almost fell backward when it flew open.

A silent sob of relief shook her entire body. Samantha clutched the windowpane and scaled the wall with her toes. She struggled to pull her body up. When the gash in her calf scraped the wall, a burning pain shot up her leg. She clenched her teeth, determined to ignore the agony and escape the basement.

"Get out here, you coward!" Collin yelled. "My nine and I got something we'd like to discuss with you!"

That was all Samantha needed to hear to pull herself out of the window. She tumbled onto the side of the house and hopped up, then hobbled toward the front yard.

The delivery truck was pulling away from the curb. She bit her bottom lip and limped into the street, shuffling alongside the truck in an attempt to stay hidden from Collin's house.

Her breathing quickened as she rummaged around inside her pocket for her car key. When the remote fell into her palm, she yanked it out, frantically pressing the fob.

Samantha tumbled onto her car and snatched open the door. She quickly climbed inside, picking up her injured leg and groaning while dragging it over the door sill. She fumbled with the key for several seconds before it finally slid inside the ignition.

"Let's go, let's go, let's go," she cried out, turning the engine, then slamming the door shut. Her right foot got caught underneath the brake pedal as she rushed to get the hell out of there.

"Come on!" Samantha screamed. She wiggled in her seat until finally freeing her foot, then stomped on the brake and threw the gearshift into Drive.

Her chest filled with thick waves of panic. She peeled away from the curb and tore down the street as thin streams of air poured from her mouth.

"Calm down," she choked, pressing her hand against her neck and massaging it rigorously.

Just before she turned the corner, Samantha glanced in the rearview mirror. She watched as Collin came rushing out of his house, his head swiveling from side to side as he searched the block. He was still holding his gun in his hand.

"This was too much," she sobbed. "This was *way* too close."

Her entire body shook uncontrollably when she realized just how close she'd come to getting herself killed.

Samantha grabbed her cell phone and called Gregory. The call went straight to voice mail, and it took everything in her not to completely break down.

"Gregory," she choked, "it's Sam. I spoke to Kenzie earlier today, and she told me that she thinks Collin is in the drug business. So I…" She paused, unable to admit that she'd broken into Collin's house. "I just *really* need to talk to you. No, actually, I really need to see you. Please call me as soon as you get this."

She disconnected the call and sped down the street, anxious to lock herself inside her house and wait on Detective Harris to get there.

Chapter Ten

"Seriously, Samantha," Gregory stressed as he paced her living room floor. "What in the hell would possess you to break into Collin's house? I thought you were kidding when you made that, that *outrageous* suggestion over dinner. What were you thinking?"

"For the tenth time, the door opened accidentally. I stepped through it. Maybe someone was in jeopardy," she said, clearly pretending. "Besides, I was triggered by the phone call with Kenzie. Plus Collin violated my home first, remember? On more than one occasion, might I add. Now, I can agree that what I did today was dangerous. But Collin deserved it."

Gregory turned and faced her, his eyebrows shooting up so high that they practically touched his hairline. "Wait, you actually think there's a difference between breaking into someone's house and what you did today?"

"Yes," Samantha snipped, defiantly folding her arms in front of her and plopping down onto the couch. "There is."

The detective could see the lingering fear behind her rebellious glare. He knew she was fighting to conceal how shaken up the run-in at Collin's house had left her.

"Well, let me ask you this," he said. "Did Collin invite you over?"

"No."

"Was he home when you got there?"

"No."

"Did you have permission to enter his house? Or did you just stroll through the door without—"

"Yes, I did just stroll through the door. The open door. As I said, someone could have been hurt and—"

"And you should have just called for help, not gone in," he said.

"Okay, okay," Samantha interrupted. "I get it. I shouldn't have gone inside Collin's home. But I did. And as a result, I got my hands on some explosive information," she insisted, grabbing the notebook she'd found in his trunk. "Accidentally. I found it accidentally and meant to put it back, but things happened," she said, hardly making an effort to cover her guilt.

When Gregory threw her a doubtful side eye, Samantha patted the seat next to her.

"Please," she continued, "come on. Sit down so we can put a plan together on what we're going to do with all this new intel that I—"

"Excuse me," Gregory interjected. "But what exactly am I supposed to do with the *new intel* you stole out of Collin's house? Go to Chief Wentworth and tell him that his son is selling drugs, and the reason why I know is because Samantha Vincent entered his home illegally and lifted his drug ledger? I just—I can't…"

Samantha watched as Gregory, frustrated, ran his hands down his goatee and stared up at the ceiling.

"Actually, I don't think you're going to be able to go to Chief Wentworth and talk to him about any of this," she said matter-of-factly.

"Oh, I know I can't. Because, like I said, the route you took to obtain that information is completely unlawful, and—"

"*Gregory.* Please, sit down. You don't even know the

half of it. There's way more to Collin's drug operation than you think."

He paused and dropped his head, then finally walked over to the couch and took a seat.

"What in the world have I gotten myself into?" he muttered.

Samantha stopped thumbing through the notebook and turned to him. "Listen, I know what I did was…sketchy. And the last thing I want to do is drag you into a situation that could jeopardize your job. But the men we're dealing with here are dirty. They *need* to be called out and apprehended."

"I understand all that. But—"

"Hold on, Gregory." She reached over and gently placed her hand on his forearm. "Let me finish."

Her touch penetrated through his shirt and caused a sensual rush to shoot straight through his chest. It shut him up immediately.

"Now, as you already know," Samantha continued, "I tried to go the legitimate route and seek justice the right way. However, considering what I'm about to share with you, I can no longer color within the lines. But I can't do this alone. I need to know that you're all in. One hundred percent. Are you down?"

The detective stared at the floor, unable to look her in the eyes for fear of what her gaze might do to his judgment as well as his libido. After several moments of contemplation, he nodded his head.

"Yes. I'm down."

"Whew! Good." Samantha sighed and relaxed her hunched shoulders. "I'm so happy to hear that."

She moved in closer to him and opened Collin's notebook. As their thighs brushed up against each other, Gregory struggled to focus on the contents of the book rather than her electrifying touch.

"So like I was saying," Samantha continued, "this ledger proves that Collin is running a major drug ring. What surprised me is that the ins and outs of the entire operation all appear to be right here in the notebook."

"Wow. That's crazy. In this day and age, you'd think he would've kept this information locked away on a secured computer. I can't understand why Collin would have something like this just lying around his house."

Samantha flipped through the book's pages. "Well, sometimes we get lucky."

"You certainly did. So what'd you find in it?" he asked, willing himself to focus on her words rather than the exotic floral scent of perfume pulsating off her neck.

"A lot of what you see here are coded or abbreviated words. But I did a little research online while I was waiting for you to get here, and I think I've cracked the codes on what a lot of them mean."

Gregory studied the bright blue columns filled with random terms, numbers and addresses. "Okay, I already recognize some of this terminology. But I'm interested to hear what you came up with."

Samantha turned to the back of the notebook. "For starters, I think Collin put the most important information on the last pages. See where it says *Chef's Menu*? I think that's code for drug recipes."

"Yeah, I'm familiar with the slang terminology where people refer to drug dealers concocting drugs as chefs cooking in the kitchen."

"Exactly. Then next it says *Diane*, as if that's the name of a person who'll be preparing the meal. But I think that's code for diamorphine, which as you know is the main ingredient in heroin."

"Oh, wow. I agree. Good catch."

Gregory glanced over at Samantha, watching as her supple lips spread into an appreciative smile. He fought off the urge to lean over and kiss her.

"Thank you," she said. "I'm just getting started. You see where it says *meat with a side of fennel*? I actually think Collin's referring to meth and fentanyl."

The detective's eyes widened as he studied the list. "Hmm. Once again, I think you're correct."

"And here where it says *oysters*?"

"Let me guess," Gregory chimed in. "Oxycodone."

Samantha leaned back and threw him a sly smirk. "See, we're on the same page. I told you we make a great team."

"Yes, we do," Gregory murmured, his ardent tone intimating that he meant more than just business.

She eyed him curiously before turning her attention back to the notebook. "And you already know the meaning behind the rest of these ingredients. Flour, cornstarch, powdered milk, sugar…"

"Yes, ma'am. Fillers that would bulk up Collin's product and increase his profit margin."

"You got it." Samantha raised her hand in the air and gave the detective a high five.

"And look," she continued, flipping through several pages. "I think these addresses belong to Collin's clients and possibly some of his drug runners. The dates listed track when the transactions occurred, and I think the numbers represent how much money he puts out and how much he brings in."

"Wow…" Gregory's eyes shifted from the book to Samantha. "You know, while I don't condone how you got ahold of this ledger, I have to admit, I am in awe right now. Your analysis is really impressive. Now we just need to figure out exactly how I should present this information to Chief Wentworth. He's going to be devastated when he finds out Collin's involved in all this."

Samantha closed the notebook and gently placed her hand on Gregory's thigh. "Yeah, about that…"

Without thinking, he covered her hand with his and looked her directly in the eye. "What about it?" he whispered, unable to project his voice properly due to a stirring sensation in his lower abdomen.

Samantha glanced down at his hand then looked back up at him and cleared her throat. "When I was paging through the book, I stumbled upon a list of pickup locations for the drugs. Guess whose name was at the very top of the list?"

"Whose?"

"Chief Wentworth's."

Gregory felt his entire body go numb. He fell against the back of the couch as a pang of nausea hit the pit of his stomach.

"You have got to be kidding me," he moaned. "So he's in on all this, too?"

"According to this ledger, yes."

The detective balled his hands into tight fists. "This is starting to feel exactly like what I went through in Chicago all over again. The reason why I came to Gattenburg was to get the hell away from all the corruption and foul behavior. And now this." He leaned forward, propping his elbows onto his knees. "I just feel so sick. And betrayed."

Samantha reached out and caressed his back reassuringly. "I'm so sorry, Gregory. I really didn't want to have to tell you that. But at least you know whom you're dealing with now. And you know why I had to act in such an…unorthodox…manner. We're talking major corruption here."

"I do. And I appreciate you telling me."

The pair gazed at one another silently before the buzz of Gregory's cell phone interrupted the moment. He pulled it from his pocket and stared down at the screen, then jumped up from the couch.

"I cannot *believe* this!" he exclaimed.

"What's going on?"

"One of the detectives just texted me. He received word that the bodies of the three missing Westman's workers were found up in Galena in the Tapley Woods."

"Ugh," Samantha moaned, gripping her stomach. "Did he say how they died?"

"Apparently from a drug overdose. Whatever was in their systems was very potent and very lethal."

"That is such devastating news…" Samantha stood up and slowly approached the detective. "Gregory, you know how I've been saying we've got to figure out what's really going on inside Westman's Automotive Factory?"

"I do."

"Well, I think I have. And I believe it's directly linked to those men's deaths."

"Okay. Let's hear it."

Samantha took a deep breath as the pair sat back down on the couch. "I think Westman's is doubling as a drug lab. And Collin's testing his product out on the employees who are addicts. If that's the case, I wonder how long he's been in business and what Jacob knew."

Gregory stared up at the ceiling. "Maybe Jacob found out that Collin was selling drugs and threatened to turn him in. Or what if Jacob was actually in business with Collin and got caught up in a deal gone wrong?"

"I can't see that being the case," Samantha refuted. "Jacob supposedly went to talk to Collin about the Westman's workers after they went missing, remember? If they were in business together, I highly doubt he would've bothered to inquire about their disappearances."

As Samantha spoke, Gregory realized he was more focused on her lips than the words coming through them.

Get your head in the game, man, he told himself. He grabbed the drug ledger and thumbed through the pages in hopes of finding specific instructions on exactly how Collin cooked up his product.

"You know what?" Samantha continued, hopping up from the couch before bending down and grabbing her injured leg. *"Ouch!"*

"Are you okay?" the detective asked. "Do you think we need to add a couple more bandages to your wound?"

"No, I'm fine. I just need to take it easy and avoid making any abrupt moves. But anyway, I was going to say that I think Collin was using those poor Westman's employees as guinea pigs. He was probably testing the drugs out on them in an effort to try and find the perfect combo before selling them on the street."

Gregory nodded his head in agreement. "I could definitely see him doing something like that. And because he isn't that bright, I'm sure his measurements were way off."

"I have *got* to talk to Kenzie. I just need to figure out a way to get her to speak with me again. I have to convince her that I'd never reveal her identity."

"Yeah, that would be great if you could get a conversation going with her again. I have a feeling she knows a hell of a lot more than what she's shared so far. If we could get some concrete evidence from her, I could definitely build a more solid case against Collin and Chief Wentworth and present it to the district attorney."

Samantha pointed at the detective. *"And,"* she began slowly, "maybe Kenzie could somehow find a way to get me inside Westman's after hours so that I can see what's really going on inside that elusive concrete jungle. Because I'm thinking that if he does have some sort of underground drug lab set up in there—"

"Samantha," Gregory interrupted, "you are not, I repeat, *not* going to break into Westman's Automotive Factory under any circumstances. And I mean that. Not only is it against the law, but it's beyond dangerous. Look at

what happened to you today when you broke into Collin's house. He could have killed you!"

"But he didn't."

"But he *could* have. And because you unlawfully entered his home, he would've gotten away with murder after pleading self-defense. I don't know what I'd do with myself if something happened to you. So moving forward, let's go about this the right way. The *legal* way. Are we clear on that?"

Gregory braced himself, expecting Samantha to snap back with some sort of snarky comment. He was pleasantly surprised when she looked directly at him with a softened expression.

"Yes," she whispered. "We're clear."

He watched as her eyes searched his face, as if there was something more she wanted to say. He held his breath, waiting for her to speak. But she remained silent.

"Okay, then," Gregory said. "So we're good."

"Yes, we are. I'll give Kenzie a call first thing tomorrow morning. Hopefully she won't ignore me." Samantha stretched her arms over her head, then rubbed the back of her neck. "I am so exhausted…"

Detective Harris opened his mouth to speak. But nothing came out as he watched her cropped sweater rise above her stomach, revealing her smooth, taut midsection. When she threw her head back and ran her perfectly manicured hands through her wavy hair, he stared down at the floor and rubbed his temples rigorously.

"So while you try and get ahold of Kenzie, I'll start digging around in some of the files down at the station," he told her, determined to focus on the mission at hand rather than his feelings of sexual excitement. "See if I can find information on drug busts that have occurred in the past year or so. There might be a statement buried in a report made by a drug dealer or addict that could provide us with some clues. You never know."

"I think that's a great idea. And in the meantime," Samantha said, inching toward the kitchen, "I think we deserve a treat for all that we've been through today."

"Oh yeah?" Gregory couldn't help but chuckle at the sight of her sweet, mischievous grin. "What did you have in mind?"

"I don't know," she shrugged coyly. "Maybe two cups of Hannah's Heavenly Hazelnut coffee and a couple of her frosted cinnamon rolls. What do you think?"

"I think that sounds delicious."

"Good. Follow me into the kitchen?"

"I'm right behind you."

Gregory stood up and let Samantha lead the way, forcing himself not to eye her curvaceous backside as she sashayed in front of him. "But let me help you."

She spun around and gave him a wink. "Oh all right, if you insist."

"I absolutely insist."

As the detective entered the kitchen and pulled two mugs down off the shelf, he mentally rewound the day's crazy developments. From the moment he'd heard Samantha's frantic voice mail message to finding out she'd broken into Collin's house to learning that Collin and Chief Wentworth were running a drug ring together, it had by far been his wildest day in Gattenburg.

But now, Gregory was just glad that he and Samantha were on the same page and had come to an agreement on how they would proceed with their joint investigation.

Joint investigation.

Those were two words the detective had never thought he'd speak again when it came to partnering with a woman. Yet here he was, finally ready to move past his painful experience in Chicago and take on the investigation of a lifetime with Samantha by his side.

Chapter Eleven

Samantha was so irritated that she could literally feel her skin crawling.

She had called Kenzie several times, leaving voice mails then following up with text messages, making it clear that she really needed to talk to her. But Kenzie still hadn't responded.

Whether Kenzie was avoiding her or not, Samantha was determined to share with her the new developments in the investigation of Jacob's death and see if it would help shake loose any other information. So much so that she'd driven down to Westman's Automotive Factory and was sitting inside her car, waiting for Kenzie to come outside for lunch so that she could make one last-ditch effort to speak with her.

Samantha craned her neck and stared out the window from her discreetly parked car, which sat half a block away from the factory. Her eyes were glued to the back door that led out into the parking lot.

Kenzie usually left the factory sometime between eleven and noon to head over to Victor's Café for the all-you-can-eat lunch buffet. Samantha's plan was to follow Kenzie to the restaurant, delicately approach her before she went inside and ask if they could sit down and talk.

Samantha's stomach turned as she anticipated Kenzie walking out the door at any given moment. She knew she was probably doing too much by showing up at her job unannounced. But Samantha wasn't too proud to admit that she was getting desperate. She and Gregory were getting too close to cracking Jacob's murder case and busting Collin and Chief Westworth to turn back now. Samantha just hoped she could convince Kenzie to spill whatever information she may have been holding, which could ultimately help solve the entire investigation.

She peered in her side-view mirror and noticed a white van coming toward her. Flashbacks of the incident at Hannah's flooded her mind. Samantha's heart began to beat so furiously that she could feel it in her pulsating temples. She quickly slumped down in her seat and turned away from the window, hoping that whoever was driving the vehicle wouldn't notice her.

When the van sped past her, Samantha emitted a deep sigh of relief, not realizing that she'd been holding her breath the whole time. She slowly sat back up and noticed the back door to the factory open. Her cell phone buzzed, but she ignored the call and kept her eyes glued to the exit.

Several men walked out into the parking lot. Samantha peered through the windshield, looking to see if Kenzie would follow them. But the door slammed with no sign of her.

"Ugh," she moaned. "Will you come out already?"

Samantha glanced down at her watch. It was after twelve o'clock. She'd been sitting in that spot for over an hour, and her body was tweaking with impatience.

She jumped at the sound of her cell phone buzzing again. Samantha pulled it from her handbag and saw a text message notification from Ava displayed on the screen.

They hadn't spoken since running into one another at Hannah's. Samantha wasn't planning on telling her or Kenzie that she'd gone into Collin's house and found the drug ledger. She would just have to figure out some other way to let them know she'd discovered his drug operation.

Samantha swiped the security code into her cell phone and tapped on Ava's message.

"Please have some good news for me…" she said aloud. Her voice trailed off as she began reading the text.

Are you available to meet up? We need to talk ASAP! I just spoke to one of Jacob's old friends at Westman's and found out Kenzie is missing! I'm really worried about her, especially after hearing that those missing workers were found dead…

Samantha inhaled sharply as her eyes stung with unshed tears. "Wait, wait, wait," Samantha uttered, scanning the message over and over again as if she'd misread it. "This isn't happening. This *can't* be happening!"

She tightened her grip on the phone as her hand began to tremble and anxiously dialed Ava's number. The call went straight to voice mail.

Before she could leave a message, the phone vibrated against her ear. Samantha pulled it away and checked the screen. Another text from Ava popped up.

Sorry, can't talk. In a meeting. Can you meet me at Hannah's in 30 minutes?

I can, Samantha replied. I am sick to my stomach right now after hearing that Kenzie is missing. I'm actually sitting outside Westman's. I was hoping to run into her and get more info on the factory. Is it okay if Detective Harris meets with us, too? I want him to hear everything about Kenzie's disappearance.

She sent the message, then looked back up at the parking lot. Collin's huge pickup truck was parked crookedly across two spaces. She glared at it, imagining herself smashing the windows and lights out with a baseball bat.

Just as her phone buzzed again, Collin came strolling out the door. Samantha's eyes narrowed in disgust at the sight of him spinning around arrogantly and high-fiving several of his cronies who'd walked out behind him.

She stifled a sob, watching while he threw his head back and cackled loudly as if he didn't have a care in the world. He and his boys jumped inside his truck, and Collin turned the music up full blast, revved the engine, then sped out of the lot.

The familiar sound of that thunderous roar caused her body to shake in a fit of anger.

"You *animal*!" she yelled while hot tears burned the corners of her eyes.

Samantha checked her phone and saw that Ava had responded to her text, confirming that she was fine with Gregory joining them.

Okay, thanks, she wrote back. I'm heading to the coffee shop now. See you there.

She started the engine and sped down the street, fighting off the urge to catch up to Collin's truck and ram her car into it.

SAMANTHA FELT AS though she were in a daze. She was sitting at a discreet back corner table in between Gregory and Ava, staring straight ahead at nothing in particular.

The coffee shop was fairly packed. Gregory had suggested that they meet elsewhere so not to be seen by law enforcement or one of Westman's workers. But Ava was in between conference calls and needed a quick, convenient place to talk.

Hannah sat the group as far away from the front windows as possible. Once she assured Gregory that her shop was too bougie for the automotive factory workers and too short on doughnuts for the Gattenburg PD, he agreed to stay.

As convincing as Hannah had been, however, Samantha still found herself jumping out of her seat every time the front doorbell jingled and a customer entered the shop.

There was a frigid chill lingering in the air. Samantha was still wearing her hat, coat and scarf but couldn't seem to warm up. Not even the piping-hot mocha latte she'd been sipping on could stave off the cold.

Hannah swore she'd turned the heat up full blast and even started a fire in the wood-burning fireplace. But Samantha knew that it wasn't the coffee shop's temperature that had her blood running cold. It was the news of Kenzie's disappearance chilling her to the bone.

"So this friend of Jacob's you spoke to," Gregory said to Ava. "Did he mention the last time he'd seen Kenzie?"

She took a deep, wavering breath. Her shifting eyes and downturned mouth were a clear indication that she was terrified.

"He did, actually. It was over a week ago. They work on the same assembly team, so of course her not being at the factory stood out to him."

Gregory slowly nodded his head before taking a sip of his double shot of espresso. "Did he ask anybody around the factory whether they knew anything, or if she was out sick or on vacation?"

"No, unfortunately. Those factory workers aren't stupid. They see what's happening around there. Plus, they're all afraid of Collin. They know what he's capable of. And they also know that Chief Wentworth is going to have his son's back no matter what. So no one wants to risk putting that type of attention on themselves."

Samantha's left eye began to twitch uncontrollably. She felt as if she was about to implode. "We have *got* to do something about this. What's this guy's name you've been talking to?"

"Taylor. Hudson Taylor."

Gregory quickly pulled a notepad and pen from inside his bomber jacket and wrote the name down.

"Did Hudson mention whether or not Kenzie's family has reported her missing?" Samantha continued.

Ava lips twisted in clear frustration. "So here's where the situation gets murky. Hudson is friends with Alex, who you all know is Kenzie's boyfriend. According to Alex, Kenzie sent him an email a little over a week ago claiming that life was getting to be too much for her. She just wanted to get away from it all. Ditch Gattenburg and start a new life elsewhere."

"Oh *please*," Samantha grunted, rolling her eyes at Ava. "I hope Alex didn't fall for that. Does he actually believe that email was sent to him by Kenzie?"

"He doesn't have reason to think otherwise. Kenzie never shared with him her issues with Collin, or Westman's, or the missing men who turned up dead. All Alex knows is that Collin's her ex. Which in turn means he hates him. So she went out of her way to never bring him up."

Gregory continued writing notes furiously in his pad before looking up at Ava, his forehead crinkling with concern. "Is this the same boyfriend I've heard about who's allegedly very controlling?"

"Unfortunately, yes," Ava responded, "it is."

"Umph," the detective grunted. "Well, I need to start by checking to see if a missing-persons report has been filed on Kenzie's behalf."

"I seriously doubt it," Ava said. "Kenzie is estranged from her family. She's been in and out of trouble over the years. Her volatile relationship with Alex was the final straw. Between his substance abuse issues and erratic behavior, her family refused to stand by and watch her ruin her life again after she'd gotten clean."

"I didn't realize Kenzie was dealing with all those issues," Samantha said. "That is really sad."

"It is," Ava agreed. "And Alex seems to believe that email really came from Kenzie. So as far as he's concerned, no crime has been committed."

Samantha felt a burning wave of anger wash over her. "You know, as crazy as he may be, I seriously doubt that Alex has anything to do with her disappearance. This is about Collin, Westman's and what she knew. So I hope that law enforcement doesn't try and put this off on him."

Samantha suddenly felt her body beginning to overheat. She tore off her hat and scarf, then glanced over at Gregory, waiting to hear what he had to say. He nodded his head at her and pointed at Ava.

"Do you think there's any way your friend Hudson could get Alex to forward a copy of that email to him?"

"I don't know, but I can certainly ask."

"Good," he told her. "Then if he can send it to you, I can take a look at it and have a computer forensics investigator check it out."

Samantha felt her chest tighten at the thought of Gregory pulling someone from the Gattenburg PD into their investigation.

"Wait," she said to him, "do you think that's a good idea? Especially with the, uh—" She paused, glancing over at Ava. "The *new intel* we just received?"

Ava sat straight up in her chair. "What new intel?" she asked, her head swiveling back and forth from Samantha to Gregory as if she were watching a tennis match.

Samantha hesitated. She glanced over at Gregory. He didn't chime in, but his soft, sympathetic expression silently told her that it was okay to share what they'd uncovered about Collin.

Just don't mention breaking into his house, she reminded herself.

"Ava," she began before looking around the shop then lowering her voice, "what I'm about to share with you must remain strictly between us. Okay?"

"Of course." She patted her hand against her chest and took a long sip of her caffè macchiato. "Now I'm getting nervous…"

"Collin is running a major drug ring, and we need your help. And we think that has something to do with Jacob's murder as well as the Westman's employees who turned up dead after they OD'd on drugs."

"Actually," Gregory added, "we think that has *everything* to do with Jacob's murder and the factory workers who turned up dead—after OD'ing on lethal drugs we believe they got from Collin, no less."

Ava's mouth fell open, but nothing came out. Tears pooled along the rims of her eyes. Samantha reached over and held her hand.

"That dirty mother…" Ava whispered. "But honestly? I'm really not surprised. What I don't understand is how Collin's drug ring would tie into Jacob's murder, though. He wasn't involved in anything like that."

"Are you sure?" Gregory asked, his low tone filled with skepticism. "Because you never know what he may have been doing behind your—"

"I'm *positive*," Ava interrupted firmly as she glared at him. Her stone-cold expression silenced the detective immediately. Samantha gave Ava's hand a squeeze.

"Hey," she said softly, "Gregory didn't mean to offend you. We just want to make sure no stone is left unturned."

"When it comes to my brother's death," Ava snapped back, "there are no salacious stones to turn. So let's just drop that whole theory. Why don't we talk about finally taking some serious action against Collin instead?"

Samantha gradually removed her hand from Ava's grip and sat back. She watched as her friend began to unravel, abruptly scooting to the edge of her chair and waving her hand wildly in the air.

"Detective Harris," Ava continued, "do you think you have the guts to confront your boss and tell him that his son is out here killing people? I know you're new to the force and all, but we need some new blood to step up and straighten out Chief Wentworth. Because a majority of the men who've been working for him are too weak to do it. He's got them all wrapped around his finger."

Gregory closed his notepad and folded his hands on top of the table. Samantha knew he was hesitant to tell Ava the extent of Chief Wentworth's involvement. So she took it upon herself to do so.

"Why are you looking at me like that?" Ava asked Gregory before turning to Samantha. "What's going on?"

"Ava," Samantha began, "we believe Chief Wentworth is a part of Collin's drug operation."

Ava stared back at her blankly. "Wait, *what*? W-why do you think that?" she stammered, her voice trembling with shock.

"I'm sorry, but I can't divulge that information. Please understand that Gregory and I are working hard to get to the bottom of it."

"Which is why it's so important for you to try and get that email Kenzie supposedly sent to Alex to me," Gregory told Ava. "The origins of that message could be the key to solving this case."

"Meaning it could finally prove once and for all that Collin is our culprit?" Ava asked.

"Exactly," Samantha confirmed.

Ava's cell phone buzzed. She dabbed the corners of her eyes with a napkin, then stared down at the screen.

"Oh no," she moaned. "My conference call started early. I need to get back to the office."

"Well, thanks for meeting with us," Samantha told her, "and for sharing that info about Kenzie."

"Yes, thank you, Ava," Gregory added while tapping his pen against the table.

"You're both welcome. And, uh... Detective Harris? I apologize for snapping at you the way I did. It's just—I guess I..."

"I understand," he said as her voice trailed off. "But an apology isn't necessary. This is tough for you. That's why we're doing all that we can to solve your brother's murder and get to the bottom of these disappearances."

"And I truly appreciate it." Ava stood up and slung her red suede handbag over her shoulder. "I'll reach out as soon as I hear back from Hudson on that email."

"Hey," Samantha chimed in, "do you think Hudson would be willing to talk to me? I really need to connect with somebody who's on the inside at Westman's."

"I don't see why not. He's just as concerned about the deaths of Jacob and the rest of the factory workers as we are. At this point, Hudson's actually worried about his own safety, too. I'll find out when I ask him to forward that email to me."

"Great, thanks. And Ava? Be careful out here."

"I will," she replied softly, placing her hand on Samantha's shoulder. "You do the same. Now that we know what Collin's really got going on, that puts a totally different spin on all this. He's got a lot to lose. And knowing him, he'd do whatever it takes to hold on to it. I just can't believe Chief Wentworth is in on this with him. I've known that man all my life. He's always been a fool for his son, but...*damn*."

"I can't believe it, either," Gregory said. "One of the reasons I came to Gattenburg was to escape the corruption running rampant throughout the Chicago PD. So to find out what's going on here is beyond disheartening. But I will say this. I let the situation in Chicago get the best of me. I'm not going to let that happen here."

"Why not?" Ava asked. "What's the difference between Chicago and Gattenburg?"

"That situation in Chicago was way bigger than me. I would've been in too deep trying to fight the majority of my precinct, politicians, the mafia." He paused, turning to Samantha with a fiery look of determination in his eyes. "Besides, I have a vested interest in Gattenburg. I have something to prove by solving this case and too much to lose if I don't. In more ways than one…"

Samantha peered back at the detective. The intensity in his gaze told her that he was referring to more than just the crimes occurring throughout the town. The thought of him being this invested in the investigation for her sake moved Samantha to the point where she was left speechless.

"Well, I appreciate everything you're doing," Ava told Gregory just as her cell phone went off again. "I'd better get going. We'll talk soon."

"Take care, Ava," Gregory said.

"Talk to you soon." Samantha watched as Ava slunk out of the restaurant. She felt a sharp pull in her chest at the sight of her hunched back and distraught expression. She was becoming a shell of herself. It was clear that Jacob's unsolved murder was eating away at her.

Samantha slid her hand across the table and gently placed it on Gregory's arm. When he covered her hand with his, a jolt of tingling energy charged up her arm.

"Thank you so much for coming today," she told him. "I hope you know how much I appreciate you being here with me throughout all this madness. You don't have to help me, especially considering how this case has become such a conflict of interest for you. Yet you still choose to do so anyway. That really means a lot to me."

"I'm happy to help, but thank you for saying that. Judging from all this new information that continues to pour in," he said while flipping through his notepad, "we've got our work cut out for us."

"Yes, we do, starting with getting inside Westman's Automotive Factory."

Gregory ignored Samantha's suggestion. He polished off the rest of his coffee, then pushed away from the table.

"This was a good meeting," he said. "And helpful. Thanks for inviting me. But before this conversation takes a turn for the worst, I'd better get back to the station."

"Oh, so it's like that?" Samantha asked, watching as he stood up.

"Yes, Sam. It's like that. I'm not about to entertain the idea of breaking into Westman's. You already know how I feel about that. For now, I'm gonna focus on whether a missing-persons report has been filed on Kenzie. Then I'm going to reach out to my IT forensics guy and give him a heads-up on that email we're hoping to get from Ava. I'll be looking into the other drug busts, too, like I'd mentioned. I'm curious to see whether any patterns will emerge."

Samantha stood up and followed the detective toward the coffee shop's back door. She waved goodbye to Hannah and walked out into the alleyway, where they'd parked their cars in hopes of not being detected.

"So let me ask you this," Samantha began. "Would you consider bringing Alex down to the station to question him about Kenzie's disappearance?"

"I would. First, it will be good for others to see me pursuing a suspect, to let them think I don't believe Collin or any Wentworth is involved. But also, just to eliminate Alex as a suspect. Because at this point, I do believe that Collin is one hundred percent responsible for Kenzie's disappearance along with the rest of these crimes. Now it's just a matter of gathering enough evidence to take to the mayor."

"That was my exact thought when I asked the question. Get Alex alibied and out of the way so that we can focus on bringing charges against Collin."

Samantha paused, watching as Gregory clicked his key fob. Despite the unfortunate circumstances they were meeting under, she found herself not wanting to leave.

"By the way," he said, "I meant to tell you that my IT guy is back in Chicago. So there won't be any sort of conflict of interest when I ask him to look at the origins of that email."

"Oh, so you caught that look of concern on my face when you mentioned him earlier?" Samantha asked, smiling at the unspoken connection she and the detective shared.

"I did. But we got sidetracked when the subject of Collin's drug operation came up. So I just wanted you to know that we're good on that end."

"Awesome. Glad to hear it."

The pair stared at one another, neither of them wanting to part ways.

"All right then," Samantha finally said after several moments of silence. "Talk to you soon."

"Talk to you soon. Oh, I've meaning to ask you, has the patrol car been showing up and keeping watch on your house?"

"It sure has. Thank you again for getting that set up."

"No problem," Gregory told her. "Call me if you need me."

"I will. Thanks."

Samantha climbed inside her car and pulled out of the alleyway. On the way home, her thoughts shifted from Gregory to the dire situation at hand.

Now that Kenzie was missing and they knew for a fact that Collin was manufacturing dangerous drugs, her concern for the entire town was at an all-time high.

And although Gregory was completely against it, Samantha knew she had to figure out a way to get inside Westman's Automotive Factory.

Chapter Twelve

Gregory looked up from his desk through the open door of his small office. Chief Wentworth was walking around the precinct, sipping a cup of coffee while chatting with police officers scattered around the floor. The sight of him acting as if he didn't have a care in the world, as if he wasn't involved in Collin's drug operation, turned his stomach.

After searching several missing-persons databases, from the Illinois clearinghouse to all four federal systems, Gregory discovered that Kenzie's family hadn't reported her missing. He assumed they'd fallen for the email message she'd allegedly sent to Alex.

The detective had also begun digging through old drug files. But so far, there was no connection between them and his current investigation.

Just as he refreshed his email inbox yet again to see whether there were any new messages, his cell phone buzzed. He glanced over at the screen. Seeing Samantha's name caused a string of rapid-fire palpitations to explode inside his chest.

Dude, calm down...

"Detective Harris," he said coolly, acting as if he didn't know who it was.

"Hey, Gregory, it's Sam."

"Hey, what's going on?"

"I come bearing gifts."

"Do you now? What've you got for me?"

"I just received the email from Ava."

Gregory jumped up from behind his desk and closed the door. "Wait, you mean you got *the* email from Ava?"

"Yep. Hudson was able to talk Alex into sending it to him, and he passed it on to Ava."

"That is fantastic," he said, hurrying back to his desk and opening his laptop. "I need you to forward it to my personal email address."

"I'm sending it right now. And while I do that, let me tell you this. Ava found out from Hudson that he actually tried some of the drugs that Collin is manufacturing."

"Really? Wow. I wonder whether he's a recreational user or a full-blown addict."

"According to Hudson, he's a *former* addict. Jacob was the one who encouraged him to get clean and recommended him for the job at Westman's. He was hired, and after he completed the one-week second-chance program, one of his assembly team members at the factory invited him out to celebrate."

Gregory groaned and dropped his head in his hand. "I already know where you're going with this. But go on."

"At one point during their night out, the guy tempted Hudson with a drug he promised would be stronger than any black tar or street heroin he'd ever tried. He called it TKO."

"TKO, huh. Because of its ability to knock people out, I'm assuming?"

"You got it."

"Clever," Gregory snarked. "Do you know whether Hudson happened to mention the guy's name he was out with?"

"Nope. According to Ava, he refused to snitch."

"Of course…"

"So anyway, after Hudson took the drug, he OD'd and

woke up in the hospital the next day. Couldn't remember a thing."

"Well, you and I saw that crazy list of ingredients in Collin's ledger. So hearing that someone OD'd on his product comes as no surprise."

Gregory once again refreshed his email inbox. Samantha's message from Hudson popped up.

"Hey, your email just came through. I've got my IT guy, Wayne, on standby. I'm shooting it over to him right now."

"Good. I can't wait to hear what he comes up with. Oh, and Ava was able to convince Hudson to talk to me. I'll see how much information I can get out of him. And I'm going to suggest we sit down and talk in person. I think a face-to-face would be more effective than a phone call."

"I agree. I always get way more information out of people in person than I do over the phone or via email. I wonder if he'd be open to me being there as well."

"I'm not sure. My gut tells me that the prospect of talking to a detective might turn him off. But I can certainly ask."

"Cool. Make sure you let him know that you and I are on the same team."

"I will."

When the pair grew silent, Gregory began fidgeting with a stack of papers sitting on his desk. He felt himself growing anxious. The detective realized it was because the conversation with Samantha was winding down, and he didn't want the call to end. He also wanted to do more, to protect her. He didn't like the thought of her doing these meet-ups alone.

At what point did you let your guard down and get this attached? he asked himself.

"So, um," Gregory continued, "do you think we should get together and discuss our next moves, aside from waiting on Wayne's analysis of the email?"

His knees bounced rapidly as he awaited her response.

"Yes, I think that's a good idea," Samantha replied without hesitation. "As a matter of fact, we can meet up at my place. I never did make that dinner for you that I promised."

Gregory sat back in his chair and grinned widely before pumping his fist in the air. "You most certainly didn't. And if I recall correctly, you were planning on cooking something up that would outdo the meal I prepared for you."

"Hold up now. I don't think I said all that," she laughed.

"Uh-uh, don't try and back out now. You said what you said. Now be a woman of your word and show me what you're working with. In the kitchen, that is," he quickly added.

"Oh, I'll show you what I'm working with all right," Samantha murmured. "Actually, I'm free tonight. If you're available, let's make it happen."

Gregory shifted in his seat, unable to stave off a feeling of arousal so strong that it had him gripping the sides of his desk. "Let's do it."

"Great. I'll run by the grocery store and pick up a few things. See you at my place at around seven or so?"

"Seven works for me. How about I bring the wine?"

"Sounds perfect. See you tonight."

"See you then."

Just as Gregory pulled the phone away from his ear, Samantha called out his name.

"Hey! Before you go…" she said, her tone filled with mischief.

"What's up?"

"I know you've been really busy, but have you checked out my blog lately?"

"Not in the past few days. Why? Did I miss something?"

"Yes, you did. You missed a lot, actually."

"Uh-oh," Gregory uttered, pulling his laptop in closer and typing the web address for *Someone Knows Something* in the internet's search engine. "What are you up to now, Miss Vincent?"

"Let's just say I'm trying to shake things up around this town and bring more awareness to Collin and his drug ring. I want answers, Gregory. And I want Collin, his cronies and Chief Wentworth to be brought to justice. Clearly some of our police force is corrupt. You know several of them are probably being bribed and profiting off Collin's operation. So I'm using *Someone Knows Something* to call them out."

The detective sat silently for a moment, clenching his jaw while searching for the right thing to say. "Listen, Sam. I need you to be cautious. And low-key. Things are getting more and more dangerous out here. You don't want to draw too much attention to yourself right now."

He cringed when she sighed, frustrated, into the phone.

"That's not my intention," she insisted. "But we're getting so close to cracking this case. I don't wanna let up. The fact that Jacob's investigation went cold and authorities aren't looking further into the deaths of the Westman's workers is making me sick."

"I know it is. It's making me sick, too. That's why you and I are doing all that we can to build a strong case against Collin and Chief Wentworth to present to the district attorney. But I'm only going to get one shot at this, so I have to make sure my reporting is flawless. We just have to be patient and stay the course. Let my IT forensics guy figure out the origins of Kenzie's alleged email. Get everything we learned from Ava, Kenzie and Hudson officially recorded in a written statement. And turn over Collin's drug ledger—even if they can't use it at trial, it might still help."

"*And* share with the district attorney our findings once we get inside Westman's Automotive Factory and figure out what's really going on in there. I want photographic evidence of the drug lab that I am convinced is set up somewhere in that factory—"

"Samantha," Gregory interrupted, the bark in his voice immediately silencing her. "Listen to me. There will be no breaking into Westman's Automotive Factory. Did you suddenly forget what happened when you broke into Collin's house? You almost got yourself killed!"

"But I didn't get—"

"This is not up for debate, dammit!" Gregory hollered, pounding the desk so loudly that several of his colleagues peered through the window on the door into his office. The detective held up his hand, letting them know that everything was okay. "Now, I'm serious," he continued into the phone, this time lowering his voice. "I don't want anything to happen to you, Samantha. Can't you understand that?"

"Yes," she replied quietly. "I do understand that."

Gregory's intense reaction to Samantha caused his throat to tighten. He could tell by her low tone that he'd rattled her. Knowing how resolute she could be, he knew that wasn't a bad thing.

"I don't want to press the issue," Samantha continued, "but I also don't want the DA's office to find some sort of loophole that would enable Collin and his father to get away with this. We need to have all the evidence we can get our hands on when you go to speak to him. Photographic proof would be the nail in their coffin."

"Well, I don't want you to end up *inside* a coffin trying to obtain that photographic evidence," Gregory shot back. "We'll have enough proof. Trust me. Proof that will stand up in court."

"I wonder if you could somehow get a warrant to search the factory."

Gregory couldn't help but chuckle at her tenacity. "You just aren't gonna let up, are you?"

"Nope."

"Well, I don't know about obtaining a warrant. But in the meantime, I'll continue to focus on what I am able to get my hands on."

"You do that. And I'll focus on getting to the grocery store so I can get started on this delicious dinner I'm about to cook up for you."

Hearing that caused the detective's stress level to drop from ten to one. "That sounds good. I'm looking forward to it."

"So am I. See you soon."

"See you soon. Bye."

Gregory disconnected the call and reclined in his chair, folding his hands behind his head. He closed his eyes, his lips curling into a crooked grin at the thought of dinner with Samantha.

But when visions of intimate moments on the couch next to her over wine and deep conversation crept into his mind, his eyes popped open.

"Come on, man," he grumbled, sitting straight up. "Stay focused…"

He refreshed his email inbox. A message appeared from his computer forensics expert.

What's up, man. Just wanted to confirm that I received your email. I'll run an analysis on it and see if I can locate the server name and IP address. From there, I should be able to track down the owner and his/her location. If I have any trouble, I'll reach out to the internet service provider. You already know I've got the hookup with them, so I won't have to go through any red tape or present a warrant if I need to request additional information. I'll circle back with you once I know more.

Thanks,

Wayne

"My dude," Gregory said, slamming his hand down on the desk victoriously. He replied to Wayne's message and thanked him, then forwarded the email to Samantha.

We're well on our way to getting to the bottom of all this, he wrote before sending it.

When he heard a commotion outside his office, Gregory looked up and saw Chief Wentworth walking back into his office.

Gregory was tempted to go ask him if he'd had a chance to look over the police reports that were filed on the vandalisms at Samantha's house. But considering the new intel he had on the chief and his connection to Collin's drug ring, the detective decided against it. The last thing he wanted was to bring attention to himself and Samantha and cause a disruption in their investigation.

Follow your own advice, he told himself. *Just be patient and stay the course.*

And with that, Gregory pulled Samantha's blog back up and began reading her latest post, which she'd aptly titled "We're Getting Closer to the Truth, My Friends…"

Chapter Thirteen

By the time Samantha walked out of the grocery store, darkness had already fallen over the town. She peered into the parking lot in search of her car. When it didn't immediately come into view, she clicked on the key fob until taillights blinked over in the far right corner.

Samantha glanced around the lot before stepping out onto the asphalt. There were very few cars scattered about between the neon-yellow lines. Most of the townspeople usually did their grocery shopping on the weekends, including her. But since her impromptu dinner with Gregory was planned at the last minute, she had no choice but to make a last-minute run to the store.

"Shoot," Samantha muttered when one of the handles on her shopping bag tore. She bent down and grabbed the steaks and potatoes before they went tumbling to the ground.

Just as she gathered the top of the bag and twisted it into a knot, the sound of a revving engine roared behind her.

A stinging cloud of dread seeped through Samantha's pores. Her entire body stiffened up. She looked ahead at her car, her vision blurring with fear. It appeared to be miles away.

"Please, please, please," she begged, willing her heavy feet to lift off the ground and get her to the vehicle. But it was as if she were in the midst of a nightmare. Everything around her began to move in slow motion and she was stuck in one spot, literally unable to budge.

But when the sound of screeching tires pierced her ears, she let out a loud scream and darted through the parking lot.

Samantha refused to look behind her for fear that it would slow her down. When she reached her car, she fell onto the trunk trying to get around to the driver's side.

"Come on," she whimpered, clutching her bags tighter. "Come on!"

The heel of her boot slipped into a crack in the asphalt. Samantha fumbled, gripping the bumper on the back of her car while barely avoiding falling to the ground.

Get up, get up, get up!

She scrambled to her feet, shuddering as a gust of blustering wind rushed past her.

Samantha whipped around and was blinded by bright yellow headlights. A car was careening toward her at full speed.

Once again, she found herself unable to move. A stiffening shock invaded her limbs. Her body felt as though it was cemented to the ground.

As the car zoomed closer toward her, Samantha realized that it was the same dark sedan she'd seen in the alleyway the night her garage was vandalized.

Her eyes widened with terror. She struggled to peer inside the windows to see who was behind the wheel. But she couldn't see through the dark tint.

Samantha recoiled against the back of her car as the vehicle raced past her. She dropped her grocery bags and screamed in terror. The car tore through the lot and onto the street then disappeared into the night.

"Ma'am!" a woman yelled as she ran toward Samantha. "Are you all right?"

Samantha clung to the back of her car, trembling with fear as tears streamed down her face.

"I... I think so," she stammered, her shaky voice indicating that she was far from okay.

She watched as a woman scurried past her and picked her groceries up off the ground.

"I saw what just happened to you," the woman said, reaching down and helping Samantha stand up straight. "What was with the crazy driver of that car?"

"It's a long story," Samantha sighed. She patted her damp face with the sleeve of her coat, then took her bags from the woman. "Thank you so much."

Samantha spun around and rushed inside her car. Her hands struggled to grip her phone and dial Gregory's number. When she finally got the call to go through, he picked up on the first ring.

"Hey, I was just thinking about you," he said. "I'm really looking forward to our dinner tonight."

Before Samantha could say a word, she burst into tears.

"Wh-what's going on?" he asked. "Are you crying?"

"I'm at the grocery store," she sobbed, "and when I came out into the parking lot, somebody tried to run me over!"

"Wait, somebody *what*?"

"Somebody tried to hit me with their car!" she cried out, clenching her heaving chest.

"Okay, calm down," the detective said soothingly. "Are you still at the store?"

Samantha could hear him rustling about, then heard a door slam. A feeling of relief rushed over her knowing he was already on his way there.

"Yes. I'm in the parking lot. But I don't feel safe staying here. At all."

"Okay. Why don't you head to your house and I'll meet you there? The squad car should be watching over your place. At this point, though, I'm honestly not comfortable with the idea of you staying in your home. If it's okay with you, I'd like you to pack a bag and come stay with me."

Samantha opened her mouth to speak, but she couldn't even formulate the words to express how thankful she was for Gregory.

"Are you still there?" he asked after several moments of silence. "I hope that suggestion didn't make you uncomfortable."

"No, it didn't," she whispered. "Not at all. That's extremely generous of you to offer. And I will take you up on it. Thank you."

Samantha started her car and pulled out of the lot. Her head swiveled back and forth as she searched for the dark sedan, afraid that it would come flying at her out of nowhere. But the street was empty.

"I'm on my way to your place now," Gregory told her. "I'll stay on the phone with you until you get there."

"Thanks," she replied, a rush of gratitude managing to overpower the burning fear churning throughout her body.

"No problem. I know you're tough and all, but what you went through tonight must have been terrifying. I'm so sorry this is all happening to you, Samantha."

"I'm scared, Gregory," she blurted out in spite of hating to admit it. She wasn't used to feeling this vulnerable. But no cold case she'd ever covered had hit this close to home, to the point where she was in such danger.

"I know you are, Sam. I clearly need to step up protecting you. The good news is that we're closing in on Collin. The bad news is, he knows it. So he's amping up the threat against you in hopes that you'll back off. If it's any consolation, he's unlikely to do anything in such a public place. He wants to scare you enough that you'll stop investigating."

Samantha felt a streak of anger shoot through her. She squeezed the steering wheel and pressed down on the accelerator.

"That'll never happen," she insisted. "I don't give a damn how scared I am, or how crazy Collin gets. I refuse to let up until he is behind bars. *Period.* I will not quit until we get justice for Jacob."

"I understand that, Sam. But like I keep telling you, you can't risk losing your life over this. Maybe you should let up on the blog posts for now. Go dark for a minute. Let him think you backed off. Focus on the results we're waiting to get back from my IT forensics guy. We've also got Hudson on our team now. Have you tried to set up that meeting with him?"

"I did. I reached out to him earlier this afternoon. I'm just waiting to hear back."

"Okay, good. Hopefully you'll hear back soon."

The pair grew silent for several seconds. Samantha could feel the pressure as the situation began to close in on them.

Yet as thoughts of staying at Gregory's place crossed her mind, she realized that it was all bringing them closer together.

"I'm a few blocks away from your house now," he told her. "How far away are you?"

"I should be there in a couple of minutes."

"Okay. I want you to pull your car into the garage—"

"Which I did get fixed, by the way," Samantha interjected.

"Glad to hear it. Once you pull your car in, I'll go inside the house with you while you pack a bag. Move as quickly as you can, grab what you need, then we'll take my car back to my house. Cool?"

"Sounds good. Oh, and I'm so sorry about dinner. You have Collin to blame for missing out on the filet mignon, double-baked potatoes and grilled asparagus I was planning on preparing tonight."

"Do you really think I'm about to let Collin ruin our dinner plans? I still have every intention of indulging in our meal. We'll just pull a little switch up and I'll take the reins and whip up the meal for us. I've got a fantastic red wine that'll go well with those steaks you bought, too."

"You're so good to me. That would be wonderful. I could really go for a glass of wine right about now. Or three…"

"Well, lucky for you I've got a couple of bottles," Gregory laughed. "And I just bought a new set of furniture for my deck. Why don't we sit out there and eat? I can cook up the steaks on the grill, light up the heat lamps and fire pit. Then after we enjoy a nice, relaxing meal, we'll plot out our next moves on gathering the evidence to present to Mayor Elliot."

Samantha felt her stiff back slacken as Detective Harris put her at ease. "I'd like that. We can do it over the cheesecake I bought for dessert."

"Mmm, now my mouth is watering…"

When she turned down her block, Samantha was relieved to see Gregory's car parked in front of her house.

"By the way," he said, "I just pulled up in front of your house."

"I see you. I'm pulling up now."

Samantha drove up beside Gregory, waving as he nodded and waved back. She could tell by the look in his shining eyes that he was just as pleased to see her as she was him. She lowered the window.

"Thank you so much for coming to my rescue yet again," Samantha told him.

"Ah, don't even mention it. At this point you're working harder for the Gattenburg PD than our actual employees. I consider you one of us now. Therefore, I owe it to you to look out."

"I appreciate you."

"It's my pleasure…"

The twosome sat there gazing at one another before Samantha noticed the squad car that'd been keeping watch over her house blink its headlights at her. She tapped her horn and waved.

"I'm really grateful that Officer Barris has been keeping an eye on my house. Thanks again for setting that up."

"No problem." The detective shifted in his seat and glanced behind him. "All right. Enough with the small talk. We'll have plenty of time for that once we get to my place. Why don't you go ahead and pull into the garage, then grab your things? I'll meet you at the front door."

"Will do."

Samantha turned into her driveway and clicked the garage door opener. As she waited for the door to rise, she glanced in her rearview mirror and watched as Gregory stepped out of his car.

He threw on his black leather motorcycle jacket while strolling toward her front door. The cool, confident swagger in his gait, mixed with his sexy good looks and gym-honed physique, had her wondering how she would get through staying at his house without slipping out of her bed and into his.

"GREGORY, THIS WAS absolutely delicious," Samantha said, dabbing the corners of her mouth with her napkin. "I hate to admit it, but my meal probably wouldn't have been as good as yours."

"Nonsense. Stop trying to boost my self-esteem. I'm sure yours would've been better."

Samantha felt a tingling heat creep up the back of her neck underneath the intensity of Gregory's gaze. She picked up her glass of cabernet and took a long sip, focusing on the rim as opposed to his seductive stare. She knew that if she looked him directly in the eye, she just might jump across the table and do something wildly inappropriate.

"Well," she continued, discreetly patting away the beads of sweat that had formed along her hairline, "the filet mignon was grilled to perfection. The twice-baked potatoes were crispy on the outside and nice and tender on the inside, just like I like them. And the charred grilled asparagus was tender and full of flavor."

Gregory's lips spread into a gradual smile. Samantha pressed her fingertips against her mouth and threw him a chef's kiss.

"My compliments to the chef. This was amazing."

"Why, thank you. You know what they say—when you cook with love in your heart, the meal is always delicious."

Samantha cocked her head to one side and felt herself swoon at the sound of those words. "That is what they say, isn't it?"

"It is…"

Gregory refilled their glasses, then set the bottle back down, his expression growing somber. "So, I've tried to avoid talking about what happened to you tonight for as long as I possibly could, but we do need to discuss it."

She swallowed hard as the elevated energy in her mood quickly spiraled upward. "I know we do. I'm okay. We can discuss it."

He swirled his wine around in the glass before continuing. "So you're sure the car that almost hit you is the same vehicle you saw in the alleyway the day your garage was vandalized?"

"Yes. I'm positive it was the same car."

"But neither you nor the woman who helped you today were able to get a good look at the license plate?"

"Unfortunately, no. We didn't. That would've been such a huge help, too."

"It would have. But that's okay. I've been trying to keep an eye out on all the dark sedans I see across town and run their license plate numbers. My plan is to pull them over and ask questions if anything suspect comes up in the system. So far, they've all turned up clean."

"Humph. Well, hopefully something will turn up soon. We know Collin drives that obnoxious pickup truck, so my guess is that it's one of his boys."

"That's my guess, too."

Gregory took a swallow of wine, then leaned back in his chair. "Listen, I really hope you took what I mentioned earlier to heart. I want you to start keeping a low profile. Not only should you go dark on the blog for a while, but start being more low-key around town, too. I'll continue to have Officer Barris keep an eye out on your house. Now that we see Collin and his associates are playing dirtier, we'll be keeping a closer eye on you, too."

The thought of being confined and having to watch her every move irritated Samantha to her core. But deep down, she knew the detective was looking out for her best interest.

"Okay," she reluctantly agreed. "I can do that."

"You can?" he asked, sounding surprised. "That's it? You're not gonna give me any type of pushback?"

"Nope—" she shrugged "—because I know you're right. I may be tenacious, but I'm not stupid. It's obvious that Collin is willing to do whatever he can to silence me. I've seen firsthand what's come of Jacob and the other factory workers. I don't want to suffer the same fate."

"And I don't want you to. So I'm glad we're on the same page."

Samantha took several sips of wine while staring thoughtfully into the flames flickering in the fire pit. "At this point, I know that getting Mayor Elliot involved is our best hope. So I'm willing to stand down while we gather the necessary evidence to present to him."

Gregory held his hand up and gave Samantha a high five. "It's so awesome to hear you say that, *partner.*"

"And it's so awesome to hear you call me partner. Remember back when you wouldn't even talk to me about this investigation? Look at you now."

He chuckled self-consciously. "Yeah, well, what can I say? You presented a pretty compelling case. Then you charmed me with your good looks and alluring personality. So technically I had no choice."

"Oh, is that what I did?" Samantha laughed.

"It sure is."

The twosome stared at each other across the table. Through the corner of her eye, Samantha noticed Gregory's hand slowly sliding toward hers. Just as their fingertips touched, the heat lamp above them went out.

"Oh no," he muttered, glancing up at it. When he stood up and tinkered with the on/off switch, the fire pit's flames began to die down.

"What is happening right now?" Samantha asked.

"I know, right? Are our heat sources trying to tell us something?"

"Yeah, that we need to wrap things up out here and go back inside," she told him.

"Maybe so. Because it looks like this heat lamp is out for the count. I just bought this thing, too. Oh well, it'll be going right back to the store tomorrow."

As Gregory poured water over the fire pit to snuff out the remaining flames, Samantha stood up and began collecting their dishes.

"By the way," she said, "since I didn't hear back from Hudson, I sent him another text message asking if he'd be willing to talk with me tomorrow."

"Good. Hopefully he'll say yes, then offer up some pertinent information to add to the file we're building for Mayor Elliot." The detective paused, staring at Samantha thoughtfully. "But I don't know. After what happened tonight in that parking lot, I don't want you meeting with Hudson in person. It could be dangerous if you two are seen together. Try and make it either a phone call or video chat."

Samantha slid the patio door open, then turned to Gregory and nodded her head. "I think that's a good idea. Better safe than sorry."

She paused, contemplating her next thought before continuing. "Hey, there's something else that's been on my mind. I know you want me to be low-key moving forward and all, but I really want to share what happened to me tonight with Ava. She needs to be careful out here, too. Everybody in town knows she's working to get justice for Jacob, which means she could possibly be in danger. Wouldn't you agree?"

"Yes, I definitely agree. No one involved in this case can be too careful at this point." Gregory grabbed the rest of the dishes and followed Samantha inside. He set everything in the sink then turned to her. "You know what? I'm going to fill out a police report and take a statement from you on what happened in that parking lot tonight."

"Don't you think that'll draw unwanted attention to us?"

"I do. Which is why I'm not going to actually process the report. I'm just going to fill it out and add it to the file that we're building for the district attorney, along with the vandalism reports on your house that I actually did process."

"You mean the ones that Chief Wentworth promised to look into then completely forgot about?"

"Yes, those," Gregory chortled, pulling the cheesecake from the refrigerator and placing it on the counter. "I just need the mayor to have a record of every incident and each piece of evidence we've gathered. That should make it easy for him to draw up charges against Collin, Chief Wentworth and everyone else involved in the drug ring."

"Speaking of everyone else, did you find any reports on drug busts that may be linked to Westman's?"

"Only one. It involved a temporary employee who

worked there briefly during the summer. He nearly OD'd after a night out with several of the assembly workers."

"Let me guess. No charges were ever filed against anyone."

"Unfortunately, no," Gregory sighed. "I did some digging into Chief Wentworth's background, too. I expected to find evidence of him using that drug money to make major purchases, take lavish vacations, something. But surprisingly, he lives a pretty modest lifestyle."

"Hmm, interesting. Maybe he pays for everything with cash and keeps his toys stashed away in another town."

"Maybe…"

Samantha poured the last of the wine into their glasses and handed one to Gregory. After they each took a sip, he reached over and covered her hand with his. "So how are you feeling now? Are you all right?"

"I'm still a bit shaken up." She shrugged. "But being here with you is certainly helping to keep me calm."

He caressed her hand while gazing at her sympathetically. Samantha responded by intertwining her fingers within his.

When he began stroking her palm with his thumb, the arousing sensation caused a nagging voice to go off inside her head.

Don't get distracted before you complete your mission…

She cleared her throat and slipped her hand from his grip. "So anyway," she continued, "thank you for tonight. Especially that delicious meal."

The detective paused, as if surprised by the abrupt way in which she disrupted their intimate moment and changed the subject.

"I'm glad you enjoyed it," he told her. "Are you ready for dessert?"

"I am. I'll grab a couple of plates and forks."

Gregory pulled a can of whipped cream and a container of mixed berries out of the refrigerator. "Look what I've got."

"Ooh, nice. Those'll go great with the cheesecake."

"I thought so, too."

He cut two slices of cake and slid them onto the plates, then topped them with the garnishes.

"I'll tell you what," Gregory continued. "Why don't we take our dessert and wine into the television room and get lost in some trashy reality TV show? No more talk of Collin, Chief Wentworth or their drug operation. Let's just decompress and enjoy the rest of the evening together. How does that sound?"

"That sounds perfect."

Samantha trailed behind Gregory as he led her down a hallway into the den. The pair got comfy on his chocolate-brown leather couch while he grabbed the remote and turned on the television.

"So look," she told him, "I'm not trying to watch anything pertaining to sports or pimped-out hot rods."

"Well, I'm not trying to watch any makeup or modeling competitions."

"Awfully presumptuous, aren't you?"

"Aren't *you*?" Gregory rebutted before they both burst out laughing.

"Listen, why don't we find some middle ground here? What about *90 Day Fiancé*?"

"Ninety day what?"

"90 Day Fiancé!" Samantha repeated. "It's this crazy reality show about people in the United States who connect with foreigners overseas."

Gregory shook his head while punching buttons on the remote. "Okay, that sounds absolutely insane."

"Yeah, but I see you're doing a search for it, so obviously you're interested."

"Obviously," he retorted before nudging Samantha's arm. "Found it. Let me see what this madness is all about…"

As Gregory hit the play button, Samantha reclined farther back into the couch and slid a piece of cheesecake inside her mouth. While her day had been traumatic, she was overcome by a sense of peace and protection being in the detective's presence.

But in the back of her mind, Samantha had an uneasy feeling that the worst was yet to come.

Chapter Fourteen

Gregory glanced down at his watch. It was a little after three o'clock in the afternoon. He was still at the station, refreshing his personal email inbox like a madman.

His IT forensics guy, Wayne, had promised he'd get back to him with some answers on Kenzie's email before the end of the workday. But the detective still hadn't heard from him.

Gregory had been able to schedule a last-minute appointment with the district attorney at four o'clock that afternoon. He was eager to report on Wayne's findings, along with the information that he and Samantha had gathered.

"Come on, dammit," Gregory grumbled, once again pounding the touchpad on his laptop. Still no new messages.

Just as he pushed away from the desk, his cell phone rang.

"Detective Harris," he barked without even checking the caller ID.

"Hey, is everything okay?"

The sound of Samantha's voice on the other end of the phone quickly put Gregory at ease.

"Hey, yeah, everything's okay. Well, actually, no. It's isn't. I thought I would've heard back from Wayne by now regarding Kenzie's email. I'm getting worried, because it's been radio silence on his end. I hope this isn't gonna end up being one of the rare cases where he's unable to track the message."

"Well, the day isn't over yet. So just relax and give him a little more time. Maybe Collin was smart enough to send the email through a virtual private network rather than his own internet service provider. If so, its origins would be harder to trace. Either way, I'm sure you'll hear back from Wayne with some news soon."

Gregory gnawed at his thumbnail. "I hope you're right. I'm just feeling an immense amount of pressure because we're running out of time here. We've got to get this report to the DA before Collin strikes again. I don't want anybody else to turn up missing, or dead, or worse. Especially you…"

He paused and took a deep breath, unable to go on.

"Just breathe, Gregory," Samantha said calmly. "You're good. *We're* good. We are making some great strides here. Don't start letting this case get the best of you. We've come too far to break down now. According to you, Wayne is a pro, right?"

"Yes, he is."

"And he's never failed you before, has he?"

"No," Gregory sighed, falling back in his chair and taking a long sip of stale, lukewarm coffee. "He hasn't."

"Well, trust and believe that he isn't going to let you down now. I know the clock is ticking. But let's just be patient. Wayne will come through for you soon enough."

The detective rubbed his burning eyes. Between worrying about their investigation and fighting off sensual thoughts of Samantha all night as she slept in the room right next to his, he hadn't gotten much rest.

"Now," she continued, "the reason why I'm calling is because I've got some pretty explosive news to share with you."

"You do?" Gregory hopped up and closed the door when

he noticed several police officers gathering near his office. "All right, let's hear it."

"I spoke with Hud—"

"Wait, hold up a sec," the detective interrupted when he heard his computer ping.

He rushed back over to the desk and refreshed his email inbox. A new message from Wayne appeared on the screen.

"Bingo!" he yelled so loudly that the officers standing outside his office peered at him through the glass window with raised eyebrows.

Gregory threw them a thumbs-up, indicating that all was well before turning back to his computer.

"What is going on?" Samantha asked.

"I just got an email from Wayne."

"See! I told you he wouldn't let you down. What does it say?"

He rolled his chair up to the desk and clicked on the message.

"It says, 'What's up, man, sorry it took me a minute to get back to you. I got the results back on the email. It was sent through a VPN rather than an ISP, so tracking the sender's IP address was a challenge. But what the sender didn't realize is that some VPNs keep a record of users' internet movement. So I was able to log the server activity, hence enabling me to trace him.'"

"Got it. Now come on. Get to the good part!" Samantha insisted.

"Okay, okay," the detective said, "The last paragraph says, 'So you were right, the IP address that I traced the email back to belongs to Collin Wentworth.'"

Gregory heard Samantha gasp as she realized what this meant. Collin must have used Kenzie's email address to send the message, but he'd done it from his own IP address.

"Wow," she breathed. "We called it. You and I both knew Collin was behind that message. But hearing the confir-

mation from an expert is wonderful. Everything is really falling into place with this case."

"I know, right? I only wish we'd gotten the info we needed before Kenzie disappeared," the detective said as he printed out Wayne's message and added it to his file for the district attorney.

"I know. But we're doing what we can as fast as we can. And I haven't even told you what I found out from Hudson when we spoke today."

"Wait, you talked to Hudson?"

"Yes! That's what I was about to tell you when Wayne's email came through. Listen, he spilled all types of tea on Collin, his drug ring *and* the deceased Westman's workers."

Gregory looked up and noticed that the cops milling around his office seemed to be doing more than just chatting among themselves. It appeared as though they were trying to eavesdrop on his conversation.

"Hey, hold that thought," he told Samantha before lowering his voice. "There are some officers congregating outside my office, and I don't know what they're up to. So why don't we continue this conversation after I leave the station?"

"Good idea. Because we don't know who's on whose team in there. Better safe than sorry."

"Exactly." Gregory kept his eyes on the window of his office while grabbing his laptop and car key. "Listen, I know you've been cooped up in my house all day. After my meeting with the DA, why don't I come pick you up and we'll go grab some sushi for dinner? There's a new spot that just opened up over on Spranton. I hear it's pretty private and low-key. I highly doubt that we'll be spotted in that area."

"Mmm, sushi would be delicious. I'm actually in the middle of clawing my way through an article for the women's journal on how to manage your anxiety when life gets too overwhelming. Needless to say, I could use a break."

"So basically working on a piece that sums up everything you're going through right now."

"Exactly."

Gregory got up and opened his office door. The cops standing nearby quickly stepped to the side, their tense expressions appearing apprehensive. The detective acknowledged them with a slight nod, his blank stare more cold than friendly.

"These dudes are in here acting a little funny toward me," he muttered into the phone as he swaggered through the police station.

"I wonder how many of them know what their beloved Chief Wentworth is actually up to."

"Speaking of the devil…"

Gregory walked past the break room and noticed the chief holding court with Officers Baxter and Miller near the vending machine. They were cracking up laughing while toasting with soda cans and slapping one another on the backs.

"*Which* devil?" Samantha snarked. "Because there appear to be a whole lot of them in there."

"You're right. But this time I'm referring to Chief Wentworth and his cronies, Baxter and Miller," he said, keeping his voice low.

"You mean those two clowns who showed up to my house and conducted that half-ass investigation after Collin busted out my windows?"

Gregory subdued a laugh as he pushed through the station's revolving door and walked out into the parking lot.

"Yeah, those two."

"Well, hopefully your meeting with the district attorney will put an end to all this madness and these criminals will finally be charged with their crimes."

"That's my hope, too," the detective said as he climbed inside his car. "I'm feeling really confident now that we have proof of Kenzie's email being sent from Collin's IP address, along with all the other evidence we've gathered."

"Same here. And I'm looking forward to us making a toast over dinner to what I already know will be a fantastic meeting with the DA."

Gregory felt a surge of excitement at the thought of sharing an intimate dinner with Samantha unrelated to the case.

It had been a long time since he'd actually taken a woman out on a date. Memories of courting an ex-girlfriend back in Chicago came to mind. They'd spent countless nights together, sharing candlelit dinners in Little Italy and dancing to jazz music in tiny clubs in Wicker Park.

Stop it, Gregory told himself, quickly pushing those thoughts out of his head. The last thing he wanted to do was compare what they had to his old life back in Chicago.

"Hey, you still there?" she asked, snapping him out of his thoughts.

"Yeah, I am. Sorry about that. What were you saying?"

"I was saying that I'm going to hang up so I can finish up some work, then start getting ready."

"Gotcha. I missed that. I was, uh…thinking about what types of sushi rolls I'm gonna order later," Gregory lied.

"Mmm, I'll have to go online and check out their menu. Good luck with the meeting, and I will be ready when you get here."

"Thanks. See you soon."

He disconnected the call and took a deep breath.

Keep your cool. And get your emotions in check… Detective Harris thought as he headed to the DA's office.

"I CANNOT BELIEVE I let you talk me into this," Gregory said, shaking his head as a feeling of regret took hold of him.

He clutched the steering wheel while making a right turn onto Everhart Avenue, then slowly drove down the street.

"Trust me, we're doing the right thing," Samantha insisted. "This is the last piece of evidence that we need to hand over to the district attorney in order for him to file charges against Collin, Chief Wentworth and whoever else is involved in their drug ring."

Detective Harris tapped on the brake and pulled over when Westman's Automotive Factory came into view. He glanced down at the clock. It was a little after nine o'clock.

The pair had just left dinner. Gregory and Samantha had spent most of the evening discussing how his meeting with the district attorney went left after the DA insisted that the detective didn't have enough evidence to execute any warrants, let alone arrests.

Gregory decided against showing him Collin's drug ledger since it was obtained without a warrant, making it inadmissible to present as evidence in court.

After the detective and Samantha left the restaurant, she'd received a text message from Hudson. His friend was working security at Westman's and agreed to let them inside the factory after hours.

"So look," Samantha began, "according to Hudson, the maintenance crew is usually done cleaning at about nine o'clock. So we should be good."

"*We?* What do you mean we? I haven't agreed to step foot inside that factory with you. Now, for the thousandth time, this is a bad idea, Samantha. The DA isn't going to use anything you find here, so you could be jeopardizing any case we do end up putting together. And you're once again risking your life by breaking into this place in search of an alleged drug laboratory that you're not even sure exists!"

"But what if it does?" she shot back, her eyes dancing wildly as she stared across the street at Westman's. "That would be a slam dunk, *guaranteeing* a prison cell inside the Menard Correctional Center with Collin's and his father's names written on it."

"So you're envisioning them being sent to the toughest prison in the state, huh?"

Samantha threw her hands in the air and looked around in confusion. "Of course! With capital murder, kidnapping and drug trafficking charges against them, where else would they go?"

"True. But as for this second break-in you're trying to pull off? Don't do this. After we gather more evidence and present it to the DA, I'm sure he'll generate a search warrant so that the factory can be inspected legally."

"I'm not breaking in. The security guard is going to *let* me in. And I hear what you're saying, but I just can't pass up this opportunity, Gregory. Now, Hudson is already inside the factory. Should I text him back and let him know we're here?"

Gregory rubbed his eyes in frustration then stared out the window. Thoughts of all the various ways things could go wrong flooded his mind.

"I'm really looking for a way to talk you out of this," he said.

"Nothing you say can talk me out of this."

The detective shook his head in disbelief. "I cannot believe this is happening right now..." He turned his attention toward Westman's. "This security guard I see leaning against the wall eating a submarine sandwich, he's Hudson's boy?"

"Yes. And he was friends with Jacob, too. So he wants to see Collin get locked up just as badly as the rest of us. The only reason he's still working at Westman's is because he has a family to support."

A pang of doubt rattled inside Gregory's chest. "I'm telling you, Samantha. I am not feeling this. At all."

She rolled her eyes and slumped down in her seat.

"But," the detective continued, "with that being said, I can go in and meet with Hudson instead of you. It'd be too dangerous for—"

"No," Samantha interrupted. "Trust me. Hudson won't meet with you alone. I have to do this myself."

Gregory paused, watching as she slowly glanced over at him.

"I don't want a repeat of what happened during the incident at Collin's house, where you were all alone having to fend for yourself. While I may not agree with what you're doing here, my conscience won't allow me to let you do this by yourself. I'm an officer of the law. This meeting is with an informant. That will keep it aboveboard."

"Thank you, Gregory," she replied softly.

"Don't," he said. "Don't thank me. I'm not happy with this."

"Oh, come on," Samantha said. "You'll be thanking me when the district attorney presents the photos I'm about to take to the jury once Collin and Chief Wentworth go to trial."

"Let me handle any photos. Remember, it's a meeting with an informant. I take the lead," he said.

"You know what? I—"

Samantha was interrupted when her cell phone buzzed.

"Saved by the bell," she said before grabbing it off her lap and peering down at the screen. "That's Hudson texting me again. He said that if I'm coming to meet him over at the side door, because there's no security camera posted above the doorway."

Gregory looked up at the parking lot's back door and noticed a camera hovering over the entryway.

"He's just now figuring that out?" he asked, his words tinged with doubt.

Samantha ignored him. "Beechwood Street—that's where the side door entrance is located."

Without saying another word, Detective Harris took off, speeding down the street and around the corner. He drove in silence, his jaw set tight, his anger and apprehension growing.

Once at the Beechwood entrance, Gregory threw the car into Park and turned off the headlights.

Samantha stared at him with wide eyes filled with anger. "Can I expect you to still be here when I come out?" she asked curtly.

"I'm going in with you," he said, not looking at her.

"If you do that, Hudson will bolt."

"I told you—I take the lead. Or this isn't happening."

In response, she opened the door and got out. When he did the same, she turned and stopped.

"Don't. Don't come with me. I promise I'll be careful. I won't compromise the investigation. If you come with me, it's over."

It's over. The investigation or them?

Gregory pushed out a sigh. He knew Samantha would do this with or without him. He had to play by her rules now or deal with the fallout of her going at it alone when he wasn't around to protect her.

"Okay," he gritted out. "I trust you. Now you trust me. If I think you are in trouble, I will come in there. I made a commitment to look after you, and I'll honor it."

"Thank you," Samantha mumbled, her voice barely a whisper. She sent Hudson a message letting him know she was on her way inside.

Gregory stayed in the shadows and watched as she approached the factory's steel-gray side door, every muscle and nerve in his body yelling at him to go after her. He stayed put, watching as the door opened just as she reached up to knock.

The detective craned his neck, trying to catch a glimpse of Hudson. But the bleak, dimly lit entryway was too dark for him to make out the figure standing on the doorstep. Within seconds, Samantha slipped inside and the door quickly slammed shut.

"Please don't let anything happen to this woman," Gregory said to himself, closing his eyes.

Thoughts of Samantha being confronted by Collin or getting hurt while inside the factory flooded his mind.

The detective's eyes flew open as a sense of urgency rushed through his body. He couldn't just stand here and wait. He had to do something.

His eyes were met with darkness. Only faint streams of light shone down on the desolate street in the distance from the scarce streetlights.

He pulled out his phone and composed a text message to Samantha.

Have Hudson send the security guard a text letting him know I'm going to be walking around outside the factory. I need to keep a closer eye on things. If you get the sense that something's wrong, get the hell out. I'll be here for you.

He sent the message, and without waiting for a reply, crept around to the side of the building, eyeing the old, thick, frosted windows lining the factory's lower level.

Gregory stooped down and leaned into one of the windows. He held his hands against the sides of his eyes, attempting to peer inside the building. But the cloudy haze covering the glass prevented him from seeing a thing.

He stood up and stepped away from the window, ignoring the stench of rotting food coming from a rusted-out nearby dumpster. A twinge of angst pulled at his chest as he anxiously waited to hear back from Samantha.

The detective pulled the phone from his back pocket, checking to see whether she'd texted him back. She hadn't.

"Don't start worrying," he told himself, struggling to ignore the sense of panic beginning to simmer inside his head.

When a frigid wind whipped past him, Gregory grabbed a black wool skull cap out of his coat pocket and slipped it over his head. Just as he reached for his black leather gloves, his cell phone buzzed. He exhaled with relief after a text message from Samantha popped up on the screen.

Hudson let the guard know you're on the scene. You're good. We're in the factory's overflow supply room now. It's on the lower level, northeast side. Hudson thinks there's some sort of secret entrance into the drug lab here. I'll keep you posted.

Good, Gregory wrote back. Don't stay too long. Leave if you don't find something soon. Otherwise, I'll come in.

After the detective sent the message, he pulled on his black leather gloves and scanned the area. There weren't many cars driving down the road. The only sounds he heard were the wind whistling past his ears and faint rumblings of a freight train in the distance.

He reached behind him and felt for the nine-millimeter he'd tucked away in the back of his jeans. It was still firmly in place, waiting to be drawn if necessary...

Chapter Fifteen

Samantha walked closely behind Hudson. She squinted her eyes in an attempt to see what was in front of her as they tiptoed through the huge, dimly lit supply room.

Very few of the industrial strip lights hanging from the high ceilings seemed to be working. Those that were flickered off and on sporadically like something from a horror movie, the effect enhanced by creepy buzzing sounds hissing underneath the lights' surface.

She tried to ignore the eerie chills crawling up her back and focus on Hudson's thick, shaggy red hair. But when she heard a loud thud bang against one of the windows, she gasped and practically leaped onto his scrawny back.

"What the hell was that?" she whispered.

"Who knows?" he replied nonchalantly, waving his hand in the air as if he didn't have a care in the world. "Probably just a cat or something. Let's just keep moving."

Samantha pursed her lips tightly together, forcing herself not to press the issue. Ava had forgotten to mention just how much of a burnout Hudson was. His drug abuse issues were obvious, from his small pupils and slurred speech to his gaunt appearance and constant scratching. Despite the fact that the factory's basement was freezing cold, Hudson was sweating profusely.

But Samantha was trying her best to ignore all that and

stay focused on the goal. If she had to follow the lead of a drug addict in order to get Collin and Chief Wentworth behind bars, then so be it.

"It is so rancid in here," she whispered, covering her nose with her hand.

There wasn't a stream of air circulating through the dank room. Between its musty odor and the stench of sweat wafting off Hudson, Samantha felt as though she might gag.

"Let's just find what we're looking for so we can grab what we need and get the hell outta here," he mumbled, stomping his feet against the floor as if looking for a trap door.

Samantha side-eyed him suspiciously. She was beginning to wonder whether he was looking to score drugs inside Collin's lab as opposed to helping her gather evidence.

She pulled out her cell phone and turned on the flashlight, then held it up toward the steel shelving units on either side of her. They were packed with sheets of metal, heaps of plastics, boxes of rubber and stacks of fiberglass.

When they reached the end of the aisle, Hudson turned and headed down the next one while continuing to stomp the floor.

"Hey," she whispered, knowing they were the only two inside the factory but still feeling the need to keep her voice down, "while you continue to check the floors, I'm going to walk along the walls and see if I can find some sort of hidden door that might lead to the lab." She felt better on her own, and Hudson wasn't giving the impression he really knew what he was looking for.

"All right, cool. Just give me a holler if you find something."

"I will. You do the same."

Samantha broke off from Hudson and headed toward the front of the supply room. She flashed the light from her phone along the drywall, using her hand to push into it in search of a crease or crevice that doubled as a hidden panel.

After several moments of silence, Hudson howled so loudly that Samantha practically jumped out of her boots.

"What's wrong?" she yelped, charging toward the back of the room.

"Woo-hoo!" he wailed.

"Did you find something?"

"I believe I did. Check this out."

Hudson was down on all fours, yanking at a small steel hook that stuck up out of what appeared to be a trap door in the floor.

"Oh wait, there's a padlock securing this thing," he huffed.

Samantha turned to a shelf next to her and dug around inside several boxes until she found a steel pipe.

"Here. Try this."

Hudson grabbed the pipe, raised it high in the air and cracked it against the padlock.

The piercing reverberation of metal on metal caused her to flinch.

"Ooh," she uttered, hunching her shoulders up toward her earlobes as if that would help muffle the clamor. "Did that do it?"

"Not that time. But give me a couple more tries."

After several more attempts at banging the pipe against the lock, Samantha heard pieces of metal skid across the floor.

"You got it?"

"I got it!" he boomed.

She leaned in closer, watching as he grabbed the door's steel loop. He gave it a yank, but the door didn't budge.

"I think it might be stuck," he grunted while continuing to pull at the lever. On the third try, the black panel that blended in perfectly with the floor flew open.

"Yes!" Samantha exclaimed, clapping her hands frantically. She bent down, aiming her cell phone's flashlight into the opening. The minuscule stream of light didn't provide much brightness. All she could make out was what appeared to be a dark abyss.

"Can you see anything down there?" she asked Hudson.

"I'm tryin', but not really." He sat back on his heels and stared off into space. "I cannot friggin' believe this, man. I *told* those dudes on my assembly team that Collin had a secret drug lab hidden somewhere in this place. They just argued me up and down, telling me how wrong I was. *Idiots.*"

"Hudson," Samantha said, eager to get moving, "turn on your cell phone's flashlight so we can get a better look at what's down there."

He sluggishly fumbled around inside his puffy neon-green jacket for several seconds before finally pulling out his phone. After tapping the screen for several seconds, he threw his head back and focused on the ceiling.

"Damn," he wheezed, dumbfounded, his thin, cracked lips hanging open. "What's my security code?"

"You don't need to enter your security code to access the flashlight," Samantha told him, resisting the urge to push him off to the side and make her way down into the opening on her own.

"Got it," he finally said, pressing more buttons until the flashlight came on.

The pair held their lights down into the darkness. A set of extremely steep black stairs appeared. Before she could say a word, Hudson spun around on his knees and began climbing down steps.

"Be careful," she told him.

"I will. But I'm hardheaded. So if I fall, I'll pop right up and keep it moving!" he snorted before emitting an animalistic cackle.

Just get in, get your photos and get out, Samantha told herself.

While he slowly made his way down, she composed a quick text message to Gregory letting him know they'd found what looked to be the drug lab.

There's a trap door in the floor of the supply room, she quickly typed. We're heading down now. More soon!

Samantha sent the message, then carefully began descending the stairs behind Hudson.

"Do you see a light down there anywhere?" she called out.

"I think I see one hanging from the ceiling. I'm trying to find a pull string, or maybe there's a switch somewhere."

As she waited for him to locate the light, Samantha stood in the middle of the stairway and aimed her phone's flashlight around the small, filthy room.

She zoned in on two steel tables covered in blenders, scales, glass cookware and pill bottles. When she climbed down a couple more steps to get a better look, a putrid mixture of toxic chemicals and urine invaded her nostrils.

"I *knew* it," she said to herself, using her free hand to shield her nose. "I knew Collin was using Westman's to manufacture drugs. And look at what we've found here…"

"We just hit the jackpot, man!" Hudson hollered just as he turned on the light. He glanced around the room while rigorously scratching his face.

Samantha watched as Hudson threw his arms out at his sides and spun around like a kid in a candy shop. She resisted the urge to tell him to calm down and instead focused on sending Gregory an update.

Jackpot! she typed, her fingertips flying over the keypad. The drug lab! About to get pix now…

Before she could pull up her phone's camera app, Gregory's response popped up on the screen.

Get what you need then get out ASAP!

Will do.

Samantha closed his message, her hands trembling as she began taking photos of the lab. She zoomed in on the tabletops, large jugs filled with murky liquid and buckets underneath the tables.

Just when Samantha began filming a video, she noticed Hudson shoving several bottles of pills inside his coat pockets.

"Hey, what are you doing?" she asked.

Hudson didn't look up from the table as he continued grabbing every pill bottle in sight.

"What does it look like I'm doing? I'm trying to score some of Collin's TKO for free. Don't trip on it, though. He owes me."

"Isn't TKO the same stuff that put you in the hospital?"

"Whatever…" Hudson panted, sweating profusely while feverishly stuffing as much product inside his pockets as he could. "That was probably just a bad batch."

"What a shame," Samantha muttered underneath her breath.

"Ooh, I'm gonna film a live chat with my boys so they can see all this!" Hudson announced.

"Hudson! *No.* That is not a good idea. We need to keep this place under wraps and focus on getting all the evidence turned in to the authorities. Your boys do not need to know about it."

"Aw, come on, man! Let me have a little fun here."

Samantha's eyes squinted warily at him. "I thought you brought me here to help get justice for Jacob and the rest of the Westman's workers. Not steal a bunch of deadly drugs and video chat with your boys for clout. Come on. Get it together. Don't lose focus on what we're trying to accomplish here."

"All right, fine," Hudson mumbled.

He reluctantly slipped his phone in his back pocket. But as Samantha continued filming her video of the lab, she noticed Hudson lurking around one of the tables and slipping more drugs inside his pockets.

Just let it go and get the rest of your footage, she told herself.

Samantha walked farther into the lab and began taking close-up shots of several propane fuel cylinders. A text message notification from Gregory popped up on the screen. She tapped on it.

You have got to get out of there NOW! it read. Collin and his boys just entered the factory!

Samantha's stomach dropped down to her knees. "Hudson!" she shrieked. "We've gotta go. Collin and his boys just pulled up!"

"Ha-ha, nice joke. They couldn't be here. Him and his crew are hanging out down at the strip club tonight."

"Well, obviously they had a change of plans," Samantha insisted, struggling to make her way up the steep set of stairs. "Detective…a friend…just texted me saying he saw them coming in. Now let's get the hell out of here before we get busted!"

Hudson casually strutted over to a metal cabinet, his filthy white sneakers screeching loudly across the floor.

"Hey!" Samantha hissed as she watched him rummage through the shelves. "This is not a drill. Let's go!"

"Yeah, yeah, I'll be up in a sec."

She couldn't wait. She climbed the stairs, hoping he'd follow. When Samantha reached the top, she froze at the sound of muffled voices coming from beyond the supply room.

"Nah, dude!" someone yelled. "The strippers can wait.

They won't care about us being late once I show up with a few bags of that TKO!"

She immediately recognized that sinister voice. Collin.

Samantha spun around and frantically waved her hand in Hudson's direction. But he was buried too deep inside the cabinet to notice.

"They already know what's up!" Collin said, his voice getting closer. "Big Vick is holding our VIP booth at the club, so we're good. The girls, the bottles…everything will be at our table when we get there."

Just as Samantha pulled herself out of the drug lab, she heard the door to the supply room fly open. Footsteps thumped loudly toward the back of the room.

Oh nooo, she thought as memories of her near misses with Collin came to mind.

"I'll make it quick," Collin said. "Just let me grab the product, then we'll be out."

"Cool, man. Do your thing," Samantha heard one of his cronies reply.

She stayed low and darted toward the back wall, then crouched down in a corner behind a shelf stacked with sheet metal.

"Hey!" Collin yelled. "Who the hell left the door to the lab open?"

Samantha cringed at the rage in his tone, swallowing hard as a lump of nausea crept up her throat.

"Not me," each of his boys quickly replied.

All Samantha could think about was Hudson still being down in the lab and what Collin would do if he found him. She prayed that he'd found a good hiding spot.

"I swear I can't trust you fools to do anything right!" Collin continued to rant. "What if the wrong person would've come up in here and found the lab?"

"There's only a few of us who have access to the supply

room, though," someone tried to reason. "Only your boys who are closest to you can even get back here."

"I don't give a damn about that!" Collin hollered. "I've got a couple of assembly team leads who have the door code but don't know about the lab. I'm telling you man, y'all better wake up. Don't make me have to unleash my other side. *Trust* me. You do not wanna meet him."

Samantha squeezed her phone in her quivering hand. As she heard the men climbing down the stairs, she composed a text to Gregory.

Collin and his boys are heading down into the drug lab and Hudson's still down there! I'm hiding in the supply room. Should I make a run for it or stay hidden?

While she waited for the detective to respond, Samantha struggled to hear what was happening down in the lab. Just when her phone buzzed, she heard yelling coming from the lab.

"What in the hell are you doing down here?"

She bent down and pressed her ear to the floor.

"Hudson!" she heard Collin bark. "Were you actually dumb enough to creep inside my factory and break into my lab? Wait! Are those my drugs falling out of your pockets? So you're stealing from me, too?"

Samantha swallowed hard. She checked the phone for Gregory's reply.

Stay put! Do not try to run. Don't risk being seen.

The thought of having to stay inside the factory made her shudder. But she knew Gregory was right.

Okay, she wrote back. Collin and his boys are in the lab. They found Hudson.

As soon as Samantha hit the send button, she heard more yelling coming from the lab.

"No, no, *no*! Please, Collin, don't!" Hudson pleaded.

"I am not the one to be messed with," she heard Collin shout. "I can't believe you had the audacity to try me. But hear me when I tell you that you'll never get the chance to do it again."

Samantha clenched her hands together and pressed them against her lips.

"Please, please don't hurt him," she whispered just as Collin yelled, "Hand me that pipe!"

"Come on, man," Hudson begged. "I promise you it'll never happen—"

He was silenced by the brutal sound of a bone cracking.

Hudson emitted an animalistic howl. Samantha covered her mouth, stifling the scream that almost flew out.

"Why'd you do that, man!" she heard Hudson shout. His words were garbled by pain.

"You know why I did it!" Collin yelled. "And you know why I'm about to do this, too."

The sound of another cracking bone numbed Samantha's eardrums. She shook so hard she could barely hold her phone.

"Get him outta here," Collin commanded.

Samantha scrambled to her feet and repositioned herself farther behind the stack of metal. Jumbled voices echoed up the stairs, followed by heavy, stuttering footsteps. Had Hudson given her up? Or had he been too addled to even remember she was here?

She crossed her arms in front of her tightly, shivering uncontrollably at the thought of being found.

When her cell phone began vibrating like crazy, Samantha silenced it completely then opened a string of text messages from Gregory.

What is all that noise? I'm at the door and coming in!

No! she quickly replied. Don't! Collin and his boys are on their way out. They just beat Hudson up!

Samantha sent the text, then braced herself as gurgling moans rippling through the supply room.

"Why didn't you just kill him?" one of Collin's cronies asked.

"Where's the fun in that?" Collin snarked. "I like to teach lessons. And you have to be alive to learn them. Hudson needs to know that Collin Wentworth is never, *ever* to be crossed. These broken bones will be a nice little reminder of that."

"So does this mean you're gonna just keep torturing him instead?" another one of the guys chuckled.

Samantha grimaced at the sound of amusement in his deep, gravelly voice.

"I might," Collin replied. "But I definitely wanna keep him around. Hudson's a good little lab rat. Let's me test out any drug on him that I want before putting it out on the street. Now grab him and let's get out of here."

Just as Samantha heard the men dragging a whimpering Hudson out of the room, her cell phone rang loudly. She stared down at it in horror.

Instead of silencing it, she'd accidentally turned the volume up full blast.

"Whose phone is that?" Collin asked.

A surge of fear detonated inside Samantha's chest. She shook uncontrollably while grappling with the button that turned off the ringer.

Her heart palpitated erratically as she leaned to the side and peered out at the men through a crack in between the shelves.

Hudson was sprawled out on the floor and appeared to

be unconscious. Two of Collin's flunkies were standing on either side of him, holding his arms.

"It wasn't my cell," both of them muttered, shrugging while looking around the room.

"Did one of you fools leave your phone down in the lab, or is somebody else in here with us?" Collin spewed, his voice rising with each word.

Samantha held her breath. She froze.

The sound of shuffling feet filled the air. Collin's boys had dropped Hudson's arms and were scrambling around the room.

"So you weren't in here alone, were you, ole Huddy boy?" Collin asked, kicking him savagely in the leg. "And you didn't even bother to *tell* me?"

Samantha curled up into a tight ball, every muscle in her body tense as she braced herself to face Collin's wrath. Her jaws clenched together tightly when she heard Hudson emit a heart-wrenching growl.

"It…it was my—my ph-phone," he sputtered.

"It was your *what*?" Collin yelled, ruthlessly kicking him again.

"It was my phone," Hudson repeated before coughing and gagging. A clump of blood gushed from his mouth.

Samantha pressed her teeth into her fist while she waited for Collin to respond. His boys stopped in their tracks one shelving unit away from where she was hiding.

"Dumbass," Collin muttered. He held his arm in the air, signaling for his boys to come back. "Hey! Let's get the hell out of here. Mitch, text Big Vick and tell him we're running late, but we'll be at the club after we make a quick stop. I need to figure out where to dump this pile of garbage," he spat before nudging Hudson's shoulder with the pipe.

Thank you, thank you, thank you, Samantha thought, beyond grateful that Hudson had looked out for her but still worried for him.

She glanced down at her phone and saw that Gregory had sent her about ten text messages in a row. She opened the most recent one.

If I don't hear from you within the next minute, I'm coming in!

Her fingertips raced across the screen as she responded to the message.

No! Don't!

Send.

They're coming out now!

Send.

And Hudson's still alive.

Send.

I'll be out as soon as they're gone. Stay low and meet me by the door where I came in. Is the guard still out there?

Samantha sent the last message then peered through the shelves. Hudson's feet had gotten caught in the doorway. One of Collin's cronies kicked the door open and yanked the rest of his body out of the room.

She quickly checked her phone for Gregory's reply.

Collin sent the guard to lunch when he got here. I see everybody coming out now. Start making your way to the door. I'll let you know when the coast it clear.

On my way! Samantha typed, both shocked and relieved that she was making it out of the factory alive.

When she stood up, her wobbly legs almost caused her to crash to the floor. She gripped a stack of boxes behind her and steadied her gait, then hurried through the supply room.

She peeked through the door before stepping out. The factory was empty. They didn't have round-the-clock shifts. Just as she crept past several workstations, her cell phone lit up with another text from Gregory.

It's clear. They just pulled off. I'm at the side door. Meet me there now!

Samantha couldn't get to the door fast enough. She darted past a row of equipment assembly systems and crashed through the exit so forcefully that she almost stumbled to the ground. Gregory was standing on the other side. He immediately grabbed hold of her.

"It's okay," he said, lifting her up and embracing her tightly. "Come on. I got you."

Samantha finally allowed herself to breathe. She closed her eyes and leaned into the detective, her feet barely touching the ground as he led them to the car.

"Thank you," she whispered into his chest.

"I'm just glad you're okay."

When he planted a soft kiss on her forehead, Samantha wrapped her arms around him and gripped the back of his jacket.

"I swear I didn't think I'd make it out of there alive."

"Well, you did. And from this point on, I'm never gonna allow you to get in harm's way again. Never. Now let's get out of here."

Gregory held Samantha in a grip so tight she had no doubt he'd keep her safe forever.

Chapter Sixteen

Gregory's heart rate didn't stabilize until he and Samantha were back inside the car and pulling away from Westman's.

He glanced over at her. Her creased brow and down-turned lips gave away her shock and fear. She must have been petrified in that factory, yet she'd stuck with it, all to get justice for Jacob and the rest of the factory workers.

When he reached over and covered her hand with his, she jumped a little and gasped.

"Are you okay?" Gregory asked her.

"I was just thinking," she panted, "I bet you could probably catch up with Collin and his boys to see where they're taking Hudson. Maybe I can even try and get some pictures of Hudson's injuries. *Man*, I wish I'd thought of that while we were still inside the factory. But I was so terrified, and—"

"Samantha," Gregory snapped, interrupting her rant. "Please. Stop it. I can't believe that's where your head's at after what just happened. I don't want you going anywhere near Collin again. I mean, seriously, haven't you had enough? What you went through tonight was absolutely horrifying."

She threw her hands in the air in exasperation. "But we need to help Hudson! He helped us! We've come too far to let up now. We've got Collin right where we want him. If we have proof of the drug lab *and* evidence that he brutally assaulted Hudson, there's no way he wouldn't be thrown in jail immediately!"

Gregory bit down on his jaw, struggling to choose his words wisely so not to further upset Samantha.

"We will help Hudson. I will call it in—that we saw someone being beaten and dragged from the factory. I'll reach out to officers I can trust. But you've already put your life on the line not once, but twice trying to collect evidence against Collin. That's done."

Samantha turned toward the window and covered her eyes.

"So that's it?" she asked. "You're not gonna go after him yourself? You're supposed to be serving and protecting the community. Or have you forgotten your job description?"

"Says the woman who broken into Collin's house *and* Westman's Automotive Factory," he shot back. "If I was one hundred percent perfect at serving and protecting the community, you'd be sitting behind bars right about now." He pulled out his phone and was about to dial when Samantha grabbed his arm and pointed up the road.

She leaned forward and squinted her eyes, struggling to get a better look.

"Gregory," she breathed, pointing at the writhing figure, "I think I see a body lying over by the curb."

"What the…" He turned on the engine and drove to where she'd indicated, and the pair jumped out and ran over to the body.

"Hudson!" Samantha screamed when she realized it was him. "Are you okay?"

"Nooo," he wheezed feebly while gripping his chest. "My ribs…my leg…"

"Just hold on," Gregory told him. "We're gonna get you to the hospital—" He brought up his phone, still in his hand.

"No!" Hudson yelled before moaning loudly and dou-

bling over in pain. "Don't take me to the hospital. I don't want anybody to see me like this. Then they'll start asking a bunch of questions, and…"

As his voice trailed off, Samantha gently touched his shoulder. "Hudson, you are severely injured. You need to see a doctor."

"My sister's a nurse. I'll have her come check me out," he grunted through clenched teeth.

"I don't think that's a good idea, Hud—"

"Samantha, *please*," he whined. "I'm in too much pain to go back and forth with you. Just take me home."

She turned to Gregory, who glanced over at her. After several seconds, he sighed in apparent defeat. "What's your address, Hudson?"

"Wait, so you're just going to take him home?" Samantha whispered. "He's in such bad shape!"

"Do I have a choice? The man made it clear that he doesn't want to go to the hospital and will refuse medical treatment."

"Fifteen thirty-one East Oak Street," Hudson gasped before slumping down.

The detective looked over at Samantha and nodded his head. "Let's get him inside the car."

She carefully lifted Hudson up by the shoulders while Gregory slid his arms underneath his legs. Hudson emitted an agonizing cry as the twosome struggled to slide him inside the back seat.

"I think Collin cracked a few of my ribs," Hudson groaned after Gregory and Samantha jumped inside the car. "And my right leg feels like it might be broken."

"Just hang on," Gregory told him. Once the man was situated, Gregory and Samantha got inside the car, and he gripped the steering wheel as he peeled away from the curb.

As Gregory pressed down on the accelerator, Samantha twisted her lips in frustration.

"After all this," she said to him, "I really hope you'll be contacting the district attorney first thing in the morning. We definitely have enough evidence for him to file charges against Collin and his cohorts now."

The detective remained silent, staring out the window in deep thought as he continued to Hudson's house.

GREGORY STOPPED AT a red light after he and Samantha dropped Hudson off safely at his home. They'd stayed just long enough to make sure the sister arrived to take care of him, and then were on their way.

The detective turned to her, his tired eyes filled with concern. "I didn't want to discuss the situation with the district attorney in front of Hudson. But listen, if I take this new evidence to him, Collin could easily claim that he acted in self-defense after Hudson broke into the factory."

He paused, waiting for Samantha to argue against his point. When she didn't, he went on.

"And," he continued, "I can assure you that Hudson won't report the assault, because he's an addict who knows he was in the wrong tonight. It actually seems as if he feels somewhat beholden to Collin."

When Samantha slowly nodded her head in agreement, Gregory leaned back in his seat. His tense muscles relaxed after realizing that he was finally getting through to her.

"Yeah," she began, "I can see Collin and his boys coming up with any sort of story they want. They could claim that Hudson broke into the factory to steal auto parts, had a weapon, tried to attack them, anything..."

"Exactly. And of course Hudson would be too afraid to tell the truth and report the drug lab."

"Especially considering Collin caught him stealing drugs from it. Speaking of which..."

When the detective stopped at another red light, Samantha pulled out her phone and showed him the photos she'd taken of the lab.

Gregory let out a sharp breath. "He's running a full-blown operation in there."

"Yes, he is. I'll show you the video I filmed when we get back to your place."

Gregory noticed the dejected tone in Samantha's voice. He reached over and gently clutched her hand.

"Hey," he murmured, "come on. Don't get discouraged. You're almost at the finish line. *We're* almost at the finish line. Even though tonight got out of control, you accomplished your mission. But I think that from this point forward, we have to lie low and move smart."

"I know. I'm just ready for all this to be over with," she sighed, wiping away fresh tears. "I want Collin off the street. That man is way more dangerous than I thought. I wish we could just bypass the district attorney altogether and take this case straight to Mayor Elliot."

"Well, keep in mind that when we take Collin down, Chief Wentworth is going down with him. And I'm sure several other law enforcement officers are entangled in their web of illegal dealings, too. According to the DA, he's already informed Mayor Elliot of the case since the chief of police is involved. So that's a good thing. But we still need to make sure the evidence we present was obtained in a legitimate manner, or else every criminal involved could get off on a technicality."

Samantha sighed and threw her head back against the headrest. "I understand. I just hate having to stay silent, knowing what's really going on. I can't even use my blog to vent my frustrations because you've forced me to go dark for the time being."

"I *advised* you to go dark," he argued, steering the car down his block. "Not forced. I can't force you to do anything, Miss Independent. Let's take tonight, for example…"

Samantha stared down at her hands while fidgeting with her fingernails. The minute Gregory pulled into his driveway, she hopped out of the car and sauntered toward the house. He quickly climbed out and followed her to the door.

"Look," he said, "you and I are conducting an intricate, complicated investigation here. This is going to take time."

"I know. Can we just go inside now? I need a drink."

The detective stared down at her. She kept her eyes on the ground. The corners of her mouth were curled into a frown. It was clear that she was hurting. She was just as frustrated as he was, and he knew she understood that everything she'd collected would have to be verified or collected again with warrants and more.

"Hey, come here," he whispered, instinctively taking her in his arms and embracing her tenderly. He reveled in the feeling of her hands gliding across his shoulders, then clenching behind his neck.

After several moments, Gregory's palms slid down Samantha's back and rested on her hips. He pulled away and took her chin in his hand, raising her head until she looked him in the eyes.

"Why don't we pull the plug on this conversation for now?" he suggested. "Let's go inside, and I'll light up the fireplace then pour you that drink. How does that sound?"

"That sounds good."

As the pair entered the house, Gregory hoped that Samantha would be able to relax while he took some time to think. He knew they needed to wrap this case up soon before she took another risk to get it done herself.

The danger and threats were at an all-time high. Gregory had come too close to losing Samantha tonight. He couldn't let it happen again.

Chapter Seventeen

The next morning, Samantha couldn't stop herself from pacing the living room floor. Gregory had just left for work, and her mind was still racing from yesterday's events.

She'd tossed and turned all night. Conjured-up images of Hudson lying on the factory floor after being beaten by Collin flooded her mind. The agony on his crumpled face as he writhed in pain haunted her dreams during the few moments that she was able to fall asleep.

"Stop it," Samantha told herself, shaking her head rapidly as if that would push the thoughts out of her mind. She trudged over to the kitchen counter and grabbed her cell phone.

Don't do it...

She sighed deeply and put the phone back down, then once again paced the floor. A restless anxiety rushed through her limbs, making it impossible to sit still. She wondered what time Gregory planned on doing a discreet drive-by past Hudson's house, which he'd promised he would do at some point during the day to try and check on him. She'd attempted to convince him to let her ride along, but the detective flat out refused.

"Are you serious?" he'd asked. "What if someone saw us together? That could ruin everything we've been working toward, not to mention put us both in serious danger."

Samantha had to admit that Gregory was right. But now here she was, alone in the house and eager to keep moving forward on the investigation, all while feeling forced to take a step back.

She shuffled into the kitchen and poured herself a second cup of coffee, then took a seat at the dining room table. Samantha realized she had to do something to get her mind off Hudson, Collin and last night's catastrophe. So she opened her laptop and began editing her most recent article for the women's journal.

After giving it one last read, she emailed the piece to her editor. When she closed her inbox, *Someone Knows Something*'s home page popped up on the screen.

Samantha hadn't posted any updates on Jacob's murder in days. Her fingertips were itching to type. She missed the blog. The fact that she hadn't been able to keep the community updated on her investigation and interact with readers left Samantha feeling empty and disconnected. But as Gregory insisted time and time again, continuing to cover the case wasn't worth risking her life.

Her eyes wandered down to the lower right-hand corner of the screen. There were twenty-four unread messages in her blog's inbox.

Do not open them. Do not open them, she kept telling herself.

Reader questions or comments could easily trigger her need to investigate more, and Gregory had been right to caution her about getting evidence legally. But she was dying to know what the townspeople were saying about Jacob's case. Maybe there was a lead here.

She squinted her eyes, tapping her fingernails on the keyboard while staring at the screen. Temptation forced her to slide the cursor toward the message in-box. Just as it hovered over the unopened envelope, her cell phone rang.

The shrill ringtone practically jolted her out of her chair.

She glanced down at the caller ID, hoping it was Gregory. But no name appeared on the screen. The call registered as unknown.

Oh no...

A weight of panic dropped into the pit of her stomach. She grappled with whether or not she should answer the call. Maybe it was just spam, a telemarketer. By the time she decided to grab it, the call went to voice mail.

Just as she set it back down, the phone rang again.

"Yep, this is not good..." she muttered, bracing herself before finally hitting the accept button on the third ring.

"Hello?" she uttered into the phone, struggling not to sound as timid as she felt.

"Hey, Sam! It's Ava."

"Oh, thank goodness!" Samantha breathed. "You have no idea how happy I am to hear your voice. I thought it may have been—"

"Wait," Ava interrupted, "let me guess. You thought it might be Collin?"

"Yes. How did you know?"

"The security guard who was working at Westman's last night called and told me some of what went down. He knows I'm trying to find out what happened with Jacob and keeps in touch."

"Girl," Samantha practically choked, "it was unreal!"

"Wait," Ava interjected, "before you get into that, I've got some good news to share with you."

"Well, I could certainly use some good news right about now. What's up?"

"Kenzie is alive and well."

Samantha jumped up from her chair as tears of joy immediately filled her eyes. "Is she? I am so happy to hear that! How'd you find out?"

"Her boyfriend, Alex, called me early this morning and told me that she reached out to him last night."

"Really," Samantha said, now pacing the floor. "So, where is she? And why'd she just up and vanish like that?"

"She's hiding out in Alabama at her great-aunt's house. Long story short, she was terrified after Jacob and the other Westman's workers were killed and afraid she'd be next."

"Well, that's perfectly understandable. But wait, what about the email she'd allegedly sent to Alex that ended up coming from an IP address belonging to Collin?"

"Good question. According to Alex, Kenzie sent the message from one of the computers located in Westman's break room. So even though it came through Collin's IP address, she was in fact the one who wrote it."

"Wow," Samantha breathed, walking over to the window and peeking outside. "I can't say I much blame her for abruptly skipping town like that considering all the madness surrounding the factory. I'm just glad to hear she's okay. But wait, speaking of madness, did the security guard at Westman's tell you that Collin beat up Hudson? *Really* badly?"

"Wait, *what*? No! He did tell me that Hudson had somehow gotten injured when he saw Collin and his boys drag him out of the factory. But I don't think he realized that Hudson had been beaten."

"Well, he was," Samantha confirmed, "with a steel pipe, no less."

"I cannot believe this," Ava choked. "I've been trying to get ahold of Hudson to see if he's okay. But the calls have been going straight to voice mail, and he hasn't responded to any of my text messages."

Samantha walked back over to the dining room table and slumped down in her chair. "I am so worried about him. He was bludgeoned pretty badly. And Collin just hauled him out of the factory then tossed him onto the street a few blocks away from Westman's like a bag of trash."

"That man is so disgusting."

"He really is. Luckily Gregory and I spotted Hudson and picked him up. But he refused to go to the hospital and insisted we take him home."

"Unreal…" Ava sighed, pausing briefly before continuing. "Wait, weren't you inside the factory with Hudson?"

Samantha hopped up out of her chair and began pacing the floor again. "I was. And being in there while Hudson was assaulted was an absolute nightmare."

"But how is it that Collin caught him and not you, too?"

Samantha cringed as the memory of Hudson refusing to leave the drug lab popped into her head. "I warned Hudson when I heard Collin and his boys walking through the factory and told him we needed to get out of there. But he was too busy stealing drugs to listen to me—"

"Hold on," Ava interjected. "What do you mean, he was stealing drugs?"

"Oh girl, we've got a lot to catch up on. Hudson and I found an underground drug lab inside the factory. And despite Hudson having gone through Westman's drug rehabilitation program, he's clearly still an addict. Because he was in there trying to snatch up every bottle of dope he could find."

"Wow. And here I was, thinking he was clean."

"Not at all," Samantha continued. "I got out of the lab in time, but wasn't able to leave the factory before Collin and his boys came in. So I was hiding behind a shelf in the supply room when they discovered Hudson. And bless Hudson's heart, he saved me by not telling them I was there."

"This entire situation just keeps getting worse and worse."

"It really does."

"So what now?" Ava asked. "Is Detective Harris *finally* going to turn in all this evidence you two have gathered so that Collin and his boys can be arrested?"

"He will. Eventually…"

"What do you mean, *eventually*?"

"Ava, there is so much more to this story than you know. Things aren't as cut-and-dried as they may seem. Just know that Gregory is doing all that he can to get justice for Jacob and the other Westman's workers. It's only a matter of time."

When Ava grew silent, Samantha became nervous, thinking that she'd hit a nerve.

"Are you still there?" she asked her.

After a few moments, Ava spoke up.

"Yep, I'm here. I'm just trying to figure out when enough is going to be enough. How many more people need to suffer at Collin's hands before he gets locked up?"

The question left Samantha speechless. Because deep down, she felt the exact same way. But ultimately, her loyalty remained with Detective Harris, and she had to trust his process.

"You know what we should do?" Ava continued. "You and I should go by Hudson's house and check on him. What do you think?"

Samantha's eyes widened at the suggestion. She took a long, contemplative sip of coffee.

"Ava, please don't tempt me."

"Come on. I'm serious. This is all getting out of hand. I want to make sure Hudson's okay. In an extremely discreet way, of course."

"You know, before Gregory left for work this morning, he did say that he'd take a drive past Hudson's house to check on him. It probably wouldn't be a good idea for you and me to go by there, considering Collin and his boys may be watching the place. So, as much as I'd love to go with you, I'm going to have to pass. I promised Gregory I'd stay out of trouble."

"You? Stay out of trouble? Since when?"

"Since that disastrous confrontation at Westman's last night."

"Humph. All right then. Suit yourself."

"And Ava? I'd strongly suggest you stay away from Hudson's house as well. It's just too dangerous. Let's leave it to a professional and see what Gregory comes back with."

"So you don't want to check on Hudson with me, even though he's the one who led you to the drug lab?"

"I can't, Ava. I'm sorry."

"So that's it? Have you suddenly forgotten that we set out on this journey to get justice for Jacob *together*? That was your promise to my family and me. But now that you've linked up with Detective Harris, you suddenly wanna start separating yourself from me?"

A streak of guilt burned Samantha's throat. She opened her mouth to speak, but nothing came out but a breath of hollow air.

"And just think, I actually believed we were friends."

"We are friends. I just… It's just that—"

"No, no," Ava interrupted. "You don't have to explain yourself. I've already heard enough. And on that note, I'd better let you go. I don't want to end up saying something that I'll regret later."

"I hate that this is where we are right now. But just hang tight. I promise you, Gregory and I will be making some major moves soon. Trust me on this."

Samantha waited to hear Ava's response, but she said nothing.

"Can you at least promise me you won't go to Hudson's house?"

"I don't know…"

"Listen. I'll send Gregory a text message right now and

find out what time he's planning on going by there. As soon as I hear back, I'll let you know. Okay?"

"Fine. But just know that my family and I are running out of patience, and you and Detective Harris are running out of time. If you two don't make something happen soon, then the Jennings family will take matters into our own hands. And trust me, you do not want that problem."

Ava's ominous words sent a chill through Samantha. Before she could respond, Ava continued.

"I'll be looking out for your message once you hear back from Detective Harris. I just hope Hudson's okay."

"So do I. I'll circle back with you soon."

Samantha disconnected the call. An uneasy feeling stirred in the pit of her stomach as she composed a text message to Gregory.

Hey, just got off the phone with Ava. She knows about Hudson and what went down at Westman's last night. She's extremely angry, and the Jennings family is getting impatient. What time are you planning on driving by Hudson's? Ava's really worried about him and I'd love to give her an update before she does something rash...

Samantha sent the message, then glanced over at her computer. A new notification had popped up on her blog. Temptation won out.

She clicked on the comment. When it appeared, she immediately regretted her decision.

Stop digging, bitch, or you'll be digging your own grave next...

GREGORY SAT AT his desk, combing through Jacob's case file. He'd studied it time and time again. But he was giving it yet another look, just to make sure he hadn't missed anything.

At this point, the detective could literally recite every word in the report verbatim. Once he reached the last page, he realized that there wasn't a thing he'd overlooked. He'd hoped to find something he could hang a search warrant on.

He sighed deeply before closing the file. In spite of his coffee being cold, he drained the cup, hoping the last few sips of caffeine would help give him a boost. After last night's madness at Westman's, he'd barely slept and had been dragging all morning.

He refreshed his email inbox. There were no new messages. He'd been planning on driving by Hudson's house to check on him during his lunch break. But since things were quiet around the station, he decided to take advantage of the downtime and go now.

Gregory grabbed Jacob's file. After shoving his keys and cell phone inside his pocket, he walked out of his office.

On the way to the exit, he was surprised to hear Chief Wentworth call out his name.

"Hey, Detective Harris, can I see you in my office?"

Gregory stopped abruptly. He looked through the chief's doorway and saw him sitting behind the desk, one of his hefty arms propped up on his elbows as he thumbed through a report.

"Of course."

"Close the door behind you."

Gregory stepped inside the office apprehensively and closed the door. He eyed the chief, searching the blank expression on his chubby face for some sort of indication as to why he'd called him in.

"Have a seat," Chief Wentworth told him.

Just as he grabbed hold of a chair, Gregory's cell phone buzzed. He pulled it from his pocket and saw a text message from Samantha appear on the screen. He slipped it back inside his pocket and sat down.

"The reason I called you in here is because I wanted to

let you know I hadn't forgotten about the police reports that were filed on Samantha Vincent."

"Oh..." the detective muttered, the tension in his shoulders easing up at the sound of those words. "That's good to hear."

"Just know that the investigations are still active. I'm really trying to get to the bottom of who was behind those attacks on her house. I'm not coming up with much, since there were no eyewitnesses. And the DNA tests came back inconclusive on the evidence you submitted on that first report. Well, with the exception of Officer Baxter's fingerprints, which showed up on one of the bricks you collected."

"Of course," Gregory quipped.

"Speaking of Officer Baxter, I enrolled him and Officer Miller in a crime scene investigation refresher course. Like you'd said, their inspection of Miss Vincent's home and subsequent reporting was shoddy to say the least."

Gregory stared across the cluttered desk at Chief Wentworth, momentarily at a loss for words. He watched the chief run his hands over the silver-gray stubble lining his plump jowls.

"I, uh...*wow*," the detective said. "Thanks, Chief. I have to admit, I hadn't expected anything to come out of that."

"Yeah, well, there's been a lot happening around here. My main focus has been on the department's budget that Mayor Elliot and I are working to finalize. So some of my other priorities have fallen by the wayside. But I'm back on top of things."

Detective Harris watched the chief closely as he casually reclined in his chair and scratched at his sparse crew cut. Knowing he was involved in his son's deadly drug ring was hard to swallow.

"That's good to know," Gregory replied, maintaining a poker face that rivaled the chief's. "I guess I just assumed you'd forgotten about the investigations."

"Never assume, Detective. You know what that makes us both," he chuckled.

Before Gregory could respond, Chief Wentworth's phone rang. He held up a finger, gesturing for the detective to excuse him, then picked up one of two cell phones that was sitting near his landline.

"Chief Wentworth," he barked, his thick eyebrows furrowing deeply into his wrinkled forehead. "Hey, Larry. Yeah, I've been waiting on your call. What have you got for me?"

The chief swiveled back and forth in his worn, squeaky leather chair. His mouth hung open as he listened keenly to the voice on the other end of the call.

Gregory studied the contents on his desk. Stacks of papers surrounded Chief Wentworth's computer monitor and laptop. A few disposable cups were scattered in between the piles. There was a file hanging off the side of the desk underneath a black letter tray. The detective focused on the name scrawled across the tab, which read Axel Guzman.

Detective Harris's eyes blinked rapidly as he racked his brain trying to recollect where he'd heard the name. And then it dawned on him. Axel Guzman was a major drug dealer connected to a notorious Midwest drug cartel that he'd become familiar with while working in Chicago.

Gregory's heart pounded out of his chest. His mind churned in a thousand different directions. If Axel was involved in Collin and Chief Wentworth's drug ring, that meant he and Samantha were no longer just investigating a little drug lab located in the basement of Westman's Automotive Factory. They were entangled in a full-blown mafia-level operation.

"So you got him?" Chief Wentworth said into the phone. "Are you *sure* you got him?"

The chief turned his back to Gregory and stared up at the certificates hanging on the wall. The detective focused on him while scooting toward the edge of his chair. He slid Axel's file off the desk and tucked it in between the reports in his hand.

"All right then, Larry," Chief Wentworth continued. "Good work, per usual. I appreciate you. Yeah, I'll shoot you the payment the usual way. No problem. Yep. Thanks for the great work. Oh, you know I'll be needing you again, sooner rather than later, I'm sure. Okay, I'll be in touch."

He disconnected the call and tossed his phone onto the desk. "Sorry about that, Detective. Just had a little business that I needed to take care of."

"No problem," Gregory replied, anxious to get out of the station and pore over Axel's file with Samantha.

"So that's all I've got for you," the chief continued. "Got anything for me?"

He sat for a few moments, as if thinking of something he needed to report. "No, I think I covered everything at our last update meeting."

"Okay, then." Chief Wentworth glanced down at his watch. "I need to get out of here. I've got a luncheon down at city hall that I need to get to. Everything else going okay for you? I hope Gattenburg's not moving too slow for you compared to all that action you had going on back in the Windy City."

"No, not at all. Everything's going great for me here in Gattenburg. I'm actually enjoying the slower pace." Gregory paused, studying the chief closely before continuing. "You know, one thing I had been concerned with was those Westman's workers whose bodies were recovered in Galena. While their fate was unfortunate, I'm glad their cold cases were finally solved and the families received closure."

"Yeah," the chief sighed, staring solemnly at Gregory. "That was definitely a tragic situation. My son, Collin, implemented an excellent rehabilitation program for recovering addicts at Westman's. Sadly, it doesn't always work for everyone. My heart goes out to those young men who overdosed as well as their families. Like you, I'm glad their cases were solved."

Gregory stared back at his boss, shocked by what appeared to be a genuine show of sympathy.

Chief Wentworth stood up and tugged at his snug navy slacks. "*Whoa*, I guess it's time for me to start that low-carb diet my wife's been nagging me about. But anyway, why don't you and I circle back later this week? I feel like I haven't been giving you enough face time since you've joined the force."

Gregory was slow to respond. He stood up and followed the chief out of the office. The detective couldn't help but wonder whether his boss was trying to get closer to him because he was on to his and Samantha's investigation.

"That would be great, thanks," Gregory told him despite feeling otherwise. He clutched the files in his hand even tighter, eager to get out of the station.

Chief Wentworth stopped at the front desk. Gregory quickly brushed past him and jetted out the door.

He walked through the parking lot and inhaled the crisp air, relieved to finally be away from the chief.

On the way to his car, Gregory noticed Officers Baxter and Miller hovering near the back of the lot. In between puffing on cigarettes, they simultaneously threw him looks of disgust.

"What's up, guys!" Gregory called out, stifling a laugh as he climbed inside his car. He wasn't surprised when neither of them responded.

The detective sped out of the lot and headed toward Hudson's house. On the way there, he pulled out his cell phone. Five missed calls from Samantha appeared on the screen.

"Oh no," he moaned. "This can't be good..."

He immediately dialed her number. She picked up on the first ring.

"Gregory!" she panted, "where are you?"

"I'm heading to Hudson's house to check on him. Why? What's going on?"

"I've been receiving death threats for the past hour. Phone calls, text messages, comments on my blog. They're all coming in anonymously, but I know it's Collin."

Gregory's jaw tightened. "What is he saying, exactly?"

"That he's going to hunt me down and slit my throat."

"My God…" Gregory floored the gas pedal. "Make sure all the doors and windows are locked, and just hang tight. I'll be there in a few minutes."

When she didn't respond, he continued.

"Just calm down," the detective told her. "Collin doesn't even know where you are."

"Someone is calling me on the other line."

"Don't answer it."

Samantha sat silently on the other end of the phone.

"Are you still there?" Gregory asked.

"I am. I was just checking to see whether a name registered on the caller ID. I think it's Ava. I should take it. She may be getting death threats, too."

"Okay. Go ahead and answer it."

"Hold on."

As she clicked over to the other line, Gregory sped through a yellow light. He'd never been one to scare easily, but in this moment, his entire body burned with fear.

"Gregory!" Samantha whispered into the phone after clicking back over. "Collin is dead!"

"Wait, what?" he asked, convinced that he'd heard her wrong.

"Collin is dead!" she repeated, louder this time. "Ava just told me!"

"How does she know that?" Detective Harris asked skeptically.

"Hudson called and told her. Collin and his boys had

stopped by his house to warn him that he'd better keep his mouth shut about the incident at Westman's. When Collin was walking back to his truck, someone drove up and shot him!"

Gregory tore down his block and pulled into the driveway. "I'm here. I'll be inside in a—"

Before he could finish, Samantha threw open the front door and ran out to the car. The detective jumped out and embraced her tightly. He caressed her back as she sobbed into his chest.

"What is happening right now?" she cried.

"Everything's going to be okay," he whispered.

"No, it isn't, Gregory. Somebody is on a killing spree in this town, and we've been after the wrong person this entire time! Our investigation is back at square one. How is everything going to be okay?"

He pulled away from Samantha and rested his hands on her shoulders. Aching pangs filled his chest at the sight of her wild, terror-filled eyes.

The detective led her inside the house and quickly closed the door behind them.

"We're going to Mayor Elliot's house," he declared. "Tonight."

Samantha turned to him, her entire face lighting up. "Really?"

"Yes. This situation has gotten completely out of hand. At this point I don't know who's out to get whom. I just had a talk with Chief Wentworth before leaving the station, and he seemed perfectly fine. As a matter of fact, I was surprised to hear he's investigating the crimes that were committed against you and took further action against Officers Baxter and Miller."

"I am so confused right now…" Samantha shuffled over to the couch and fell into the cushions. "This entire situation has my head spinning. I wonder if Chief Wentworth knows that Collin's been killed yet."

"Good question." Gregory checked his phone. "I haven't gotten any calls or text messages. But judging from the way these guys roll, they probably wouldn't report the crime. They'd hide Collin's body and seek revenge."

"Judging from the way these guys roll, I wouldn't be surprised if Chief Wentworth had something to do with it."

Detective Harris stared at her, absorbing what she'd just said. He slowly walked over to the couch and took a seat next to her.

"You know, it's funny you say that. When I was in the chief's office, he did have a rather interesting phone conversation that I overheard."

"Did he? With who?"

"Some guy named Larry. The conversation just seemed…odd. Chief Wentworth was saying things like, 'So you got him? Are you sure you got him?' Then he told the guy that he'd done a good job and he would send him his payment."

Gregory glanced over at Samantha and saw that she was staring back at him in shock.

"Are you thinking what I'm thinking?" she whispered.

"That Chief Wentworth put a hit out on his own son?" He had a hard time getting his head wrapped around that.

Samantha nodded her head while she massaged her temples. "Well, if the chief thought Collin was getting too careless in the way he was handling their drug operation, then yes. Absolutely. I've seen firsthand how ruthless these men can be."

Gregory grabbed the files he'd taken from the police station. "And to add to the suspense, I found a report in Chief Wentworth's office on Axel Guzman—"

"Wait, Axel Guzman—where have I heard that name?"

"He's a drug dealer. Part of a big Midwest cartel."

"Oh my God…" Samantha covered her mouth with her hands. "Do you think he's working with Chief Wentworth and Collin?"

"That would be my guess. And you already know how he moves. The man is a savage. If Collin crossed him, he also could've been the one to have him killed."

Samantha was visibly shaken. She ran her hands over her arms, as if trying to warm herself up.

"I want to take this to the mayor, but he's not available until this evening. Let's go check on Hudson, then head there."

They gazed at one another, the energy between them palpable. In that moment, Gregory realized that the imminent danger surrounding them had only brought them even closer together. He wanted this case over so she'd be out of danger and in his arms for more than just protection.

Chapter Eighteen

"I am really not looking forward to telling Mayor Elliot about Chief Wentworth and Collin's drug ring," Gregory muttered to Samantha as they headed to the mayor's house. They'd already done a quick check on Hudson, who was recovering from his injuries.

"I know," Samantha said, gripping the thick file of information that she and Gregory had compiled tightly. "He is going to be crushed. He thinks the world of the chief."

She stared out the window, thoughts of the day's outrageous events flashing through her mind. "I still can't believe Collin is dead."

"Neither can I. But in all honesty, we shouldn't be surprised. Look at all the damage he's done and bridges he's burned all over this town."

"Very true." Samantha turned to the detective, her eyelids lowering with doubt. "But at this point, I'm wondering whether Collin's only guilty of manufacturing illegal drugs and injuring Hudson. What if he isn't the one behind the deaths of Jacob and the other Westman's workers?"

The detective raised his eyebrows curiously. "That's a definite possibility. But at this point, things have gotten way too baffling to assume anything. That's why we're going to Mayor Elliot. Maybe he'll be the one to pull the truth out of Chief Wentworth."

"I hope so."

Gregory turned down the mayor's block and eased up on the accelerator. As he approached the house, all the lights appeared to be out.

"I wonder if he's home," Detective Harris said before pulling up to the curb and parking the car.

"There's only one way to find out." Samantha ignored the jitters flitting throughout her entire body. She closed her eyes, said a quick prayer, then grabbed the door handle. "Come on. Let's do this."

The pair climbed out of the car and approached Mayor Elliot's grand, pillared white porch. Gregory searched the street, checking to see whether anyone was in the vicinity.

"Looks like the coast is clear," he said.

Samantha reached up to ring the doorbell. Right before her finger hit the button, a bloodcurdling shout came from the back of the house.

She jerked her hand away and grabbed the detective's arm. "What the hell was that?"

Gregory reached back and pulled his gun out of his waistband. "Go back to the car. Lock the doors."

"No way."

He muttered a curse and heaved a sigh. "Let's go check around back. Stay behind me."

Samantha didn't release her grip on the detective's arm as he led her along the side of the house. They approached a tall wooden gate. Just as he slowly opened it, another ear-piercing shriek ripped through the air, drowning out the sound of the gate's creaking wood.

"*Help!* Please, somebody help me!"

Gregory turned to Samantha. "Wait, that sounds like Chief Wentworth!"

He led her into the dark, vast backyard. They slunk up the stairs leading to the deck. Samantha held Gregory tighter as they crept alongside the brick wall, then paused at the edge of sliding glass doors. A set of semisheer white curtains partially covered them.

"Can you see anything?" she whispered.

Gregory turned to her and held his finger to his lips, signaling her silence. She nodded her head, then cringed at the sound of more yelling.

"Just sign the damn papers, Wentworth!"

"What is going *on* in there?" she mouthed.

Gregory took a slight step to the side and peered through the glass. She peeked past him and peered through the curtain.

"What the…"

In the dim light, she saw Mayor Elliot standing over Chief Wentworth with a knife to his throat. The chief was tied to a chair, his distorted expression twisted in terror.

"Sign them! *Now!*" the mayor shouted as he shoved a stack of papers in the chief's face.

Samantha quickly stepped away from the door. Every one of her limbs trembled as she processed what they were witnessing.

"I'm not signing a damn thing!" Chief Wentworth shot back. "You killed my son, and you think I'm gonna take the blame for it? You're out of your mind!"

"What is happening right now?" Samantha whimpered, shaking her head in utter confusion.

"Your son was a loose cannon, Walter!" the mayor spewed. "He was getting out of control. Killing the townspeople with his deadly drug experiments. But after he savagely beat Hudson, who just so happens to be the district attorney's stepson? That was the last straw."

Samantha and Gregory turned to one another, gasping in unison after hearing the information about Hudson.

"Collin would never—" Chief Wentworth began. He was abruptly silenced when Mayor Elliot pressed the knife into his throat.

"That's your problem!" the mayor yelled. "You raised your son to be a punk! Thanks to you, he never paid for any of his wrongdoings. And now? He's right where he belongs, and you're going to take the blame for him almost taking my entire drug operation down."

Samantha and Gregory both froze. Mayor Elliot was involved in Gattenburg's drug ring.

When Chief Wentworth cried out in pain, Samantha turned to Gregory.

"You have got to do something! *Now!*"

Without saying a word, the detective used the butt of his gun to break the lock on the door. He threw it open and aimed the weapon at Mayor Elliot.

"Drop the knife!" he yelled.

Chief Wentworth let out a sigh of relief when he laid eyes on Gregory and Samantha. The mayor, however, appeared stunned. But his mouth quickly twisted into a shrewd smirk.

"So how much did you two hear?" he asked condescendingly.

"Enough to know that you're running a drug ring and killed Collin," Gregory shot back. "Now drop the knife and step away from Chief Wentworth."

"Aww, how sweet," Mayor Elliot said. "Look, everybody, it's the new kid on the block, trying to be a hero. Listen, you and your little fake journalist friend here need to get the hell out of my house. Trust me, you don't wanna get involved in this."

"Don't listen to him," Chief Wentworth pleaded. "Help me. The mayor's trying to force me to sign a statement confessing that I'm involved in his drug operation and responsible for the murders of Jacob and Collin—"

"Shut up!" Mayor Elliot yelled, slicing the chief's jaw with the knife.

"Ahh!" Chief Wentworth hollered in agony. "Shoot him, Harris. *Shoot* him!"

"Drop the weapon, Elliot!" Gregory once again insisted. "I'm not going to ask you again."

Smirking, the mayor tossed the knife across the room. When Gregory turned to retrieve it, Mayor Elliot fled the room.

"Untie him," Gregory yelled to Samantha, nodding toward the chief before running after the mayor.

Samantha swooped in and began tugging at the knots restraining Chief Wentworth.

"Are you okay?" she asked him.

"My boy is dead," the chief whimpered. "He's dead!"

"I'm so sorry," she replied while frantically untying him. "Come on. Let's get you out of here and call for backup."

Samantha bent down and wrapped Chief Wentworth's arm around her shoulders, helping him out of the chair. He leaned into her, his hefty frame causing her to stumble. She swiftly regained her footing and led him out the door toward the front of the house. On the way there, she managed to grab hold of her cell phone and dial 9-1-1, spitting out the information about what was going on and telling the dispatcher she didn't need to stay on the line.

"I can't believe my boy is gone," Wentworth mumbled. He fell against the side of the house, sobbing into the palms of his hands.

Samantha bent down and wrapped her arm around the chief.

"I mean—I knew Collin was trouble," he continued. "But I had no idea he was into all this. It's my fault. I should've disciplined him more. I shouldn't have let him get away with all that I did over the years."

Samantha grabbed a tissue from her coat pocket and held it to the chief's jaw. She couldn't ignore his pain, despite his connection to the harm that'd been done to so many.

"Collin chose this life," Chief Wentworth declared. "But he just didn't have it in him to walk the straight and narrow. I hope you know I had nothing to do with any of this."

"Collin kept a drug ledger that implicated you."

The chief nodded his head solemnly, the corners of his damp eyes crinkling with sadness. "I know. I just found out about all this from Officer Barris. He confided in me while we were down at city hall this afternoon."

"Wait, Officer Barris knew about the drug ring?"

"Yes. He did. He'd just recently found out about it after Officers Baxter and Miller tried to recruit him into Guzman's crime syndicate. Guzman and Mayor Elliot are behind all this. And they've been paying off several Gattenburg police officers to turn a blind eye and keep quiet."

"I knew those two were somehow involved. That's why they blew off the vandalism investigation at my house. They've been working against my cause to get justice for Jacob Jennings all along."

"Barris also found out that Guzman is the anonymous owner of Westman's Automotive Factory. He registered the ownership under a different name so that it wouldn't be affiliated with him."

"And so he could use it produce illegal drugs," Samantha added. "Without it being traced to him."

"Exactly. Those drugs that Collin was formulating were so potent. And deadly. Some concoction he was trying to perfect called TKO is what killed the three Westman's workers. They were testing it out one night inside the factory. After they OD'd, Guzman ordered *my* son to dump their bodies in the woods somewhere outside Gattenburg. And Collin did it."

He paused, his voice cracking as he began to sob uncontrollably. Samantha wrapped her arm around him, patting his back until he gathered himself.

"And poor Jacob," the chief continued, his distorted

words practically inaudible. "He was just trying to find out what happened to his coworkers when he went to talk to Collin. But Collin made the mistake of telling Guzman, who turned around and killed Jacob with a deadly overdose in order to silence him."

Samantha blinked back tears, thinking of how Ava would take the news.

"I'm in shock right now," Chief Wentworth muttered, staring straight ahead as if he were in a daze. "I came here thinking Mayor Elliot would help me apprehend my son's killer. Instead he attacks me, and I find out he's in on the whole operation. He's the one who convinced Collin to list my name in the drug ledger so that if it were ever confiscated, I'd be implicated and forced to cover for them."

"I'm so sorry, Chief. I, um—I actually have Collin's drug ledger in my possession."

"You do? How did you get ahold of it?"

"It's complicated," Samantha said just as she heard yelling come from inside the house.

"Drop the gun, Elliot! *Now!*"

Bang. Bang. Bang.

Samantha inhaled sharply, immobilized by the thought of Gregory being shot.

"Let's go!" Chief Wentworth yelled. He pulled her up and led her toward the street. They crouched down behind Gregory's car.

Samantha stared out at the mayor's house. *Come out, Gregory, please come out.*

"I've gotta get in there!" she insisted, jumping up. "I need to make sure Gregory's okay…"

"Samantha, *no!*" Chief Wentworth grabbed hold of her. "Detective Harris is well trained and knows how to handle himself. You might endanger him if you go in. Help is on the way."

As soon as he spoke those words, sirens blared in the

distance. Samantha spun around and saw flashing lights heading their way. She jumped up and waved her arms in the air. Officer Barris was the first one to pull up and jump out of his car.

"Detective Harris is inside the house and Mayor Elliot is trying to kill him!" she yelled.

"Got it!" the officer called out, leading a trail of officers through the front yard. They broke down the door and barreled inside.

She couldn't wait any longer and started rushing toward the door herself.

Before she got far, Gregory came limping through the front door with policemen on either side of him, his left leg covered in blood.

Samantha ran to the detective at full speed.

"Are you okay?" she managed to say, her voice choked.

"I will be," Gregory muttered through clenched teeth. "Mayor Elliot shot me. It just grazed me. Officer Barris stopped the bleeding."

Samantha knew he was downplaying his injury for her sake. As he spoke, she saw him wince in pain.

"We need to get you to the hospital, Detective Harris," Officer Barris told him. "The ambulance is waiting."

"I'm coming with you," Samantha insisted. "There's no way I'm letting you out of my sight."

"I don't want you to…"

As the group headed toward the ambulance, they stopped to check on Chief Wentworth. He was leaning against a squad car now, holding a fresh handkerchief against his wounded jaw.

"Detective Harris," the chief said, "I can't thank you and Samantha enough for what you did tonight. You two saved my life."

"I was just doing my job, sir," Gregory replied. "With

the help of the best criminal journalist in town. Samantha was crucial in getting to the bottom of all this."

"Thanks," she whispered, a smile of appreciation spreading across her face.

"Well, you two make a great team," Chief Wentworth said. "Now get out of here. Get to the hospital and have them stitch up that leg."

"Will do, sir. And you have my condolences. I'm really sorry about what happened to Collin."

Chief Wentworth nodded silently, his lips tightening as he blinked back tears. "Hey, before you go, Detective, I have something I want to share with you."

"What's that?"

"After tonight, I'll be retiring. And I'm going to recommend you as my replacement. I had my eye on you for this slot when I hired you."

Gregory stared at Chief Wentworth in disbelief. "Wow. I… I don't know what to say, sir. Thank you."

"You're welcome. It's well deserved. We'll talk more about it later. For now, get to the hospital. And while you're there, start thinking about the capital murder, aggravated kidnapping and drug trafficking charges that need to be brought against Elliot and Guzman."

"Yes, sir."

The group said their goodbyes, and the EMTs came over and helped Gregory inside the ambulance. Samantha climbed in behind him and took a seat next to the stretcher.

"Congratulations, *Chief Harris*," she said.

"Hmm, thanks. That has a nice ring to it…"

The detective tried to shift his body but froze, wincing from the pain of the gunshot wound.

"Are you okay?" Samantha asked, moving in closer to the stretcher.

"I'll survive."

Samantha reached out and covered his hand with hers. "I

cannot believe this night. And I *really* can't believe Mayor Elliot is in cahoots with Axel Guzman and at the helm of the drug ring. I had a chance to speak with Chief Wentworth while you were inside the house. I've got a lot to catch you up on."

Gregory rested his head against the back of the stretcher and closed his eyes. "I can imagine. Hey, can you do me a favor and check my phone? It's been buzzing like crazy. I don't have the energy to do it myself."

"Of course. Where is it?"

"Inside my coat pocket."

Samantha grabbed the phone and tapped the notifications. "There's a message here from Officer Barris. Ooh! Things are moving fast. It says that Axel Guzman was caught down in the drug lab at Westman's. Both he and Mayor Elliot are currently under arrest, along with Officers Baxter and Miller. Collin's boys are being questioned right now, and they're cooperating with the police."

"That is great news. I still can't believe I left Chicago thinking life would be slower and easier for me here in Gattenburg. Oh, how wrong I was…"

"Yeah, well, at least we're finally getting justice for this town. You should be glad you came and proud of all your hard work. None of this would've been resolved had it not been for you."

"And you."

Samantha tightened her grip on Gregory's hand. "Thank you. After all this, I can't wait to get back to blogging and follow up on this crazy, twisted case. You know what else, Chief Harris?"

"What's up?" he chuckled.

"Tonight just reaffirmed that life is short. I have to go after my dreams. So, with that being said, I've decided to quit my job with the women's journal and focus on my *Someone Knows Something* brand full-time. I'm talking launching a podcast, creating a cold case web series, developing partnerships and sponsorships, the works. I'm about to go global."

Gregory opened his eyes and turned to her. "I think that sounds amazing. You know, what's interesting is that tonight showed me I need to go after what I want, too."

"Oh really? And what is it that you're ready to pursue?"

"You."

Samantha paused, feeling as if everything around her had come to a complete stop.

"What do you think of that?" he asked.

"I think you should go for it…"

Just as the ambulance turned into the hospital's driveway, Gregory wrapped his arm around the small of her back and pulled her in close. He held her chin in his hand and kissed her passionately.

Samantha leaned into him, relishing the feeling of his full, supple lips. She felt every word they hadn't spoken in that kiss. Their shared triumph in solving the Gattenburg murders, how they'd come out of the ordeal unscathed, the love they shared for one another—it was all there.

When the ambulance came to a stop, she gradually pulled away from him.

"Mmm," Gregory sighed. "That was nice."

"Yes, it was," she murmured, her lips still tingling from his touch.

"I'm so glad I don't have to hide my feelings for you anymore."

"So am I. Because it was becoming quite the struggle."

"It was, wasn't it?" he quipped just as the EMTs opened the back door. Gregory took Samantha's hand in his. "You and I have a lot to discuss. And I'm hoping part of that conversation will be about us building a life together."

"It most certainly will."

She watched as the paramedics pulled him from the vehicle. He stared back at her. There was an unspoken, unbreakable bond in their gaze.

And in that moment, Samantha knew that Gregory was the man she would spend the rest of her life with.

* * * * *

FALLING FOR HIS SUSPECT

TARA TAYLOR QUINN

For Tim, I am thankful every single day
that you have what it takes.

Chapter One

"Sis... I'm sorry to call you so early...but..."

"Josh?" Jasmine Taylor glanced toward the window as she sat up, noting the darkness between the cracks in the closed blinds. "What's wrong?"

Heart pounding, she pushed her legs out from under the covers and over the side of the bed. Her brother wouldn't be calling predawn just to say hello.

"Danny called." Her brother named his best friend from high school, who also happened to be a cop. That didn't assuage anxiety any as her brain quickly jumped from one family member to the next. Anyone they'd get middle-of-the-night calls for. Mom and Aunt Suzie, who lived together back in New York, where they'd grown up, were on a cruise with a group of people from their church. The privately litigated, no-contact agreement with their dad probably precluded notifications.

"There's a warrant out for my arrest, Jas. I plan to turn myself in first thing this morning. I need you to keep Bella. Please..."

"Of course." Every nerve in Jasmine's body jittered. Standing in her bedroom, she forced her knees to find their strength. Fear would not win. Whatever the police had found was a mistake. No matter what. Josh was one of the good guys. Through and through.

She was already pulling on black capri pants and reaching for the cropped white blouse she usually wore with them. "I'll come get her."

"I'm actually on my way to you. I'll be there in about ten minutes."

Coming from his home in Santa Barbara, he'd have had to have been on the road over half an hour before he called. And had to have pulled his three-year-old out of bed in the middle of her night.

"What's going on?"

Josh was the only guy she really trusted.

"Heidi's going on," he said, sounding frustrated in spite of his soft tone. "She filed a complaint of spousal abuse."

"What!" She shook her head. And then, "Heidi?" Her squeal was decibels louder than she'd have liked. "What the hell?" His ex-wife was the abuser—she was the reason why Josh, a businessman who also ran a string of nonprofit sports training centers for at-risk teenaged boys, was raising a toddler daughter on his own.

"She wants shared parenting," he said now, his voice lower than ever, as though his most likely sleeping toddler would hear, and understand, the conversation. "She threatened to claim I was abusing her if I didn't comply."

"That's stupid." Jasmine said the first thing that came to mind. Because...this was Josh. They were each other's safe places. "She's already been convicted of abuse, which is why she lost custody to begin with. And the law says you have to wait five years before a judge can give it back, right? Claiming you're abusive isn't going to get Bella back to her, either. But it could leave Bella in the hands of Child Protective Services if the system got wonked and someone believes her." She heard her words aloud. "Not that that's going to happen," she quickly assured him. "You know it's not. You've got a lifetime of people who will back you up. Besides, she'd have to have some kind of proof."

"She fell and sprained her wrist," he said, sounding more defeated than she'd ever heard. Even when he'd had to admit that he was a victim of domestic violence. Again. "She's claiming that I grabbed her, yanked her and sprained it."

"With your bare hands?"

"Yes."

"She'd need pictures of bruises to corroborate that." Brain in fully awake, fighting mode now, Jasmine strode to the kitchen to put coffee on for him, checking Bella's room on the way to ensure that it was clean and ready as it always was. She had a room for Josh, too. One he'd occupied during the dark days after his marriage had fallen apart—while he'd been in the process of fighting for his daughter and buying a new home for them both.

A home without destructive memories lining the walls.

"Heidi had a guy at the gym grab her wrist as resistance, as she tried to push past him, and then took a picture of the marks he left. She showed me the photo."

"Before she fell?"

"Yeah, the wrist isn't bruised in the picture."

"Is there a time stamp on it? If her doctor's report for the sprain doesn't match up with the photo time frame…" She knew her stuff. Not just from the years of growing up with an abusive father, but because she spent forty hours a week teaching elementary school at The Lemonade Stand—a unique, resort-like women's shelter in

Santa Raquel. She'd spent countless more hours volunteering at the Stand when her classroom hours were over. You spent enough time there, you heard all the stories.

"She claims they match. At this point I have no way of knowing…"

"Danny'll sort it all out." Josh's friend would have Josh's back with the police. And Jasmine had faith. Because Josh had given her the ability to believe in a better life each and every time he'd protected her from another blast of their prominent father's temper.

And now they had Bella to protect.

"Is Bella still asleep?" she asked, reminding herself that they were survivors. And had had their family blessed the day Bella had been born—in a way neither of them had realized could happen. The little one's innocence and natural joy…

While Bella's advent into their lives filled Josh and Jasmine with joy, it hadn't been the same for her mother.

Heidi herself had also been a victim of domestic violence. At first, she had been protective and tender with her little one…

But over that next year, dealing with a crying infant who never let her sleep through the night, jealous of Josh who got to go to work every day and be with adults… she'd changed. Had grown into a state of almost constant irritability. Counseling had helped. Josh had taken Heidi on a couple of small getaways, just the two of them, and things had improved each time. For a while.

"Yeah, sound asleep," Josh was saying, his tone a bit more relaxed. "Barely peeped when I put her in her car seat. I have her blanket and baby pillow propped around her."

The baby pillow had been Jasmine's back in a day

when parents hadn't known better than to put a little pillow and blanket in a crib with a baby. She'd given it to Bella when the toddler had been having trouble transitioning from her crib to the princess bed that came next.

"If you get to the station quickly enough, you could possibly make it back before she even realizes you've been gone," she told him. "You'll be released as soon as they process you..."

If not, she'd take Bella to work with her. While not a regular by any means, her niece had been a guest at the Stand's excellent daycare several times.

Moving from the coffeepot to the front window, Jasmine peeked out through the blinds, watching for Josh's headlights.

"I need to talk to you about that," Josh said, barely above a whisper. Then added, "I'm here."

She was already out the front door.

AN ARROW SLICED the pit of Detective Greg Johnson's stomach when his phone rang just as dawn was striking. In his modest beach bungalow's home gym, he glanced toward the cell he'd left on the bench with his towel and continued to do crunches.

Nine. Ten.

He'd made his reps. But his phone was four rings in. He grabbed the phone with one hand and his towel with the other, wiping sweat as he said, "Yeah."

"You know it's me," a petulant female voice said. "Why do you answer like that?"

Guilt jabbed at him.

"I'm working out, Liv. You know that. Every morning from five to six." She used to complain about it, the way he'd leave her in bed to wake up alone every morning, rather than starting her day within the safety of his arms. Or cuddled up to his back.

Of course, she could have just gotten up with him.

Her silence irritated him, which brought along a bit of residual guilt, which irritated him even more. "What's up?" he asked. It'd been a couple of months since she'd called him in a state. The longest they'd gone since their two-year-old breakup.

He hadn't missed those calls.

More guilt.

Accompanied by a need to lie flat on the bench he stood beside and press against every ounce of the 350 pounds hanging from the bar. One hundred and fifty pounds over his weight. Piece of cake compared to dealing with Liv.

"I called now because you don't like it when I interrupt as you're getting ready for work. And you don't like when I call you at work…"

After five. He'd told her, umpteen times, that it would best if she called him in the evening. But then, he'd always picked up every time she'd called outside the parameters. Because she only called when she was struggling. And he had the ability to help.

He couldn't not answer.

"What's up?" he asked again. He'd told her when she'd left him to call if she ever needed him. He'd meant the offer.

"Rick called me stupid. I just… I think that's verbal abuse, isn't it, when your partner tries to personally belittle you? Especially when you're already struggling?"

He dropped his towel. Sat on the bench. Workout over.

"You have a bad night?" he asked. Rick calling her stupid didn't ring true. Middles of the night were her worst times, though the home invasion that had scarred her had been in broad daylight. She hadn't been physically hurt, other than some bruising, hunger and dehydration, but the a-hole had tied her up and left her there to die, instilling a sense of inadequacy and periodic helplessness with which she still struggled…

"Yeeaaahhh." The tears started. Dread filled his gut. He kept his thoughts on task.

"Is Rick there?" Greg not only genuinely liked the guy; he admired the hell out of him. The man had some mysterious vault filled with empathy.

"He's in the shower," Liv said, sniffing. "I've never seen him so angry…"

The Richard Haley Greg knew was a saint. His mother had been a victim of human trafficking before she'd had him, and he'd grown up tending to her fears. And seemed to understand Olivia in a way Greg never could.

But you never really knew, did you, unless you were in the relationship? Liv had misinterpreted Greg on almost a daily basis. So maybe Greg had Richard wrong…

"Tell me what happened."

"The anxiety…you know how it gets…that I can't always help it…"

When he'd first started seeing her, six months after his office had prosecuted the invasion, she'd been on prescribed medication for anxiety. During the course of their three-year on-again, off-again relationship, she'd traded those in for illegal substances for a short stint. She'd been sober their last year together, though. And two years after that, still was. He'd had dinner with the couple two nights ago.

"There's no way I can go in to work…"

"Which is why you arranged it so you could work from home," he reminded her.

"I know, but...it's a bad one, Greg. I couldn't be alone today. And Rick...he didn't get any sleep, either, and..."

Everything in him tensed. Not in a good way.

"He lost his temper with you?"

"Not at first."

If the man had hurt her...if he'd so much as broken a hair on her head...

He took a deep breath. Liv had a way of getting him to overreact—also not in a good way. He couldn't always separate the drama from reality with her.

"When then?"

"When I called into work and said that he was sick and would be working from home today."

Oh God. Running a hand through his hair, Greg grabbed his towel. Threw it, along with the T-shirt he pulled off one-handedly, into the laundry bin on his way toward the shower.

"You called *him* in sick," he said, trying his damnedest to keep all inflection out of his voice.

"Yeah."

"Why?"

"Because he can work from home, just like I can, but if I called myself into work, there'd be no reason for him to stay home. Calling in sick for him gives me a reason to call myself off to care for him."

Calling in sick for him made her look like the strong one. Every once in a while he got how her psyche rolled. Whether or not she got it, too, was a mystery to him.

"You don't think he'd have a reason to stay home if you were sick?"

More likely, she hadn't trusted that he would and, as she'd admitted, she hadn't wanted to be alone.

Her lack of response to his latest question was respite, at least. He still had to deal with whatever Rick had done or said. As a cop he couldn't hear something of concern and just walk away. As Liv's ex, he didn't think he'd ever be able to fully walk away. Not because he loved her. But because he didn't.

Because he felt for her. And felt horrible about his inability to tend to the aftereffects of her trauma on a daily basis. "What did Rick do when you told him you'd called in sick for him?" he finally asked, after listening to sniffles for a lot of seconds.

"He said...he said...he said it was a stupid thing to do!" She was crying again, but after years of deciphering her words through tears, he was pretty sure he'd heard them right.

"He didn't call you stupid. He said what you'd *done* was stupid."

"It's the same thing." More sobs followed. He tried to ignore them. She couldn't help the emotion. And he'd never understand the seemingly uncontrollable intensity of it.

"No, it's not. You've kind of put him in a tough spot, saying he's sick when he's not. He's now either forced to show you up for a liar with your employer or lie to his employer." Who happened to be one and the same.

Greg was sure he was being too harsh. But she knew him. And she'd called him. He gave her what he had.

"Yeah," she said, sounding more like the woman he'd been drawn to once upon a time. "I already called back and told them that I was wrong about him not feeling well, and that I'd be working from home today."

"Does Rick know that?"

"Not yet." He could hear the huff and puffs of air as she started to cry once again. "I'm afraid he's going to leave me…"

A fear he'd heard so often…and could never assuage. *I'm afraid you're going to leave me, Greg. Are you going to leave me, Greg?*

"You made this one right, Liv. You always do. He knows that. Just as he knows what he signed on for. So why would you think he'd leave you?" He had the thought that maybe Rick had finally had enough. Hoped he was wrong about that.

"You did."

He'd wanted to. God, he'd wanted to. He had a bit of a savior complex—him always feeling like he needed to rescue people. Made him good at his job, but not so good in relationships, as he never factored in his own needs until it was too late.

"No, Liv. You left me, remember?"

"Only because you made me feel unwelcome."

He probably had. There'd been days he'd dreaded going home when he'd known she was going to be there.

"You're a smart, capable woman," he told her. "You're witty and loyal and nurturing. You've increased product sales by more than fifty percent in the five years you've been at your current position. Your team loves working for you. Think about those things, Liv. Think about the fact that you have way more good days than bad."

It's what had kept him sane when they'd been together.

"Yeah. You're right. I just…when the fear takes over… I feel like such a freak…"

"Talk to Rick. Ask him how he feels about you."

Another twinge as Greg considered the idea that

Rick's feelings might have changed in the past forty-eight hours, but he didn't think so.

God, he hoped not.

"He's just getting out of the shower. I have to go. Thanks, Greg."

Rick was getting out of the shower. Greg was getting in. Wondering if he'd ever find someone who fit him as well as Rick fit Liv.

Chapter Two

Just seeing her brother in his typical dress pants, shirt and tie made Jasmine feel better. Business as usual. With a little sidebar trip before the day really got started. They'd sort this out.

"It's just another ditch in the road," she told him after he'd carried his daughter in and settled her, still sleeping, in her room.

Another ditch in the road. A line from a Savage Garden song they'd been drawn to as teenagers. Abuse. Destruction. Mom takes kids and leaves. And then, because there are bills to pay, goes back.

Until, in their case, she didn't. Jasmine had been seventeen, Josh fifteen, when Mary Taylor had finally found the courage to stand up to her soft-spoken, powerful and abusive husband. She'd made a deal with him—she wouldn't go to the police as long as he put a million dollars apiece in a trust fund for each of their children and didn't ever contact her again. She'd taken a hell of a beating for her efforts while he told her he'd make mincemeat of her reputation, say she was crazy. He even threatened he'd have her committed. Until Josh had walked in the room and shown him a picture he'd just snapped of his father's fist raised over his cowering mother. Oscar Taylor had been so enraged with Mary that he hadn't heard Josh come in.

One look at the photo and that anger had seeped out of him. A balloon without air. He'd sagged right before their eyes, still staring at the photo. As though, until that moment, he hadn't known who he'd become.

When Josh had turned twenty-one, he'd taken a good chunk of his inheritance to start Play for the Win. Not only was he chairman of that board, but he was also now into various other investments, helping their trusts grow. Until he'd gained sole custody of Bella, he'd been at the Santa Barbara Play for the Win facility, working with the kids, at least three times a week. Just as she spent so much volunteer time at The Lemonade Stand. They'd survived their youth and were paying it forward.

In her kitchen that September Tuesday morning, with a cup of coffee in his hand, Josh hadn't yet said a word. Putting ice in an insulated glass, she poured herself the one caffeinated soda she allowed herself a day. She wasn't a coffee drinker.

"You know this is just more of Heidi's crap," she told him. That was her job, to make sure the funk didn't get him. Just like he was the person she called when fear tried to play with her.

He looked her in the eye. Her silent gaze told him what he needed to know. When he nodded, she knew he'd heard. Took a sip of her soda.

"I need you to keep Bella, Jas."

Jasmine coughed, sending carbonated liquid into her nasal cavities. Her eyes watered while her mind flew. Take Bella? What kind of nonsense was he talking?

Heidi had done a number on Josh for sure. But Jasmine had thought he was beyond it. Beyond Heidi's ability to get to him.

"Heidi would rather see her with Child Services than with me." Her brother's tone was firm, calm as he looked at her. "She's descended to a new low."

"Yeah, but we'll—"

He shook his head, cutting off her fight call before she'd uttered it.

"I won't have Bella pulled into this."

Of course not. Neither would she. That little girl was going to grow up abuse-free. Not just physically, but psychologically, too. That wasn't negotiable. For any kids either of them brought into the world. Patterns that might have some pull on them would not repeat themselves. They'd promised each other. If either of them ended up in a situation like their mother, they'd get out.

She nodded. Listening for any sounds emanating from the handheld child monitor receiver sitting on the counter. When Bella had been a newborn, Jasmine had carried the device even into the bathroom with her when she'd been on babysitting duty. More recently, she had to know when the little girl was out of bed. Bella had a curiosity that didn't quit and almost no sense of fear.

Both Jasmine and Josh celebrated that lack of fear—even as they'd acknowledged that the little girl needed to develop just a healthy dose of it.

"Don't you think this is a little drastic?" she asked softly, hoping Josh could tap into her calm, like she'd tapped into his so many times in the past. "Even if you're not home before she's due to go to her nanny, you'll be home sometime today…"

"She's asking for Bella to be removed from the home

immediately. They could make that a condition of my release. I can't risk it, Jas."

Sickness spread through her. Insidious fear. Powerlessness. "She always has a home here. You know that," she said. Bella could slide right into her life with very little effort. That wasn't the point. Josh didn't deserve to lose the brightest bulb in his life. And Bella didn't deserve to lose him, either. They *weren't* powerless.

Evil couldn't do this to him. He shouldn't have anything real to fear. Which was why she had to keep Bella like he'd asked. It dawned on her why he was asking. "Heidi doesn't have any family for her to go to, so I'm it," she said. "If she's already here, moved in, with day-care in place, chances are Child Services won't disrupt her while they investigate Heidi's allegations."

Josh wasn't running scared. He was thinking clearly. Practically.

"Exactly."

"And if she's here, you'll be able to see her whenever you want."

He shrugged, turning enough that she couldn't see his face as he sipped his coffee and picked up his keys. "Depends on what the court decides, initially. I won't let Heidi push me into making a mistake. If I have to go a few days without seeing Bella while they investigate bogus charges, then I do. I'm going to play by the rules."

As she'd expect him to.

The whole thing sucked.

Other than that, she had the unexpected gift of Bella for a few days. Having come to the painful conclusion that, because she'd made the choice not to have a partner relationship, she might never have a child of her own, she'd poured every bit of nurturing instinct into Bella since the day her niece was born.

"I've got a couple of suitcases and bags of her things out in the car," Josh said, setting down his cup and heading for the door. "I want to get her moved in, and get me out of here, before anyone comes after me and grabs her, too."

Taking things from her brother at the front door as he made a couple of trips, Jasmine tried not to cry. How it had to hurt him, turning over his daughter's things. He adored Bella more than anything on earth. From the second she was born, Josh had glowed with love and pride for her.

"I'll keep her happy," she told him as he stood on her porch, ready to take off.

"I know you will, sis. That's why she's here."

"You sure you don't want a second cup of coffee?" Dawn had come, but it was still early.

Shaking his head, he reached a hand behind her neck and gently pulled her to him for a quick hug. "I want to get ahead of this. Turn myself in before they come for me. Danny says that's the best way to keep it low-key."

Right. Because while Bella was by far his greatest concern, she wasn't his only concern. As founder and chairman of Play for the Win, he had well over a thousand kids benefiting from his good reputation. A scandal could hurt them all.

Because of one damaged, bitter and vindictive woman.

"Call me as soon as you can," she called to Josh as he strode, head high, down the walk. With a backward wave, he acknowledged her request.

"We'll video talk every night before Bella goes to bed," she told his already retreated back.

She wasn't sure he heard her. And, feeling helpless in spite of herself, she let the tears fall.

THE HOUSE GREG was headed to was nice. He'd been to Santa Raquel many times in the past. Liked the small, beachside town. And had never been in any of these moneyed neighborhoods with expanses of private beach. Not a lot of crime happened there and he didn't run with the kind of crowd that would produce invitations to gated communities. He was the guy who came to town for a few hours on the public beach.

Nineteen eighty-five. He found the address. Jasmine Taylor's home, while on a stretch of private beach, was set a quarter of a mile up from the water. And it was fenced off.

Not that safety was on his roster of concern. Child Services had already had their go at the perp's sister over the past few days and deemed her suitable for temporary custody of the toddler. Greg was there to interview the sister for evidence against her brother.

Vibrant flowers lined her walk and trailed out of large terra-cotta pots on either side of the massive double front door.

Unlike most of the homes spread far apart on the secluded street, 1985 was single story. But still had four bedrooms.

Ms. Taylor lived nice for an elementary school teacher. But then he knew she, like her brother, had a trust fund to back her up. The brother had hired a snake of a lawyer, refusing to cooperate with the prosecutor's office in any way.

Greg knocked. Not sure what to expect in a woman who was worth more than a million dollars and still spent her days at work teaching young children how to add and subtract.

The police had arraigned her brother on a single misdemeanor charge of domestic violence. At the status conference the prosecutor had offered a no brainer plea agreement. Even Josh Taylor's lawyer had told him that if he pleaded guilty, he'd get no more than a slap on the wrist and probably some mandatory counseling. It was his first offense and he contributed an inordinate amount of good to the community.

Josh had refused to listen to any talk of deals or settling out of court. He seemed certain he was going to prove his innocence and had the money to spend doing it.

Which meant Greg had to work all that much harder to see justice done. Josh Taylor had nearly broken his ex-wife's wrist. The guy had to be accountable to that. At least by an admission and submission to counseling.

The door opened. Greg stood still, forgetting for a split second why he was there. There was nothing that remarkable about the woman standing before him. Nothing shocking about a woman wearing a long, black skirt that looked like it was made out of lightweight material. Her white T-shirt with black lace flowers hugged her figure nicely, but in Southern California nice curves were the norm. The dark hair that curled around her shoulders looked clean, the big brown gaze…everyone had eyes.

He'd broken out into a sweat in his light gray suit.

"Detective Johnson?" Her voice, quiet and yet somehow laced with authority, drew his gaze to her mouth. What in the hell was wrong with him? She wasn't his first good-looking interview. Not by a long shot.

Liv's drama must be rubbing off on him. Another reason to get himself fully out of her life.

"Yes, I'm sorry I'm a few minutes late." He found his spiel in the nick of time as he held up his badge. "I didn't count on so much traffic on the freeway."

"Yeah, the number of people who live up here and work between here and LA is growing every year." She didn't really smile, but it kind of seemed like she had.

"Auntie JJ! Auntie JJ! Look what I drawed!" A tiny, lisping little three-year-old voice came barreling around the corner and out to the foyer with the little girl carrying some kind of board that had a pencil-type article hanging from it by a cord.

"Come on, kiddo! Auntie JJ told you she had to work for just a minute and would be right back." Another female voice, slightly garbled and older, sounded just before another woman came into view.

"It's okay, Maddie." Jasmine—he assumed Auntie JJ was the woman who'd answered the door, and that the toddler was Anabelle Taylor—took the board from little fingers as the pudgy cheeks, framed by dark hair, turned up to her. "That's really good, Bella!"

"It's Daddy and me riding horses to supper!" Greg thought he heard. From what he could see, the board was covered with scattered scribbles.

"What are you having for supper?" Maddie asked in that unusual voice, taking the board from Jasmine and leading the little girl down a hall. "I'll close the door this time," the blonde said, glancing back at Jasmine, who nodded.

"Maddie and her husband and kids live at The Lemonade Stand with Lynn Bishop, our full-time nurse practitioner," Jasmine said, leading Greg out through a set of French doors at the back of the house to a deck furnished with upholstered wicker furniture. Wicker. For a two-hundred-pound guy.

He briefly noticed the large expanse of yard beyond, followed by as much beach and then the ocean. Paradise.

"Maddie works at the daycare and offered to sit with Bella while you're here," Jasmine was saying.

His job was to find out anything pertinent that wasn't in the formal reports. And to get her to tell him whether or not her brother had ever exhibited signs of domestic violence. During initial plea negotiation it had come out that they'd grown up in an abusive home—not that that fact alone made someone suspect. At all. Taylor's lawyer had offered the information in his client's defense, saying that Josh had helped save his mother and sister and was determined to live a violence-free life. As was his sibling. But fact was, victims often grew up to have victims. He didn't make the facts; he had to know them, to use them, to do his job.

She didn't offer him anything to drink—in spite of the nice teapot centerpiece on the wicker-wrapped glass-topped table in front of the couch. She took a rocker off one corner of the table. He lowered himself carefully to the couch, facing the ocean in the distance. He could barely make out waves moving in the dusk but didn't hear their sound.

"Maddie was a victim of domestic violence. First at home, when she was growing up, and then she was a victim of her husband."

Maybe she thought he needed a crash course in the world of domestic violence. No way she'd know that he'd successfully investigated—and earlier in his career, prosecuted—more cases of it than he could count.

"I'm not here to investigate you or your choice of babysitter," he told her, the first words he'd been able to get in since he'd shown her his badge. "I'm a detective, employed by the prosecutor's office." He'd told her so earlier when he'd called to make the appointment.

She nodded. "I know." Both hands on the arms of her chair, she rocked. Back and forth. Back and forth. Slowly. Portraying a sense of calm he wasn't sure she really felt.

Because she was a woman with secrets?

Could she hide something without appearing to be doing so?

She was a survivor. He heeded that knowledge.

But Liv was a survivor, too. And had moments of utter control.

"I'd like to have Maddie back before eight," she told him, not ungently. "She's happier when she can tuck her kids into bed herself."

That gave him an hour. For a five-minute interview.

For the first time in years, Greg wasn't sure of himself. Wasn't getting a good read on his interviewee.

There was no way he was thrown off balance by the woman in front of him. Wouldn't happen. Not after Liv.

Damn straight.

That wasn't going to happen.

Ever again.

Chapter Three

The second she realized she was feeling relaxed, Jasmine put herself on notice. The man sitting across from her, while recognizably attractive with his short, thick dark hair and surprisingly vivid green eyes, was huge. As in tall. And broad. One good shove from his index finger could send her backward.

And he was there to get her to turn on her brother. Not to find out the truth. His job was to assist the prosecutor to build his case.

Not to help her and Josh.

She usually felt safe around law enforcement. Was drawn to them. You'd think she wouldn't be, after an unsuccessful relationship with a cop who'd taken his street persona of being in charge way too far. He'd once told her he'd handcuff her to the kitchen table if that's what it took to keep her from going out with some friends he thought were bad for her. But no. Jasmine was attracted to people who exhibited confidence. People with power. Most particularly to cops. They'd always been her symbol of safety. She just had to call the cops. Just had to get to them. The police would help her.

Detective Greg Johnson was there to hurt them. She couldn't like him.

But when he asked her about The Lemonade Stand, about her job there, teaching the elementary-aged children who were residents, she found herself answering him like they were old friends.

"I've got grades one through six," she told him, thinking it would have been better if she'd faced the ocean rather than the house. That seemingly unending water mass was like a talisman. Reminding her of her strength. "But I rarely have students in all six grades at a time. The kids are generally never there more than six weeks—that's the state-allotted time a woman can remain at a shelter. The Lemonade Stand is privately owned, though, so exceptions can be, and are, made when deemed appropriate."

"Why would anyone ever not deem it appropriate for a woman to stay longer if she had nowhere to go?"

"Six weeks should be enough time for her to make some kind of arrangements. The thought is that if you don't force someone who's been victimized to take back control of her life, she'll remain a victim. The shelter is a safe place—and for a woman who's just left a home of terror, she could easily just settle in and want to stay."

"So how much teaching can you actually do?"

"A lot. I teach to state mandates for public education, focusing on the basics kids will need to pass on to the next year. Reading, writing and math proficiencies. But since I have all grades in one classroom, I do a lot of one-on-one work. Much like school systems that share buses and start different schools at different times, my kids' days start at staggered times. That way I can get one age group going on something before the next one comes in and needs my time."

"Sounds like a tough gig."

"It's actually the best job I could imagine," she told him. "I've been where those kids are. I love being able to work with them. To show them gentleness and love and understanding from a position of authority. I want them to know there are adults in charge of them whom they can trust."

So maybe they wouldn't constantly be drawn to, feel safe with, people who tried to control them—with an overactive need to seek approval from those people—once they reached adulthood.

Sadly, children who grew up with abuse were more prone to end up with partners with abusive tendencies. It made no logical sense to her. She couldn't explain it. But she knew the statistics were high.

And true. Because she was one of them.

"So that's why you do it."

"Do what?"

"Your work. You and your brother are both quite well-off."

"Me more than my brother now, since he gave half of what he had to Heidi when they divorced. Just offered it to her, not because he'd been ordered to do so." Her job was to show this detective, this big man in her space, that Josh was one of the good guys. One of the very best.

"So what about you? You've never been married?"

"Don't you have that information in your report?"

His shrug didn't tell her much. He did or he didn't?

"Why does that matter in proving that my brother didn't hurt his ex-wife?"

"It could tell me where you stand in terms of spousal negotiations…"

If she had a bias for him to be concerned about, it would be her love for her brother. But even that wouldn't let her hide any abuse. No way would she expose Bella to it. Not for anyone.

"I've never been married," she told him. "I've had three serious relationships but got out of all three before anything legal transpired." That should do it for his investigative purposes.

Why she hadn't turned in Desmond the cop was a question for another conversation. With her counselor, not this detective.

A conversation she'd already had. Multiple times.

Why she'd never filed charges, never brought anything into the legal realm, when all three of her choices—two male and one female—had ended up being abusive in one way or another, was more of that "other" conversation.

"Are you currently in a relationship?"

His green gaze glinted as he watched her. In the back of her mind a thought hung out—surely that wasn't an investigative question—and yet, meeting his gaze, she shook her head.

Because she wanted to answer him.

She wanted to please him.

It's what she did.

And...

"Has Josh been by to see Bella?"

There. That's what they did. People in authority, people you needed sucked you in. Made you feel safe. Cared for. And then, *wham*! So you'll give them what they want from you.

"No. He was ordered to stay away from her, except for supervised visits, since his arraignment two days ago. He's waiting for the paperwork to clear Child Services." This detective had to know that. And she had nothing to hide.

"Josh is going to do this by the book," she told him, straight on. "Bella is his world. Keeping her safe and happy means more than life to him. And to me, too, for that matter. He didn't hurt Heidi. This is all new to you, but we've been dealing with her, and her insidious vindictiveness, for years. This is a new low for her, granted, but it's of the same cloth."

"I've spoken with Child Services," Detective Johnson told her. She wasn't sure why. Was he warning her?

If so, it was unwarranted. And unnecessary.

"Then you'll know Josh is complying."

"I also know that Heidi's been in counseling and is committed to getting her rights to her daughter back."

Heidi had earned the right to supervised visits after completing a year of counseling successfully. And the restraining order Josh had been granted at the time of her arrest eighteen months before had been dropped.

Jasmine hadn't felt good about either development.

"Do you know that she threatened Josh? Told him she'd accuse him of domestic violence if he didn't agree to shared parenting with her?"

The woman he was trying to protect was dangerous. Maybe Jasmine was the one who had to show him that. They certainly didn't seem predisposed to believe Josh.

"This whole thing was planned. Just like the time Heidi claimed that Josh had stolen from her when, in fact, he'd merely taken what had been granted as his by the divorce. Or the time she claimed that her ring had slipped around on her finger without her knowing when she slapped him on the neck and left a big gash with her diamond?"

She could go on. And on. It would all be in his record. If he'd bothered to read about Heidi's past.

"The past is past," the detective said, almost as though he'd read her mind. He wiped at the back of his neck with his hand, perched there on her sofa like he thought it might give way beneath him at any moment.

She shivered. September's Friday evening air was balmy. Not warm, but not cold, either. The motion-sensor lights on either side of the deck had come on. Maybe she shouldn't have brought him out here to her peaceful place. In the mornings she liked to sit with her soda and watch the waves in the distance as they raced up to the beach.

With the sun having set, they weren't visible behind her. But she knew they were there.

"We are who we are." She shot the platitude back at him. And then, "Did she tell you she'd threatened him?"

"He did."

"And you don't believe him." It wasn't a question.

"She has proof of assault, Ms. Taylor. I understand your emotional investment here. I applaud your faith in your brother. But in my job, I have to deal with facts."

His pat on the head felt like a major thump. Disappointment flooded her when anger probably would have been more appropriate. She recognized the failing.

"You want facts? Well, how about the fact that the picture of the fingerprints on Heidi's wrist are on her left wrist and it's her right one that's sprained?" She'd discovered the discrepancy the first night after Josh's arrest and release—after they'd video-called Bella's bedtime story and hug. Her brother had shared the evidence against him with her.

No one had said he couldn't contact his daughter. Thank God for modern technology that made it so easy to almost be in the room together.

She had the detective's attention now. He'd leaned forward, turned his head slightly. Wasn't patting her on the head anymore.

"How do you know this?"

"Because I know her wrists. The fingerprints fit the sprain, but if you look at the picture with the prints, before the bruise appeared, you'll notice a freckle just beneath the wrist bone. You won't be able to see it in the bruising, I'm sure, but you look at her left wrist, you'll see it there."

"A freckle."

"Yep. Bella has one, too. In the exact same place. It's more like a little birthmark, really, but so small you wouldn't notice unless you saw it on a baby who'd never been exposed to the sun and had no other freckles anywhere on her body."

He wanted facts. She'd give them to him.

And...had that been a brief twinge of admiration in his eyes? She'd pleased him?

She smiled. "If you want the truth, Detective, if you want the real facts, then we're on the same side here."

His shrug was beginning to annoy her. Partly because it drew her attention to those big, protective shoulders.

Protective over someone else.

Not her.

She neither needed, wanted, nor would accept protection. She couldn't, lest she fall prey to bad choice number four. A woman could only stay strong through so many unhealthy relationships.

"You're saying you'll give me the truth?" he asked.

"Of course."

His gaze was compelling in the softness of the outdoor lamp as darkness fell. "Have you ever known your brother to lash out in anger?"

"No. I've seen him put himself in between my face and my father's backhand. I've seen him grab me up and leave a room with my father's belt slapping against his back. A belt that had been meant for me."

Because she'd dared to talk back when her father had told her that she didn't know what she needed. She'd said she wanted to start babysitting and earn her own money. She'd been fourteen.

"And I've seen him take Heidi's pummeling without raising a hand to stop her because he knew she was fighting herself, and her past, as much as him. He'd turn his back to her slaps, put distance between them, but he wouldn't walk out on her. He really loved her."

"She says she really loved him. But that, now that she's been through counseling, she knows she has to get her daughter away from him."

"Bella's the reason Josh left. Heidi picked her up in anger, started to shake her one evening when she was crying. Thank God Josh was there. He got the baby away from her before she did any damage. And just kept on walking. They came here that night, and I can guarantee you, my brother was devastated."

"Did you know they were seeing each other again?"

"For Heidi's supervised visits, yes. A counselor was there. Josh didn't stay. But he allowed the visits in his home so Heidi could be around Bella with all of her things. So Bella could be at home to see her mother." She'd worried every time. "I wasn't happy when the restraining order was dropped, but Josh thought it was the best thing for all of them. As long as Heidi was healthy, and he believed she was, Bella needed her mama."

"And you witnessed him turning his back when Heidi attacked him?"

"Yes. I also saw her slap his face. Until then he'd kept her abusive outbursts to himself. When I questioned him about it, he said it wasn't a big deal. He could handle it. He understood that she didn't mean or want to hurt him. She'd grown up in a violent home and just reacted without thinking sometimes."

Feeling really good about the detective now, as he actually sat there and listened to the truth, Jasmine started to relax again. He could help them.

He could let the prosecutor know they had no case and get him to drop the charges.

He could smile at her and she'd smile back.

But he didn't. He stood up. "Thank you for seeing me," he said. "I'll be in touch if I have any other questions."

She didn't want him to go. Didn't immediately hear the alarm bells in the back of her brain, at that. But she stood, too. She had to get Maddie back, then bathe Bella and call Josh for his daughter's bedtime story and virtual hug before bed.

"So…you think the prosecutor is going to be willing to drop the charges?" she asked, to prolong the moment anyway.

"He can't."

Of course he could. That's how the system worked. No evidence. Charges dropped. "Why not?" She was cold all of a sudden, out there in the dark on her porch with a man whose throat was above her head.

"Heidi has an eyewitness to Josh grabbing her."

It was a lie. Another one of Heidi's ploys.

"You've talked to this witness?"

"Not yet," Josh said. "We're going to try to do this without her."

"Why?"

"Because she's only three years old."

It took her a second to get it. But…wait… "Bella? You mean Bella?"

"Unfortunately."

"You think you're going to question a baby? My three-year-old niece?"

"I won't be. But if it comes to that, someone with the proper training will do so."

This couldn't be happening.

"And there's nothing you can do? This prosecutor, can't you talk to him? You said you wanted the truth. I swear to you, whatever Heidi's telling you is a lie. Or her own made-up variation of a small piece of truth. Like Bella saw the two of them together, or something." Bella's imagination was remarkable. Wonderful. And… imaginative. She'd thought squiggly lines were her and her father riding horses to dinner. She'd never even been near a horse, as far as Jasmine knew.

Could she be led to think she'd seen her father hurt her mother?

Oh God. If Josh had even held Heidi's hand, the child could be convinced to say he'd grabbed her wrist.

No.

She couldn't panic. All those years… Josh had fought her battles with Jasmine and even taken his own beatings. He was her earth. Her water. She wasn't going to let him down now.

"I know Josh didn't do it," she blurted before she could think. And then couldn't stop the next words from emerging.

"I know he didn't. Because… I did."

Chapter Four

"You want to rethink that?" Standing on the deck, facing an ocean he mostly couldn't see due to the darkness that had fallen outside the reach of the lights, Greg did what he could to force Jasmine to meet his gaze.

She held her own for a few long seconds. Then looked away.

Swallowing disappointment that had no place in his system in that moment, in that situation, he noted that she'd lied to him.

He'd wanted to trust her.

"Because, you know," he continued, "I can check alibis and probably prove, pretty easily, that you weren't present when Heidi's wrist was...damaged."

She glanced back at him, and for a second there he saw Liv's eyes, imploring him. Needing something from him that didn't exist. He felt compelled to help people. Needed to help her. He understood the reasons behind her struggles. He just wasn't a guy who was good with so much drama in his home.

"I didn't do it, and that was a ridiculous thing to say." Her words were soft and yet...strong, too. Nothing like Liv's needy tone that generally accompanied that vulnerable gaze. "Please, please, don't put that on the record, or whatever. In your report. If I'm a suspect in any way, I could lose Bella, and…"

He had her. The gift was right there for his taking. She needed him to keep quiet. He needed her to talk.

The fact that he'd never risk a child's life on something as innocuous as a nonsensical statement made out of desperation to save a loved one didn't have to play in here. She didn't know what he was and was not capable of. What he would or wouldn't do to help get a conviction.

She didn't know that while he served at the pleasure of the prosecutor's office, he was there to see justice done, not to get convictions.

He'd earned enough of those all on his own, when he'd been the county's lead prosecutor. And he carried the burden of them, too.

"I'll make a deal with you," he said, speaking slowly as he did a quick mental check on the idea as it occurred to him. Giving himself the go-ahead, he continued. "You agree to speak nothing but the truth from here on out, you cooperate with me every step of the way, and I'll forget I ever heard you implicate yourself."

She loved her brother. He needed the real abuser to take accountability or, chances were, the abuse would escalate.

"Since I've had every intention from the very beginning to cooperate and to speak the truth, I agree with your stipulations," she said.

Nodding, he turned away, figuring he'd done his job there for the moment.

His hand was on the knob of the French door when she said, "But I have a stipulation of my own."

Slowly rounding to face her, he waited.

She seemed to have no trouble whatsoever meeting his

gaze then. "If I'm going to give you everything I might have or find out, I need to be able to trust that you'll keep an open mind about Josh. That you'll weigh everything against the possibility that he's innocent. Not just what I give you, but everything you get. That you entertain other theories…"

What the hell? He had her on the hook, and she was…

"Because I know that Josh didn't do this. And I also know that he and I aren't enough this time. If Heidi is losing it to this point—willing to see her sweet baby go to Child Protective Services just to hurt Josh—there's no telling what she'll do. Giving her a voice, as the prosecutor has now done by charging Josh, gives her a strength she's never had before. Josh and I have been fighting her illness for years. We know her. We know the signs. But this is bigger than just us now. With her having support of the system, we're going to need professional help to stop her. None of us are safe until she's exposed as the liar she is."

He heard her passion. But he'd learned through his years with Liv that passion didn't always come from a place of truth. Sometimes it was born of other emotions, like fear. And versions of facts that, while believed by the speaker, weren't always as real as they seemed in the moment.

"I know that somewhere there is evidence that will prove Josh's innocence and show Heidi for who she really is. You're the one doing the investigating. You have the authority to go places and ask questions we can't. You're the one with the prosecutor's ear. We need your help," she told him.

His gut dropped like lead.

Another woman asking for empathy. Greg didn't tell

her he wasn't her guy. That his ex was proof that he'd been grossly shorted in the empathy department.

To the contrary, he let her believe that he'd comply with her request. He needed her cooperation.

He'd keep an open mind, follow whatever theories presented themselves, because that was what he always did. He did not want a preconceived ending. But she was asking for more than that. She wanted him to prove her brother's innocence.

And Greg believed, without doubt, that her brother was guilty. Not because Heidi had played him, but because she hadn't. There'd been no needy plea for sympathy when they'd met. She'd looked him in the eye and spoken with conviction.

Heidi Taylor loved her ex-husband.

And he'd physically hurt her.

GRABBING A SWEATER off the back of a chair, slipping into it, Jasmine followed Greg toward the front door.

She had to tell her brother not to give up. That they had someone on the inside willing to look for the truth. Bella's existence made him more vulnerable than he'd ever been before. Heidi knew that and was determined to kick him in the knees. Over and over again.

Josh had been through so much, had stayed strong and rock-solid through most of it. He didn't deserve any part of what Heidi was handing out. He'd loved the woman faithfully. Had put up with years of growing abuse— would have continued to do so if she hadn't turned on Bella.

"He chose Bella over her," she said aloud as the detective, reaching for the front doorknob, turned back to her. "That's why she's doing this. He put up with her abuse, loved her through it, until she turned on Bella. It's eating her alive, that his loyalty switched from her to someone else. That he'd protect someone else over her. She'll do whatever it takes to get her away from him."

Even at the toddler's expense. Heidi's own child.

Greg had said he wanted the truth. That he'd listen to it, look for other theories. This wasn't just a theory. It was the *only* truth. "She's jealous of her own daughter."

It was up to Jasmine to help Josh. She'd been shown the way.

The big man in her hallway wasn't the least bit intimidating as he met her gaze. "I need to hear about the past. Everything you can tell me. I need the whole picture."

"Of course." It wasn't a smiling moment. She felt like smiling anyway. She'd been given a way to make things right.

His long look settled her nerves even more. "I know you have to get your sitter back, but can you make some time tomorrow?"

"I'm out of class at three. Bella can play at the day-care until five."

"You're all right with that? Being apart from her that long?"

The question was odd. Had her studying him for a second, as though she should be on guard.

"I just...don't want to make things harder on you," he said. "With her being newly separated from her father and all."

Right. He'd been being thoughtful. She had to watch her trust issues or she was going to blow this.

"I have lunch with her," she told him anyway. Just in case he'd been questioning her care for her niece. As though she'd be willing to just brush the toddler off, leave her in the company of others during this trying time in her life. And then, to assure him that his demand on her time wasn't going to be a detriment to either her or Bella, she added, "And it's not all that uncommon for Bella to spend a few days with me. Each time, she always goes to the daycare at the Stand. I keep her any time Josh has a late meeting or needs to be overnight in LA or farther afield on business. That's why she has a room here." She motioned behind her. "And the people at The Lemonade Stand...we're all family. And Maddie works at the daycare and she's taken Bella on as one of her own."

Detective Greg Johnson was watching her, standing there in his light gray suit like he had all kinds of authority.

Which he did.

And he'd made a deal with her. At the moment, he was their hope.

While she stood there babbling out of both sides of her mouth. In case she could trust him, and in case she couldn't.

Time to get a grip. Josh had been the strong one for her so many, many times in their lives. It was time for her to carry the weight for both of them.

Her brother was one of the good guys.

No way she was going to let him fall now.

GREG ALMOST SENT someone else to meet with Jasmine at The Lemonade Stand the next day. Almost. The woman was getting to him, but sending someone else would require him to admit that he wasn't up to the task. That he wasn't able to do his job.

So he showed up. In suit and tie—lighter brown this time, short-sleeved tan shirt on under his jacket, brown dress shoes shined. He'd shaved just after six that morning, in the shower after his workout, but by three the growth was shadowing his jaw again. He chose not to do anything about that.

While Greg had worked with the High-Risk Team—a group of professionals who pooled knowledge and information to help prevent domestic violence deaths—it was the first time he'd ever actually been to this shelter. Hidden as it was between the cliffs and ocean and the innocuous street of shops that fronted it—shops that he knew were all owned by the Stand's founder and there to service its clients with everything from computer training to jobs—The Lemonade Stand wasn't hard to miss unless you knew what you were looking for.

He knew to take the mostly hidden drive into the nondescript parking lot that fronted a single, plain door giving entrance to a small, plebeian reception area. He'd been told to wait there—the only unrestricted area—for someone to come get him.

He'd been cleared for entrance onto the grounds of the shelter, but clearance didn't give him access. And he was ten minutes early.

There were a few seats along one wall. Plastic chairs with metal legs. His chose to explore further while he waited. Generic linoleum. Plain walls. He made a second pass. Noticed the same crack in the wall on the third time by, too. His legs needed a little stretching after being boxed up in his vehicle—a blue SUV purchased expressly because he could push the seat back far enough to drive comfortably.

So…he had energy to expel. And another seven minutes to wait. To not think about the woman who'd been on his mind most of the previous night. And a good part of the current day, too.

Stood to reason—his mind always got wrapped up in whatever case he was working, and hers was the current one. *One* of them. It wasn't like a first offense, a noninvasive domestic charge that the prosecutor was willing to plead out, needed his full day's attention.

Jasmine Taylor was the one who'd upped the stakes on this one. Challenging him to keep an open mind. As though he wouldn't always do so.

That thought was an irritating sting inside of him, warning him about getting complacent. About going for the obvious. About believing without complete proof.

As a prosecutor he'd been forgiven for doing so. Had even, at times, been expected to trust without all the evidence.

Which was why he was no longer a prosecutor and was a cop instead.

And also why he could never just believe someone without proof.

Heidi Taylor had proof. More than just a photo.

Jasmine had been right about that freckle. But the doctor's report specified an approximate time of injury, not just based on the patient's visit, but on the level of discoloration. Of swelling. His estimation—a scientific report the doctor had testified to in court—put the injury at a time that Heidi claimed to have been with Josh. A time when she most definitely had not been at the gym. At least not officially. Members had to get in and out with an ID card. Heidi's hadn't been used within the doctor's twenty-four-hour window. Which didn't mean definitively that Heidi was telling the truth.

But Greg had spoken with the doctor that morning. Had that opinion verified. Firsthand. Face-to-face.

He'd told Jasmine Taylor he'd get the facts.

And now she was going to give them to him, too. That was the deal. He was sorry that she was going to have to testify, at least to him, against her brother, but that wasn't his fault. Preventing further abuse lay on him, and he was going to get the job done.

Heidi had admittedly abused her husband—physically and verbally—in the past. And she'd lost control and had shaken her daughter. She'd told him all of it without him even pressing her. But she'd been through counseling and continued to go. She was healthy and wanting to be a part of her daughter's life again, and Josh Taylor was trying to prevent that from happening—by abusing his wife. If the man didn't get help, chances were he'd one day strike out at his daughter, too. Maybe not until she was a little older, until she tested him, pushed him too far...

Of course, Heidi could be manipulating Greg—but the prosecutor and the judge, too? "Detective Johnson?"

The voice, coming from a speaker near a heavy locked door, was not Jasmine's. The door opened, and a fiftyish-looking woman in a pair of blue pants with a matching jacket and blue leather flats stood there. "I'm Lila McDaniels Mantle, managing director of the Stand. Jasmine's running a couple of minutes late," she said.

While he'd never seen Mrs. McDaniels Mantle in person, he'd been hearing about her for years. She'd taken on a benefactor's idea—to create a haven for abused women and children to heal, under the theory that victims of domestic violence already felt so ugly inside that treating them physically well was a basic component to speeding up the healing process—and made the idea a huge success. The numbers of women who left the Stand to lead successful lives, as opposed to those who fell back into victimhood, were far greater than the state's norm.

"I'm happy to wait," he told her, taking stock of the smallish woman.

"No, I'll take you down," she said, and while her tone was soft, Greg didn't feel like he had much choice but to follow her. "I told Jasmine the two of you could use my private suite for your conversation," Lila said as she showed Greg through a doorway and then another passcoded entry and down a hall. She moved too quickly for him to get much more than a glimpse of many of the rooms he passed—some with open doors, some not. Some larger community areas with several family room–like seating areas. A library. A big cafeteria area. A few women passed, some in pairs, some alone. None of them met his gaze or offered a greeting of any kind.

The lack of friendliness was a bit off-putting. Until he gave himself a mental shake—with a little berating on the side—and realized that the women in these hallways were most likely victims. Almost surely victims since they weren't wearing The Lemonade Stand shirts he caught glimpses of on three different women in a couple of different rooms. Logic would follow that a man in their midst could very well make them uncomfortable.

And a man of his stature…

Walking beside Lila McDaniels Mantle, he hadn't felt so big—the woman had a way of taking control and seeming much larger than her size—but Greg suddenly felt like hunching his shoulders a bit. Needing to make himself smaller.

The managing director didn't speak to him at all—didn't give him any kind of tour as she hurried him through the halls and toward a door marked with her name. But she smiled at every single woman in their midst—not seeming put out at all by those whose eyes never rose from the floor.

"You can wait for her here," Lila McDaniels Mantle said, showing him to a conversation area in her office. "She'll take you through to the suite when she gets here."

The woman was matter-of-fact. Not friendly, but not at all unfriendly, either. Because she wasn't sure she could trust him?

On Jasmine's behalf, she was probably right. Because he had every intention of using the woman to get her brother's conviction.

But it was the right thing to do. Surely, Lila would see that. Want that. An abuser held accountable. For Jasmine's sake, even. As hard as it would be for her to have to admit the truth about her brother—in the long run, she'd be better off with him either healthy or serving time. That was the idea here—to prevent domestic violence from happening.

Against Heidi. And Bella. And Jasmine, too.

"I'm watching out for her," he told the director as she took her purse out of a drawer.

"She thinks you are." Mrs. McDaniels Mantle held his gaze with a steady stream that didn't falter. He sensed her warning, whether through the look, or something else he didn't know. "Josh Taylor saved his sister's life. And every day his work, his personal efforts, are saving hundreds of lives in this state."

"I'm aware of his work. Of Play for the Win."

He was doing his job. Doing it well. And felt guilty as hell for some reason that was baffling the hell out of him. And kind of pissing him off, too.

The director looked as though she had more to say. But shook her head and went for the door. "I'm very late for lunch with my husband," she said. And then stopped, turned back, came to rest directly in front of him.

"We all have jobs to do," she said, seeming to choose her words carefully. "And lives to save," she added. "The key is to figure out whom to save."

He was going to save them all. Or as many as came into his circle of influence.

"And you do that by figuring out why you're saving any of them at all."

He wasn't following. Frowned. Wished he'd remained standing. The woman was nothing like he'd imagined her.

And everything like he had.

"Why you?" she said to him. "Not why should lives be saved. Why should you be the one saving this particular life?"

What the hell…?

Greg stood, not sure he was going to bother with a response, or even stick around and wait for his appointment. He was in some frickin' twilight zone. Definitely not a place for a guy like him who didn't understand needy women well enough on a good day.

His mother was about the only woman he ever got. She was a rock. Happy. Capable. Always there. Always ready. And friends from high school, college, even the prosecutor's office. Women who understood there were boundaries, and respected them, too.

Women with reasonable expectations…

"Oh, Lila, I'm so sorry I made you even later…"

The voice was fresh air blowing into a confined space. Something a little more normal. Definitely expected.

"Jasmine," he said, feeling as though he'd known her

for a lot longer than a day, judging by how familiar she seemed to him. How glad he was to see her there. "If now's a bad time, we can set up something else…"

He couldn't get the offer out fast enough. He'd heard the resort was acres and acres of lush beauty with a beach and ocean below. Sacred gardens. Woods. Lovely bungalows. That reality and his current one didn't mesh. At all.

"No." Jasmine met his gaze. "I'm ready. Just had a new student come in this afternoon, and I wanted to make sure he felt comfortable and wouldn't dread coming back to us in the morning," Jasmine continued as Lila McDaniels Mantle, with one more glance at Greg, told Jasmine she was happy to help anytime and then said goodbye.

Leaving Greg feeling relieved.

And like Jasmine Taylor had just saved him from a fate worse than failing.

Chapter Five

Meeting him at The Lemonade Stand had not been the best choice. The second she saw Greg Johnson standing there in Lila's office, she'd recognized her mistake. The Stand was her safe place. A little haven in the world where warm fuzzies were free to roam at will.

They now roamed right over to the detective. She wasn't going to fall for him. Wasn't even going to entertain the idea of feeling safe with him, either.

He was there on business. And while his business was incredibly personal to her heart and happiness, he wasn't included in the heart part.

Wanting to lead him straight out to the parking lot, to have their meeting standing on the curb if need be, she thought of Bella and straightened herself out. She wasn't a vulnerable young woman anymore, looking for someone to be her partner through life, to share the ups and downs, to love her like no one else ever could.

She was a grown woman who'd learned the hard way that she was better off living alone, loving those who needed it most. And trusting Josh to have her back.

"Would you like something to drink?" she asked as she let them both into the private suite behind Lila's office. "Lila always has tea on hand."

The living quarters were small, and yet, a place where Jasmine could picture herself being perennially happy. With the rose-colored wing-back chairs made of the finest silk and claw-footed end table, the antique china in a hutch, silk roses in a solid crystal vase, and pictures of faraway places on the walls, she always felt like she could lose yourself to joy in that room. The small adjoining kitchen with table and chairs, and the separate bedroom, were decorated with equal combinations of feminine opulence and whimsy.

So unlike the Lila that ran The Lemonade Stand with a firm, practical, loving hand.

Greg declined refreshments. He shot a pointed look toward the lovely, welcoming couch and pulled out one of the kitchen chairs. Jasmine busied herself brewing some lavender tea.

Maybe she should have thought a bit more before immediately accepting Lila's offer to have this meeting in her quarters. Greg Johnson's big presence was a bit much.

Didn't fit.

And yet she wanted him there. Was happy to see him.

"What do you need to know?" she asked, bringing her tea to the table and sitting down opposite him—not that he was really facing the table. More like he'd pulled the chair out away, facing the biggest expanse of unoccupied room in the small space.

Josh would be the first to tell her that she had to fight any attraction she might feel to the man she was certain was going to help them. Because she had no other friends whom she was vulnerable enough with to confide her lowest lows, her brother had been the one left to pick up her pieces each time she'd ended up broken from another failed relationship. She didn't need him to tell her, though; she had looked her issues in the eye and taken them on as the baggage they were—lessons to her, but not in charge.

She couldn't honestly tell herself that that baggage had had no hand in choosing her outfit: a knee-length black-and-white-striped stretch cotton dress or her favorite pair of thin, soft black leggings. The outfit, while completely circumspect for school, showed how slim she was, while making the most of breasts that, while not overly large, had a shape that seemed to attract attention. And while Bella had been smearing peanut butter on the table while she ate her toast, Jasmine had plugged a curling iron into an outlet within view and spent a little time working on the ends of her hair.

Earning her an "Auntie JJ looks peetty" from her niece as they headed out the door.

"How old were you and Josh the first time your father got violent at home?"

The question felt like a slap. Her fault. She'd let herself spend too much time with the baggage…

He'd come there for information that would help Josh. Nothing there to feel good about. Except giving it so that her brother could be free from the nightmare that was Heidi.

"I was four the first time I remember knowing that I had to get Josh upstairs in my doll closet and be really quiet until Mom came to find me," she said, with very little emotion. The story had been told. It was out. No longer a memory with the power to cripple her.

"Your mother told you to go?"

Dipping her tea bag, she lifted it out of the cup, dropping it onto the side of the china saucer.

"No," she answered eventually. "I wasn't even sure

she'd find us. I have no idea what I was planning to do from there. Spend the rest of our lives in my closet? It was a separate walk-in closet in my room that my parents built into a dollhouse."

"Your father, too?"

She nodded. He'd had a good side. A great side. A side that allowed you to love him. A side the world saw. So did all three of her exes.

And Heidi.

"Mom says that the first time I protected Josh was when I was three and he was one. He was just learning to walk and couldn't take many steps on his own. My father was in one of his rages and apparently I laid Josh down on the floor and got down beside him, pulling a blanket up over the top of us, as though we wouldn't be seen. According to my mom, when my father saw that, he stopped yelling in midsentence and walked out."

A decent man had lurked inside him.

"So you grew up with violence? It wasn't just something that happened later."

"It's all we ever knew."

"Did he ever hit you?" Greg asked.

"Not when Josh was old enough to stop him."

"But before that?"

She shrugged. More old news. Dealt with. No more power to hurt.

Ah, but she was there to help Josh. "Yes. He broke my tooth when I was six. I have a permanent cap on it." That was one she remembered specifically. "He had an active backhand," she said. "It was a part of our lives, almost as frequent as Saturday morning cartoons. And some weeks, as prevalent as bedtime prayers."

She thought about how that sounded. How…horribly

victimized it made them all sound, living like that for so many years.

"He was also generous. Encouraging us to show interest in things and then supporting that interest, both with time and money. He was at every game and school play. Took an active role in holiday shopping and made a wonderful Santa on Christmas mornings."

And by afternoon he'd have a bourbon, retreat to his home office to work, and come out raging if something wasn't going his way.

"He'd say the most awful things," she said aloud, without conscious choice to do so. "From calling one or the other us an imbecile or stupid, to telling my mother she was worthless. He'd tell us his rages were our faults. And if anyone dared talk back, he'd throw a backhand."

"So his anger was work related?"

"Not necessarily. One Christmas he flew off because the swing set he was trying to put together fell over and the top bar hit him in the head. He just had a lightning, vile temper."

And the rest of the time, when he wasn't angry, he was a regular husband and father. One who'd amassed enough wealth to provide them all with whatever material things they wanted or needed. He was always generous and seemed to take real joy out of giving to them.

"You said that he didn't hit you after Josh was old enough to protect you."

"I said, since he was old enough to stop our dad," she corrected. They were dealing with the truth here, not versions thereof. "He was tall for his age," she added. "I told you about it last night. The way he grabbed me up and left the room…" She said she'd been fourteen, which she had been. But Josh's protection had started even before that.

Which would be pertinent for Greg to know.

"When I was ten, in fifth grade, Josh and I were play-ing a video game one night after dinner. My job was to clear the table, and I forgot. We'd been playing before dinner, too, and I was beating him at the game." Not that it mattered. But it stuck in her mind. "My father came in and saw me there and told me that if I didn't get in the kitchen and get the table cleared, I was going to get a spanking."

He hadn't been in a temper. But he'd been serious about the spanking. She'd known that. She'd also known that her mother had already cleared most of the table. Mom had known about the ongoing video game, and they only had half an hour more to play before home-work and bedtime. Mary had liked that she and Josh got along so well together. Played together. She hadn't told Jasmine she could be excused, but when she'd seen them trying to finish their game, she'd smiled and left to clear the table herself.

Their father had only cared that one child wasn't meet-ing their responsibilities.

"He told Josh that if he didn't get up and help me, he was in for it, too."

Josh had looked at him—and lost a point on the game. "When Josh protested, saying he hadn't done anything wrong, that clearing the table wasn't his job, our father's face turned red, and I knew there was going to be trou-ble."

She sipped tea. She'd been over the event multiple times, in joint counseling with Josh when they were younger, and as an adult, too. They'd learned from this incident and were able even to joke about it between the two of them now.

Looking at the detective, she was glad that she'd tended to her issues, done the work, so she could be healthy and healed. She'd hate to be less than her best in front of the man who was there to save them from this current nightmare.

"We both stood up as our father approached." She gave a shrug, a small smile in memory of those two kids who'd stood up for themselves way back then, having no idea about what standing up for yourself really meant.

"I knew I was going to get it, but I also knew that Josh was safe behind me. When my father hit me, Josh could run and get Mom. Or just run…"

She could still remember so clearly knowing that. That Josh would be safe. What she couldn't remember was why on earth she'd opened her mouth.

"I told my father that my teacher said that no one should hit kids," she said, shaking her head. "He flew into a rage," she continued, throwing the rest out there without needing to call up any memories. "I hunched, tucking my face, and suddenly Josh was there, pushing in front of me, putting himself right in front of my father's approaching blows. I couldn't believe it. He was supposed to run for Mom. To get himself safe. I was the one who hadn't done my job. I pushed back at Josh. Hard. There was no way I was going to let him in front of me."

She stopped for a moment. Breathing as she knew to do. Allowing any residual negative emotion to wash over her and fade, as she knew it would. Taking another sip of tea. Lavender was calming. She also liked the taste of it. A pleasant sensation to replace ones that were less so.

She had this.

"But he got in front of you anyway?" Greg asked, confusing her for a second. She then remembered that she'd told this story because it was about the first time Josh had protected her from their father. The detective was waiting to hear how Josh had saved the day.

"No, he fell and broke the glass inset on the coffee table, gashing his shoulder blade. We spent the next few hours in the emergency room while Josh got twenty-four stitches on his back. The shard of glass missed his neck by a couple of inches."

Thank God for that.

For saving her sweet and wonderful brother from more severe consequences due to her ghastly mistake.

Their father had had a lot to say to her during those hours. "You see what happens when you try to disobey a parent?" She could still hear his next words: "My rules are set for a reason. They're designed to teach you life lessons, not school lessons. Discipline is necessary. Without it you and your brother will never be able to live happy, productive lives."

Their mother, looking sick and loving and concerned, had nodded at that as Jasmine, who'd been huddling against her, turned to look up. The nurse had come in then to check on Josh, who'd been eating chocolate ice cream, and to let them know that they were processing the paperwork for the accident as a result of siblings roughhousing so they could go home. There'd been no reason to think of Josh's injury as anything other than what her wealthy, respected parents reported. There were no prior visits on record. No visible evidence of previous injuries.

She hadn't looked at her mother during her father's next speech, ten or so minutes later.

"None of this would have happened if you'd just listened to me to begin with. Your teacher's job is to give you math and science skills. My job is to raise a decent, moral human being who will be a positive contribution to society, not a drain on it. I always only want what's best for you. That's something you're too young to understand now, but you'll get it later. When you grow up and have your own kids. But this you need to get now—I have an obligation to you, and to society, one that the law gives me, to raise you kids. Until you are eighteen, my word is your law."

You'd think she'd have gotten it. Learned to keep her mouth shut. She had, eventually, at least when it was her own concerns at issue.

"Were you punished for pushing him?" Greg Johnson's words pulled her back from the brink of falling back too many years. To before she'd had adult counseling, when such memories still had the power to take over her brain.

"No," she said, fast-forwarding back to Lila's office. To giving testimony to the man helping them. "My parents knew I was only trying to keep Josh from taking my punishment."

Josh had made Jasmine swear a promise that night. If he ever stepped up to help her, she had to let him.

He was bigger than she was, he'd pointed out. And he wouldn't just stand by and watch his sister get hurt.

She'd agreed. Hadn't felt like she'd had much other choice, based on his reasoning and the fact that he was lying propped up oddly in bed with a sling. He wasn't going to stop trying to save her, no matter what she said, and she couldn't take a chance on him getting injured again.

She'd agreed, too, because no matter what anyone said, she knew him being hurt was her fault. For a second there she'd been mad at Josh for rushing forward, for putting himself in danger. She'd always wondered if maybe she'd shoved too hard because of that.

Coming back to the present, she answered more of Greg's questions, sipping her tea, feeling almost as calm as she sounded. Counseling, working through things, really did work. You could grow up in hell and find a way back to living with joy.

It was true what they said about facing your fears taking away their sting.

Until they backhanded you out of the blue.

Like Heidi was doing.

And then, if you lived right, if you were lucky, a good detective caught your case. Sometimes you didn't have to do it all alone.

Sometimes protection knocked on your door looking for truth.

Chapter Six

Greg didn't spend a lot of time in his office. It made him itchy. Seriously. For ten years he'd practically lived on the second floor of the county court building, home to the prosecutor's office. Area restaurants knew his number by heart. He'd dial, they'd pick up and ask if he wanted his usual.

When Liv had come into his life, he'd eaten at home more. And then less, again, the more he'd needed to escape from her.

He was what he was. And at the exact moment he entered his office on Friday afternoon, he knew he wasn't going to change. It just hit him. No matter how much he might wish he was a different kind of guy, capable of understanding softer emotions in a more supportive way or understanding them at all—he wasn't that guy. He wasn't Rick. And definitely not Josh Taylor. Not only was he not an abuser, he also could not, in any way see himself dedicating his life to raising a toddler singlehandedly.

The whole idea of it gave him hives.

The kid would get its feelings hurt for some reason unclear to him, and he'd need to go lift weights. Again and again.

Once a day, from 5:00 to 6:00 a.m., was enough for him. A guy his size couldn't afford to get much bigger.

He had to get Jasmine Taylor out of his head. All this soul searching wasn't good for him. Cramped up his thinking. Put him in a foul mood.

As did the folder he found sitting on top of his desk. Left there by William Brubaker, assistant prosecutor in charge of the Taylor case.

He read the paperwork, a new filing related to their case, but completely separate from it as far as the court system was concerned. It had been left for him as an informational piece of the puzzle, not one requiring immediate action on his part.

Heidi Taylor's lawyer had filed a suit with the court to have Bella removed from Jasmine Taylor's custody, claiming, of all things, that Josh's sister had been abusive in the past.

Fake confession aside, there was no evidence that Jasmine had ever hurt her niece, as noted in the filing. No proof even of any hint that Bella had been hurt by anyone other than Heidi. And because Child Protective Services had just recently vetted Jasmine and placed the child with her, the only nearby living relative Bella had other than her parents, Bella was to continue to remain with her temporarily while allegations against Jasmine were investigated. There were no grounds for a restraining order. And yet, Heidi had convinced her attorney to file the motion.

It seemed the woman would rather have her child in foster care than at home with her aunt. Just as Jasmine had claimed. Against his better judgment, he picked up his cell. Pushed to dial another cell. Private to private.

"Greg? Detective Johnson, I'm sorry, what's up?" Jasmine's voice was breathy, like she'd either picked up on the run or was emotionally distressed in some way.

"Is this a bad time?" He knew her classes were through for the day. She could be out with Bella. Or even home already.

"No. I was just moving some bookcases into my classroom," she said. "They were donated today."

"There's no one there to help you do that?"

"Of course there is. I just didn't want to wait!" She sounded...happy...about used bookcases. He thought about hanging up on Jasmine.

About Liv's good moods doing complete 180s on a dime and him being dizzy with the quick turn. But Jasmine wasn't his girlfriend, past or present, he reminded himself.

"Have you heard from the court today?"

"No, why?"

"Have you been inside The Lemonade Stand all day?"

"Yes, why? What's going on?" He didn't miss the sharpening tone. Or blame her for it, either, really.

"Just didn't know if anyone had been to see you. Heidi filed a motion to try to have Bella moved to foster care."

"What!" The shrill tone had him pulling the phone back from his ear. Shrugging out of his suit jacket and, hand in his pocket, strolling over to the window. He didn't have an ocean view. Or even a city one. He saw mountains. And liked what he saw.

Mountains he could climb. Had climbed every peak within his current view. Multiple times.

"On what grounds?" Her question broke into his mental reveries.

"She fears that you have abusive tendencies."

Silence fell on the line. He let it sit there.

Many seconds later Jasmine said, "She fears— I've never— She has absolutely no grounds— What kind of mother would rather see her three-year-old in foster care than with a family member she knows and loves?"

He'd asked the same question moments ago. Seconds ago, too. And yet, Jasmine had put herself under suspicion with that false confession.

"One who is truly that afraid for her child's safety?" His only goal was the truth.

"One whose need to lash out and hurt someone is more powerful than her maternal instincts," she shot right back. "She'll be telling herself Bella will be just fine in foster care for a short time. That the state will watch out for her, which they will, of course. But to what emotional toll on a sensitive and bright little girl who will be scared to death away from the homes and loved ones she knows?" Jasmine's voice rose. So did Greg's gaze—to the top of the tallest peak. He'd been up there the previous spring. With his father. Had a picture of it on his phone.

"This is just…wow. One part of me can believe it, but… No, I really can't believe it. Not even from her."

She started to ask Greg questions, and he had to cut her off. Let Jasmine know that, at that point, his involvement was only informational, that there was nothing more he could tell her or do for her. Which raised a question she didn't ask, but probably should have. "Why are you still talking to me, then?"

He brooded over it the rest of the afternoon.

JASMINE DIDN'T WANT to leave The Lemonade Stand that day. For so many reasons. Some parts of her, in spite of all her healing and good emotional and mental health, suddenly craved the sanctity inside the Stand. The women there, they were all as one inside those walls. No one could get her there. Serve her any notices. Or worse.

No one could touch Bella, either. At least not easily. They'd have to do a lot more than file a lame motion to breach the security of protection, figuratively and literally. Harper Davidson, the newly remarried head of security, and her staff of fifteen, lived life on alert.

Lila would let her stay. All she'd have to do was let the managing director know that she didn't feel safe going home.

Something stopped her from going that far, though. The bungalows at the Stand were at nearly full capacity. The spaces that remained should be left for women afraid for their lives. Jasmine wasn't. Heidi wasn't going to do any physical damage to her. Or to Bella, either, for that matter.

And Jasmine had to go home.

Josh was getting his first supervised visit with Bella that night. Coming over to Jasmine's for dinner. She'd made his favorite—chicken alfredo—the night before and it was waiting in the refrigerator for her to reheat.

She'd tell him about Heidi's new motion and they'd figure this out. Hopefully she'd have a chance to speak with him without the social worker present. Video calls were wonderful, but she needed some in-person time for this one, weak though that made her feel.

She wasn't weak. And Heidi was not going to win.

BELLA WAS SO happy to see her dad that night she peed her pants. Jumping up and down and laughing, she stopped suddenly and looked up at him. Josh knelt down to his daughter.

"I just let go a little," she said, scooting her tennis

shoe—shod feet apart and looking at the small darkening trickle heading down her little pink leggings. And then she giggled and held her arms up for him to pick her up.

Lifting her into the air above his head, both hands securely around her little body, Josh said, "Bet you can't make me pee," and flew her like an airplane into the house to change her pants.

Marianne Lyons, the social worker, had gotten out of a car across the street as soon as Josh pulled into the driveway. She followed right behind him into Jasmine's house. They'd yet to be introduced, but Josh had told her he'd met Marianne twice that week. While Josh didn't like having her in his life, in his relationship with his daughter, he trusted the woman and felt like she'd truly do what was best for Bella. In the end, that was all that mattered to Josh.

Dinner was actually quite nice. Marianne sat at the table and ate with them, but she was more like wallpaper then a dinner companion. Bella had been introduced to her, but she was so glad to be with her daddy, who entertained her the entire meal with silly games and antics to get her try new tastes and eat every one of her green beans, that the social worker could just as easily have not been there. Watching Marianne as Josh played on the floor with Bella in the new toddler-size playhouse he'd brought in after dinner, Jasmine was really impressed. Jasmine couldn't figure out what in particular she did to fade, but whatever it was, she did it so well the entire evening passed almost naturally.

Josh was allowed to put Bella to bed and read her a story on his own—Marianne just stood out in the hallway, watching through the crack in the open door. Then Jasmine, having just finished the dishes, mentioned that she'd like a moment to have a private word with her brother. The older woman offered to stay, to sit in the living room and listen for Bella, so the siblings could have some time together.

"I'm hoping that after another visit or two we won't need Marianne here," Josh told her as he followed her out to the deck. "My lawyer is writing a motion to ask the court to allow you to be our chaperone."

Her stomach knotted so tightly she wished she hadn't eaten any of the dinner. Still in the navy leggings and long blue plaid shirtdress she'd worn to work that day, she thought about loosening the thin belt around her waist.

She told her brother about the motion Heidi had filed that day instead. One she'd yet to see. She jumped right in. Had to get it over with.

"I have no idea how this works," she told Josh as she sat in the same chair she'd been in the other night with Greg and, elbows on her knees, leaned in toward her brother. Part of his face was in shadows, but the motion-sensor lights let her see the immediate tightening of his lips. "Do I get served?" she asked.

"She must not have filed a restraining order or you'd have already been served."

"She had no grounds to file one." Jasmine had never so much as spoken harshly to Bella or been in any way abusive to Heidi, either. To the contrary, she'd loved the woman like a sister—continuing to try to get her to get help for herself when it became obvious that she'd crossed a dangerous line.

"She's become pretty well versed on California family and domestic violence law over the past couple of years," Josh said. "She had to know that with no proof, no evidence, she'd lose a bid for the restraining order, so didn't go that route. She doesn't want to throw doubt on her credibility."

A sense of familiarity washed over her. Oddly calming. She and Josh had spent the past two years in huddles just like this one. Discussing Heidi. Deciphering. Josh understood his ex-wife better than anyone. And the way to beat her disease was to know what she was thinking and somehow expose that to those who were working on her behalf.

"I just have no idea if that's a good thing for us, or not," Josh was saying. "Is she rational enough that she knows she can't go that far? Or is she so far gone she's being almost diabolical in her approach to this? Calculating every single aspect of some thoroughly developed plan…"

Heidi was smart. Sometimes too smart for her own good.

Fear stabbed Jasmine, swift and cruel, heightened by her own false confession. "She's afraid that I have abusive tendencies… My God, Josh, what do I do to prove that there's no basis in that? How do you prove that someone's fear is ungrounded?" She stopped when she heard her voice getting louder. And heard the high note of panic, too. Josh didn't need to deal with her on top of everything else.

This was her time to be strong for him.

But…

"My job… I could lose everything. There's no way I'd have clearance to work at the Stand if I can't even qualify for custody of my own niece."

She'd grown up a victim. Many victims became abusers. It wasn't fair. Wasn't even profiling. It was just fact.

Could Heidi use that against her? Would it be enough to lay doubt?

Was that what this was about? Hurting Jasmine?

"I'll call my lawyer in the morning," Greg said. "If the motion's been filed, he'll be able to see it. And tell us what to expect. What the next step will be. But, for now, we can ask Marianne." He stood.

"Wait," Jasmine told him. "Are you sure we should bring her into it? I mean, what if the motion gets thrown out? We don't want to alert Child Services… It could lay doubts and then maybe they won't let me supervise your visits."

She wasn't sure how that worked, really. The court would have to trust her not to side with her brother and leave him alone with Bella, right? Did they do that?

"Let me talk to Sara at the Stand," she said, speaking aloud what she'd been thinking on and off all evening. If she'd had her head about her, she'd have asked Sara that afternoon before she left work. As it was, she'd been so determined to not give in to fear that she'd just picked up Bella as though it was any normal day and dared to go home. "She's not a lawyer, but she works closely with attorneys in domestic violence cases, testifies in court. She'll keep things confidential and at least give us a clue what to expect, what to do, even it's just to say to talk to our own legal team." If nothing else, Sara would help Jasmine get control of her fear enough to be able to help, not hinder, the situation.

"There's a good possibility the motion will just be thrown out," Josh said, taking a seat and meeting her gaze. The worry lines on his forehead gave her a physical ache. "She completed her batterer's treatment program, but as you said before, the law generally doesn't revisit custody for a proven abuser for five years. It's only been two. Which means Heidi won't get Bella, regardless. Bella would just go in the system. And the courts always try to find a suitable family member for placement first."

Which would be Jasmine herself. Unless it wasn't.

Logically she knew that Heidi was really reaching this time. That she couldn't possibly win. "There's no evidence at all," she reminded herself. And him. "Other than the time you stopped her from shaking Bella, Bella's never known violence of any kind. That baby has never even had a bruise on her little body that I know of…"

"Just the time she fell backward when she was first sitting on her own and hit her head."

He'd called the doctor immediately, Jasmine remembered. And then called her. She'd driven to Santa Barbara, fearing concussion or worse, only to find barely a little bump on the back of the baby's head. Heidi, who'd still been in the picture then, had been out shopping, and she'd come rushing home, too. And then teased Josh for being overreactive. Still, for the next two months, Josh had followed the baby around with pillows, putting them all around her any time she was sitting on the floor.

"Heidi's hurting herself with this motion more than anything," Jasmine said now, pulling herself out of the spiral of fear and back into reality. "She's showing herself for the mean-spirited person she is, which can only help your situation." Back on top. Being the helper rather than the helpee.

"And the fact that Detective Johnson called me about it right away… He's the one investigating her claim against you, and he's on our side, Josh. We've got this."

Josh nodded, his expression easing. "You're right," he said, and then grinned. "She was so happy to see me

she peed her pants," he said. "God, I love that kid. It's…
She's… Having her…it's a feeling I never could have
imagined," he said. "I wake up in the morning and know
she's alive and healthy, and…it's just…" He shook his
head. "It's the best, Jas. You need this, too. You deserve
this kind of inner happiness and peace. It's like a built-
in joy that doesn't go away."

"I love her, too, Josh," she told her brother. "She brings
magic to my life every single day."

They'd been through this multiple times, in various
versions. Josh wanted her to fall in love and have babies
of her own.

She'd tried to help him understand that she'd had her
three strikes and she was out. By her own choice.

That one thing she'd learned about herself was that
she truly was one of those people who was happier alone.

And yet, as she passed Bella's room on her way to bed
that night, she stood there a long time, thinking about
what Josh had said.

She was alone by her own choice. Because she couldn't
make good choices. Just where relationships were concerned, she reminded herself, taking soft, quiet steps as
she moved into the carpeted nursery and stood by Bella's bed.

Only one of Bella's chubby cheeks was exposed as the
toddler lay curled in the fetal position, her favorite blanket and little crocheted ballerina doll cuddled up with her.
Calming as she watched her little niece's chest move up
and down with reassuringly repetitive breaths, Jasmine
reminded herself that she was a survivor.

Blowing a small kiss near Bella's ear, she let herself
out as stealthily as she'd gone in. Brushed her teeth. Got
in her nightgown and slid under her own covers, reach-

ing over to triple-check the baby monitor that would alert her if Bella made a sound.

She closed her eyes and found herself engulfed immediately in another kind of darkness. The kind that hit victims when they least expected it. The kind that you could push away during the day, when others were around, when you were engaged in other endeavors, but that awaited to attack you, from the inside out, when you let your guard down.

She wasn't normal. Hadn't grown up in a healthy, happy home. She'd pushed her brother so hard once he'd had to have stitches. She'd been mad that he was putting himself in danger and she'd pushed too hard.

No. Her rational mind told her. She knew her psyche was playing with her. Told it to stop. And still, as she drifted off to sleep, she was reminded that Heidi knew about her past. Heidi knew she was her father's daughter. And that it was possible that somewhere deep inside Jasmine some of her father's same vile temper could be lying dormant.

Chapter Seven

Greg spent the weekend with his parents in Las Vegas. They'd just moved from Boston to Seattle, and all three of them were eager for some rest and relaxation, Johnson family style. None of them were good at just sitting around. They always had to be going and doing, and Vegas had long been a family favorite getaway, even before he'd been twenty-one. They'd done the shows. The food. The racetrack—as in driving race cars around a real track. And at night, he'd lie in luxury in his room in the suite they'd always reserved, watch movies and order whatever he wanted from room service while his folks spent a few hours in the casino. They never stayed out late—had always returned in time to wish him good-night…

More recently, Greg was the one who spent more time gambling. And he didn't always make it back upstairs in time to tell them good-night. He didn't share a suite with them anymore, either.

But the weekend away was good. Just what he'd needed, he told himself as he landed in LA Sunday night, retrieved his car from the garage and drove up to his home in Santa Barbara. He'd gone hours without thinking about Jasmine Taylor and was ready to carry on with the case from a more distanced standpoint.

Heidi Taylor had grown up a victim. She'd married a victim. Become an abuser. And was now a victim again. That theory was completely believable. He'd done enough work with the High-Risk Team, both as a prosecutor and an investigator, to be well versed on domestic violence profiles. The disease, what it could do to the psyches of all involved, was insidious.

But it didn't have to be fatal. Or lifelong. Heidi had gone through treatment. She knew herself, the laws, the signs of relapse, the dangers. If she thought Jasmine Taylor was a danger to her daughter, Greg needed to talk to her about that. He had to know what she was saying to others. What she believed. And why.

It was the only way to prepare William Brubaker, the prosecutor on whose case he was now working, for trial.

He had a couple of other cases on his desk as well. Interviews to do. A couple of visits to make. One a simple burglary count, and the other a murder case. He spent most of Sunday night studying every single page of notes again, looking for anything that would give him an edge to use when he went the next day to re-interview witnesses.

It was the kind of work he was good at. The kind of work he was comfortable doing.

And by lunchtime on Monday, he had two new witnesses willing to testify on other cases. He hadn't forced them to do so, or coerced them, but a previous testimony from a young girl had jumped out at him the night before. That account had led him to a group of children who led him to a couple of women who were willing to talk to the prosecutor. Greg had just happened to find their vulnerabilities.

Usually when there was the will, there was a way, and one thing Greg had in abundance, when it came to seeing justice done, was the will to make it happen.

In a dark suit and tie, with a somewhat wrinkled white shirt, he was feeling pretty good about himself as he headed back to his office for an interview with Heidi Taylor. He'd called the woman earlier that morning, to set up the early-afternoon meet. And was eager to get to it.

If the day's luck continued, he could get a mini climb in that afternoon and still be home with a beer in hand by sunset.

A couple of prosecutors at the office, fellow lawyer buddies, had tickets to a game in LA that night. They'd invited him to join them, and he was thinking about maybe doing that. Instead of the climb and the beer. Either way, the evening was going to be good.

Well deserved.

That afternoon, he waited while Heidi took a seat at the table in a conference room down the hall from his office and turned on the recording device before closing the door and seating himself across from her.

"First, I need you to know that while I'd like to ask you some questions regarding the custody motion you filed last week, you are under no obligation to answer me, and I have absolutely nothing to do with that case," he said. "Do you understand?"

She nodded.

"Can you answer out loud, please? For the recording?"

"Yes, I understand." She didn't smile. Or frown. Her look was earnest as her hands lay on the table in front of her.

"My interest in that filing has solely to do with anything that might come up with the court that could affect our case."

"I understand," she repeated, nodding again. Whether she'd curled her hair for this meeting, or it stayed naturally that way, he didn't know. But the waves gave her a sense of vulnerability, in his opinion. Her hair had been in a ponytail the other times he'd met with her.

If she was trying to work him, as Jasmine Taylor would have him believe, the move could be deliberate. He made a mental note. And followed it with another—to keep Jasmine's views out of this interview. And out of his perceptions, too.

He was there as an unbiased party, interested only in the truth.

"Have you ever seen Jasmine Taylor act in any way abusively toward your daughter?"

"No."

She didn't even hesitate.

"Never. No."

"Has the child ever reported anything to you that makes you suspect Jasmine has mistreated her?"

"No."

"Does she raise her voice to her? Or has Bella ever indicated that she'd done so? Or indicated impatience of any kind?"

"No."

Confused, he took a second to reassess. A second that allowed Jasmine's words a say in his head.

One whose need to lash out and hurt someone is more powerful than her maternal instincts. He shut it down. He had no proof of that assertion. And Jasmine was understandably prejudiced.

"I read your motions. You said you didn't feel Bella was physically safe with her. You're afraid Jasmine is going to physically abuse her."

"That's right."

"On what basis?"

"Have you ever been abused, Detective? Or witnessed familial abuse?"

"No. But I've worked many cases involving domestic violence."

"So you're familiar with the patterns of abuse."

"Yes."

"She fits the pattern."

To one way of thinking, anyone who'd ever been abused fit the pattern. Which was why profiling was mostly illegal and definitely frowned upon. You couldn't judge a person solely but what had happened to them.

"Many, many, many victims of domestic violence move on to have happy, healthy, productive lives and relationships," he said. No judge worth the robe was going to grant Heidi her motion based on amateur profiling alone.

Chances were, it wouldn't even be heard. It would be tossed.

"Jasmine has...issues."

Giving her a voice, as the prosecutor has now done by charging Josh, gives her a strength she's never had before. The voice slipped in. He showed it out.

Heidi leaned forward, as though telling him a secret. He noted the maneuver. "Jasmine knows she's got it in her to lash out," she said. "She's afraid of herself."

"How do you know this?"

"She told me so."

"When?"

"Several years ago, but something like that...it doesn't

just go away. You know what you're capable of, and deep down, she knows she's capable. She just hasn't had an instance yet that drove her to breaking point. She's a time bomb waiting to go off."

Greg was listening. And at the same time knowing there was no way Heidi was going to be able to prove what she was saying in a court of law, which made it all moot. Especially to him, because the only thing he was there to find out was if she had anything to say that would hurt William's case against Josh Taylor. Anything that might make his star witness—Heidi Taylor—seem less credible.

"I know exactly how she feels, Detective, because I was her. I knew I had it in me, too. And, like her, I thought I had it under control. Until I didn't. I've since learned how to recognize early signs and take action so that nothing like that will ever happen again. She's still living in denial."

"And Josh? You think he was living in denial, too?" Why hadn't any of this come into her testimony with William? It was actually quite compelling.

She shook her head. "Josh wasn't like us. He didn't have any doubts. He was certain he'd never, ever hurt anyone he loved. We three talked about it. When Josh and I first got together, all of us were tight. We talked about all that stuff. Because we found understanding between us. I thought I'd finally found my little piece of heaven when I met Josh and Jasmine Taylor. I thought God had finally found me. Blessed me."

He thought she was going to tear up. Automatically braced himself not to go into Liv mode. Not to be an unsympathetic ass.

She reached for a tissue, held on to it. Looked at it for a moment, and then back across at him.

"Josh isn't Oscar Taylor's biological son. He couldn't possibly have been born with his dad's temperament."

Greg didn't like surprises this far into a case. They pissed him off almost as much as drama did.

But...he wasn't that far into the case. Had, in fact, only received it six days ago. And the perp's biological parentage really didn't hold much bearing on his case.

"Jasmine *is* Oscar's biological child, and it eats at her," Heidi continued.

There's no telling what she'll do. Josh and I have been fighting her illness for years. Giving her a voice...

"She's been in three committed relationships," Heidi continued, passion in her tone, and yet, maintaining control, too. Upping his respect for her another notch. "And she ended all three of them. She'd never say why, but I knew. She was afraid of herself. As soon as things started to get a little intense, you know, real life instead of new love, she'd bail."

"To your knowledge, did she ever get violent in any of those relationships?"

"No. That's the whole point. She got out because she was afraid she'd get to that point. I could see it in her every time. Because, remember, I've been there. So what happens when Bella is sick all night and whiny and Jasmine has to get up and go to work, but finds out that she has no water because a pipe burst? What happens when she's stuck with a full-time toddler all alone and can't bail?"

He understood the concern. And knew that no one could be convicted on what-ifs. Or even be considered unsafe because of it.

Even if there was truth in what Heidi was saying, he figured Jasmine had a handle on it. She was thirty-one years old. Most likely had learned to live with herself. But that aside, he didn't believe, for one second, the woman would have taken in her niece if she had any fears that she had the capacity to hurt her.

"She hasn't ever shown any aggression or anger toward Bella, but she's hurt Josh before," Heidi continued. He had to listen. Had to know the whole truth.

"When Josh was only eight, she pushed him into the coffee table, and it took twenty-four stitches to put him back together. That scar… It haunts me when I think of her alone with Bella. Trying to work full-time, run a house by herself. And now taking on single parenting for someone else's child…"

The telling might have been more effective if he hadn't already heard the story. In full context.

Still, for his purposes, Heidi seemed to have valid points. Convincing points. Not enough to convince the court to remove Bella Taylor from her aunt's home, probably. Almost assuredly. But enough to maintain her credibility as a witness against her ex-husband.

With her having support of the system, we're going to need professional help to stop her.

He was feeling pretty certain that there was nothing in the filing of this new and separate motion that was going to hurt William's case against Josh Taylor.

To the contrary, it could help. Giving Heidi yet another avenue to be heard. So he was done there.

With her having support of the system, we're going to need professional help to stop her.

Stop. He reminded himself, and the irritating voice

in his head, that he was done. He had the information he needed.

The new motion would give Heidi another chance to show herself before the court as a healed woman who only wanted what was best for her young daughter. A woman who knew that she had to get Bella away from the Taylors, just like she had to get herself away…

None of us are safe until she's exposed as the liar she is.

Greg ended the interview. Went for his climb early. He tried to concentrate on the good work he'd done that day—and found himself, instead, with a maybe messed-up brown-eyed schoolteacher taking his thoughts hostage.

He had to get rid of Jasmine. Mentally, that was. Get her out of his head. He'd find the truth, and that's all he could do. He wasn't Jasmine's savior. Couldn't be. Didn't even want to be.

He couldn't afford to be.

Chapter Eight

Jasmine wasn't served that weekend, or Monday, either. When she'd spoken to Sara Havens Edwin, head therapist at the Stand, she found out that if the motion was thrown out, she likely wouldn't hear about it. She was told not to worry about it in any case. With no evidence, the court wouldn't take Bella away from her. Most particularly since Josh was the custodial parent and Heidi wouldn't even be considered for such a role for another two or three years.

Most of which she already knew.

Validation was good, though. Heady. As was the knowledge that Greg Johnson had called her to give her a heads-up when there'd been no reason for him to need to have done so. Not in an official capacity. He was letting her know Heidi's moves, so she and Josh could be prepared.

He was helping her protect her brother and niece.

She thought about calling him often over the weekend, as she took Bella grocery shopping, to the park, down to the beach. Instead, spent an afternoon baking chocolate chip cookies with the toddler, letting her dump, "stir" and help put cookies on the trays. She talked to Bella about different ingredients. Put a tiny taste of flour on her tongue and then sugar. Let her feel the difference between the two of them with her fingers. And thought about Greg Johnson and the way he was helping them.

Was it too good to be true? Was she being naive, or worse, stupid again, to trust the cop? To believe that someone would really protect them?

Still…the weekend passed with many joyful moments. Josh called each night. Saturday night they played a memory game together on video chat with big flashcards of colors laid out on Jasmine's floor. Bella had the most matches most of the time. Josh teased her, and she laughed and showed him her "flips." She was learning to do somersaults in a little pre-dance class at the Stand.

When it was time to say good-night, he brought his lips right up to the phone to kiss her cheek, and then Bella turned her lips to the phone where all that showed was his cheek.

It wasn't perfect. Perfection would have had her brother right there in the room with them. Or her visiting with him and Bella in Josh's living room.

But it was good. *Really* good.

Heidi was inconveniencing them. She wasn't going to hurt them. Or change them.

She managed to stay predominantly hopeful and positive on Monday, too, going into the new week with strength and determination, until Lila called her to office just after the end of classes. An unsolicited meeting with the managing director wasn't usually just a pat on the back for work well done.

After checking on Bella, happy to see her niece avidly engaged with story time, she presented herself to her boss with trepidation.

Had word of the motion somehow reached Lila? Was

it going to be a problem after all? Her job…it was more than just an occupation, a way to earn money to pay for bills. She had enough money to pay bills. Her work was her life. A way to contribute something meaningful, to make lemonade out of her lemons.

Heidi, who worked at a call center, knew how much Jasmine loved going to work every day. Could her former sister-in-law really become so vindictive that she would stop at nothing to cause pain to her as well as Josh? To ruin their lives as she'd ruined her own?

Lila answered her knock immediately. She showed Jasmine to a seat on the couch off to the side of her desk—not to her inner sanctum. Not a good sign.

Glancing at the director, Jasmine tried to get a sense of what was coming, but she couldn't read much on the stoic face. Lila's hair was in its usual bun, secured with a jeweled clasp instead of just the pins she used to wear.

Tempted to look around, she didn't. One thing life had taught her was to face her challenges head-on. It was the only way to have a chance at preventing them from rear-ending you.

"I had another call from Detective Johnson today." Lila, who took a seat next to her, rather than in a chair across from her, came straight to the point. And for a moment, relief pounded through Jasmine instead of dread. "He was asking questions about you…things about you personally. I thought you should know."

Greg was interested in her? Personally? Her heart fluttered in a good way. A *very* good way.

She tempered her smile. Just because the man was interested didn't mean she was changing her life choice to remain single. But damn, it felt good to have someone watching out for her…

It had to be because of Heidi's motion. He'd said he had nothing to do with it, that he wasn't involved in any aspect of that case, but he'd know that if Heidi continued to come after her, it could have an impact on her job.

"If you're asking for my permission to give him personal information, you have it. I trust you to be circumspect," she said, while making a plan to call the detective himself and let him know that if he had questions, all he had to do was ask. She'd told him she'd be completely honest with him. That promise hadn't just encompassed Josh's case.

Maybe they could be friends. A good friend would be nice.

Lila, who wasn't smiling at all, shook her head. "His questions were more on the lines of someone investigating you," she said. "He wanted to know if I had any concerns..."

"Concerns? About my work? My teaching ability?" Confused, she tried to fit the new data into what she already knew. What would Greg Johnson care if she was a good teacher? Unless he was believing Heidi? Or there was some weight to her motion?

If it just had to do with him investigating her regarding the criminal case against Josh, then wouldn't he have questioned Lila the previous week when he'd been to the Stand?

"He didn't specify. And I didn't ask. I simply told him that if I had any concerns about you at all, you wouldn't be teaching in one of my classrooms. I was left with the impression, though, that I was only one of many people he'd spoken to, or would be speaking to. I thought you should know."

Lila's unusual blue-gray eyes held Jasmine's gaze

steadily, as though waiting for her to catch up. And then she did.

"Desmond." She said the one word and saw Lila's nod. "Detective Johnson just called. I suggested that he might want to wait and speak with you before making any other calls, but I can't guarantee he'll do so. He's got a job to do, and he doesn't strike me as a man who'll let anything get in the way of that."

If Greg Johnson called Desmond, he'd be unleashing more than he knew. "I have to believe he hasn't called him yet or my cell would be going off." Pulling it out of one of the two big pockets on the front of her tunic, she checked. Her heart pounded in earnest now. Hard enough for her to feel it in her chest.

"I'm sorry," she said to Lila, rising. "I have to call him before he gets to Desmond."

Nodding, Lila moved over to her desk. Jasmine could have left the office to make her call. She didn't.

Greg Johnson's voice mail picked up.

"Detective Johnson, this is Jasmine Taylor. I need you to call me before you contact any other people in my life asking about me. Please. It's important."

She hung up and looked over at Lila. "He'll call," she said, not sure why she felt like she had to convince Lila.

The woman, standing still, moved some papers around on her desk. Maybe purposefully. "I'd never met him before, but I know of some of the work he's done for the High-Risk Team. With Emma Martin, in particular. You've met her, right?"

Jasmine nodded, wishing her chest wasn't knotted to her throat with tension. Prosecutor Emma Martin had most recently worked a case involving a resident at the Stand. The girlfriend of a prominent drug dealer who swore her boyfriend wasn't responsible for a face so swollen it was hardly recognizable.

"He'll call," she said again, glad to know that Bella was happily and safely ensconced in the Stand's daycare.

"I'm just wondering if perhaps you should stay here until you hear from him," Lila said. "At least give him a chance to call back. Especially with that little one in tow. Desmond hasn't made a chargeable mistake yet, but something like this could throw him into high gear."

Desmond Williamson. Her ex whose brotherhood all gathered around him, honored him as a great cop.

In his circle he was revered—just as her father still was in his own. Men like them, they always found a way to come out okay. Partially because of the great work they did outside the home. No one ever saw the people they became once behind the locked doors of their own abodes.

"I can handle Desmond," she said now. "He's not going to risk his career—"

"You don't need to go through that again."

With a sad smile, she met Lila's concerned gaze and said, "But the good news is that we both know I can handle it if I have to do so."

"I'd feel better if you'd gotten a restraining order out against him."

"It could have ruined his career, which would have unhinged him, and then I'd be looking over my shoulder for the rest of my life." Some men, like Desmond, like her father, you could bargain with. They'd go away if you left their lives intact.

The only problem was, her way, her mother's way, of dealing with the problem put others at risk. Jasmine lived with that knowledge. And knew that Lila supported her choices, regardless. Even if Desmond had gotten convicted, a first offense, for a dedicated cop…he'd have had a slap of the wrist at best. He could have lost his job, but even that wasn't a foregone conclusion. They had programs for officers who'd committed domestic violence. Some that allowed them to remain on the job. And Desmond had been so careful to skate on the line, but not cross it completely. He'd never actually landed a blow with the hand he'd raised to her.

"I've still got some work to do in my classroom, with the rearranging," she said. "Maybe Detective Johnson will call in that time."

"If he doesn't, why don't you and Bella join me for dinner? Here. In my suite."

That Lila would stay for her—and Jasmine knew full well that was what the director was offering—meant more than she'd probably ever know. The director's support, her belief in Jasmine, helped Jasmine to believe in herself.

Nodding, she told Lila she'd call her within the hour to let her know if they'd be staying or not.

GREG CALLED JASMINE Taylor back after he got out of the shower, still standing in his bathroom in his underwear. His call to Lila had been on the way home from his climb. It didn't completely surprise him that the managing director had gone straight to her employee.

Maybe he'd known she would. Maybe that's why he'd called her first. To know that someone would have Jasmine's back in his stead.

She expected it to be him. It wasn't going to be. But she wouldn't be left adrift, either.

"You want to know about me, I've lain my life open to you," she started in, obviously recognizing his number on her cell as soon as she picked up. "I told you I'd tell you anything you wanted to know. Come search my home. Take my computer and analyze it, if you need to. But don't… Please, Greg, I'm asking you not to go around talking to everyone I've ever known."

"I'm an investigator. Talking to people about other people is what I do."

"I'm not the one on trial here."

"No, but I believe you're holding things back from me." He gave it to her straight. Sometimes it was the best way. "I need to know what and why. Someone you or Josh knows might know what neither of you are telling me. I'm talking to people he knows, too, by the way."

"You're not involving Play for the Win, I hope—at least any more than you can help. Ultimately, we want you to do whatever you need to do to get to the truth so these charges can be dropped, but…"

Turning his back on his face and near nudity in the mirror, Greg leaned his butt against the counter, looking at the unmade bed. He'd meant to put the sheets in the wash before he'd left that morning.

"So you understand that I need to talk to people," he said.

"I'm not afraid of what you'll find out, if that's what you mean," she said. "But…you bringing me up to other people—look, I've had some people in my life that might be only too glad to give you false impressions, which is fine, you'd have to figure out what to believe, but in at least one case, there could be other repercussions…"

Sounded a hell of a lot like drama to him.

"Someone else is going to be hurt if I talk to them about you?" he said, trying to decipher fact from supposed fear. Or imagined scenarios. Not that she'd given him any reason to believe that she had Liv's vivid imagination when it came to fearing the worst.

"Look. I just… I really appreciate that you're searching for the truth like you told me you would. I appreciate that more than you might ever understand. But…could you just hold off long enough for us to talk about this?"

"Isn't that what we're doing?"

"I'm still at school. At the Stand. Anyone can walk in… I need to get Bella from daycare. It might be better if we do this later."

"Your brother has a hearing on Thursday."

"I know. I'm not… We can talk tonight if you'd like. Maybe it would be better in person. So you can watch my body language or whatever you do. Bella's bedtime call is at eight. If you come right after that, we'll have whatever time you need, uninterrupted. And you can look at my computer or whatever else then, too, if you'd like. I'll give you whatever records you want or need. Just, please…hear me out…before you contact anyone else…"

He hadn't planned to make any further calls that night anyway.

"Why do you think I'm holding back on you?" Her question came while he was still pondering the advisability of doing what he wanted to do and taking her up on her offer to look at her computer. He didn't have a warrant. But he would like to get a peek at any emails between her and her brother—not that she wouldn't delete any incriminating ones before she gave him access.

Why did he think she was holding out on him? Her question hung there.

"There are patterns…things that victims experience kind of globally, not all of course, but a lot, and I see none of those for Josh. He grew up in an abusive home.

Where are his issues? No one's as perfect as you make him out to be." Why this woman brought out the straight truth from him sometimes, he didn't know. But he noted it happening. Would keep an eye on it.

"Of course he has issues. He'll discuss them with you if you ask."

"I can't talk to him without his lawyer present, and his lawyer is advising him to say nothing."

Which meant that her brother's lawyer would probably tell her to remain silent, as well. She could very well be realizing that herself. "I talked to Heidi today. She brought up some things that need explaining," he added.

Because he didn't want to take a chance on losing her cooperation?

Or because he was just a little bit bothered by how cleanly Heidi's new motion fit with the criminal charges filed against her ex-husband. If he were a confessed and convicted abuser, Josh's opinion would have admittedly held more weight than hers when they appeared before a judge. For all he knew Heidi's family law attorney had come up with the whole idea to file the custody motion just to help her win her case against Josh.

"So...you'll stop by tonight? We can talk then?"

He'd met with witnesses at later hours. In bars and parking lots. Jails and homes.

He hadn't planned to work that night. "Yes. I'll be there."

He waited for a bit of gushing. For her relief. Knew her emotion was going to wash right over him.

She calmly thanked him and hung up.

Chapter Nine

She'd changed clothes. Jasmine had gone back and forth on that one. Did she answer the door in a floral shirtdress with leggings? Or in jeans and a loose blouse with tennis shoes on her feet? She almost never wore those. Found them…bulky and uncomfortable. And somewhat unattractive, too, as far as shoes went.

Ditto for the oversize blue-and-white-striped buttonshirt that covered the pretty floral stitching on the pockets of her jeans. Her hair pulled back in a ponytail, she hoped her message was clear. She wasn't trying to pretty up anything about her. Or impress him.

She most definitely wasn't coming on to him. Lord knew the last thing she wanted to do, inviting him over after dark, was to encourage him to think of her in a personal way. Yes, she'd had thoughts about them maybe becoming friends. But she went back and forth on that, too. Given her track record, did she trust herself to have a friend like Greg Johnson in her life?

And did she really want to find out that he was like all the rest of the people who attracted her? Bad news underneath?

Because if she was as into him as her reaction to him would have her believe, she could bet there was some not-

good stuff beneath his surface. Maybe, during his interrogation, she could learn a little bit about him, too. Like,
was he married even though he wore no ring?

Did he have a girlfriend? Live with someone? Have
any children?

He knocked on the door just then, wearing jeans, too.
And a blue-and-white shirt that fit him to perfection. The
buttons didn't quite pull at his chest, but there wasn't any
extra room there, either. Not like her baggy cotton. His
tennis shoes, black to her white, looked newer than hers.

When she'd been in high school, the kids with new-
looking tennis shoes had been considered nerds. The lu-
dicrousness of the thought hit her almost as quickly as
the thought itself, but it calmed her shaking nerves, too.

Heidi had had a supervised visit with Bella the day
before. The caseworker had come to Jasmine's to pick up
the toddler and had returned her right on schedule. Bella
had been clingy the rest of the evening. That's what she
had to keep in mind. Her niece. And getting this mess
fixed, showing Heidi for who she was, so that Bella could
have a secure, happy home environment.

"We can talk in here," she said, leading Greg into the
great room that served as both living and family room.
Her light brown leather sectional, matching chairs and
entertainment center separated most of the room from
the back quarter that held a couple of antique chairs, a
bookcase and the piano that she'd learned on, growing up.

She didn't offer him anything to drink, but he carried
a bottle of water with him. She took one of the chairs.
He sat on the love seat portion of the sectional, putting
his plastic water bottle on a coaster on the table in front
of him.

The man had manners. Kudos to those who'd raised

him. Of course, he could have learned them on his own—overcoming a horrendous childhood to make it good in the world...

"Did you grow up around here?" The question popped out.

He shook his head. "I went to high school in Colorado and Arizona, two years each," he told her. "Grade school and junior high were Utah, Colorado, Oregon and then Washington State—Seattle."

She leaned on the arm of her chair, in his direction. "Seriously?" she asked, unable to prevent her interest. As a teacher, she knew how rough it could be on kids to move around during the critical years of bonding and first friendships. "Was your father in the military?"

"My parents met in college," he said, somewhat laconically. "Mom's into employee management and getting the best out of the people who work for you. My father's the numbers guy. They formed a business even before they formed a marriage and have made an impressive success out of both."

He wasn't a shy man. Or overly modest. His honesty impressed her. "What's their business?" And did it have that many franchises, that they'd needed to move so much?

"The Rescuers," he said, shaking his head. "There are a lot of companies out there that wait for a company to show signs of struggle and then swoop in and acquire them."

"Acquisitions," she said, nodding. "That's what my father does. He took over from his father. So...you're telling me our parents are in the same business?"

That was... Wow. Weird. And kind of... So did his father have a razor-sharp temperament, too? Did Greg?

Was that the warning sign she needed so she didn't let herself fall for him?

"No. My folks are the antidote," he said. "Or at least they try to be. They go into struggling companies on a two-year contract in order to turn them around."

Which explained why he'd moved around so much. And…completely the opposite from Oscar Taylor, the taker. Not that that gave her any leeway to fall for Greg Johnson.

"Must have been hard for you, though, moving around so much. Do you have siblings?" She didn't know what she'd do without Josh. And figured her growing up, while hard, still had some great memories attached, largely because of her brother.

"No siblings," he told her, lifting an ankle across his knee as he sat back, an elbow on the couch arm. He seemed relaxed.

She liked him there.

"My mom couldn't have kids," he told her. "She'd been in a car accident when she was a teenager, and it left her infertile."

So he was adopted. Why he was putting that out there she didn't know, but she was glad he had. Maybe he was just being kind, giving a bit of himself since he was prying so completely into her private life.

Maybe he just found her easy to talk to. People had told her they found her so, many times. Her friend Wynne said that she'd never met anyone she could talk to like she could talk to Jasmine.

"Were you adopted as a baby?" She wanted to know.

"Yes."

He didn't seem to be in any hurry. Wasn't looking around, seeking out her computer or nosing into closets and drawers. Could be he got more out of a person by the questions they asked. Or just by watching them...

Could be she watched too many psychological cop shows.

"Do you know anything about your biological parents? Have you ever sought them out? If you don't mind my asking?" Being a cop, it might be easier for him to find out things that others wouldn't be able to access. And she knew how it could mess with a guy, wondering about what genes he'd inherited on his Y chromosome. Or maybe that was just when your adoptive dad was too destructive to show you how to be a man.

"I was abandoned in an office building bathroom with the umbilical cord still attached," he said, watching her steadily now, making her more certain that she was under some kind of trial.

Her eyes widened. Her mouth fell open. She could feel them both, but not soon enough to stop them. "Are you serious?" she asked, and then quickly, so he didn't think she was seriously doubting him... "Were there security cameras? Did they see who left you there?"

"No. And while the police spent months searching out every clue, they never found whoever took me there. Or found out who gave birth to me."

"Maybe she had you there, in the bathroom."

"That was one theory. The scene was clean, though, so doubtful. All of the women who worked in the building and were known to be pregnant checked out."

"Wow. Who found you?"

"My mother. She and Dad had just started work for a smallish organic food company with offices on the third floor of the building."

She hardly knew the man. He'd been in her life less

than a week. And at his candor, feeling a surge of compassion for that abandoned baby boy, Jasmine had maybe just fallen a tiny smidgeon in love with him.

INTERROGATION 101. FIND a way to identify with the subject. Josh Taylor had been adopted by Jasmine's father after he and Mary got married. A search of records between his phone call with Jasmine that afternoon and the evening's visit had told him that much.

He was adopted, too.

She had sympathy for her brother. It would put her at ease to know that he understood a basic concept that had helped form Josh Taylor the man.

Greg wanted to believe that was why he'd started burping out his private affairs to a woman who was not only a stranger, destined to remain so, but one he didn't even fully trust.

Except he did trust her not to be harmful to other human beings. He'd done what research he could on the internet. Found a blog written by a former resident at The Lemonade Stand and comments on the post. He'd read all of the records that William had in Josh's file—some provided by Josh's attorney earlier that day in preparation for Thursday's hearing. He'd thought about his conversations with Lila McDaniels Mantle. Brief though they were, given the director's reputation, they were also very telling. Jasmine wouldn't be working at the Stand if Lila had a single doubt about the safety of children around her.

And he'd considered Heidi's testimony, too. The abused woman had admitted that she had no evidence whatsoever that Jasmine had ever hurt anyone—except Josh all those years ago.

"Heidi tells me that Josh isn't your father's biological child," he said, maybe not with the most finesse. His successful morning, his climb, the hot shower afterward had left him a bit too relaxed.

"That's right," she said, with little more than a raised eyebrow.

"You didn't think to mention that to me the other night?" Out on her deck. She'd told him she'd tell him the complete truth.

"It honestly didn't even cross my mind," she said. And then frowned, looking at him. "But it should have. I'm asking for your help, and him not being biologically related to an abuser might help. I just... Wow, I'm sorry. I don't think of Josh in terms of our father. Because I know he's not my dad's child."

"Environmentally, he is."

She tilted her head, as though to acknowledge the statement.

He thought of her question about finding his biological parents. "Has Josh ever looked for his father?"

"He didn't have to look. Mom was only ever with one other man. The identity of Josh's father was never a secret between her and my dad. They told Josh together when he reached puberty."

Not at all like his own sorry tale, biologically speaking. Feeling a bit soft for having shared his own story, in light of Josh having been adopted, he asked, "Did he take it hard?"

"Are you kidding? He ran into my room all excited because the ass wasn't his real dad. And then he stopped dead still in the middle of the room, looking sick, because he knew that Oscar was still my real dad."

Yes. About that...

Heidi and her patterns. And her testimony that Jasmine had told her about having fears about herself. Fears that she might have the capacity for her father's vile anger deep inside her.

"Has he been in his touch with his father?"

"Once. Shortly after he found out about him. They met once, for hamburgers. The guy was married, no kids, and no desire to have any. He played in a band. His wife was their lead singer. They traveled all the time. Lived in a one-bedroom trailer. And when Oscar found out he and his wife did drugs, that was that. When Josh was old enough to reconnect, he said he had no reason to do so.

"The guy has always been kind of a nonentity in our lives. Surreal, you know? After having me, my mom left my father because he already had anger issues, though she didn't tell us that part until after she and my dad divorced. Anyway, while they were apart she met Josh's dad in a bar where he was playing a one-man guitar gig, had one night with him, and when he found out she was pregnant, he told her she had to get an abortion. My father, who was still in the picture because of me, offered to take her back, to love Josh as his own, to take care of all of us, and she figured that was the best choice. In his own way, Oscar loved us. Just not enough to get help for his temper. Or even to admit that he's ever done anything wrong."

"He signed private legal documents not only giving you and Josh a fortune, but agreeing to stay away from you. Obviously he knows he did something wrong."

She shook her head. "He signed them so that my mother wouldn't go public with her accusations against him. He'd built a solid reputation along with a great deal of wealth during the years of their marriage. Mostly I think he signed them because of Josh and me. We were old enough to be heard by then. I think he knew our mother would never stand up to him on her own. And he also knew that she couldn't keep us quiet. I don't think he thought for a minute that he'd get convicted if he was charged. And chances were he might not have. He just didn't want the hit to his reputation. He hobnobs with senators and billionaires. He still believes that we bring on whatever bad happens to us."

"You seem pretty prosaic about it all."

"Years of counseling," she said, with a shake of her head and a small smile. "It took a long time for me to talk about my father without bitterness. But the truth is, things happen and you either accept them and move on, or you let them steal the rest of your life from you. Oscar isn't getting mine. And thanks to his money, Josh and I can both work to make the world better for at risk children after growing up as we did. Thanks to Oscar, I can afford to donate every cent of my salary right back to The Lemonade Stand, as I'm sure Lila told you. There's justice in that."

Lila hadn't told him. Greg took the news with a bit more than a mere mental note. Not that he let on to her. Jasmine Taylor worked a full-time job for free. Not on a volunteer basis, but she just didn't take her paycheck home with her.

Impressive.

"Heidi mentioned your three failed relationships," he said, pulling out the big guns to get himself back on track. "She thinks they were abusive or bordering on it."

Color left her face. Noticeably. She didn't bow her head, or start any nervous tweaks or twitters, but he had the distinct impression that he could feel her sudden tension.

So she *had* been holding back.

And if she had her own secrets, didn't it stand to reason that she'd hide her brother's, as well? Maybe without even realizing she was doing so?

It was a theory. One that he preferred over her having been lying to him all along. It shouldn't matter either way, though, since the outcome was the same.

An outcome that was his only reason for knowing her, talking to her, at all.

"Why was she talking about my relationships?"

"Because I asked her about the motion she filed on Friday. If there's anything that's going to come up there that will affect the state's case against your brother, I need to know about it. She didn't name names, though, and I didn't ask for them. As of right now, I don't know them. I was just getting ready to dig deeper and find out on my own when I got your call. I'm hoping you'll give them to me."

She could make of that what she would. If she wanted to continue fooling herself that he was there to protect her and her brother with the truth, that was on her. He wasn't looking for her truth, but the real truth.

"She's using my past relationships to prove that I'm unfit to care for Bella?" The horror in her voice was stark. And painfully clear. "Because I made some bad relationship choices, I'm unfit to keep a child safe?"

As she said the words, she seemed to shrink in on herself. "I get it," she said slowly, her voice a mere thread compared to what it had been a moment ago. "I mean, look at my mother. But... I'm not in a relationship. Nor do I have any plans to be in one. To the contrary, I've made a firm decision *not* to get involved again. To be forever single and live alone. Because of those relationships. Because of what I learned about me through them."

Because Heidi was right? Had Jasmine found herself dangerously close to exploding, as her father had?

"What did you learn?"

"Seriously?"

She'd been using that word a lot that night. He wondered if it was a thing of hers. Everyone had their things. He kind of liked the way she said the word. With a bit of a sassy lilt in her voice. Which had nothing at all to do with why he was there.

Or why he'd asked the question.

"Seriously," he said back.

"I learned that, as happens with many victims—and survivors—I am attracted to people who portray characteristics that can easily turn abusive. People in positions of power. People who exude strength. Not to say that most people with either of those characteristics are abusive, but that's where it starts with me. And somehow my psyche homes in on the ones with the negative aspects that turn something good into something very, very wrong."

One of those patterns Heidi had talked about. But not the one Heidi had mentioned in terms of Jasmine.

"So they challenged you and you got angry?"

"To the contrary." She lifted her chin and looked him straight in the eye. "They challenged me, and I took it. I did everything I could to please. And when they got angry anyway, I did what I learned to do in high school when my mom and Josh and I left my dad. I walked out. Three times. Leaving each of them in wherever we'd been living. Two cottages and a condo. I used those, and my agreement to never bad talk them, to negotiate for the things I wanted. My personal things. Artwork I loved. A cat, once. He's since died."

She added the last matter-of-factly. Greg sat there watching her. Staring, really. He had no idea what to make of any of what she was telling him.

A person didn't just make up stuff like that.

This person didn't. His gut was telling him that much.

It had told him some things about Liv, too. Some right. Some not.

And why in the hell did he keep thinking about Liv when he was with Jasmine? He wasn't getting involved with Josh Taylor's sister.

Must be because of the previous week's phone call. He was due to have dinner with Liv and Rick again the following evening. She'd called just before he'd headed over to Jasmine's that evening. Was in a good place again. She and Rick wanted to treat him to sushi to thank him for being such a good friend.

A card would have been nicer. But there was no way he'd tell her so. Or turn down her invitation. Liv was a good woman. Smart. And he actually enjoyed hanging out with her and Rick. They felt like family—and God knew he had so little of that.

Thinking of which, he should be heading home. Get some sleep. He'd need a full hour's workout in the morning if he was going to be seeing Liv. And 5:00 a.m. came early.

Just one more thing…

"Who is it you don't want me to talk to?" he asked. He'd thought about her phone call a lot since it had come that afternoon. More than he'd have liked. And he figured it out, too. That she'd been panicked in particular. Not in general.

"I'd rather you not talk to anybody, but there's only one person I'd beg to have you skip. I'll tell you anything you want to know. I'll even open up my private counseling files about him to you, or have my counselor do so at my request. I'll tell Lila to tell you everything she knows and thinks about my relationship with him. As long as you don't bring me up to him."

He sat forward. Noting everything at once, the changed tone in her voice—not whiny. Not dramatic. Just stark fear. The way her hands were clasped together, as though all they had were each other and were afraid to let go. The sharp points in her eyebrows. A trembling at the corners of her mouth.

For the first time since he'd met her, Greg felt completely and truly protective of Jasmine Taylor.

This was not good.

Chapter Ten

She'd sworn she wouldn't do this. Part of her agreement with Desmond Williamson had been that she would not speak poorly of him in public. His job was everything to him. If she exposed him for what he was, there wasn't going to be any stopping him. He'd wait his time. He'd know exactly how to stay under the radar. And when he saw a chance, he'd kill her.

Not all abusers were killers. But there was no doubt in her mind that police sergeant Desmond Williamson would kill her if he thought she'd betrayed him. What would he have left to lose?

If Greg went to talk to him about her, she was as good as dead then, too. Because Desmond would believe that she'd talked. Heidi knew all of that.

Her counselor knew. The lawyers knew. Lila and Josh knew. Period.

Heidi had known exactly what she was doing when she'd told Greg Johnson about Jasmine's exes. She was pulling Jasmine back into the life.

Because she was jealous that Jasmine and Josh had made it out. That they were living healthy, productive existences. That they had her daughter.

Jasmine understood.

She just had no idea how to fight her. How to win this one.

She had to trust Greg to keep whatever she told him to himself. It couldn't come out in court. In either of Heidi's cases. She'd deny it if it did. She'd have to. She would not testify.

If there was one thing Jasmine lived by with all of her being, it was keeping her agreements with her abusers. Those agreements bought her freedom on a psychological level with them. The only way to really win.

Her decision not to ever involve herself in another committed relationship guaranteed her future freedom.

No more.

No more tries. No more failures. No more abusers.

She'd told Greg she'd tell him the complete truth. Give him whatever information he needed. She'd been referring to Josh. To everything she knew about him. And Heidi. And about her own current life—which was no threat to Bella.

But it could be if Desmond came back in the picture.

She'd just told him she'd tell him about her relationships as long as he stayed away. And so there he sat, waiting. Expectant.

And she couldn't get words to come up from her throat and out of her mouth.

Was there a way to buy time? To make this go nowhere until Josh's hearing on Thursday? If the judge dismissed the charges, then the rest would die right along with it. She just had to buy herself a couple of days. Would a faked stroke work?

She gave herself a mental shake. It would work if she wanted to show herself as a lying nutcase. She'd already been duplicitous with him once. She wasn't going down that road again.

But could she trust him?

Did she dare trust him?

Making that decision meant she had to trust her own judgment where he was concerned, and she couldn't do that.

She felt like she could. She wanted to.

But he was a cop. Someone with power. She was attracted to him, which was the kiss of death where her trust in her judgment was concerned.

He dropped his foot from his knee to the floor. Sat forward.

"I've been in three relationships," she said too quickly. His finger tapped a slow beat against the leather of the couch. Information he already had. In triplicate.

"The exit agreements…they give me the assurance that there will be no contact from any of the three of them unless I seek it out myself, as long as I don't speak ill of them. I can't break that legal agreement without putting myself in danger. …"

"You're protected by law when it has to do with a criminal case."

"My relationships have no bearing whatsoever on Josh's case." A prosecutor could argue the point. Might win, depending on the judge. She couldn't take that chance because…

"It's not the law I'm afraid of," she told him. "A lot of abusers aren't, either. I know you've worked on the High-Risk Team. You must know the statistics. You're a cop. You have to know that restraining orders are largely ineffective when it comes to keeping abusers away from their victims."

She had his attention. And he had hers, suddenly, too, sitting there in his jeans looking so strong. Intent. Like he could make things happen.

She should trust him. To keep her information confidential. And to protect her, too. What if he was the good guy life was finally going to send her and she cut off her nose to spite her face?

No. She was scared. Falling back into patterns her psyche couldn't afford to consider.

"It's getting late," he said, sitting forward. "If you have a name to give me, and a reason why I shouldn't talk to him or her, I'm listening. Otherwise I need to get going. I've got a long day tomorrow, and my morning starts early."

She wanted to know about that, too. The start of his day.

"Do you have a wife at home?" she asked. Should have already asked. Had no good reason to ask. He wasn't wearing a ring. And whether or not he was, wasn't her business.

"I live alone."

Wow. Good. That he'd given her what she needed. She didn't need it.

"You ever been married?"

"No."

He was a nice guy. Humoring her with answers to questions she had no right to ask. As though he knew she was stalling—and was letting her.

His lack of marital ties was not good news to her. No matter how much it felt like it was.

"If I talk to you about him, and he finds out, he'll kill me." The words dropped out simply. No fanfare. No emotion. There they were. Hanging between them.

"If you'd like to speak with my counselor, or Lila, they'll confirm what I just told you. That's why Lila called me immediately after you'd called her. To give me a heads-up that you were talking to people I knew."

"Why would *he* kill you? Because I'm asking him if he knew you or had anything to tell me about you that could give me insight into your relationship with your brother?"

"Because if you bring me up to him, he's not going to believe that's all you want to know. He's going to assume that I told you about him. A detective tracking him down to ask him questions about me would be the trigger. The only thing that keeps me safe is the fact that he loves his job more than anything else—including his own life. A great quality in light of what he does. But if he thinks he's going to lose that job—and he probably would, if he was ever charged and found guilty of abuse—there won't be any stopping him. He'll blame me, and I won't walk another safe step on this earth."

There was no panic now. No fear, even, in that moment. Just her cold, stark truth.

GREG WASN'T GOING to fall prey to the drama. As soon as she'd said she would be killed, he took a step back. Way back.

As far back as he could go and still remain seated on her love seat in her home with her just feet away shining conviction out of her every pore.

The truth lay someplace between them. He didn't want to leave without it.

The woman wasn't falling apart. Wasn't shaking or panicking. She wasn't begging him.

She wasn't Liv.

Still didn't mean he could help her.

"What does he do for a living?"

"He's a sergeant with the Los Angeles police. He's got an exemplary record. Has won medals. Saved a lot of lives. He's the first responder who charges in even when bullets are flying. And if you think I'm exaggerating, I can show you an article or two to prove the authenticity of my statements."

He sat back. He wanted to disbelieve her.

He didn't.

Could it be that this cop had noticed tendencies in her and got himself out? That he knew things that would help Heidi's case? And that Jasmine was trying to keep him from finding that information?

The theory was valid enough to be considered. He gave it half a minute. Lila knew about this relationship. And Jasmine was still working for her.

The director had warned Jasmine immediately upon Greg's phone call. The timing of Jasmine's call to him was proof of that.

Could he pursue the Heidi theory anyway? And risk putting Jasmine Taylor's life in danger?

"Tell me more about your relationship with him," he said. And then added, "Without giving me his name. Let's call him Mike. My choice so nothing can be read into it or inferred from it. He's Mike for our purposes. Tell me what you can without giving me any more clues to his identity."

Her head tilted. She studied him as though she was able to read inside his mind. He wanted to take her hand, pull her over to the couch with him and take her in his arms. To make it possible for her to tell her story while being held.

That was so unlike Greg that a wave of discomfort

shot through his system. And landed. He was tired, but...
what the hell was wrong with him?

"We dated for...a while. Long enough that people recognized us as a monogamous couple. Serious enough
to include our families in our lives." She paused, seeming to be looking at him, but Greg was certain her sight
had turned inward. He wanted to tell her she could stop.
And didn't.

"At first, I loved it when he showed signs of posses-
siveness. I loved having someone to belong to. Someone
who wanted to belong to me. *With* me. And when he had
an opinion on everything I did, I saw it as him taking
an interest. Until his opinion clashed with mine and he
expected me to see that his was the right way. I did, at
first. Doubting myself..."

She blinked, seemed to see Greg sitting there. Really
see him. Recognize him. And to realize what she was
doing. The clarity in her eyes, the unease swarming in her
space...she was exposing herself to him, and he wasn't
going to turn his gaze away. She didn't, either.

He noted.

"I'd met a woman, Wynne Anderson—" She broke
off abruptly, rather than just fading, leaving him with
the distinct impression that she had more to say there.
He'd come back to it.

"*Mike* didn't like her. Thought she had too much influence over me. I agreed with her opinions, some of
which he strongly opposed, and she became a problem
between us."

"Wynne Anderson? The state representative?"

"She is now. She was a city councilwoman when I
knew her. The youngest woman ever to have that honor,"

she added. "She was speaking at a Lemonade Stand fund-raising dinner and sat at my table."

"Didn't she just get married? To that female golfer, what was her name?"

"Andrea Long, and yes."

While her gaze didn't drop, Jasmine was definitely less bold in her delivery than she'd been earlier in the evening. Hands clasped, she rolled her thumbs around and around each other—kind of like he'd seen his great-grandmother do when he used to visit her at the home.

"So you know them. Andrea and Wynne?" He was kind of impressed. Name-dropping wasn't big on his list of impressionable items, but still…pretty much everyone in California knew about Wynne. Her party had her pegged for Washington and didn't seem to mind spending the bucks to let everyone who breathed California air know about it.

"Yes. I know Wynne. I've met Andrea, but just briefly." She nodded. Seemed content to sit there without resuming the point of the conversation.

He thought about letting it go. He could find the cop she was talking about easily enough. Or not. If William didn't need more information on the Taylor siblings…

Jasmine had asked him to get the truth. Something he already required of himself. To see real justice done, not just the law's version of it.

"And Mike didn't like her?" he prompted.

She shook her head. Straightened her shoulders. Feminine, slim shoulders that seemed to carry a lot of weight.

And carry it well.

"*Mike* made his feelings obvious almost from the start. He didn't agree with her politics, and if I did, she was brainwashing me. He made it clear he didn't want her around and didn't want me hanging with her or her crowd. When he told me he'd handcuff me to the kitchen table if that's what it took to keep me safe from her, I thought he was exaggerating. Then I woke up one morning with one wrist handcuffed to the bed rail, and I knew. Lying there, chafing my wrist as I tried like hell to get free, I admitted what I'd known for a while. My relationship with *Mike* wasn't healthy.

"That morning I'd been going to meet Wynne and a couple of other women for coffee before I had to be at the Stand to teach. *Mike* came back from a run shortly after I'd missed any chance of making it to see them. He acted completely surprised and immediately contrite when he saw me chained to the bed. He said he'd put the cuffs on me as a joke. Had thought I'd wake up before he left and call out to him, and then when I hadn't, he'd forgotten. He took them off immediately. Kissed my wrist. Insisted on putting cream on it. Checked it over. Apologized again and again. That night he brought a diamond bracelet home to me—only I'd already moved my personal stuff and myself out. He did some police work. Found me. Brought me the bracelet and other gifts. Until I threatened to get a restraining order."

He could figure the rest. She'd made her deal with the man—she wouldn't report him, they'd pretend he'd locked her to the bed as a joke, he'd keep their residence and his job, and she'd have her freedom without contact. Lucky for her he'd cared more about his job than he had about her.

Greg knew without being told that the handcuffs weren't the only time *Mike* had abused Jasmine. They'd just been her breaking point. Not going after the bastard was going to be tough. He'd be lifting weights before bed, for sure.

"You were in three relationships," he said aloud. "What about the other two?"

"I'll give you their names if you need me to, but I'd like to speak to them first."

He might need them. In the future. Depending. But not at that point. "I'd appreciate that." So she was on speaking terms with her other exes, apparently. Having made deals with them, not reporting any wayward behavior, giving up her home each time...

"You talk to the other two, then?" Why was he pushing this?

"One of them. The second one. *Mike* was the first, and absolutely not. Ever. And if he comes near me, I will call the police. The third...under our legal agreement, he cannot contact me or speak of me, but I am able to contact him."

He believed her. Everything she was saying, she'd know he could corroborate or not, if he forced the issue. He had her over a barrel with Josh's hearing on Thursday. She'd do whatever she had to do to help her brother.

He'd found out what he needed to know for now. Heidi's new motion wasn't going to adversely affect William's case against Josh Taylor. And there didn't appear to be anything in Jasmine's life that was going to help William's case against her brother—not that Greg was going to find easily.

He had what he needed.

And he still wanted more.

He asked her if she planned to be in court on Thursday. It was just an arraignment hearing—a chance for the judge to hear information from Josh's attorney and rule on the motion to dismiss—and then, if he chose to proceed, to set court dates. There was no major reason for her to be there. There'd be no testimony at that point. But she said she'd already arranged to take off work—while leaving Bella in daycare at the Stand. Said she wouldn't leave her brother to stand alone.

Greg, who'd never had a sibling, had an odd sense of missing out on something. Bed, that's what he was missing. He needed some sleep before dinner with Liv.

Telling Jasmine he'd see her in court, he left. And stood outside until he'd heard her dead bolt slide securely into place behind him.

Chapter Eleven

The case wasn't dismissed. Jasmine had trouble sitting still and calm as she heard her brother's motion denied. His lawyer had prepared them. They'd been assigned a female judge, Beatrice Grand. She tended to side with victims in abuse cases. And legally, if there was any doubt at all in the judge's mind regarding Josh's innocence, she had to hear the case. It didn't mean he was guilty. Or that they'd lose the case if it went to trial. It only meant that the judge found sufficient evidence against Josh to proceed. Josh, through his lawyer, Ryder, entered a not-guilty plea, and a settlement conference was scheduled to take place in two weeks.

The one unexpected piece of news… Heidi had opted not to go through with a permanent restraining order against Josh. She told the judge that while she wanted him to pay for what he did to her, she didn't fear that he'd come after her, and she wasn't out to ruin his life.

Another ploy on her part to get the court's sympathy? To show her as the more reasonable, wanting-to-get-along ex-spouse?

Whatever the reason, it was better for Josh, overall.

Still, Jasmine knew Josh had to be crumbling inside as he stood with his attorney before the bench. He nodded when asked if suggested court dates were okay with him. Judge Grand told him that she was going to recommend that he maintain visitation rights, but that his visits remain supervised, and Josh thanked her.

Within two minutes of having the case called, they were through. Jasmine had managed to get through the whole thing without looking to see if Greg was in the courtroom. She hadn't seen or spoken to him since he'd left her house Monday night. She wished she could say the same about his presence in her thoughts.

He'd been there constantly. Going through her days with her. At the grocery, when she'd bought noodles to make lasagna because Bella and Josh both loved it, she'd wondered if Greg liked Italian food. While she'd cooked Tuesday night for Josh's Wednesday dinner visit, she'd pictured Greg in her kitchen opening a bottle of wine to go with the pasta dish.

He'd shown up in other more intimate spaces as well. But sitting there in court Thursday afternoon, Jasmine was never more aware that Greg worked for the other side. The other side of the case. People working on it were sitting on the other side of the courtroom.

She knew Heidi was there. Had heard the woman answer when the judge asked if she was present in the courtroom. She just hadn't looked.

Was Greg sitting with her brother's beautiful and manipulative ex-wife?

Were he, and maybe the prosecutor, too, taken in by her seemingly fragile countenance? Her soft voice?

She couldn't blame them. She and Josh had both been fooled, too, for a while. Until they'd heard that kind, tender voice screech with hateful insults…

"Hey, sis, Ryder's asked me to hang back for a brief meeting with him." Josh was there, standing next to her as she picked up her purse and prepared to leave the courtroom. Reaching up, she hugged him, her heart filled with tears and her mind with so many things she wanted to say to him. And she would, later that night when he called.

Eyes squeezed shut, she poured all of her love and support and encouragement into that hug, felt Josh's usual, less emotional, pat on her back, and opened her eyes— to find herself staring straight into Greg Johnson's gaze. The detective, in a brown suit and matching sedate tie, stood alone toward the back of the room.

"I'll call you," Josh said, leaving her there—seemingly unaware of the detective's gaze on her.

And why wouldn't he be? This wasn't about her. Her brother's mind needed to be solely on that lawyer meeting and finding out what he needed to do to get his daughter back at home with him.

Greg left the courtroom as she headed toward the door, not waiting to hold the door open for her. She was simultaneously relieved and disappointed.

Because her emotions were running high. Josh's case hadn't been dismissed, which made her feel vulnerable. Hearing Heidi's voice behind her, not the words she was speaking, but her voice, she hurried her step. And pushed outside the courtroom to see Greg standing there in the hallway, speaking to another suited man—another attorney from the prosecutor's office? Another detective, like himself?

Passing them was the only way to the elevator that would take her to street level and back to The Lemonade

Stand to collect Bella. Head turned, Jasmine wrapped her arms around her middle, hooking her fingers into the belt loops on her long-sleeved navy T-shirt dress, and moved quickly. Made it without incident. Pushed the down button and was gratified when the ding signifying an arriving car sounded almost immediately. Placing herself squarely in front of the designated door, she stepped inside the empty car, pushed for the ground floor and... Greg slipped inside with her just as the doors started to close.

She'd pulled her hair up and back into a bun before court, going for a proper, respectable look. And now couldn't hide behind the long dark curtain it often afforded her. It would look just too weird and creepy if she were to suddenly yank off the scrunchie holding it in place.

"I need to speak with you." Greg's tone wasn't all that friendly, adding to the surreal court experience. Her brother on the defendant's side. Being accused of abuse.

And Greg no longer on their side?

"What's up?" she asked, forcing herself to look at him. Needing to really see him, and yet, not at all sure anybody ever did.

Or if *she* ever could, at least. Her issue. And maybe him, too.

"You've been holding out on me." His chin was firm, his gaze harder than she'd seen it.

Frowning, she shook her head. Really? Was he kidding? She'd told him about Desmond! "I have not!" she stated, insulted. He could accuse her of wanting to—of liking him too much, thinking about him too much. Then, he'd have her.

But this?

Two floors had passed. They had ten more.

"You didn't tell me that Heidi was living with your brother."

Had he gone mad in the two days since she'd seen him? "You knew they were married. And had a child. One would assume that meant they shared a house." Her words bore sarcasm without apology.

And more intonation than the situation warranted.

How could he doubt her? She'd given him more of her true self, told him more about her relationship with Desmond, than she'd ever told anyone. Including Josh.

"I'm sorry I failed to point out that while they were married, they also lived in the same home," she added, jabbing the ground-floor button again, as though the act would make the car reach its destination more rapidly.

"Not while they were married," he said. "For the past three months."

Four more floors to go. Then, two. She stared at him.

"Are you kidding? You think my brother had Heidi…" She shook her head. And the door opened to the lobby. Jasmine stepped out. Greg kept in step with her and then, with a light touch to her forearm, stepped in front of her.

"I know he did," he said, softly. Convincingly.

She shook her head. No. This way-too-attractive man of power was not going to convince her of things her own mind knew better than to believe.

"I've got proof."

He had *proof*? Her mind went briefly blank. She was aware of her surroundings. Of people coming and going. A little girl holding the hand of a young woman. Someone in a red dress that just walked past.

Did they all think the day was normal? Or did they know it wasn't?

"What proof?"

Heidi was staying at Josh's? Had her brother betrayed her?

"Neighbor's testimony, for one."

And Bella. It dawned on her. Bella would know if her mommy had been sleeping at Daddy's house. Was he about to tell her they were planning to compel the child's testimony?

She shook her head again. Thought about shaking it so hard her hair fell out of her bun. Hard enough that reality would return, the judge would dismiss Josh's case and life would go on.

The world stayed exactly the same. Her in the lobby of the courthouse with a detective she'd somehow fallen for in the space of nine days and she now couldn't trust. And Josh was upstairs getting ready to fight a case that hadn't been dismissed. People were swarming around them.

She wasn't sure what to say. But knew her brother was the one person in the world she could trust.

Greg was studying her. Thinking she was his bug under some personal microscope? Had he *detected* how she was struggling not to think about him every minute of the day?

He couldn't involve Bella. Couldn't use an innocent three-year-old in the fight between her parents. She'd take her niece and run if she had to.

"You didn't know."

Greg's tone had noticeably softened. So much so that her entire being yearned to relax into him. She forbade it. Immediately.

"It's more of Heidi's lies," she said, just a few words away from begging him to believe her. To leave Bella out of it. To help them. "It has to be."

He didn't nod, but the one simple tilt forward of his head felt to her like the same thing. Like a *yes*. "Just ask him for me, will you?"

She wasn't going to ask her brother about the allegations. She was going to tell him about what Greg had said, as soon as she knew he was out of his meeting and they were alone. She nodded like some smitten idiot, letting him hold her gaze captive.

But… "Why don't you ask him yourself?"

He tilted his head slightly to the side this time. "His lawyer will be present."

Oh. That made sense. He wanted an honest answer. "You think his lawyer will…"

"…tell him not to say anything."

Right. She'd been going to ask if he thought Ryder Michaels would ask Josh to lie. And where that thought came from, she didn't know. Like they could trust this detective who worked for the other side over her brother's paid attorney…

"You asked me to find the real truth," he reminded her.

She had. Still needed him to do so. Lord knew they weren't going to be able to fight Heidi on her own with a judge who leaned toward female victims and a prosecutor falling prey to her manipulative and creative spins on tiny pieces of truth.

Josh was going to sink under the weight of it all if she couldn't figure out a way to hold him up. Temporarily losing custody of Bella. Losing his motion. And now hearing that Heidi was claiming to have proof that she'd been living with him. That she'd somehow apparently managed to get his own neighbors to corroborate the story.

"I'll talk to him tonight," she said, before she could think and knowing as soon as the words were out that she shouldn't have put a time on it. Should have left herself an opening of time before he'd be expecting an answer...

"Jas? Is that you?"

With a small lift of her spirits, she swung around when she heard the feminine voice off to her side coming closer. "Wynne!" She reached to return the hug she knew was coming. A hug that was a little longer than either of them hugged others, one that held a love that, while benign now, would always be present between them.

"What are you doing here?" Wynne's words asked as her warm, personal gaze asked if Jasmine was okay. She included a sideways glance toward Greg in the silent question.

Jasmine understood immediately, of course. Wynne needed to know that Jasmine wasn't in trouble. That she hadn't fallen under the spell of power and supposed protection once again. Jasmine's counselor had pointed out to her that, in truth, she never did fall. She always got out before she lost herself.

She was a strong, capable woman.

One who could struggle when it came to falling in love.

"Heidi's accused Josh of abuse," she said softly, moving more closely to the state representative who always seemed to have people around her these days. "I'll tell you about it later."

"What? Heidi's back at it *again*?" Wynne glanced toward Greg a second time. He'd chosen not to wander off on his way, as Jasmine had half hoped he would, but rather, stood there, watching the two of them. And she remembered that he'd been impressed that she knew Wynne Anderson.

"Where are my manners?" she exclaimed with a last

glance at Wynne, needing the other woman to keep her counsel until they could talk alone. "Greg, this is Representative Wynne Anderson. Wynne, Detective Greg Johnson. He's working on my brother's case. We're just coming from a preliminary hearing."

Glancing around, Wynne asked, "Where's Josh?" And then held out her hand to Greg. "Nice to meet you," she added, almost as though it wasn't an afterthought. Jasmine knew her better than that, though. Wynne had reservations about Greg.

Old jealousy rearing its head? Or valid concerns of a close friend?

"Josh is still upstairs with his lawyer," she said, trying to walk the three of them toward the door where she could make her escape before her too-complicated world exploded into painful shards.

Wynne stopped after just a couple of steps. "I actually have to get upstairs myself," she said. "I'm late for a meeting. But…you going to be home tonight?" The look she gave Jasmine was adamant, in an almost sisterly way.

"Yes." *Please go. Let me go. Make him go. Let's all be gone…*

"I'll call you," Wynne said and with a quick "Nice to meet you" aimed in Greg's direction, she sped toward an opening elevator door.

Turning her gaze back to Greg, Jasmine found him watching her. "You know her well."

"I told you I did."

"You're close."

"We used to be." She started walking. Needing to get Bella and keep the child close until she figured out the best way to win the current war they were facing.

There was no doubt they'd win. They were survivors.

"We don't talk that much anymore," she continued, since talking about Wynne seemed to be getting her closer to the door, the parking lot across the street, her car. "She's busy, I'm busy..." Wynne hadn't known about the charges against Josh.

"Does she know what Desmond did to you? To keep you from meeting up with her?"

"No."

He kept looking at her. She didn't meet his gaze. On emotional overload already, she was in no state to get into the Wynne thing. Had no idea where he'd stand on the sexuality spectrum and didn't have the energy to find out.

Balmy air and a glorious blaze of sunshine hit them as they walked past a security guard and made it through the door.

"Once she got heavier into politics, you didn't have as much in common?" he asked, hands in his pockets. They walked in tandem toward the streetlight that would hopefully change by the time they got there and let her just head straight across the street without another delay.

She shrugged at his question. "We just got busier with other things," she said and then cringed inside. What things was she busier with that she hadn't already been busy with during the time that she and Wynne Anderson were close? She'd already told him she was teaching back then. And other than the recent advent of Bella into her daily routine, what else did she do?

Truth was, she still respected and appreciated Wynne's opinion on any matter she brought up to her. The woman was incredibly smart. Analytical. And generally spot-on when it came to powers of observation, as well.

She'd just been way too possessive for Jasmine. Wanting them to be so far into each other's lives they never went anywhere alone. Not personally, at least. And then, once, Wynne had screamed horrible, demeaning things at her when she'd failed to comply and didn't seem to want the same things for them. She'd later come to understand that Wynne had been dealing with her own tensions, her political aspirations and sexual orientation at war with each other, as well as her own insecurities about being a lesbian. The fact that Jasmine was bisexual made it more difficult for her to trust that Jasmine wanted her and only her. It was Jasmine's belief that Wynne had shocked herself as much as Jasmine when she'd lost control that last night. She'd accepted the break in their relationship without a fight. Had asked only that Jasmine not say anything about her outburst and had taken an extended vacation, "caring for her ill mother across the country." In reality, she'd put herself in private anger counseling, just in case, in another state.

But Jasmine just wasn't up to telling any of that to Greg Johnson as they walked across the street. Or admitting out loud that Wynne's wife seemed to feel a bit threatened by Jasmine.

She didn't want to think about any of it.

"So, you'll talk to Josh tonight?" Greg asked as she reached her car.

She'd said she would. He knew that she talked to him every night for Bella's good-night story. And he'd know that after their day in court, of course they had to talk about his case. "Yes." She pushed the button on the door handle that unlocked her car electronically in partnership with the fob in her purse.

He turned away, tapped the hood of the car as though a form of goodbye, and then turned back. "Jasmine?"

"Yeah?"

"Is Wynne the second one?" She knew what he was asking. The ex-lover that she still talked to.

With one foot in the car, she hesitated. Was cornered. Him there, asking for truth. Her not wanting him to have it. But needing him to trust her so that he'd believe her about Josh…

"Yes."

Chapter Twelve

Greg waited for Jasmine's call. He knew Bella went to bed fairly early. He didn't actually start watching the clock until nine. By ten he was actively staring at his phone. Checking to see if he'd missed a call.

Forcing himself to focus on things other than Jasmine Taylor. Fighting a mind that wanted to give him a continuous thread, running over and over, including every picture his memory had stored of her. From the moment that she'd opened her door to him almost two weeks before until she'd told him that Wynne Anderson had been her lover and then ducked into her car and drove off without looking back.

She hadn't even given him a chance to react, to show her that he saw her exactly the same, whether she'd had a female lover or not. She was loyal and kind, steadfast in her devotion to her loved ones. Her sexuality was a part of her. It didn't define her.

And she hadn't trusted him to get that.

At 10:20 he had a text.

Talked to Josh as requested. Will be available to speak with you tomorrow after class.

She wanted to talk in person, then? His body jolted. No reason. Just a jolt. He started typing immediately. Phone is fine.

He wanted to hear what she was going to tell him now. Didn't want to wait overnight. He knew that Heidi had been living with Josh. There was security camera coverage of her car in his driveway all night. Provided willingly without warrant by Josh's next-door neighbor. What Greg needed to know was whether Josh was lying to Jasmine or Jasmine was lying to Greg.

Why he needed to know he didn't question at the moment. He was working a case. And if that particular piece of information didn't directly affect the case, well, then, that would be something he'd figure out some other time.

Okay, good, I'll wait to pick up Bella from daycare until after you call

What? No…wait.

What about now

He hit Send. Waited. A minute. Ten.

Talking now I mean

More waiting.

Had she gone to bed? Put her phone on charge and left the room? Gone out to sit on that private deck and let breeze from the waves caress her skin after a long, hard day?

Dropping his phone on his nightstand, Greg decided waiting to speak was a good idea and went in to take a cold shower.

JASMINE DIDN'T SLEEP well that night. She spent a lot of the time in a rocker lounger in Bella's room wrapped in a fleece blanket, dozing on and off. Being close to the baby girl she'd defend with her life was her only priority during those dark hours.

Josh was scared to death. He'd already resigned from the board of Play for the Win. The idea that scandal might make parents and guardians leery of letting kids participate in activities or be associated with the organization disturbed him. But even then, he knew that he could always start again, somewhere else, with the same idea. It wasn't like the charges against him, if they stuck, would get him jail time. Not likely. Not on a first offense.

What was sending her younger brother into panic mode was the idea of losing Bella. He just couldn't fathom life without her. But more than that, the idea that his precious baby might become a ward of the state…

Jasmine had promised him, from the depth of her soul, that she wasn't going to let that happen.

Which was why protecting Bella was her first priority the next afternoon when she sat, cell in hand, waiting for it to ring. Bella needed to be at home with her father.

Not with her aunt. Not being questioned by child psychologists who would use her answers to try to convict her father of a crime he didn't commit.

Greg Johnson was the surest way to make that happen—and maybe the biggest stumbling block to it happening as well. He was coming to her for answers.

Somehow she had to capitalize on that to secure Bella and Josh's future.

The thought made her slightly sick. She didn't use people.

But what if he was using her?

The thought had occurred to her every time she'd jolted awake the night before. She'd had a brief conversation with Wynne before Andrea got home and Wynne had to go. Wynne had warned her not to fall into her old pattern. Not to trust until trust was earned…

Her phone rang.

"I have something to show you," Greg said in response to her polite "hello." "I'm almost to The Lemonade Stand. Can you meet me outside and take a little drive with me?"

She already had her bag packed up and on her shoulder, in preparation for collecting Bella as soon as the call was through. "I'll stop at the daycare and meet you outside," she said before second-guessing herself. He was the key to her family's future. Whether he was trustworthy or not.

Giving Maddie the fruit snack pouch she'd packed for Bella and letting her know that she'd be back as soon as she could, Jasmine stopped at Lila's office to let the director know where she was going.

She wasn't getting in the man's car without letting someone know. Detective or not.

Greg was waiting for her in the dark blue SUV she'd seen in her driveway both times he'd been over. When she saw his jeans and flannel shirt, she wondered if she should have asked where they were going. Her leggings and long-sleeved, midthigh-length sweater had been fine for the mid-September Santa Raquel morning, but the wedges she had on weren't going to make it if he had anything athletic in mind, like a walk...

He didn't get out and open her door. She opened it herself. Climbed in. "Where are we going?"

The car was warm. Smelled of him. A wave of sweet goodness washed over her. She basked in it for a second. Then she buckled her seat belt.

"I have something to show you," he said. "It's not far."

She liked the mystery. And heard Wynne telling her not to fall...

She liked not having to deal with Josh and Bella and losing her family for a second. They'd have their talk. She had no doubt about that. They both were determined to get what they wanted and needed. His want. Her need.

But if he was open to being friendly with each other, or doing something nice, in the midst of taking care of business, if he was experiencing any of the same personal pull that she'd been fighting the past two weeks, then... she was game. To a point.

He had classic rock playing. Not booming. Just playing. She looked around. The car was clean. No bits of shoe grit on the floor mats. No spare clothes or wadded receipts anywhere to be seen. The console's two cup holders were empty. No pencils or other paraphernalia collecting there.

The dash system was touch screen.

She loved hers.

He turned and turned again. Seeming not to notice that she was sitting there. And still, she felt comfortable. Glad for the odd moment to spend with him without having to be on guard.

Curious.

Maybe they were going to get a coffee or something,

or sit by the ocean in some scenic layover he'd noticed on his way in from Santa Barbara.

If that's where he lived.

It occurred to her she had no idea.

"You work in Santa Barbara," she said. "Do you live there, as well?"

"I have a place just outside town." He was watching the road. And she felt her first fissure of tension.

He made another turn. Slowed. They were nearing a park by a large cliff that looked out over the ocean. She knew the place. Had been there once for a picnic with Josh and Bella. And knew that though there was a cliff face, the other side wasn't a straight drop to the water. It was a wooded hillside that was angled enough to get down with relative safety.

Not in wedges, probably, and there was no reason for them to—

Greg slowed the vehicle more, and she thought he was going to turn in. Getting outside, talking in the park, was maybe a good idea…

He didn't stop, though. Just slowly drove past. She looked at the park, wondering what on earth he was doing. Looking for. She was done playing his game.

"What's going…" The word *on* never made it off her tongue. A vehicle was parked in the last spot, behind a dumpster. She recognized the Play for the Win logo on the door. And then saw the couple sitting across from each other at a picnic table made out of stone. They were in earnest conversation.

And she knew what they were talking about.

"I'M PART OF the High-Risk Team's crew doing extra drive-bys at Heidi's place." Greg started with the spiel he'd rehearsed as soon as they were past the park. He hadn't been sure she'd just ride with him without an explanation, but he'd needed her to see for herself.

No explanation on that one forthcoming. He could have just told her what he'd seen. If she were any other possible witness he suspected of hiding information, he'd have just told her, as part of a shock interrogation attempt to get information from her.

She'd know about the drive-bys from being familiar with the High-Risk Team. Though she might not have known that they'd taken Heidi's case.

"I saw your brother parked, his car running, far enough down the street to not be seen with her, but, of course, I couldn't ignore his presence. Before I could park and approach him, ask him what he was doing there, I see Heidi coming down the street in her car, toward him. He pulled out in front of her. She followed him. So I followed them."

Not one to fall prey to tension, so much as to be prepared for others' possible over-the-top reactions to it, Greg pulled over at another, much smaller, cliff-side layby and waited. Would she start to cry? Turn on him— the messenger—with anger?

He wanted to reach out to her. Pull her to him. Let her know she wasn't alone and... What the hell? Bothered by his reaction, he pictured Josh and Heidi back at the park, sitting across from each other. Wishing Heidi hadn't made that particular choice. Just as William had been adamantly against Heidi not getting a permanent restraining order.

Without her cooperation, there hadn't been enough evidence for the judge to order one for her own protection. Josh Taylor had physically harmed his wife. Once that they could prove. That made a bad day. A man who perhaps grabbed her arm too hard in the heat of the moment. Still punishable. Worthy of record. Not yet an ongoing threat. That they knew of.

That Heidi was ready to say.

Something that, unfortunately, wasn't all that unusual in domestic violence cases.

Until Josh hurt Heidi again, all the court could do was handle the one charge.

And chances were, based on statistics, and on the extents of Josh's subterfuge, he would hurt his wife again.

And someday, maybe even his daughter, too.

"Josh wants to give me permanent custody of Bella before his rights are possibly severed." Jasmine's voice cut the car's silence, slicing through him. She was staring out the window toward the horizon beyond the cliff's edge— the ocean they couldn't see from their vantage point. She hadn't looked his way since she'd buckled her seat belt.

And suddenly the confines of his vehicle, the scent of her, was…uncomfortable to him. "You want to get out and walk?" he asked.

She shrugged, unbuckled, let herself out. And leaned back against the front end of his car, facing the ocean. Not the walking—the expulsion of physical energy—he'd envisioned. But he leaned with her. Next to her.

Close enough to touch her if the need arose. A ludicrous thought. Left over from Liv days—without the sense of suffocation he'd felt back then. Must mean he was finally getting rid of some of the guilt his ex had saddled him with.

"So he admitted to you that he's guilty?" he asked softly. Wishing the situation had turned out differently even though he'd known all along how it was going to go.

He'd seen the way Josh Taylor's glance had darted around the room when he'd asked the man about the morning that Heidi had been hurt—the varying versions of the story.

"No!" She turned then, standing upright, facing him. The afternoon sun put glints in the long dark hair tumbling over her shoulders to cover her breasts. "Of course not!" She studied him, eye to eye. "I thought you were open to the truth. All along, you've just been using me to get a conviction?" she accused, but without the drama he'd been expecting accompanying the anger.

The anger wasn't really there, either. More like disappointment. Bitterness.

Vile things to have slung at him. He didn't want to hurt her. To add his name to the crushing list of people who'd let her down in her life.

And as he met her gaze, he grew confused. Using her? That had come a bit out of left field. She was upset about their growing relationship when her brother was almost convicted?

Their relationship. Like they had one.

"I want the truth," he told her, looking her straight in the eye. Leaning in so she could feel the strength of his words. Know their validity. Then he added, "You said you talked to Josh last night. Let's start there."

"What about him and Heidi back there?" She nodded toward the direction from which they'd come. "Shouldn't we go make sure things are okay?"

He shook his head. "I alerted an officer I know on the High-Risk Team. They'll have someone drive by and check things out, but legally, we can't stop them from talking to each other. Your brother canceled his restraining order six months ago and, as you know, Heidi refused the one offered to her yesterday."

"Yeah, didn't you wonder about that?" she asked then, turning back to face his side, while he continued to lean against the SUV, his hands on the hood on either side of him. She crossed her arms over those breasts. "She's accusing him of abuse but isn't afraid of him?"

"She doesn't think he's a permanent threat. Doesn't think he'll seek her out to hurt her. She says he only gets violent when they're fighting, and she doesn't plan to fight with him. She doesn't want to ruin his life..."

He stopped when he realized she'd heard most of it in court the day before and realized her question hadn't been about the legalities. "I think Heidi cares about Josh," he told her. "She truly doesn't want to hurt him. At the same time, she needs to send a strong message to him that hurting her—or anyone—isn't okay. For Bella's sake as much as her own. And for his sake, too." He'd been in the room when William had talked to her before court—trying his best to get her to go for a permanent restraining order, explaining that doing so would strengthen their case.

"She's going for sympathy with the court," Jasmine said and then shook her head, her mouth turning downward, like she wasn't expecting to be believed.

He was losing her. He couldn't lose her.

Didn't matter that she wasn't proving to be a source of information to help William's case. She was involved. She needed the truth.

And for some ungodly reason, he needed to help her see it.

Chapter Thirteen

Jasmine didn't really see what good talking with Greg was going to do. He'd made up his mind that he had his proof. That Josh was guilty. While she couldn't find any reasonable explanation for Josh to have misled her, she knew there would be one. An explanation. She just had to talk to her brother. And she couldn't trust Greg to be open-minded. The way he'd jumped automatically—with a tone of expectation—to the idea that Josh had confessed guilt to her the night before...

Wynne's words rang in her ears. Because they'd been in her own mind, too. She knew herself. Knew her weaknesses.

Greg Johnson played to them perfectly—whether he meant to or not. Wanted to or not. Just thinking about how she'd felt climbing into his car—like it was a tiny oasis of good feeling—made her cringe.

Had Josh risked everything, having this meeting with Heidi?

Confused, hurting for her brother, afraid for all of them, she shored her defenses.

"Why does Josh want you to take full custody of Bella?" Greg's question was soft, his expression looking like he really cared, pulling her out of the muck into which she'd sunk and back to the problem at hand. Back to what really mattered.

She had to be honest with him if she had any hope he'd see the truth.

"He's afraid that Heidi's going to be successful at manipulating the court, that he's going to get convicted. While the sentence probably won't amount to much, it sets a pattern that he doesn't see ending. He doesn't want his daughter to grow up in a home that is disrupted every time her mother comes after her father. He also fears that if he's convicted, the court will determine that he's not a fit custodial parent, even though there's not one bit of evidence that he's ever, or would ever, hurt that baby girl…" Her throat clogged, and she swallowed. Then continued.

"Despite what Heidi might have convinced herself to believe, even if Josh gets convicted, she's not going to be eligible to take custody of her daughter. Because of the charges against her before, and the proof that she hurt Bella, she has to wait a minimum of five years before she'll even be considered as a safe parent. And if Josh is deemed unsafe, Bella could become a ward of the state. If I have her, they can both talk to her every day, video call with her, have their visitations, get to spend holidays with her and go to school functions… We're still a family, and providing Bella with a secure and stable home life at the same time." Josh had it all worked out.

And as much as she'd love to raise her niece full-time, as badly as she wanted to be a mother/aunt to the toddler, her heart broke every time she considered her brother's home without his baby girl.

"Josh knows that I've decided to remain single, and he sees this as a win for me, too," she continued. If there was a chance Greg was open to the truth, she was going to put it all out there so he could get it. For Josh and Bella. "I've always wanted children…"

The man had turned to face her, his gaze so warm she shivered like she did when she first stepped into a deliciously warm bubble bath. She wanted to immerse herself. To soak in it. And know the peace that came from being able to just relax and feel good for a moment.

"What did he say when you asked him if Heidi had been living with him?"

His gaze was inches from hers. His face inches from hers. She desperately needed to know if he was digging for dirt or sincerely looking for truth—she just couldn't tell.

Didn't trust herself to be able to tell where he was concerned.

And wanted him to hold her, regardless. To just squeeze her up against that body and do things to her that made them both feel so glorious that the world and its troubles didn't seem so all encompassing.

"He said that she'd asked to be allowed to spend the night sometimes, so that she could be there when Bella went to bed and when she got up in the morning. So her daughter had a sense of her being a real part of their home life."

"So he let her move in?"

"No." It was important that he get this. That he get that Josh—both a victim and a survivor—was a very capable, loving father. "He just let her spend the night sometimes, for Bella's sake, because he agreed that it could be better for her to know her mother in a more normal light, once or twice a week, depending on his schedule and Heidi's emotional state. She slept in a downstairs guest bedroom. His and Bella's rooms are upstairs. And he installed a motion-sensor light that would alert him immediately if she tried to climb the stairs during the night."

"She could have tampered with the light."

"She'd have had to do so from upstairs, and he checked it before he went to bed each night. He always sleeps with his door open. And, just in case you're wondering, he also has a child safety gate at the top of the stairs in case Bella gets up."

He appeared to be paying avid attention. She still couldn't tell what he was thinking. Or believing. His gaze seemed softer still. More personal, too. She wanted to get distracted by that. To distract him. And couldn't afford to do either.

"He's a guy who thinks of every eventuality and protects against them," she said. "Not a man who'd ever hurt anyone. All those years... He'd stop my father, but he never gave back. He defended, but never attacked. It's just not Josh."

He nodded. But whether or not it was in confirmation, she didn't know. Wasn't sure she could trust herself to know.

She wanted to trust him, though. So badly.

"Josh is meeting with Heidi today to discuss giving me custody of Bella, at least for now. I assumed, with all that's going on, that he'd do it virtually, but obviously not. He's going to offer, at my suggestion, that the two of them go to counseling together at whatever point it's deemed appropriate. That they work together to become good and healthy parents to Bella. He's telling her that I'll make visitation as easy and home friendly as the courts will allow—she's currently only allowed supervised visits, which I'm sure you know, and I'm sure you heard yesterday that that's all Josh gets right now, too."

He nodded again. Felt like confirmation that time. Did that mean the prior one had not been?

"She doesn't really have a say at this point, as he's been Bella's full custodial parent, but he wants Heidi's buy-in. He wants her to be willing to sign whatever papers are necessary to give me full guardianship. We aren't sure about all the legalities, but he wants us all agreed before he calls his family lawyer to put things in action." He'd actually talked about adoption if it came to that, but she'd cut him off at that point. There was no way he was going to give up Bella to that extent. No way.

"I didn't know he was going to meet with Heidi in person," she added, again. "I would have warned him against that." And wasn't sure Josh would have listened on that one. Which could be why he hadn't told her. If he was falling for Heidi's lies again, they were in much more serious trouble than she'd even thought.

"You think he still loves Heidi?"

She shrugged. Had asked herself the same question many times. "Maybe," she said. "I think he definitely loves the person she can be when she's in a good place. But I know he sees the other side clearly now, too. Mostly, I think he knows what it's like to grow up not knowing your biological parent, and he doesn't want Bella to go through that. At the same time, he recognizes that it's not healthy for her to be around an abusive mom. I think he's hoping that the counseling, the divorce and losing custody have helped Heidi change."

"But you don't believe that it has?"

"I'd hoped, but, no, not really. She just didn't seem... I don't know..." Heidi had said the right things the time or two she'd seen her, but there'd been a missing...something, too. It was like she wasn't fully engaged, and Jasmine had worried about what would happen when Heidi let it all loose. Would she be able to control it?

"And now that she's pulling this stunt, and I find out she was working him for partial custody when she'd already been told by the state that she wouldn't be eligible for five years… I know she hasn't changed."

He pushed a lock of hair away from her face, grazing her skin. She stared up at him. "Are you sure you're open to seeing the change? To believing it can happen?"

He wasn't asking about Heidi, now. It was like she read words in his eyes. He wanted to know if she could believe that her brother had changed from who she knew him to be? Wanted to know if she believed Josh had become an abuser?

Or was he just needing reassurance that she'd know if he had? That she'd be able to see if he had?

She'd grown up a victim. He knew her history with adult relationships. She understood his doubt.

"I know I'm able to see it," she told him. And then added more, even though she was opening a door she'd rather not have him enter. "I've seen it in Wynne."

She wasn't ashamed of her relationship with Wynne. Of having had a same-sex partner. She just didn't expect others—men, mostly—to understand. Or not get all weird about it.

Noah had thought it was cool. Until he found out that it didn't make her open to threesomes.

And while Greg most definitely didn't send out that kind of vibe, she didn't want to find out she was wrong and be disappointed some more. It wasn't like she and Greg were ever going to be anything. It didn't hurt to want to think good thoughts about him.

"You still care about her," he said, seeming to take a

step back without moving his feet. Cars flew by occasionally. She'd been aware. Paid no attention. And suddenly felt as though they were on display, standing out there with his SUV between them and the road.

Who was going to think twice about seeing them out there?

"I do." She wasn't going to lie. Most particularly not to him. If he caught her in one little white stretching of the truth, it could be over for Josh. After seeing William Brubaker in court the previous afternoon, she was fairly certain the man was determined to win his case. Regardless of whether or not Josh had abused his wife. She figured he believed Josh had done it. That he believed Heidi. And his mind was closed to any other scenario.

"Is it hard for you? Seeing her married to someone else?"

"No!" She heard how loud her voice had become and softened her tone. "Not at all. I want her happy, and it wasn't going to happen with me."

"Because you couldn't give her a second chance? You said all three of your exes were abusive, so I'm assuming she was? And agreed to leave you alone as long as you didn't ruin her political aspirations by going public with her abuse?"

He paid attention to what she'd told him. There was no doubting that much.

"Because she's a woman who faces public scrutiny, and backlash from political opponents, every day in her public life, which gives her a tendency to be insecure in her private one." She told him another truth she hadn't spoken to anyone else. Because she had to. For Josh's sake.

Or was it because there was something about this man

that compelled her to be her real self with him, in a way she'd never been able to be with anyone else?

Oh God, was she in trouble here? Falling for this guy for real?

Did that mean that underneath all of his avowals of wanting honesty, and his good-guy demeanor, he had a mean streak, too?

"And I'm too sensitive to other people's emotional nuances to be at peace with that. Wynne's a strong, public person. She has to be to make the differences she's making. I'm someone who likes to keep my private stuff private."

She couldn't decipher his expression as he continued to watch her. And couldn't have him thinking she didn't know her own mind. Or wasn't perfectly rational and reliable.

"Wynne was there when I got the rest of my stuff out of the place I'd shared with D—*Mike*." She'd almost used Des's real name. She had to be more careful. "She stood up to him, not backing down, when he made a verbal slur or two. And when we left, she was so understanding—in an emotional way. She sat with me as I worked through it, sharing the emotion with me. It was…oddly compelling. Of course I know now that I was susceptible, due to the relationship challenges I face. Wynne fit my pattern. Anyway, a deep friendship was solidified that night, and I found myself relying on her as things happened in my day and wanting to be there for whatever she happened to be facing. I knew she was gay, but didn't care, one way or the other. I never really have thought too much about a person's sexual orientation. She was Wynne, and I was falling in love with her, with the *us* we were creating. To me, sex is a culmination of being with someone who you want to be with more than anyone else. That's what powers the need to see, to touch, to be intimate. That's what powers the arousal. Sexual attraction grows out of an emotional bond, not a predilection for body parts.

"I can be equally aroused, and satisfied, from either sex if the emotional bond is there. And, for me, it also has to be monogamous from the very beginning. Sex is the one thing you share with your partner that no one else in the world gets to share. Or have a part of. Truthfully, for most of my life, I thought everyone was built that way, but that a lot of us just followed societal norms because that's what we'd been taught. Or for procreation. It wasn't until Wynne had such a hard time accepting that I could be satisfied with just her after I'd been attracted to men, had sex with men, that I saw how different I was. She was beautiful and charming…and I never wanted anyone else when we were together…" She shrugged.

"And that's when she became abusive? When she started to think you were attracted to men, too? That you couldn't be satisfied only by her?" he asked.

His voice, the motorcycle that sped by, the sun in her eyes, all hit at the same time. She wanted to get back to the Stand. To collect Bella and go home.

And wished she'd met Greg under different circumstances. That he wasn't a cop. In a position of power.

How could he sit there so calmly, accept her so calmly? As though it all made sense to him? As though she made sense to him?

"She was never physically abusive," she said, needing to finish this off. She'd started it. It had to end. "She just got extremely possessive, and she's already got that take-charge personality. And then, once, when I wouldn't say that I was a lesbian, she was verbally abusive. It was like, in her mind, I wasn't fully accepting of who we were as a couple. The abuse only happened that once. Neither of us allowed it to go any further than that. And I didn't offer her an agreement—she asked for one. She heard herself screaming horrible things at me and immediately stopped. Midsentence. She knew we had to break up. She had other issues going on and put herself in counseling and got herself right. And while I care deeply about her, I'd already begun to realize that we weren't right for each other. Not because of the sex, but because of the lives we'd chosen to live. I wasn't happy being the partner of a politician. I dreaded the dinners, the constant smiles, the fund raising. And once that emotional bond waned, so did the sexual desire. We stay in touch, though we don't see each other all that much anymore. I get the feeling Andrea doesn't like me." She shrugged. He now knew all about a part of her life even Josh didn't know.

Her brother had known Wynne. Knew they were friends. Roommates. But…

"So, just to be clear, given the right relationship… you…feel arousal for men, too?"

Wynne was special. Important to her. Jasmine didn't regret that they'd loved each other. Or how they'd loved each other. Wynne just hadn't been the right life-partner relationship.

"I most definitely feel it," she told him.

And could have sworn she saw him smile.

Chapter Fourteen

When exactly he got the idea that he could help Jasmine and still see her brother pay for his crime, Greg didn't know. It kind of grew on him. And the more he knew of her, the more he got to know her, the more it all made sense.

Jasmine had suffered more than a lot of women before she'd even reached adulthood. At a time when she should have been carefree and exploring her own strengths, she'd been forced to protect the brother she'd loved. And then watch him protect her.

She was aware. Responsible. She took accountability. There were no chips on her shoulders that he could see. No blaming others for what went wrong in her life. There was only facing the challenge and doing what you had to do to get to the other side.

The one constant in her life, through all the battles, appeared to be Josh. Of course she couldn't imagine him in any kind of role that made him dangerous. To her or anyone else.

That crash was going to be a hard one. Probably the hardest in her life. She'd need a friend. Someone who could deal with whatever fallout she might suffer and remain calm—as Josh had seemingly always done.

Maybe he, in all of his dread of drama, his calm demeanor, his logical, problem-solving mind, was what she needed.

Maybe Liv had prepared him.

As a friend, that was. Jasmine had made it quite clear that she wasn't looking for more than that. And if she ended up with her three-year-old niece, which seemed almost inevitable from where he sat, she'd have enough to deal with without the added uncertainty of a new relationship.

But a friendship…that just *was*.

Appeared almost to be already.

Regardless, he had to stick close to her. Because the bottom line was that if Heidi was telling the truth, and he had no doubts that she was, then Josh Taylor was a potentially dangerous man. And Jasmine and Bella, as his closest family, stood a good chance of becoming his victims.

That was it. That was why he couldn't get this woman off his mind. Because he sensed that she could be in danger.

The idea made sense. Sat well with him as he hung at home Friday night, thinking about her. Picking up his phone to call her a time or two and setting it back down.

He could tell her to watch out for herself. She was never, ever going to suspect that her brother would hurt her. She'd just quit trusting Greg to be open to the truth.

He had one hell of a job ahead of him. One that might just help him find some peace for a conscience that he'd been battling since the last case he'd prosecuted. The reason he'd left the prosecutorial side and gone back to the academy to become a detective. As a lawyer, he'd once won a conviction with the evidence he had, sent a fall guy to jail and allowed a criminal to walk free.

If he was going to be her friend, help her through what lay ahead with her brother, she had to trust him. Therein lay his biggest challenge. Jasmine Taylor didn't even fully trust herself. And she most particularly didn't trust men like him who fit her pattern. He had to let her get to know him.

To tell her he'd been a prosecutor before he'd been a prosecutor's detective. And maybe tell her how badly he'd let Liv down, too.

With that thought in mind, he picked up his phone. Added her to speed dial and then tested the button.

He heard ringing. Six times. And then got her voice mail. The button worked.

SHE HEARD THE phone ring. It was on the counter in the kitchen where she'd set it after speaking with Josh that evening. He'd read Bella her story. Blew her good-night kisses. Accepted the kisses the little girl's lips put on her phone screen. And then, once Bella was tucked in, Josh had asked her to do something she absolutely didn't want to do.

Talk to Heidi.

His ex-wife needed reassurances that if she went along with Josh's plan, Jasmine wouldn't try to keep her from her child. He'd insisted that she just wanted to know that Jasmine would still give her a say in decisions regarding Bella's future.

She'd promised to call the other woman but hadn't had the chance. Heidi had shown up on her doorstep half an hour after Bella went to sleep. She'd claimed Josh had given her the code to get past security and into her neighborhood. And wanting to keep peace, and because Heidi met her gaze without that wild-eyed look, she'd let her in.

Josh was certain they could all work this out as a family. That Heidi had seemed calm with accepting that while she couldn't have custody of Bella for another three years at least, Josh wouldn't have their daughter, either. He seemed to think that he'd be able to talk Heidi into dropping the abuse charges against him, too.

And that was the only real reason she was sitting in her living room, listening to Heidi, hoping to God she hadn't made a mistake. All she had to do was listen, to let Heidi talk, to help her feel heard and understood, and then maybe they could talk about the fake charges.

"Who's calling you this late at night?" Heidi asked when the phone's ring finally quieted.

"I don't know." She knew who she'd most like to talk to at the moment, but figured that would have been a mistake, too. She didn't need more of Greg Johnson in her personal life. No matter how much she might want him there.

"It's Josh, isn't it?" Heidi stood up, and Jasmine forced herself to remain calm. If she didn't engage, Heidi would sit back down. They'd been through some pretty horrible scenes during their years as family, and Jasmine always seemed to have a calming effect on the younger woman. "The two of you, you're working me. In this together. I knew it!" Her voice grew louder still. "There's no breaking into the two of you. It's like this impenetrable wall. Always there for each other. Protecting each other. Well, I've got news for you, Jasmine. You aren't going to be able to protect him this time. You two think you're so perfect, but he's not. He hurt me, Jasmine. He *abused* me, and he's going to pay, just like I had to."

She wished she had her phone. Could be recording this. Surely the court would see that Heidi was out for revenge.

"Tell me about it." She forced herself to speak with a compassion she just didn't feel. Not anymore. Not for this woman. "But keep your voice down. You don't want to wake Bella. You don't want her telling anyone you were here or that she heard Mommy yelling."

Heidi watched her through narrowed eyes. She didn't sit. But her voice was lowered when she spoke again. "He grabbed my wrist so hard it was bruised to the elbow," she said, her eyes starting to get a more faraway look. "When I tried to pull away, he wouldn't let go, and that's how it got sprained. But that's not the first time he hurt me," she said. "It's just the first time there was any evidence."

Jasmine could hardly sit still, but she knew from past experience that if she stood, Heidi would take the move as aggressive, as though Jasmine was standing up to her, and get defensive.

She had to talk her down. Not raise the fight in her. And, it occurred to her, maybe she could get something out of Heidi to take to Greg. Something that could prove the lie to her accusations.

"What else did he do that hurt you?"

"One time he slapped the back of my head. But you can't very well see the bruise underneath your hair."

The look of concern, of horror, Jasmine knew was on her face wasn't faked. But it wasn't due to thinking her beloved brother was an abuser. Heidi had it all worked out. Without even hearing other ways Josh had supposedly hurt Heidi, Jasmine knew that they'd all be similar injuries. Ones that didn't allow proof.

She knew Josh knew them all. Their father had been a genius at hiding his abuse. Heidi listed a couple of more instances where Josh had supposedly hurt her, leaving no evidence. A trip that landed her on her ass and left her whiplashed, saying she hadn't been watching where she was going. Pulling her hair straight up on her head until she capitulated. Both stories Heidi had heard from her and Josh's past.

"So...you agree that I should have custody of Bella for now," she said when the woman fell silent, still pacing. "Since you can't have her yet, and we have to get her away from Josh." She sat on crossed fingers on that one. Feeling like she was betraying her brother just by saying the horrible words aloud.

She had to defuse the conversation and get Heidi out of her home. Then think about calling the police. Or at least Greg.

She'd let Heidi in. There was no restraining order to prevent Heidi from being there. And she wasn't attempting to see Bella without her court-ordered supervision. To the contrary, she'd come after the toddler's bedtime.

"I think I can have her." Heidi stopped right in front of her. A look in her eye that Jasmine didn't like at all. For the first time since she'd seen her former sister-in-law on her doorstep, fear seeped through Jasmine. And her first thought was Bella. Keeping herself between Heidi and the little girl's bedroom door.

"The court said five years," she said softly, still hoping to rationalize their way out of this. "It's only been two. That's not me or Josh stipulating, that's the court."

"The court says generally it's five years before I can petition," Heidi said. "But when I show that Josh is the one who's abusive, they'll believe that he was abusive back then, too, which I claimed, if you remember, and they'll realize I've been a victim all along."

"I saw you attack him, Heidi," she said now. "He hadn't done anything to you. He'd just told you that he was giving Bella to me for the weekend so the two of you could work some things out."

"He was trying to take her away from me then, too," Heidi said. "I couldn't let him do that."

An admission of abuse.

Josh had been trying to protect his daughter. With good cause, as it turned out. Thank God he'd been home when Heidi had finally lost it and started to shake the baby uncontrollably that day…had gone into the nursery and saved Bella from serious harm…

"I think you should go," Jasmine said, putting her hands on both arms of the chair as she started to rise.

With one strong shove, Heidi pushed her back down.

"Don't think you're going to pawn me off like you did before, missy," she spat. "I'm not going away this time. I know my rights. I'm the victim here. The victim!" Spittle shot from her mouth to Jasmine's face on the last *v*.

Heidi grabbed Jasmine's hair, wrapping her hand in it, even as Jasmine reached up to try to free herself. With Heidi's hand tangled at her head, she was able to stand, wincing at the sharp pain in her scalp.

Heidi yanked, but she wouldn't cry out. With her body bent sideways, she used both hands to try to free the other woman's hand from her hair. To knock Heidi off balance. Trip her up. But Heidi was quick. Agile. She'd been a runner in high school. Had always been in good physical shape.

As long as Jasmine kept herself between Heidi and Bella's door, she'd be okay.

"I'm warning you, Jasmine. You think you and Josh

are going to keep me from my daughter, *my* only real family, you're wrong. You got that?" The words came through gritted teeth.

Her head felt like her scalp could come loose at any minute. But Heidi wasn't even attempting to get to Bella. "I got it," she said.

"Good then. I don't want to hear another word about you getting custody of my daughter, you understand? Josh is going down. And I'm going to take Bella and start a new life. Away from the two of you. You're poisonous. Both of you. I won't have her growing up in your vile little family."

The woman gave Jasmine a shove, letting go of her hair only after the force of the shove gave her one more stab of pain so severe she felt sick to her stomach.

And then she was gone. Out the door, to her car and down the drive.

Leaving Jasmine with a god-awful headache, and, she saw as she looked down, a piece of evidence.

GREG HAD BEEN heading to his home gym when his phone rang. Seeing his newly entered speed dial contact come up, he grabbed it up. She'd seen his missed call.

Was calling back.

A good sign.

"Can you come over?" The words, alarming in themselves, didn't grab him as much as the weak thread in her voice.

"Of course," he said, turning from the bedroom-turned-gym toward the master suite where he'd traded his jeans for basketball shorts. "What's up?"

"I…need you to come. I don't know if I should call the police or not, but…can you hurry?"

Fumbling to get into a flannel shirt over his workout T-shirt, Greg was on full alert. "Are you hurt? Is Bella?" Had Josh been there?

"No, Bella's fine. Still asleep. And I'm…fine. Just…"

He'd button up in the car. Was working his way one-handed into his jeans.

"Is someone there?"

"Not anymore."

Her brother had shown her his true colors. And she'd called him. "You need to call the police, Jasmine." They couldn't quibble on that one. "He could come back."

"He?" For the first time since he'd picked up, he heard the fire of her strength in her voice. "Who?"

"Who was there?" She'd said not any more when he'd asked if someone was there.

"Heidi."

Not at all the answer he'd been expecting.

Grabbing his keys and the gun he didn't always carry, he headed for the garage door and listened as she gave him a two-sentence brief of the meeting.

"Hang up and call the police and call me right back," he told her, pushing the button to open the garage door and starting his SUV at the same time.

He was almost half an hour away. The Santa Raquel police were five minutes away. Max.

Heidi could still be in the area.

While Jasmine made her call, Greg sped to the free-way and made a call of his own. To the Santa Barbara police department, asking them to do a wellness check on Josh Taylor.

Just in case he'd been wrong again.

And to reassure himself that the man wasn't going to be hurting someone, too.

Chapter Fifteen

She'd been crying, Greg noticed. Her eyes were red rimmed. Completely devoid of makeup. In black fleece pants and a cream-colored fleece-looking sweatshirt, she looked fragile to him. He'd been fully prepared for that. Was ready for panic and more tears. As ready as he ever was.

He'd been prepared to help her through as best he could.

And yet she stood in her doorway, telling the officers who were leaving she was just fine, in a voice that sounded—just fine.

In the half hour it had taken Greg to get to her, she'd regained her composure. For a second there, he felt…not needed. Superfluous.

Missed a step as he strode toward her. Or rather, paused while attempting to stride toward her.

She glanced over and saw him. Held his gaze. He hurried up the walk, passing the uniformed officers on his way, flashing his ID but not stopping to speak with them.

"My brother wanted to come, but I told him to stay put," she said as she shut her front door behind them. "Bella never even woke up, and I don't want him anywhere near the place where Heidi was in a terror. She'd find a way to blame it on him. She'll find a way, anyway, I'm sure, but at least if he's home, he has an alibi. Well, not really, since he's there alone, but..."

So not quite as composed as he'd first thought. Which made more sense to him. And yet...her rambling didn't irritate him in the least. He wanted to hear it, strangely enough. Wanted any and all parts of her she'd share with him.

A thought he might examine further later. Or not.

"He's got his alibi," he said when she paused for breath. "I called the local police to do a wellness check on him, and they've already reported back. They've warned him not to open the door and to call 911 if she comes to his place. There's also an APB out on her in Santa Raquel and Santa Barbara. I'm sure she'll be in custody before morning."

Jasmine's mouth fell open. She stared at him, standing there in his jeans and flannel shirt that were both now fastened properly, and then she smiled. Not a full-bodied expression. The slight upward turn of her lips didn't encompass her eyes. Or even much of her face. But it was there.

So was he.

And that was good.

"I SHOULDN'T HAVE asked you to come all the way over here." Standing there, smiling up at the handsome detective like some kind of besotted idiot, Jasmine suddenly felt self-conscious. Far too aware that she had a huge problem of falling for the protector with power.

Because she was falling hard for this one.

For the first time in her life, she hadn't needed Josh to come racing over and hold her hand through the trauma.

Even figuratively. She'd needed to know that he was okay. Needed to warn him about Heidi. But she hadn't *needed* him. She'd known Greg was on his way, and that was enough.

"I needed to come." His response sent her into another tizzy. What did that mean? Was there some investigative reason she didn't know about that required his presence?

They were standing there looking at each other like a couple of infatuated high school sweethearts.

He took her hand. "Let's go sit down," he said, leading the way to the dining table that he'd passed before on his way out to her deck. Wrapping her fingers around his, she nudged them in another direction. Decorated in deeps reds and golds, with green accents, and earth-tone porcelain floors with hand-spun wool rugs, the family room was her peaceful place. In the daytime sun shone in from the two clerestory windows set high above the wall of windows that faced the ocean. Her home was only one story, but the cathedral ceilings gave the room a spacious feel.

She could have taken one of the two rocking armchairs, left the other for him. Instead, she led him to the sectional they complemented, rounding the big square table that held court in the middle of the entire conversation area. The wall-mounted flat-screen television was hardly noticeable to her. What she loved were the three walls filled with intermittent bookcases that not only held more than one hundred of her favorite books, but many other random things that made her feel good. The colorful painted pony she'd picked up on a trip to Chicago with Wynne. A wooden angel that was in a flying position with hearts in her hands. That had come from a friend from college upon their graduation…

He was touching the back of her head and she realized she'd turned as she'd perused the room, seeking out the feel goods automatically.

Reaching a hand up immediately, she covered the small bald spot just beneath the crown of her head. "I'm going to be wearing ponytails for a while," she said, self-conscious again. Out of nowhere came a memory of an episode of a sitcom when a jealous woman had convinced her ex's new girlfriend to shave her head.

It wasn't like Greg was attracted to her. Or that she wanted him to be. Not really. Not the part of her that knew better. And it wasn't like baldness was a turnoff anyway. Just because the writers of a television show played it that way didn't make it so...

He pushed her hand away. Rubbed his thumb gently across the spot. "Does it hurt badly?" he asked.

Oh God, not unless you called tingles running through your whole body pain.

"It's a little tender," she managed. "But...my dad used to yank me by my hair when I turned my back to walk away from him and didn't do it fast enough. I've got a tough scalp." She almost gulped on that last bit. Needing to push his hand away from her.

And to move her head slowly beneath it, too. Savoring the feel of him.

She knew she should be shaking in fear. Or residual PTSD from an attack reminiscent of years of abuse. Instead, she sat there trembling at this man's touch.

Wanting to bury herself in his arms and cry a little.

Why did life have to be so hard?

And so...wonderful at times, too?

"The police took the hair," she blurted. She couldn't let anything happen. She'd be glad later. "I guess they can get her fingerprints or DNA off it or something. Seems like a lot of resources being spent on pulled hair, but…"

He'd dropped his hand, was sitting with her, neither of them leaning back, on the edge of the sofa. Unlike the wicker bench out back, her sofa was plenty big enough to contain him. And yet she felt as though he dwarfed the room.

And he was frowning.

"What?" she asked.

He shook his head. Studied her. And then said, "It's just—your father, pulling his daughter by her hair… and…just the things I know… He should be in prison, but instead, he's a respected businessman living a good life, from what I can see. And your exes… *Mike*…" He said the word with an intonation that led her to wonder if he knew she'd been talking about Desmond Williamson. "He should definitely be in jail. And now Heidi. You don't think punishing an abuser is worth the resources needed to do so?"

What she thought was that he was suddenly in a space where she didn't want him. Jumping up from the couch, she walked around the table, between the chairs and stood just in front of the television set.

He was talking about family. About those you loved.

"They're ill, Greg," she said, trying to fight her way through the confusion he'd just splashed all over her. "But there's still good in them. A lot of good. More good than bad."

He didn't say anything for a while, and she fidgeted, tapping her bare heel on the cold floor, hugging her sides. She'd pushed Josh into a table, and he'd had to get stitches. In technical terms, that could make her an abuser. She was her father's daughter, after all. Hadn't only grown up with him, as Josh had, but she also had his genes.

"People have to pay when they commit crimes," he finally said. "It's not only the law, it's the boundary that makes society possible."

"You're just seeing it from a law enforcement point of view," she shot back. "But there are other things to consider. Like…" A little girl fearing that her younger brother was going to get hurt at her expense. Or get hurt, period.

Rubbing his hands together slowly, he sat with his forearms on his knees, watching her. And she heard her words from his perspective.

"I'm not protecting Josh, if that's what you're thinking," she said, growing more rigid by the second. "If I thought my brother had ever hurt anyone, I'd be the first one insisting that he get help. Covering for him would not only hurt him, it would put Bella at risk, and if you think I'm ever going to let anyone hurt her, you don't know me at all." Her tone was biting now. She didn't care. She hugged herself tighter. She could fight them all.

Alone if she had to.

"I don't think you're covering for him."

Greg's words knocked her off her axis. She stood there, openmouthed, not sure what to do with them.

"You believe me? You really trust that I'm not lying to you?"

"I trust you to tell me the truth. I'd already reached that point before now."

Okay. Wow. Well, what did she do with that? Dropping her arms, Jasmine moved closer to him. Plopping on the edge of the armchair closest to his side of the couch.

"So, back to what I was saying. It's not that I think

what my father, or…any of them…did was okay, it's just that…"

She didn't know what. If they went to jail, she should, too? Or—

"I just always try to put myself in other people's shoes," she said now, pretty sure she was being honest. With him, yes, but with herself. Or was it that she saw herself through her perceived views others had of her? Her counselor had suggested the theory. She'd never identified with it before.

But now…

"It's just because you're a cop," she blurted when things seemed to jumble up again. "You see the actions, not the people."

"I've only been a cop for a couple of years."

She stared at him. "But you're a detective. You don't just jump to that grade level."

So now he wasn't whom she thought he'd been? Whom he led her to believe he was? Or had she just made the leap on her own? What the hell…

"For the first ten years after I graduated from college, I practiced law," he told her, bowing his head and then raising it again to look her in the eye. "I went through the academy with the express purpose of working in an investigative capacity for the prosecutor's office. You don't always have to do time on the streets, depending on the circumstances."

Wait. What? He was a lawyer? That made no sense to her. Who went from being a lawyer to being a cop? For one thing, the pay was less. Unless he'd been disbarred? But then he wouldn't pass the background check to be an officer, would he?

"Why am I only finding this out now?" She got out the

easiest question to ask. Easier maybe because it was the one screaming most loudly in her head at the moment.

"Because I hadn't realized that being your friend was so important to me before now."

She stared. Openmouthed again. Like some dimwitted donkey who couldn't hold an intelligible conversation.

"As a detective, investigating a case, my past, or any part of my personal life, wasn't important."

He wanted to be her friend. In her life. On a personal level. She could hardly take it in. Wanted to laugh out loud. Throw herself in his arms and hang on tight.

She wanted to tell Lila. And Wynne.

She sat there, wrapping her arms around herself again. "You told me about your parents," she pointed out inanely. Looking for the lies. For the things she couldn't see when she entered into personal relationships. Those things that would smack you upside the head when you least expected them, which made you most vulnerable to them.

Heidi's attack that evening… That would be nothing compared to the possibility of having Greg turn on her. And not just because of his mammoth size, which didn't scare her at all.

"I needed you to talk to me."

"You told me about your parents because you needed me to talk to you?"

"Put people at ease, make it a give and take, and it's easier for them to talk." He dropped his gaze, and she had a sudden clear moment. An insight. And blurted out before she could question it.

"How many people have you told?" She held his gaze fiercely.

"In recent years?" He didn't look away.

Clasping her hands together in her lap, she didn't relent. "In your adult life."

"One."

"Me." He said nothing, did nothing, in response. "You told me because you wanted me to know," she replied. "Maybe it was the other, too, but you wanted me to know."

Would have been nice if he'd told her he was a lawyer, too. He'd know even more about helping her and Josh wade through the issues facing them in Josh's case. But then, he had a job to do. Giving legal advice wasn't it. And…he'd told her about his parents, even before he'd known he wanted to be friends with her. That mattered.

Rising, Jasmine went to join him back on the couch.

HE'D KNOWN TELLING her was important. That he stood to lose her trust if he didn't tell her about his past. But now, with the prosecutor thing out there and her sitting so close and still somewhat vulnerable from her recent attack, Greg wondered if maybe he'd said enough.

"What kind of law did you practice?" The first words out of her mouth told him he'd called that one wrong.

Taking a breath, much like he used to do when dealing with Liv, he dived in. "I was a prosecutor. In Santa Barbara. William and I used to sound cases off each other. We partnered with each other a time or two, as well." He'd been the lead. William had been his second.

And he didn't regret, at all, the current status of their professional partnership—him working at William's pleasure.

Her shock shone from her eyes. She didn't leave the couch. He saw that as a good sign. And knew, deep down, that he'd had to tell her. Now that he had to be her friend.

To help her through when Josh was convicted.

Because no matter what his ex had or had not done, Josh Taylor had committed a crime.

"You and William worked together? You were… You…"

He could almost feel the turbulent wave of thoughts speeding through her mind. And waited for whatever outcome she reached. He could be playing her to help his friend and peer of many years. It wouldn't be illegal for him to be doing so.

Immoral, maybe, but the court didn't care. Unethical behavior could be a problem. But there was a very clear line, and he hadn't crossed that, either. And wouldn't be if he was using her to get William the information he needed.

He wasn't using her, actually. But he wouldn't blame her for thinking he was. In the beginning, the possibility had been there, on his list.

In truth, he couldn't even tell her when he'd eliminated that option. He just knew it had left the scene.

She was quiet for so long he considered getting up and leaving. Thinking maybe that would be the kindest thing.

But his reason for offering his friendship to begin with—other than the fact that she was in for a huge upheaval when her brother was convicted—kept him sitting there.

"You're going to have to decide." He dropped the statement into the room when he'd reached his limit of doing nothing. "You trust me or you don't."

She looked at him then, and the pleading in her gaze got to him. Deep. "Can I ask a few more questions first?"

So unexpected. A calm, rational request he could grant. "Yes."

"Why?"

"Why did I come to talk to you in the first place? Why didn't I tell you I was a prosecutor?"

"Why did you quit being one? And why did you become a detective?"

He wasn't going to get off easy. Nothing about this woman was turning out to be easy. And yet, facing her, the words came much easier than he'd ever have expected.

"As an attorney, I'm bound to present only the evidence that makes it past all of the laws that protect perpetrators. I was not only stifled, but I was oftentimes dependent on the detectives who investigated my cases to find admissible evidence that would allow me to do my job in a way that sat well with me. As I grew more and more frustrated, it became clear to me that I'd be happier doing the investigating and making damned sure that I brought every conceivable angle to the prosecutor so that he could be happy doing his job well."

That was the more generic answer. One he'd repeated ad nauseam when his decision had first become public knowledge. Before that, actually. It had started with his parents.

"I'm guessing there were specific cases that prompted the frustration?"

He sat back, enjoying the largeness of her sectional. Of the room. Not sure what to do about her, though. In all of the times he'd talked about his most recent career choice, all of the times he'd given the same basic answer, not once had anyone delved deeper. Or seen beyond. At least not out loud.

Not even Liv.

"There was one," he told her. "A drug dealer, a higher-up, not one of the street hoods. We'd known about him for years. Law enforcement longer than that. They wanted him bad. His lawyer got phone records thrown out, there'd been a piece of physical evidence compromised and a star witness refused to testify. The guy walked when I and everyone else in that room knew he was guilty."

"He'll make a mistake. They always do, right? At least that's what they say on TV."

If only real life emulated the life Hollywood created— or better put, if only Hollywood told the full story. Ever.

"He did," he said, feeling the rock in his gut with as much discomfort then as when he'd first heard the news. "He raped a woman and is serving fifteen years."

Greg had been unable to get the man off the streets, and he'd gone on to rape a woman. Not Liv. But like Liv, he'd broken into that woman's home and irrevocably changed her life forever.

Liv had explained that part to him. About the joy she'd lost. And he'd never forgotten.

The day he'd won that man's conviction, after spending weeks with the victim's testimony, living over and over the grisly details of the case, the pain and suffering that should never have happened, Greg had handed in his resignation.

He wasn't going to get them all as a detective, either. There would still be inadmissible evidence. Even mistakes made. But now he had the freedom to spend every working minute of every day doing nothing but going after them…

His thoughts were interrupted by the touch of a soft hand, sliding on top of his. "I've made my decision."

He couldn't believe how hard his heart was pounding as he looked over at her.

"I've decided to let myself trust you," she said softly, her makeup-less, red-rimmed eyes wide and bright and beautiful. "And I want to be your friend."

Chapter Sixteen

She thought he might kiss her. Hoped he would.

He didn't.

Instead he told her about a woman, Liv, who sounded an awful lot like Heidi, minus the physical brutality. A woman who was emotionally scarred to the point that she struggled at times not to wallow in the drama of it all.

"Not that you and I are…like, dating, or in that kind of relationship…" Her heart sank to the cold porcelain floor beneath her feet as he spoke. "Not yet, anyway." Her heart flew up to the clouds. "But I need you to know, from the outset, what you're getting into," he told her while she managed to sit calmly a foot or so away from him, listening.

"I'm not good with the drama," he told her. "It makes me feel helpless, which irritates me."

She nodded, couldn't think of a guy offhand who *was* into it.

"I'm serious," he told her. "I can be an unsympathetic ass at times."

"Like when I called tonight and you rushed right over here?"

He was looking at her, and she wished she could tell what he was thinking. Wouldn't change what she'd said.

Or might say. She couldn't play games. There were too many real minefields to cross in life without creating more. None of which negated her desire to know his mind.

"I'm serious," he told her, effectively brushing off what she'd said as though his jumping in his car and heading to her immediately was inconsequential. "I'm not good with emotional breakdowns. I'm detached. I tend to come across as cold and retreat to my gym at the soonest possible moment."

"You have a gym?" She was learning more about him in ten minutes than she'd learned in two weeks. Facts only, but she'd been gathering her opinions about the character of the man all along.

"A bedroom with a full wall of mirrors, free weights and a home gym. There's a treadmill in there, too," he added, "but I'm not much into running as a form of exercise."

Neither was she—into running. She liked inline skating, though.

With a sideways glance at her, he quirked an eyebrow. "I'm getting the impression you aren't taking me seriously here."

"I'm not finding anything to take," she told him. "You're going on like you're some kind of freak man or something."

"Liv suffered from my inability to sit through the tough moments, or hours, with her. I've had a victim or two over the years who was negatively impacted by my lack of empathy. I tend to prefer to stick to the facts."

"Okay." She didn't know what else to say. "If you're expecting me to convince you otherwise, to tell you that I'm sure you'll come through if I need you to, or something, I'm sorry to disappoint you. Or if you're expecting me to find you lacking…same response." She'd never had anyone give a friendship precursor before. Or had one come with warnings.

He looked at her. She looked back. "You've had your share of being blindsided by the people you let into your life," he said. "I don't want to be one of those people."

In that moment, she fell in love.

HE NEEDED TO kiss her. To take her into his arms and not let go for at least the rest of the night. They'd agreed to become friends, not lovers.

He touched her sweet face, hating that she'd once again been physically attacked that night. Hating more that she'd come through it, taken it, as though it wasn't all that big of a deal.

Said far too much about the life she'd lived.

And explained even more clearly why she championed her brother so much.

Her fingers reached up, and while he was thinking she was going to pull his hand away, she touched his face, instead. "I've been wanting to do this since the first time you showed up at my door," she told him. And then, leaning forward, she pressed her lips against his.

It was just a light touch. Nothing at all come-hither. Maybe even just a thank-you. His body reacted as though he'd been prepped for liftoff, though. Immediate and intense, the response shocked him. Embarrassed him a little.

He wrapped his hand around the back of her neck and pulled her closer, supporting her head as he pressed harder against her, opening his mouth over hers, ready to coax her to do the same.

Her tongue met his without any need of teasing.

Tempting him further. Urging him to pull her body closer, then to lean over, laying them both back on the couch with him half on top of her, half beside her.

He lifted his free hand, maybe heading toward her face again, but it was shaking so hard he let it drop at her waist. Held on. And continued to explore the taste of her. Her lips moved with his, opening, accepting, giving back. She didn't quite suckle him, but they did this thing, this kind of moving against him, it was like they held his lips, caressed them—all in a kiss.

And her tongue…it slow danced, teased, like none other.

What the hell? Kissing was kissing. The get-through-it-to-get-to-it part.

He didn't rush to it. Wanted to linger right where he was. Aware of every second. He was going to make love to her. He had no doubt about that now.

But…

When his body was perilously close to exploding from the pleasure of her—and he hadn't yet even touched her breasts—Greg sat up, pulling her with him.

"I want you so badly it hurts," he said, not quite evenly—and breathing a little hard. With one downward glance, she'd know the state he was in. His jeans were pinching him. There was no point in trying to deny the fact. "But when we make love, I want it to be something we do because we're both eager to get there before we actually do get there."

So he was a frickin' poet now? A bad one? "I don't want it to be in the heat of the moment," he clarified. And then shook his head. His brain was definitely all in his pants at the moment. "I want it to be a decision we've reached before we get to the heat of the moment." At least the third time was still the charm. In some world.

"You want to give me time to make sure I know what I'm doing," Jasmine said, no longer touching him, but smiling as she faced the black television screen.

With a sideways shrug, he nodded. Probably. He couldn't be completely sure. He'd had the thought, knew that's why he'd stopped. On the surface.

It was the deeper crap. Stuff lurking there, bugging him, too. Not only was this friendship with Jasmine Taylor new territory for him—what had just happened, the kissing, that all had been pretty much different, too.

He couldn't remember a time, ever, in his entire life, when he'd struggled to stay on the surface. The surface was the only life he was capable of living. Right up top there with facts, body parts and explosive orgasms.

She probably only had orgasms when she was emotionally involved. Monogamously, emotionally involved. Sex, for her, was likely the seal on a deal. The one intimacy no one else got…

He probably needed to get home and work out.

But didn't want to get up.

Or leave her. He leaned over and kissed her again. Deeply.

And his phone rang.

The Santa Barbara police had just picked up Heidi, less than a mile from Josh's home. Another squad stopped by Josh's house to check on him and found him asleep in his bed.

He hadn't been expecting Heidi.

But she'd clearly been heading for him.

JASMINE WENT IN to check on Bella while Greg took his phone call. It was close to midnight. Jasmine was generally in bed asleep by then and wouldn't be checking on her niece, but she went anyway. She needed to reassure herself that the toddler was right there, sleeping peacefully. Content. Secure.

A peek in her door was all it took. A glimpse of those small cheeks and the covers moving up and down in the regular rhythm she'd grown used to seeing.

She stopped to refresh herself, got a look at her face in the mirror and pulled out her makeup drawer, before sliding it closed without reaching inside.

He was probably getting ready to head out. Might even be waiting for her by the front door. She didn't blame him. It was late.

She was off the next day but had no idea if prosecutors-turned-detectives worked Saturdays.

And didn't want him to leave.

Her heart skipped ahead a beat. *Oh my God!* Before that phone call, she'd made out with Greg Johnson. And had been so turned on she couldn't think about it without a resurge of that heat.

Far better than that…they'd made a formal declaration of personal friendship.

It sounded so high school.

And felt so adult. So real life. *Her* life.

Pausing when the front door came into view and he wasn't there, she also paused in her chain of thoughts. They'd said "friendship."

The kind that came with benefits, obviously. That much was pretty clear now. But…

He was sitting right where she'd left him. Her gaze went of its own accord to the fly of his jeans. Like that was somehow the reason he hadn't moved. Which was ridiculous. Guys might have a hard time moving when they were kicked in certain places, but a guy could walk with a hard-on.

"She still asleep?" he asked, watching as she curled up not too far away from him, tucking her feet up beside her.

"Yep. Amazing how so much can happen and little ones sleep blissfully through it," she said. Thinking of the violence—not what came after—at the moment. How many years had her mom suffered while she and Josh slept, unaware of the man their father really was? How many years before they'd caught on?

And become his victims, too.

But no more. Her father couldn't hurt her anymore with his blows and taunts and lashing out. And he wasn't going to infiltrate her home in any other way, either.

Bella had slept through the violence earlier that night. There couldn't be any more coming after. No chance that precious little girl would grow up with that fear in her home.

"Since you came with warnings, I guess I should, too," she told Greg before she could second-guess herself.

He grinned. "Shoot," he said, his lids lowered in a way that called out to her. She liked him this way—all relaxed and laid-back.

But had to say what she had to say.

"I'm not looking for forever," she said, making her intent as clear as possible. "Not now. Not ever."

"Ever's a long time off," he said, still with a hint of a smile—not so much on his lips, but in his eyes.

She turned, frowning, and took his hand. "I mean it, Greg. I am not going to get married. Or even live with a partner ever again."

She'd had a hard past and scars that were not going to go away.

"Because of the chance that you'd end up with an unhealthy partner."

She'd told him her dark secrets. Now he had to understand that she'd made some healthy choices and they weren't going to change.

"Partially, yes."

"You think that somewhere inside me lurks a temper that could turn violent."

"No." She shook her head. "But that's just it… I never think it. I mean, I know you aren't a violent man. But I also know that I am predisposed to not be able to discern if you were. But it's not even just that…"

She was being pushed from the inside out, as though her life depended on speaking up.

"We're in the beginning stages right now," she said. She was falling back on things she'd learned in counseling; they'd helped her to finally understand a lot of what motivated actions she'd never before been able to recognize, much less understand. "Everything's new and feels so great. There's an excitement unlike any other kind in finding someone who's a mate for our soul."

She heard the words and wished she'd dialed back a bit. Expected him to balk at the emotional, drama-ridden bit. His gaze was focused, seemingly intent. As though she not only had his full visual attention, but his auditory concentration, as well.

"However long that lasts—could be weeks or months, even years depending on how much time you spend together—things are good. Kind of like the honeymoon phase of a new marriage. But there are always parts of people that you don't know until you live through unexpected circumstances with them. Like a tire blowing out on a deserted road. Or the death of someone close. And then there are the life choices—a career change. A sudden need for adventure or the desire to wander to new places. Midlife crises. Or goals left unmet. Maybe even an unexpected need to procreate. Add to that any financial challenges, decorating difference and squeezing the toothpaste from the middle or not..."

Turning his hand over, she slowly laced their fingers together. One by one.

"Or a brother being prosecuted," he said.

And she knew what he was telling her. Something she'd already pretty much figured out for herself. Just because Heidi had shown tonight that she wasn't healed didn't mean that Josh wasn't also an abuser. There was nothing on earth that proclaimed that there couldn't be two abusers in a home. Or that one took precedence over another.

This wasn't two spouses duking it out in divorce court. As far as the court suspected, or at least had to entertain, Heidi and Josh were equally abusive.

If that was the case, they'd both have to pay.

"I know his case isn't just going to go away, if that's what you're worried about," she said now. Greg nodded.

"I also know that entering into another life-partner relationship is not healthy for me." She brought them right back to where she'd started. "I'm always going to be looking, Greg. Fearing the unknown. And by doing so, creating my own reality. Bringing on the bad. They say that what you put your mind to, you get. Or something like that. And I can't be in a live-in monogamous relationship without having those thoughts."

She knew how people could do things they'd never expect themselves to do or in a million years want to do. Desperate circumstances created desperate actions.

Like pushing your brother so hard he had to get stitches.

"So you could be in a live-in relationship if it wasn't monogamous?"

He wasn't smiling. Was he asking for...

"No," she said. "I can't be in a sexual relationship that isn't monogamous, either." Saying it out loud like that sounded so...uptight. She came with strict rules of all kinds, apparently.

"So, if we were to...say...be friends who had a sexual relationship, I'd be the only one you were sharing that kind of friendship with?" He nodded as he spoke, like he could already see that happening.

Even after she'd let him know, quite clearly, that their friendship would never be more than that.

"Yes." The word came out with a sound of intent. And maybe a bit of cheer.

She hadn't been describing their future, she'd been defining what it couldn't be, but...

"Good, then," he said, leaning over to kiss her again. "Because I'm all for a monogamous friendship with you."

He was pushing her back down to the couch. Slowly. Gently. Giving her time to object. "And you understand that it goes no further than that," she said, not objecting so much as stalling.

"I do." He was looking her right in the eye, all humor gone for the moment, as he said those two words.

She kissed him then, pulling him down to her as much as being laid down. And then stopped once more. "And this is a given, but should be mentioned—I come as a package deal with Bella right now. And for however long it takes."

"Oh, lady, I've got that one," he said, lying fully on top of her. "I believe I've just signed on for a long-term plan without having kids of my own, which I happen to like, by the way. I'm good with kids. They seem to like me, too, what little I've had to do with them. I just don't have a lot of experience so wouldn't want to say…raise one on my own, as Josh has been doing. But I'm open to learning. So…yeah, I'm fully prepared for whatever comes with Bella…"

His mouth was on hers as his voice drifted off, and she couldn't think after that.

Not about violence, or court, or never having kids of her own. She couldn't think about not having…any-thing…because in his arms, she felt like she had every-thing she'd ever need.

Chapter Seventeen

She didn't sleep with him that night. She came pretty darn close. About as close as you could come without completing the act. He was the one who'd stopped them. But she was glad he had. Even in the moment.

Being with him felt…necessary. Rushing things just didn't. They had time. *She* needed time.

And yet, as the weekend transpired, she was burning with the need to have that final connection there between them. Burning on the back burner, as she gladly welcomed her brother and his caseworker Marianne, who'd agreed to a longer weekend visitation with Bella. The little girl knew nothing about her mother's visit the night before, the violence or her subsequent arrest, but Josh still needed to see her. To be close.

They watched a couple of kiddie movies. Made chocolate chip cookies. And had hot dogs for dinner. Marianne sat in a corner of the dining room a good part of the afternoon, working on a laptop and going out on the deck to make calls.

Josh was hoping that when William Brubaker got to the office Monday morning and heard about his victim's arrest, he'd drop the charges.

She hoped, too, but didn't count on it. She did think,

though, that Josh had a better chance of winning the case, that his attorney had a better shot at showing the court that Heidi was manipulating them, lying, than he'd had before.

She didn't tell Josh about Greg. And wasn't sure why. Maybe because of Wynne's reaction. What if Josh, like her friend, warned her off? Reminded her of her relationship challenges? Told her he didn't have a good feeling about him?

Maybe she didn't tell him just because she wanted to savor her new friendship privately for a bit. Or maybe she felt a bit off, finding this new happiness while her brother's life was falling apart. Almost at his expense.

Because his life *was* falling apart. But if it hadn't been for Heidi filing charges, she'd never have met Greg. Maybe the thing to do was just as Greg had suggested the other night when he'd stopped their lovemaking. They should wait until after the case was done.

Anything else just further complicated an already complicated situation.

She couldn't have Josh worrying that she was losing focus. Or that Greg was.

For that reason, she decided that she shouldn't have Greg around Bella much, either. At three, the little girl had a tendency to blurt out whatever was on her mind with no idea of nuances or potential consequences. She didn't want Bella telling Josh that she'd had dinner with Greg. Or watched TV with him. Or that he'd been kissing Auntie JJ.

And she most definitely was not going to put herself in a position that would require her to tell Bella not to tell her father. Not about Greg. Or anything else personal.

So she contented herself with phone calls. A lengthier one on Sunday night even than Saturday.

"It's kind of good, you know," she told him while lying in her bed in the dark. "Having this time. I know you're there. That we're here. And yet I'm going about my normal life, too."

"And is normal life giving you qualms about us... being here?"

"None." Which surprised her. A lot. "It's kind of a sweet agony. Thinking about you. Wanting. Knowing I'm going to have you and yet...not having."

"Like looking at all the presents under the Christmas tree and knowing you'll get to open them, but not until later," he said, his voice a low, sleepy drawl. He'd told her he was in bed, too. In the dark.

And nude.

She was in her favorite nightgown. She had a child in the house and had already told him how she always slept with her door open. Wanted Bella to feel free and comfortable about crawling into bed with her if she wanted.

"Yeah, like Christmas," she said now, wishing he was there with her. "Except that at Christmastime, you only get to unwrap once and then the anticipation is over."

"You planning to unwrap over and over?"

"Oh, yeah." She chuckled. And then, thinking about the morning, sobered. "Josh thinks William's going to reconsider the charges against him," she said, treading a fine line. Greg couldn't tell her what the prosecutor was going to do. Couldn't tell her strategy. Not ethically.

And she wouldn't have him any other way.

"I'd like to see him with Bella," he came back, leaving her to read, or not read, more into the statement.

"I could arrange a dinner here," she said. "His next visitation is Wednesday night. You could join us."

"Let me think about it," Greg said. "I'd need to be the one to set it up. And he'd have to agree. And frankly, I don't see his lawyers allowing that. I wouldn't. Your brother's relationship with his daughter really has no bearing on this case."

Not on Greg's side of it. She got that.

"So why do you want to see them together?"

"Because I want to see the man you see."

Scooting down further under the covers, she relaxed. Well and truly. For the first time since Josh had woken her up to tell her he was bringing his daughter to her. "You believe me now, don't you? You see Heidi for who she is."

His silence could have been agreement. Or not. She didn't ask. She didn't need to. He believed her and was on their side.

GREG HUNG UP the phone Sunday night, climbed out of bed and went in to lift weights. *You see Heidi for who she is.* Jasmine's statement kept playing over and over in his mind.

She was right. He *did* see. The things Heidi had told him about Jasmine and her relationships, that Jasmine was afraid of herself, of getting violent when things got intense, about her breaking up with her lovers when she did get that angry. Heidi had sounded so convincing because she'd been describing herself. He saw that now.

And he wanted to believe, really wanted to believe that Josh Taylor was an innocent victim all the way. But he just couldn't. The doctor's report, the evidence that put Heidi at Josh's house, not at the gym, at the time of the injury…and even the photo—it was the opposite wrist as Jasmine had said. When he'd asked Heidi about it, she'd produced another one of the other limb, saying that at first, Josh had grabbed both wrists. When he'd sprained her wrist, he'd only been holding the one.

Not information he could or would share with Jasmine.

So what if Heidi was lying about *all* of it? Not about being at Josh's house—they had the neighbor's security camera footage to prove that. But what if, on the way to the hospital, she'd paid someone to hold her wrists and then jerked herself away?

Was he being ludicrous here? Thinking such thoughts?

Or opening his mind to the truth as Jasmine had asked him to do? Open his mind to possibilities he'd never imagined.

Like falling for a woman who, like Liv, had emotional residue from a tragic past to the point of not being able to have a committed traditional relationship? He wanted what his folks had, what they'd given him: a family. A happy home life. And maybe, just maybe he did want children of his own someday. Now that he was actually waking up to the fact that he didn't want to go through life alone.

He wanted to be biologically related to someone he knew.

And here he was, nuts about a woman who wouldn't give him any of those things.

Life didn't always fit the mold.

But it usually fit. So…maybe Jasmine was right for him because she didn't need what he didn't have. She didn't need someone right there in her world, her home, sharing everything with her in the moment, like Liv had needed. His lack of empathetic powers didn't even seem to be an issue with her.

And what about Josh and Heidi Taylor? Were they both abusive spouses? Or was he not looking in the right places for the truth?

He worked out hard. Slept a little. And was already in the office when William arrived the next morning. Charges were pending against Heidi—another prosecutor would handle that case—and she was out of jail, having been warned to stay away from the Taylors or her bail could be revoked. Her visitation with her daughter would continue, in a playroom at Child Protective Services only. And for only one hour a week.

William asked Greg to go talk to her. To find out if she'd be a credible enough witness to still take her case to court. He felt, as Greg did, that the evidence against Josh Taylor was too strong to ignore.

"And what concerns me the most…" William started.

"…is the fact that he continues to deny any culpability," Greg finished for his friend and colleague. "If he admitted getting angry, grabbing her wrist to keep her from hitting him, we could maybe see a way to thinking that this was a onetime thing on his part and not an ongoing danger."

Not that the holding the wrist to avoid a blow theory was valid. The injury clearly showed that Heidi's arm was down when she was grabbed.

"My guess is he's in denial, which is almost a guarantee of future violence, or he's aware of his issues and hiding them," William agreed, sipping from the coffee he'd brought in for the both of them. In a shirt and tie, and behind his desk, William looked impressive enough.

But when he stood next to Greg in court, his five-foot-two frame next to Greg's bulk, not so much.

But anyone who underestimated William, or his ability to see right to the core of things, anyone who thought William didn't have what it took to fight to the end no matter how bitter it got, would be making a huge mistake.

"Either way, without accountability and counseling, he's a danger out there." Greg, who was sitting in his usual seat across from William, voiced a concern that had been gnawing at him with growing intensity.

"Talk to Heidi," William said. "Find out what's going on with her. Try one more time to get her to admit there were other episodes with him."

"I witnessed something this weekend." Greg had to speak up. Lives could be at risk. Jasmine and Bella's lives. "An apathy to physical abuse, almost as though, as long as one came through it without major physical damage, it wasn't a big deal. My take was that it comes from years of living with abuse as a way of life. Normalizing it. So maybe Josh has been exhibiting signs of abuse that no one paid attention to. Unexpected temper flares, for instance, that those close to him would be able to understand and explain away. Slamming a door hard enough to crack a door jamb, but maybe the jamb was old and loose anyway. Spinning the truth to suit him. Maybe, as this behavior has a tendency to do, his violence is escalating."

"Find out."

He nodded. And then continued, needing to check himself in with William. "One of the things the High-Risk Team looks for is a trigger for the escalation. Usually it's financial worry, alcohol or drug addiction, a breakup. Josh Taylor has none of those."

He showed no patterns, from what Greg could see.

And he'd seen a lot over the past couple of weeks, just by talking to Jasmine. And looking into Josh Taylor's personal affairs. Everyone who knew the guy seemed to love him. Greg had been to Play for the Win headquarters. Had asked discreet questions around some of the gyms—posing as a man looking to place his son.

He couldn't help thinking that maybe Jasmine was right. That Josh was being set up by a woman who wasn't getting what she wanted. Heidi didn't have Josh. Or her daughter. And, though she'd gotten a settlement in her divorce, it hadn't been as much as she'd might have won had she not been abusive to her ex-husband. To the contrary, Josh Taylor, of his own accord, had been more than generous with her, considering the circumstances.

Still, she wasn't living as comfortably as she once had.

"Evidence speaks," William said. "Maybe instead of looking for proof of abuse, you need to look for whatever it is that's frustrating Josh Taylor."

It was the thought he'd woken with that morning. And now had the confirmation he'd been seeking that he was on the right path.

"Start with Heidi," William suggested again. "She might tell you something if you ask the right questions." And then he grinned. "But you already planned to do that, didn't you?"

Greg didn't answer. He made a six-foot shot with his empty coffee cup into the trash can.

They had a status hearing with the court in a week and three days. William would be talking to Josh's defense prior to that to try to reach a settlement agreement. If Josh would just admit that he'd lost his temper and agree to counseling, this would all go away.

And then he wouldn't have to go find the trigger that

had set the whole thing in motion. Because as much as he wanted to believe otherwise, Greg knew it was out there.

"Just let me know whether I'll be doing this with or without Heidi's testimony," William said. He was leaving it up to Greg to decide if Heidi was still going to be a credible witness.

Greg nodded. Paid attention as he and the prosecutor discussed several other cases on the docket. Made a mental list of the actionable items he'd be taking out of the discussion. And went out to do his job.

JASMINE CALLED HER counselor Monday afternoon. Dr. Bloom Freelander worked with The Lemonade Stand but had a private office in Santa Raquel. A victim herself, Dr. Freelander had almost died at the hands of her ex-husband. These days she was married to the cop who'd investigated her now-ex. Things weren't always rosy. But in the end, she'd trusted Sam. And that trust hadn't been misplaced.

It happened. Survivors were capable of loving and being loved. Not all were destined for marriage and children. But Jasmine could still love and be loved, too, couldn't she?

"It's all about the trust," Bloom told her when they met Tuesday after school at The Lemonade Stand, where the gifted psychiatrist had offered to meet Jasmine. "Abuse strips you of your trust in yourself, which emanates outward. The only way to truly and happily love and be loved is to find a way to trust again."

They talked about Desmond, and Wynne, and Noah. About her untrustworthy track record when it came to choosing lovers.

And about the fact that Wynne had been the one to

end the one incident of verbal abuse. To get help. That she and Jasmine were still good friends. That Wynne was in a healthy relationship with someone more suited to her. And that Wynne was making wonderful contributions to society, too.

Jasmine had chosen wrong in terms of a relationship with that one. But she hadn't chosen a systematic abuser.

As the hour moved by, Jasmine's confusion grew. She'd wanted reassurance. A pat on the head. She'd wanted to be told she was allowed to be excited about her new friendship with Greg. That she was making a good choice that would serve her and her family well.

"I wish there was a magic bullet," Bloom said, her long auburn curls a compliment to the colorful scarf she wore with the light purple suit. "An ability to trust isn't something that I, or anyone else, can give you. It has to come from within you. But in my opinion, you're heading in the right direction. You're open to finding an ability to trust, which is the first step. And just as important, you're aware of your challenges," she said, her smile taking any sting there might have been in that last confirmation.

Yes, Jasmine had challenges.

"Do you think there's a possibility that I am capable of choosing a good man to spend time with?" She sat in one of the many homey little rooms used for private conversations at the Stand. Though fabrics and styles were different, each had a couch, a chair or two, a coffee table and plenty of tissues.

"Absolutely." Bloom's response gave Jasmine the first easy breath she'd taken since she'd walked over from her classroom.

"I don't want to live with a partner again. Things change. People change. You never know what's going to

come out in someone. Or what they might not be showing you."

"There are people who love each other and still maintain separate lives as well. If that's the choice that makes
you happy, then it's the right one for you. I'd urge you to
be honest from the outset, though..."

"I was." She stopped. "I am," she said. And then, looking into Bloom's compassionate, knowing eyes, she told
her all about Greg. About her brother's case. About the
investigator who was open to seeing the truth. About
feelings so intense they couldn't be denied. "It's not like
anything I've ever felt before," she told Bloom, letting
the excitement, the genuine joy out as she talked.

It wasn't perfect. It was complicated, just like Greg
had said.

"But I want it," she told Bloom.

"Then go for it."

"You think it's the right thing to do?"

Bloom just looked at her.

"You can't tell me what's right." Jasmine said what
she'd been told many times in the past. "Only I can make
that choice for myself."

"We're all in this life together." Bloom repeated something Jasmine had heard before. "And each of us has our
own unique journey to complete."

"So, let me ask you this. Do you see any obvious signs
that I'm committing emotional suicide here? Or any signs
that I'm falling back into my old patterns?"

"Do you?"

"I don't," she said, frustrated, and yet understanding,
too. She wanted guarantees. Safeguards. There weren't
any. "I really don't."

"Then that's all the answer you need."

In one sense, the meeting had been a waste of time. She hadn't had any huge insights—she, with Bloom's guidance, had already done that work—nor had she received the permission she'd been seeking. But Jasmine left the appointment with clarity anyway.

There were no sure things. But she was alive, aware and determined to live, in spite of the possibility of making mistakes.

She was also, like anyone who'd learned from their mistakes, better prepared this time around.

Chapter Eighteen

He found Josh Taylor's trigger: having his daughter around anyone who had any kind of a temper. Heidi let it all fly that week when Greg met with her. She opened up about the fights that she and Josh had had over the past six months, the time he'd held her up against a wall so she didn't go down the hall and open her daughter's bedroom door to tell her goodbye when Josh had told her she had to leave. He hadn't trusted her to say a quiet goodbye to the sleeping child.

The time he'd shoved her out the back door, causing her to fall on her knees and then shutting the door with her foot still in the jamb. Luckily she'd had on hiking boots and hadn't been seriously hurt. That time she'd been going off on him about his refusal to even consider petitioning the courts to grant her partial custody.

There were others. Every time she'd been pushing him about Bella. Getting upset with him. And every time, he'd been contrite afterward. Offering to let her stay over so she could spend quality, in-home time with her daughter.

Greg met with her twice that week, getting dates and times as accurately as she could remember. Some were spot-on, based on memories she had of where she'd been or what she'd been doing, like having to cancel a walkathon the day after her foot had been shut in the door because the appendage was too sore. He followed up the interrogation with more security-camera digital footage requests for new dates and times. Asking Heidi for various receipts, which she could provide for him. Checking phone records for repeated calls from Josh that had come to her after each incident. Looking up text messages. It was all there. Not one thing that didn't fit.

Claiming that Josh and Jasmine had her trapped and were egging her on so they could take Bella from her permanently, and because of the new charges against her, she was willing to give Greg everything. Her story was that she still loved Josh, and didn't want him in jail or even out of her life, which was why she hadn't talked about the other times she'd suffered abuse All she'd wanted was shared custody of Bella. Greg had let it be known to her that her testimony in one case could help her defense in the other.

Every night that week, he also spoke with Jasmine. Hearing how her day went. Giving her what he could of his. His work was going to cause her great pain. And yet, in the end, it could save her or Bella's lives. Josh's violence was escalating. His frustration.

And he had to know he was a danger. That was why he'd asked Jasmine to take Bella. It was all adding up.

Why he wouldn't just admit he was struggling and go into counseling, Greg could only guess. He hoped like hell that with all the new evidence, the man would agree to a plea deal during the settlement conference the next week.

In the meantime, he ached to hold Jasmine. To taste her again. So much so that on Thursday night he drove to Santa Raquel, called her and asked if he could just stop by for a minute. He was leaving the next day for a weekend in Seattle to attend a function with his parents and just needed to see Jasmine before he left.

He knew that, until the court case the following week, she'd be safe. Josh's whole life was about keeping his daughter safe. And in his mind, her safety meant Jasmine. Besides, he couldn't see either of them without his caseworker present. And lastly, Jasmine was currently giving him what he needed—nightly access to Bella via video calling—and all the support a guy could ever want.

Greg still didn't like leaving town with everything unresolved.

She greeted him at the door like a long-lost lover, and he hauled her into his arms like she was one. It had been six days since he'd kissed her. It seemed like a lot longer than that.

A lifetime longer.

There was so much he knew now. Nothing that he could ethically tell her. Or help her to understand. He could only hope that when her brother was presented with the truth, he'd do the right thing for his family.

Perhaps a domestic violence admission would hurt his professional reputation. Greg was well aware that there were scores of kids who benefited from Josh Taylor's programs. But if they were run right, surely the Play for the Win board would be able to do enough damage control to keep the nonprofit healthy. Of course, how many of those programs were supported by Josh's personal investors? Some could dry up when it became known that the great defender was an abuser himself...

One taste of Jasmine's lips, and he couldn't think about any of it. She was sweet and pure and hungry power all wrapped up in one very caring and compelling package.

She broke away from him long enough to shut the front door and lead him to the room in which he'd first kissed her. Over to the sectional couch.

"So what's this function in Seattle?" she asked, picking up a throw pillow and holding it as she sat down on the couch. In leggings and a thigh-length red sweatshirt, with her hair up in the ponytail she'd already told him she'd been wearing all week, she looked innocent and so sexy to him. His jeans were pinching him again, and he dropped down beside her, determined to control himself. They weren't going to have sex until after Josh's case was over. Hopefully that just meant seven more days. One week.

"Some celebrity client thank-you dinner given by the company my parents are overhauling. A football player I used to follow as a kid is going to be there, and so they asked me to come up."

Any other time, he'd have been pretty psyched to go. At the moment, he really did not want to get on that plane in the morning. He told her what he knew about the company. Talked for a second about the two years he'd spent playing football in Colorado as a kid, and then leaned over, hands on his thighs, to kiss her again.

He'd keep them to himself. He was just going to kiss her.

She moaned, moved closer, seeming to understand that the kiss was it. Her hands, which had taunted and tantalized him the week before, were still holding her pillow. Her tongue met his. Her lips suckled his just as he'd been remembering with sweet agony all week long.

For the past few nights, she hadn't even mentioned Josh. Or the case. Neither had he. They were separate and apart from the charges pending against her brother.

"I thought I was imagining how great this feels," she murmured in between kisses, her lips tickling his as she spoke. "How right."

Her words were like an aphrodisiac. "I've missed you this week," he told her, words coming naturally from a guy who didn't talk—or hadn't ever liked talk—during sex.

He kissed her again, deeply, his tongue doing more than just playing with hers. It was like they were mating with their clothes on. With no other body parts engaged. And yet…the connection was so intimate. So…

Jasmine groaned. Stuck her tongue in his mouth again.

And her hand landed on top of the bulge in his jeans.

SHE UNDERSTOOD HIS wanting to wait. Appreciated it. She couldn't wait anymore, though. With a boldness she'd never known herself to have, she caressed Greg's rock-hard penis through his zipped fly, needing nothing in that moment more than she needed to have him be free of the constraints.

He'd stopped kissing her the second she'd touched him. He'd pretty much frozen in general. Until her hand started moving. She glanced up at him. Saw the intense gaze in his eye as he watched her, and then she glanced down to her hand over his jeans, paying acute attention to what she was doing. He moved against her. Raising his hips. Moving them slightly from side to side. Filling her hand.

When the jeans were just too frustrating to deal with anymore, she went for the zipper, pulling it down carefully.

She got about a quarter of an inch before his hand fell on top of hers. Holding everything in place. Then he gently readjusted himself, back inside his pants.

"It's just another week," he said, his tone soft—and hoarse.

"I'm no longer sure why we're waiting," she answered back immediately. "This has nothing to do with anything but you and me. I want to show you I trust you before any court decision."

"It might not go your way."

"But I know you're doing your best, Greg. That you want the exact same thing I want. The truth. I want to show you that I trust you to find it."

He moved her hand off from him. Sat up.

"What's wrong?" What had she said?

"What if Josh loses? What if he's found guilty? Or decides that taking a plea deal is better than going to trial?"

"You think I'm using you? That I'd do this…have *sex* with you to ensure that you help Josh?"

She could kind of see it. If she was Heidi. Or someone else. But…she was hurt. Disappointed. Getting ready to cry, which was plumb dumb. If he thought… He didn't deserve…

He touched her hand, and the emotional turbulence gearing up inside her subsided. She'd just told him she trusted him, and yet she thought he'd accuse her of…

"If I thought you were using me, I'd never have kissed you to begin with."

"I kissed you first." They were looking each other right in the eye now, and that place…the space they occupied together like that…she never wanted to leave it.

"If Josh loses, you might hold me responsible," he said, still holding her gaze. "And if you do, you'll wish you hadn't slept with me."

He was thinking of her. Thinking rationally.

"And I know that if you ever think that, I'll wish it,

too." He kissed her lightly. "Once we make love, I don't want you to ever regret doing so."

"I won't regret it. No matter what. We...this that's happening between us...it's completely separate and apart from Josh's case. Please, Greg. I need to be able to trust my own mind. To make love to you without knowing if Josh wins or loses. I don't want it to be mixed up with some kind of gratitude feelings for helping us. I want it to be this..." She pointed between their two faces. "You and me. Period."

Standing, she moved over to the double French doors closing the living room off from the rest of the house. Increased the volume on the child monitor over by the television set. Pulled her top over her head, and dropped it on the floor, feeling sexy as hell as she headed slowly back toward him.

GREG RELIVED THEIR lovemaking all the way to Seattle. Through the fancy dinner. He was distracted for a short time, meeting one of his childhood heroes, a man who was bigger than he was—not an ounce overweight even at fifty—and was also now a lawyer. And then it was right back to thoughts of Jasmine on top of him on the couch, her body sliding down on his, taking in every inch of him, those breasts, firm and responsive as he splayed both hands over them as she moved with him inside her. That hair—he'd pulled it down and loved how it tangled around her shoulders, getting sweaty around her temples and at her nape.

And the look on her face, pure confidence and pleasure as she'd come all over him.

Yeah, it had been one hell of a good hour. Best lovemaking he'd ever had.

And he hoped to God she didn't regret it. She'd needed him to give her the chance to be right about trusting herself. About trusting her own mind.

And he knew that when she found out what he knew— what his investigative abilities had managed to dredge up, when she found out what he'd known before they'd made love—she wasn't going to trust him, or maybe even herself, again.

Unless Josh pleaded guilty. Everything rested on that plea. If Jasmine's younger brother would own up to his problem, he'd set them all free.

And she'd know, once and for all, that she could trust herself, because she'd chosen to make love to Greg, to partner herself with him, over staying loyal to Josh's case. She'd sensed that Greg could be trusted.

Either way it went, he couldn't have said no when she'd told him that she was exercising her belief in herself. It would be like telling a child that he knew better than the child did—like a pat on the head.

And maybe…just maybe…he hoped that she'd see that her trust in him, no matter Josh's outcome, was not misplaced. Maybe…just maybe…he hoped that she really did trust him. Because they were right for each other.

Because their friendship was legitimate.

The evening soiree was nice, but he was ready to get back to his folks' place and excuse himself to bed long before they were ready to leave. They were in the process of getting to know all the key players in the company, seeing how they interacted and with whom. They'd invited Greg so that he could enjoy himself, but they were working.

He ended up sitting out in the lobby texting with Jasmine. It was the only fun thing he could think of to do alone in Seattle on a Friday night.

His folks were talking business five minutes after they were in the car. Greg was sitting in the front passenger due to his long legs, his mother in the back seat. She'd made the decision to switch seats with him when he'd hit puberty and shot up over a foot in six months, and the arrangement had been that way ever since. While his mother discussed what she'd noticed that night, Greg almost nodded off. The car's motion, the darkness, the normality of his parents discussing people he didn't know, people they'd be leaving within the next eighteen months, all relaxed him.

He barely noticed the other car when it came careening around a corner, running a light and speeding straight toward them. His father, glancing in the rearview mirror as he spoke to Greg's mother, didn't see the hit coming right at him.

"Dad!" he yelled, grabbing the wheel and swerving the car. The hit wasn't head-on, but it was crushing. Loud. Throwing them all sideways as the oncoming vehicle drove into the driver's side front fender.

It all happened so fast Greg wasn't even sure he was okay. He saw his father slumped over his airbag. Heard his mother's screams. And pulled out his phone.

HE REMEMBERED MAKING the 911 call. He didn't remember the conversation. His father wasn't bleeding profusely from what he could see. Greg was more concerned about his mother. He'd never seen her cry before—except maybe in the movie theater.

She'd gotten out of the car okay. Standing beside her husband's door, she jerked on the handle but was unable to open it because of the front fender that was now smashed up into it. "Come on!" she cried as Greg reached her side, looking as best he could in the streetlight, to see that she wasn't bleeding.

"Mom." He spoke firmly. "The ambulance is coming," he told her, trying to lead her away from the car. His father was unconscious. He'd felt a strong pulse, though. He knew better than to move him. "Are you hurt?" he asked as she yanked once again on the door.

Taking a hold of her hand, he pried her fingers from the handle and pulled her just a few inches away. Enough that he could get her attention. "Look at me," he said, hating the shakiness he could hear in his voice. It would only alarm her further.

It got her to look at him. "Are you okay?" he asked again. "Do you hurt anywhere?"

She rubbed her forehead. Shook her head. "I… No. I don't think so," she said. "Oh God, Greg, your father! Is he going to be okay? Is he?" Her voice rose as she clutched the lapel of Greg's dress coat. Her other hand grabbed hold as well and she was clinging to him. Pulling on him. "Is he going to be okay?" she almost squealed.

"I think so." He couldn't lie to her. But the pulse had been strong. He told her so. And as sirens sounded in the distance, she slumped against him, sobbing, and he wished Jasmine, with her seemingly endless emotional strength, was there to help him get through whatever was coming.

Holding his mother, rubbing the back of her head, he choked up, too. Hardly aware when a couple of tears slid down his cheeks. Seeing his father like that…

The man was in perfect health.

A rock.

Greg's rock.

Chapter Nineteen

Jasmine couldn't fall asleep Friday night. She'd been texting with Greg until he'd said his parents were ready to
head home. She'd thought he'd message her when he got
there, but she didn't hear from him. And didn't know if
their friendship had room for her to get nervous and follow up. Or if she'd seem like some kind of clinging ninny.

Josh had been quiet that night during his call with
Bella. He'd read to her. Kissed her good-night. Told her
he loved her. But there'd been none of the playfulness
that usually accompanied the ritual. Once Bella had been
tucked in, he'd explained why.

He'd heard from his lawyer, who wanted to meet with
him on Monday to go over disclosures from the prosecutor's office and talk about settlement.

"He wants me to accept a plea, Jas," he'd said. "He's
really putting on the pressure, and I just can't do it."

"Then don't." Her reply had been instantaneous, because she understood. After all they'd been through, to
admit to being an abuser when you weren't one…her
heart broke at even the thought of him doing that.

He'd told her that his attorney thought there'd be less
fallout in terms of his professional life if he settled things

quietly, got counseling and moved on. He said he couldn't lie about something so vile, though.

And he couldn't bear the thought of a DV conviction tied to his name for a minute, let alone for the rest of his life. The only way to have that charge go away was to win at trial.

She wanted to tell him to stay strong and go to trial. She knew they'd win. But she didn't. She did, however, fully support his stance, which she told him as strongly as she could. He'd met with the attorney who handled family law that day, someone Ryder had referred to them, and had a lot to talk to her about there, too. Different options. She didn't even want him thinking about giving up his daughter.

The whole idea of it was just too cruel.

And then she didn't hear from Greg when he got back to his parents' place Friday night.

He hadn't said he'd text again. Or call.

But it was the first night since their first kiss that he hadn't done so.

The first night since they'd made love.

Sometime after two, she finally settled down. She'd told him she trusted him. She had to do so. For him. But for herself, and her family, too.

She was going to get this one right.

Two hours of pacing later, of watching his mother go back and forth between the calm, contained woman he'd always known and a panicked, fear-filled, helpless near-invalid, Greg saw the doctor come toward them in the emergency waiting room.

They were the only ones there at that hour of the morning.

"He's going to be all right," the man said before the door to the room had even closed behind him. Both Greg and his mother had been checked out and cleared shortly after they'd arrived. "He's awake and talking. Asking to see you both. He doesn't believe me when I tell him that you're both fine." The man spoke with barely a breath, and Greg was intent on catching every word, while he held his mother up at his side.

The second she heard the news, she'd slumped against him, burying her face in his rib cage.

"He doesn't remember the accident, and he's got one hell of a headache," Dr. Miller added. "He's concussed, so we're going to hold him overnight, but you can stay with him if you'd like. We'll have him up in a room in about fifteen minutes or so. Someone will come get you."

"So...other than the concussion he's fine?" Greg asked as his mother stood up, still looking elegant in her black lace dress and silk shawl as she looked at the doctor.

"He's bruised, going to be sore, maybe a bit whip-lashed, but everything else checks out fine. His vitals are great."

"Thank you, Doctor," Greg said, seeing the tears roll down his mother's cheeks again. With a nod, Dr. Miller turned to go.

"Doctor?" Greg's mother called out. And when the man turned, she said, "Thank you," in as regal a voice, albeit laced with sincerity and gratitude, as Greg had ever heard.

THE NIGHT WAS LONG. Surreal. The three of them dozed intermittently in his father's private room. They'd brought in a second hospital bed, and Greg had insisted his mother use it. He took the reclining chair. She adjusted the head of her bed to a sitting position. And Greg didn't recline.

Events from the accident on kept replaying in his mind. His mother's lack of control. Not that he blamed her—at all—but he just never would have believed…

His own shakiness.

The way he'd been right there with his mother the whole time. Needing to be right there. Holding her. Dealing with the emotion, not just the facts.

"What?" she asked, causing his father to look at him, too. It had to be three in the morning.

"What, what?" he asked her.

"You're sitting over there, shaking your head."

Any other night he'd have come up with some generic yet truthful response. That night he couldn't find one.

"I just…the whole night…us, here now. We don't do this," he said.

"Your father and I both stayed in the hospital with you the night you had your tonsils out," his mother said.

He'd been about four and vaguely remembered that.

"I meant— I don't know. It's just been a weird night."

"I fell apart on him," his mother told his father. "I just…when I saw you slumped there and I couldn't get the car door open…"

"They had to jimmy it to get you out," Greg piped in.

"It's all a blur. I was so scared. I think I started to scream and yank on the door."

"You did." And he'd known what to do. How to help her. Not just with the phone call. The details. But he'd been able to comfort her.

"I don't know what I'd have done without you there," she told Greg, as though she'd been reading his mind.

She knew him well.

"I wouldn't have thought you'd think you could rely on me for emotional support," he told her. She never had before.

"Why ever not?" Both of his parents were looking at him now.

"Because. I'm not that guy. I'm the one who handles the details." They knew him better than anyone.

"Greg, what on earth are you talking about?" His mother sat up, away from the back of the bed. "You're my son. You and your father, you've always been the sources of my strength. My comfort. You remember the time I thought I had a tumor? You held my hand and told me everything would be all right, and I just knew somehow it would."

He kind of remembered. He'd been a kid. What had he known?

"You've always been such a deep, sensitive guy," she told him. He stared at her. Needing her to stop. And wishing his father wasn't sitting there, hearing this, watching him.

"I am not deep or sensitive," he told her. "I'm the guy on the sidelines, making sure that whatever needs to happen, happens."

"You're very reliable, yes, and smart, and good at keeping track of details," she told him, "but you're aware and sensitive, too."

She had the wrong man. Maybe she'd worked it up in her head that he was as she wanted him to be. Mothers had a tendency to think the best of their kids.

"You keep it inside," his mother said. "I blame your father and myself for a lot of that."

His father harrumphed, and Greg glanced over, expecting to see disagreement on his face. Instead, he was nodding.

"All the moving around. We never gave you a chance to bond with other kids. Or have a pet. Or a sense of community."

"I had you two," he reminded them. "That's all I ever needed." These people had rescued him—a thrown-out piece of humanity—from a public restroom and made him their son. How could they think...

"We thought so at the time," his mother continued. "We thought our love would be enough, but look at you, Greg, thirty-two years old and no relationship. No wife or grandkids in sight. And now I'm hearing this nonsense about you not caring?"

"My God, boy, you care more than any man I know," his father boomed. "More than is good for you sometimes, maybe."

He didn't get that.

"You let the guilt from your breakup with that Liv woman eat you alive..."

"I let her down, Dad. Because I have no empathy..."

"You didn't love her, son," his mother piped in. "It wasn't a lack of empathy. It was a lack of love. And I'm afraid, because of how you came into the world, coupled with the fact that you had little opportunity to bond as a child, that you aren't going to let yourself be open to happiness."

How in the hell had they gone from a normal family weekend, to a car accident and worry over his father's life, to him being some deep guy not open to love?

"And your career," his father said, as though pick-on-Greg night was the only thing on the agenda.

"I know, you don't understand how I could give up a lucrative law career to..."

"You might want to let me finish," the older man said in a tone that Greg automatically respected.

"Go ahead," he said, instead of the "yes, sir," he might have issued in years past.

"In the first place, I wouldn't call working in the prosecutor's office a lucrative law career. Those guys are grossly underpaid, in my opinion. However, your choice to be there was typical of you. You weren't in it for the money. You were in it because you honestly cared about justice being served. And you cared too much to have your hands tied, which is why you left. Both of which made me proud as hell."

Greg shook his head. Irritated. Maybe a little pissed at them both. But not wanting to get up and walk out.

Of course, it was late, he was exhausted, and the chair was comfortable.

"Just for the record," he spat out, "I'm not closed off to love."

"You just have to find the right woman," his mother said. "Like I found your father."

He heard her words in a different voice. In a different form. Lila McDaniels Mantle, at The Lemonade Stand, the day she was grilling him about Jasmine. "Why you?" she'd said to him. "Why should you be the one saving this particular life?"

He'd thought she was way out of line. Hadn't wanted to hear anything she might have been trying to tell him, any warning she might have been trying to give him.

"I have to say, Dad, Mom was kind of a screaming banshee tonight," he said, trying for a grin, to get them out of the emotional turmoil they'd fallen into. As a family, they tended to avoid this stuff.

At least he thought they had. Maybe they'd just been unbelievably lucky enough to be happy. A happy family that enjoyed being together.

"I thought I was going to lose you," his mother told his father with one of the looks Greg had been witnessing his entire life. The one that just told you for sure that they were connected way beyond laws of the land. "I don't know what I'd do without either one of you," she said, tearing up again as she looked from him to his dad.

He'd always thought she was just a calm, strong person. When, in fact, he'd just never had to witness her deeply afraid or hurting. Funny how a little perspective changed so much.

Funny, too, how when you loved someone, you just knew how to be there for them.

He hadn't loved Liv. Not his fault. Not something he could control. Not like she'd needed to be loved. Rick did, though.

In that moment, Greg knew that he wanted a home like he and his parents had shared. A home filled with love and loved ones. With a child to raise and teach and know better than they knew themselves sometimes.

He wanted to be biologically related to someone he knew, but even more, he wanted to be in a committed, loving relationship with a woman, in one residence, and to raise a family with her.

Expecting his father to make some kind of pithy remark that would make his mother smile, Greg was surprised yet again when, instead, his father took his mother's hand, then reached out a hand to Greg on his other side. "We just need to be thankful that the good

Lord didn't think tonight was the right time to separate us, and maybe we ought to talk about the stuff that matters a bit more."

Bowing his head, Greg wondered if the entire world had just gone mad.

Or somehow righted itself.

JASMINE WAS STILL asleep when her phone rang just after seven Saturday morning. Throwing her legs over the side of the bed, she pushed to answer so she could silence the ring as she rushed into Bella's room to find the little girl still sound asleep.

And then headed back to her room. "Hello?" she said, as though she hadn't been waiting most of the night to hear from Greg.

"Hey, is this too early? Did I wake you?"

He sounded different.

"What's wrong?"

"Nothing, I just… We were in an accident last night on the way home from the dinner…"

His voice continued on. Jasmine heard about his father being okay. About them all spending the night in the hospital. But she listened from afar.

The relief flooding through made her mind fuzzy and her body shake. She cuddled up under the covers, pulling herself together and asking for all the details. The other guy had been arrested at the scene and charged with drunk driving, with other charges expected to follow.

Greg and his parents were planning to lie low the rest of the weekend, catch up on a couple of movies, maybe play some cards. He didn't say when he'd be calling again.

She wanted to know if he'd told them about her but didn't ask.

He was okay. He'd called her.

That was enough.

Chapter Twenty

Greg had thought he'd at least text Jasmine when he got home Sunday night. He wanted to. In the end, he lifted weights instead. It had been a tough weekend; he hadn't done any physical exercise for two days and he had a lot to work off.

He thought of her as he lay in bed, hands behind his head, staring at the ceiling. His body, which should be exhausted and needing rest, ached for her. They'd had sex once. Once. How long could it take to get over it?

Because he was pretty sure they wouldn't be doing it again.

The weekend, the accident, the way he'd felt when he'd thought he'd lost his father, the way he'd been able to tend to his mother because he loved her that much and had just known what to do... He was seeing himself differently.

His parents' words had been rambling around in his head for over twenty-four hours. Finding a home inside of him.

He'd convinced himself that he had an inability to care deeply. Figured it had something to do with being abandoned in a public restroom as an infant. Kind of hard to live with that your whole life and not be defined by it—at least a little bit. He'd really thought he was permanently detached. Right. He'd been *real* detached when he'd looked over and seen his father unconscious.

About as detached as he'd been making love to Jasmine the night before he'd left.

He still didn't really remember his mother's tumor scare all that much. But he was beginning to accept that there might truth in the fact that he did care deeply. His problem was being unable to fix everything. Having things outside his control.

Like the fact that he was never going to know whom he came from. But his truth was, he didn't want to know. He had his parents.

And he wasn't going to be able to settle for a relationship without a shared home and a family to raise. He needed those things.

He deserved them.

He wasn't going to be as happy without them.

So Jasmine wasn't the one.

Or rather, she was—the one he was meant to save. Not the one he was meant to love.

Chances were, after her brother's settlement conference that week, unless Josh did the right thing and admitted what he'd done, she wasn't going to want Greg anymore, either. She wasn't going to trust him when she found out that he'd turned up the evidence that was going to get Josh convicted.

Even if Josh did take a plea agreement, which would require mandatory counseling, Jasmine might still turn on Greg. Josh could, and probably would, tell her that he wasn't guilty but was taking the plea because he had no choice. With the new evidence, Josh wasn't going to win this case. His own attorney had agreed with William on that one.

But Greg would be there for her. As long as she'd let him be. He was already getting her the truth she'd requested. For some reason, hers was the life he was meant to save. And he was damned well going to do it.

Fate had let his small family remain intact. He wasn't about to piss her off.

JASMINE WAS JUST closing up her classroom on Monday when her phone rang. She practically dropped her bag, she was fumbling so voraciously to get to the cell before the ringing stopped. It had to be Greg. She hadn't heard from him the night before—she figured he'd gotten in too late and had probably been on the phone with his parents. But he knew what time she finished teaching and…

It wasn't Greg. It was Josh.

"I took the plea agreement, Jas," were his first words. She sank down to one of the small chairs at the row of desks where she'd been standing, her eyes flooding with tears. Shivering in spite of her almost knee-length, fleece-lined red sweatshirt she was wearing with black leggings, she hugged her bag and listened, trying to determine Josh's state of mind. To know how to help him. To wipe her nose so she didn't sniffle and expose the fact that she was crying.

"Listen, I need to see you. They had all this stuff, and…anyway, I took the agreement because my attorney got them to lift my visitation restrictions," he said. "He told them that I'm in the process of granting you permanent custody of Bella and asked that I be allowed to visit without restriction or supervision, dependent solely upon your say-so."

Her heart lifted a little. She'd do whatever she had to keep Bella wholly in his life. If it was up to her, then they were home free. She could move in with him. Or he could move in with her. Either way.

"I need to see her. Jas, please? I took the agreement. Please let me see her."

"Of course." It would take a day or several before things were official, she got that. But Josh had sold himself out for strictly one purpose—the freedom to be in his daughter's life. He'd already missed three weeks. "Come over for dinner," she told him.

"I was hoping you'd bring her to the cottage." He sounded like he was starting to cry. "I've signed paperwork, but nothing is official yet, and I don't trust... I'll tell you about it when I see you. I just... I think...someone...might be watching your place and will do anything to see me suffer more. But I need to see you two, Jasmine. Please? Just for an hour or so? And remember to turn your cell phone off."

The cottage. Their safe place. When they'd been kids, they'd found the abandoned two-room shack not far from the land their father had owned for hunting. During the long hours with everyone together during their numerous California vacations, Josh and Jasmine would head to the cottage when they'd have to stay at their vacation home alone with their dad when he was on a rampage. Jasmine had done her best to clean the place up, in spite of rotted wood and splintery floors. She brought rugs from the vacation home their parents' had purchased. Some pillows she'd found in the attic. A lantern that ran on batteries. And some blankets.

When they'd grown and received their settlements, Josh had bought the place. Fixed it up. She hadn't known until one year for Christmas he'd taken her there. Surprised her with the completely renovated little cottage, complete with electric and running water.

"I'm on my way," she told him. He'd just done the unthinkable because he loved his daughter that much. Even if the paperwork wasn't official yet, the court had agreed to release his visitation restrictions. There was no way she was going to deny him this.

GREG GOT THE call from William shortly after four. He'd been out investigating a barn, an old crime scene from a cold case William had been assigned, and hadn't had good cell reception.

"He refused to take the plea," the prosecutor told him. "We sweetened the deal as you suggested, offering to remove all visitation restrictions, and he still turned it down. Said there was nothing anyone was going to do to get him to admit to being an abuser."

"You think he's a flight risk?"

"His attorney didn't think so. Says the man adamantly maintains his innocence and is confident that the truth will win out in court."

Starting his vehicle, Greg waited while the phone switched to car mode. Either the man was more out of touch than he'd thought—making him more of a danger?—or he was...

"You think there's a chance that he really is innocent?" William asked. "Just asking for your gut response," he continued. "I know what the evidence says."

A moment he hadn't expected was right there, offering itself to him. If he sided with Josh, would William drop the case? And let an escalating situation get worse?

Let Josh continue on in denial, either just public or

personal, too, until he put someone he loved in the hospital, or worse?

If he didn't, would Heidi get away with stripping a man of everything he held dear, out of spite or revenge?

"I don't know." He told the truth and rang off.

He had to call Jasmine. Not to talk about the case.

Just to hear her voice.

JOSH AND BELLA played for the entire hour. He'd greeted her with a hug. They held up their respective cell phones—a ritual of sorts—to show each device was off. Because of their shared need to always know there was somewhere they could go and be completely safe, they always turned off their cell phones before they got near the cabin. She did hers half an hour out. Josh did his when he left town.

And then he was rolling in the grass with his daughter in his arms. Jasmine had thought they'd have a chance to talk. He'd said he had things to show her. But the time was gone before she even realized it. The cottage was almost an hour from home, and she had to get the toddler fed and then it was bath and bedtime. Still, she hated to stop the fun. The sound of Bella's giggles while her father played horsey with her, the smile on Josh's face, were all that mattered.

"I hungry," Bella said a few minutes later, taking care of Jasmine's hesitation. Glancing at her brother as he lay flat on the expensive wool rug with his daughter climbing on top of his chest, she knew he knew it was time, too. His expression had grown serious. "I hungry, Daddy," Bella said, giving a bounce and giggling.

"Well, Daddy has just the thing for you, then," Josh

said, taking her with him as he rose, throwing her up in the air but never letting her body leave his hands.

He was always so careful with her.

Such a great dad.

"I'm planning to drive through for some grilled chicken," she told him. There was a place right by the freeway, not ten minutes away. "You can come with us and we can eat there, if you'd like."

"Chicken!" Bella hollered. The little girl loved her chicken. Fried. Grilled. Baked. She wasn't too fond of vegetables, but she'd eat chicken every meal if she could.

"How about macaroni and cheese?" Josh suggested, and she frowned. Most chicken places offered the side dish—Bella's second favorite food—but the one by the freeway did not. Josh knew that. They'd had a meltdown with Bella there about a year before.

"I'll be right back," Josh said. He ran out to his vehicle and came in carrying a sack full of groceries. "How about if we make chicken and mac and cheese here?" he suggested to his daughter, pulling out her favorite frozen meal.

"Josh," Jasmine said. He'd asked her for an hour. She hadn't packed anything for a longer stay for Bella, who, while potty-trained, was still wearing pull-up, disposable diapers at night.

Looking at her over the top of the bag, Josh said, "Please?" And, of course, when his big brown eyes—just like hers and their mom's—implored her, she couldn't deny him.

He'd had a bad day. The worst. So he could have hours like the one he'd just spent. They could do dinner. And if Bella fell asleep in the car seat on the way home, she could always carry her into the house and put her to bed.

It wouldn't be the first time she'd changed her niece while Bella was asleep.

Might even be better that way. Bella had cried for several minutes the last time Josh left before she was asleep.

While Josh and Bella pretended to help her, but really just played silly games in the small kitchen area, Jasmine made dinner for the three of them.

"You got a whole gallon of milk," she said, shaking her head. "It's going to spoil before you get it all the way home." Giving his shoulder a nudge with her knee as he crawled past her, she capped the container and put it in the fridge. Along with the pound of butter he'd also purchased for the quarter of a cup she needed.

They kept the refrigerator stocked with essentials that held longer shelf lives, like condiments. There was usually some cheese and a few other things in the freezer. And boxed food in the cupboards. But opened butter and milk…he'd need to take those with him.

It wasn't until after they ate and she was just putting away the rest of the dishes—Josh had offered to help, but she'd told him to spend the time with Bella—that she noticed her brother had brought in a couple of more bags. Along with a duffel.

And she got it. He was planning to stay. Maybe even until his court date on Thursday to officially record his plea before the judge. Her heart lightened a bit more. He was taking care of himself. Coming to their haven because it was where they'd always gone to get healthy.

To find security and freedom from fear. To remember that they were valuable human beings with rights. That they were strong and capable and would be okay.

All reminders that she wanted to give him. He'd known how to access them, even before she'd thought of it. That was Josh—dealing with the bad by taking action to bring out the good. She was proud of him.

They'd get through this. Heidi could be going to jail for her attack on Jasmine. And even if she didn't, there'd most likely be a permanent restraining order. They were going to be okay. Josh was going to be okay.

It was just a bump in the road.

Chapter Twenty-One

Her phone went immediately to voice mail. Again. Greg had been trying to reach Jasmine for a couple of hours, and she wasn't picking up.

Josh had obviously gone straight to her from the meeting with his lawyer. She knew what Greg had been doing the previous week—the evidence he'd turned up against her brother.

And she was clearly no longer speaking to him.

Because she believed her brother was innocent.

And because she now thought Greg had been lying to her, using her, all along?

He thought about the way she'd moved on top of him—and beneath him—just three days before and ached like he'd never ached in his life.

He needed to see her. To explain.

He couldn't explain. He worked for the prosecution. The case was going to trial.

He needed to hold her.

He needed her to trust him.

Which meant he had to let her come to him.

Or not.

Downing a cold meat sandwich for dinner, along with a protein shake, he went down the hall to his gym, turned on the television mounted to the wall and listened to voices droning on as he worked out. Doing what he could to deal with the frustration of knowing that there were so many things he couldn't fix.

LEAVING THE LIGHT on over the sink in the clean kitchen to welcome Josh after they left, Jasmine went to find Bella and get her loaded up for the drive home. They could still make it by her bedtime. Which was important; the toddler had to be up the next morning for Jasmine to be able to get them both ready to go to the Stand. Luckily she'd already prepared the materials for the next day's lessons.

The cottage had grown quiet, which was saying a lot since it was really just two rooms—the big room that served as the living area with the kitchen divided off with a half wall in one corner, and the bedroom. Josh had had a lovely full bath added on to the back of the original structure, off the bedroom.

Glancing outside, she didn't see the twosome in the yard, so headed through the bedroom door, figuring her brother was having his daughter go potty before the drive home.

The sound of splashing water hit her before she could see inside the bathroom. On his knees beside the mammoth tub, Josh was leaning over, bathing Bella.

"I thought I'd give her a bath," he said while Bella grinned up at her and said, "Watch, Auntie JJ!" At which point she picked up a squeezable, colorful letter block toy and pushed it under the water, laughing as it popped back up through the water at her.

Jasmine smiled. Made some appropriate comment to the toddler but didn't say much else. She understood. Josh was struggling. She ached for him.

So much.

If there was a way they could spend the night…

But she couldn't. She had to work in the morning. Bella had daycare. There were no official orders yet allowing Josh to spend the night with Bella, and she wasn't going to let him screw things up at this point.

Worrying all of a sudden that she'd already taken way too much of a chance of that, bringing Bella out to the cottage, afraid she'd given in to Josh at a time when he'd needed her to be strong for him, to see the bigger picture, she calmed herself down. No one but the two of them knew about the cabin. It had always been their secret. Just the two of them. That's what made it so safe.

Josh had purchased it through one of his holdings as just a piece of land. The cottage hadn't had running water or electricity. It hadn't been taxable. She was sure there were permits somewhere for adding the electric, but the water, that was on well.

Weird, maybe, but when you grew up in a home of terror, you learned to do what you had to do to live healthily in a world with very few guarantees.

Not wanting Bella to catch on to her changed mood, not wanting to ruin the last few minutes Josh had with Bella, she left them alone and went out to gather her bag and the few things she'd taken out of the backpack full of Bella's things she always carried anytime she had the little girl. An emergency juice box. A few travel toys. A change of clothes. A couple pairs of big girl panties. Usually a pull-up or two, but the little girl had grown, changed sizes, and she hadn't thought to put larger ones in. She hadn't been planning to take Bella anywhere to spend the night.

They weren't going to stay the night. She was not

going to let her brother convince her to go that far. As much as she owed him, as much as she understood, it didn't feel right having Bella away from her home overnight.

Nor did it feel right calling into work the next day. Letting her kids down.

When she heard him in the bedroom, she grabbed Bella's sweater, put their bags on her shoulders and had her keys in hand, ready to take Bella on her free hip. It would just be easier to load her in the car herself, rather than have her hanging on her daddy, not wanting to let go to get buckled into her car seat.

LEAVING JOSH UP at the cottage alone wasn't easy.

He was alone when he joined her in the living area. "Where's Bella?" She stood there, watching him as he moved toward the front door.

Locking the keyed dead bolt from the inside, he stood in front of the only door, facing her. The doors on his home were locked the same way. Something he'd done in his house when Heidi had been pregnant. Part of babyproofing the house, he'd said. She and Heidi had thought it overkill. But survivors all had their little quirks.

"What are you doing, Josh?" she asked. The poor man. This had to be killing him. "You know we have to go."

"Not yet," he said. "I just laid Bella down. She can fall asleep here, and I'll carry her out when you leave. I need to be able to show you the things that Ryder showed me today, the discovery materials." He grabbed a file out of a drawer in the bookcase along one wall. "He made a copy for me," he said. "I couldn't do it with Bella awake."

She didn't relish the hourlong drive back in the dark, but for Josh, it was a small price to pay. She'd thought they could talk while she drove home and Bella slept. But if he had things to show her, she definitely had to see them.

Nodding, she dropped her bags on the couch and went over to the kitchen table to look at the paperwork.

GREG TRIED JASMINE again after his shower. In his room, pulling on basketball shorts and nothing else, he listened as her voice mail picked up again after the second ring.

Either she was deliberately refusing his calls or her phone was off.

Jasmine wasn't the type to avoid him, no matter how pissed she got. She'd pick up the phone and tell him to go to hell. In the nicest way possible, of course.

Or demand that he admit he lied to her—also without raising her voice. Just like she'd immediately called him out both times she'd thought he might be using her.

She had a way about her—some things that were consequences of having grown up a victim—and one of them was that she didn't take a lack of truthfulness lightly.

She'd fought hard to be a survivor and was going to make damned certain that she didn't become a victim again. And, as evidence of that last thought, he offered himself the fact that she was never going to live with a partner again. She'd learned that doing so made her vulnerable.

He needed to drive by her house. He didn't have to stop. If her lights were on, he'd know she was there and okay.

Maybe he'd stop. He could figure that out when he got there. See how he felt.

Already out of his shorts and into jeans, Greg grabbed a sweatshirt, his wallet, phone and keys, and was out the door.

JASMINE STARED AT the pages of documentation, a partial transcript from a conversation between Greg Johnson and Heidi Taylor that had taken place the previous week. Pages of corroborating evidence. Grainy photos of time-stamped security-tape footage. Copies of text messages from two phone numbers she recognized well. Josh's and Heidi's.

Dizzy, she sat down. Her chest was so tight she worried about breathing for a second. All last week, while she'd been on a new relationship high, hopeful, Greg had been making sure her brother hanged.

And Josh...

"You... These texts... You threw Heidi out and hurt her foot so bad so couldn't walk?"

She didn't get it. Truly just couldn't comprehend. There must be a way to right this. She knew it. But where was it? Why couldn't she see it?

"I didn't throw her out," Josh said, pulling out a chair to sit next to her, moving it close enough that their arms were touching as they looked at the pages together. "I told her multiple times to leave. She said if I wanted her gone, I'd have to make her go. I couldn't call the police on her. Not again. She was trying so hard. And when she's in a good place, she's great with Bella. But Bella was coming down the hall and I couldn't let her see Heidi in that state, so I pushed her out the door. The foot thing was completely unintentional. I was watching for Bella, not looking at Heidi, and shut the door before she was completely out. It caught her foot."

She nodded. Able to see it all happening. Because she'd been witness to enough similar situations in the past to know exactly what Josh was talking about.

They went through all of the pages together. He had explanations for every situation. Believable ones.

And yet he'd had to plead guilty.

Sick to her stomach, she kept looking it all over, as though there was some answer there she was missing.

Some piece of clarity.

God knew she needed it. Desperately.

"Ryder says there's no way to beat all this in court. With this evidence...the judge is going to know that the things happened and then it's going to be Heidi's interpretation, her word, against mine. And with our judge, my chances are pretty much nil."

"So we file to have her removed. Petition for a new judge."

She was just spitballing. He'd already pleaded guilty.

"I have no legal grounds to do so. She's a sitting judge with a stellar record. The most I could do is file for appeal. She's been up on appeal a few times. Has only been overturned once, and it wasn't on a DV case."

She got to the bottom of the pile. The picture that had started it all. Only there was a second one there, this time. Of the proper wrist. Also taken from Heidi's phone with the same time stamp.

"What's this?" she asked.

Shaking his head, he said. "Apparently she had two photos on her phone."

"But...this one matches her testimony," she said, looking closely at it. And then the following paperwork, mentioning a doctor's report and neighborhood security coverage. "Did you look at this, Josh?"

He grabbed up the photo. Studied it like he'd never seen it before, and she was scared for him. She knew how trapped this was all going to make him feel. How hopeless and hurt.

But when he looked at her, he didn't look hurt. He looked...determined.

"I didn't take the plea."

THERE WERE NO lights on at Jasmine's place. She'd have just put Bella to bed. Could be in the back part of the house. Greg got out of his car and circled the place, noting, with comfort, the security cameras. She'd given him her code to the gate, so he'd gotten in without a hitch.

Which meant any number of other people could do so as well.

Her bedroom light wasn't on. The blinds were still open. She never left them open at night.

Jumping up onto the deck, he sat there for a minute, on the wicker couch he'd occupied the first night he'd met her. Hard to believe that had just been three weeks ago. Seemed like years of his life had passed in that space.

In the three weeks he'd known her, she'd been adamant about getting Bella to bed on schedule. Believing that a regular routine built a sense of security. And she had to be at work in the morning. Something else she was a stickler about.

Funny, how he knew her so well in such a little bit of time.

So...where was she?

She wouldn't be with Josh. The brother and sister pair were committed to following Bella's visitation rules, and with his court case coming up on Thursday—with his determination to win—no way that either of them would jeopardize things now.

She could be at The Lemonade Stand. Helping with some emergency situation there. Maddie would watch Bella.

But what emergency would require an elementary school teacher to be on hand at nine o'clock at night?

It hit him then… Heidi. The woman knew better than to go after Jasmine again. She knew she was treading a fine line between freedom and jail.

But she also wasn't stable.

On his phone immediately Greg made one call—and then hit the road himself. If Heidi Taylor thought she was going to hurt Jasmine or that little girl, she had another think coming.

This one, he was going to fix.

Chapter Twenty-Two

"You lied to me?" Josh hadn't taken the plea? There was no order to remove visitation restrictions? She couldn't be there. Not with Bella. She shook her head. "You *lied* to me?"

"I had to get you here, Jas. I had to be able to show you all this, and I'm not allowed at your place with Bella there. Look at all these things. It's like there are eyes everywhere. And Heidi's opening them. For all I know, she's sitting on my place. Following me. Taking pictures…"

It was a bit extreme. And yet…somewhat believable, too. Knowing Heidi. And seeing all of the evidence that had been collected on a misdemeanor domestic violence charge.

She couldn't even think about the finder of that evidence. The collector. Sleeping with that man…she just couldn't go there. Not yet.

"All you had to do was tell me the truth, Josh," she said. It was their golden rule. They would never, ever lie to each other. Because they both had issues and had to know that there was always someplace they could go where they didn't have to worry about misplaced trust.

"I know." He put a hand on her arm. "I'm sorry. I

just…after seeing all this, I wasn't thinking straight. But tonight…being here, a family, playing with Bella…"

She felt his hand on her wrist and saw, in her mind's eye, the photo that was right in front of her. Another wrist he'd had his hand on.

"You did it," she said softly. "You sprained Heidi's wrist."

"It wasn't like that," he said, bowing his head with his hands at the back of his neck. "She was trying to get to Bella in the playroom. She was out of her head and thinking she was going to grab her up and take her. I couldn't let her get back there. I knew I'd be able to keep her from leaving with our daughter, but I didn't want Bella to see her like that. Or be pulled back and forth between us."

Which made total and complete sense. But… "So why didn't you just say so? You were defending a baby!"

"Because it was her word against mine."

And wait… Based on the timeline, wouldn't Bella have been at preschool? Josh should have been at work.

What the hell! Was she actually sitting there questioning the integrity of the one man she knew she could trust?

"So why didn't you tell me all this on the phone? Why risk… You're due in court in three days! If anyone finds out that you spent this afternoon and evening with Bella—it's a violation of orders, Josh. If they see that you can't be trusted to keep visitation regulations, they aren't going to trust you or believe your side of things. You're compromising your integrity. And they could take your rights away, too, you know. If they can't trust you where she's concerned…"

And more. There was so much more. He'd lied to her. He'd gone against direct court orders. He'd made her stay so late…each time she'd wanted to leave, he'd stopped her.

"I needed you to see for yourself." His tone had changed from that of loving, needy brother to businessman. He sat up, looking at her.

"Needed me to see what for myself?"

He pointed to the folder. "You know who's behind all of this. Who got Heidi to talk. Who dug all this other stuff up."

Greg Johnson. Yeah, she knew. "So?"

"I wasn't sure you'd believe me if I told you."

That was rich. Considering that she'd always believed him, never, ever considered not believing him, and he'd just lied to her.

"Why on earth would you even think something like that?" She just wasn't getting it.

"You're falling for him."

She couldn't deny the fact. She wouldn't desecrate his one trustworthy place. "Whether I am or not, you're my brother. This case—you, Bella—you always come first. And you have no way of knowing whether I like him or not."

"I know you, sis. You mentioned Greg pretty much every night when we talked, in that tone of voice you get when you think highly of someone."

"So I think he's a good detective. I believed he was our best hope at getting the court to see that Heidi was manipulating them."

"And you have a pattern," Josh said, still sounding more impersonal than not. "You gravitate toward cops. You always have. Thinking they're somehow going to help us. How many times did you insist on calling them when we were growing up? And how many times did Dad make one phone call and have everyone understand that he had a drama queen, a spoiled daughter who was just mad she wasn't getting her own way?"

Four.

She could give a full account of each one.

"And you fall for people in positions of power," he said next. She held up her hand. Didn't need him to continue. She knew these parts of herself only too well.

She trusted people with abusive qualities.

Like she trusted her own brother.

He'd lied to her. But she understood his reasoning. He had good explanations.

It was all so confusing.

"Okay, I've seen. If you need me to tell you that I know Greg isn't on our side, and to promise you not to say another word to him about any of this, I'll do so. You don't even have to ask. Done. And now I've got to get out of here, Josh. It's past Bella's bedtime. If anyone did happen to be looking for me, it's going to be odd that I'm not home."

"Oh my God. You think he might be looking for you?"

"I was referring to Heidi." And Greg, too, she was ashamed to admit, so she didn't. "You said you were worried about her looking for dirt on you. And she's already been to my house once before." She didn't touch the ponytail at the back of her head, but she thought about it.

Josh hadn't even asked to see the bald spot his ex-wife had left on her.

But then, he had real problems on his hands. His future was at stake. How could she be sitting there doubting him?

"I need your help, Jas," he said now, his elbow on the table, those brown eyes filled with warmth again.

"You've got it," she told him. "We're not through here.

We'll get through this. Figure it out. I just need to get on the road first."

"There's nothing to figure out," he said. "I've got it all figured out."

Okay. Good. That was more like the Josh she knew.

"So what do you need from me?" She'd do it. She always did. He knew that.

"I need you to cover for me long enough to get out of town."

"What? Are you nuts?"

"I've got money put away in an offshore account. I'll change my identity and start a new life. Just me and Bella. I just need you to give us the chance to get out of the state. Go home. Call in sick tomorrow. Say Bella's got the flu. That'll give me twenty-four hours, which is all I need to cross the border."

She thought he was kidding. Trying to lighten the moment. Almost chuckled. Until she saw the dead-serious look in his eye.

Shaking her head, she stood up. Reached for her purse and turned toward the bedroom. Josh was there, blocking her way.

She wasn't afraid of him. He wasn't going to hurt her.

But Jasmine was so numb, she wasn't really feeling much of anything. She was going to get that baby girl, who was hopefully sleeping through this moment when her father went mad, bring her out to the car and take her home.

Whatever Josh did was on him. If he skipped town on them, he wasn't the man she'd thought he was.

Someday that might make sense to her.

"Get out of my way, Josh."

"I can't do that, Jasmine. I can't let you take her from me."

In that second, she saw truth. Josh had a breaking point. And the trigger was his daughter, Bella. Every time he'd hurt Heidi, every story he'd told her that night, every piece of evidence she'd seen, all pointed to times when Heidi was interfering with Bella.

He'd had excuses every time. Believable ones. Just as their father had.

Their father! She was that man's biological child, not him! Through all the years, she'd always been aware that she was more prone to become an abuser than Josh because she had both environment and biology against her. He hadn't been desperate to save anyone when he'd shoved Heidi outside. He just hadn't wanted his daughter to see her there. And maybe he'd wanted to spend more time with her. And the rest of them…at no time had Bella's life been at stake.

Their whole lives, Jasmine had been expecting that if violence popped up in their family again, it would be from her, and she hadn't even seen that it was there with them all along.

That Josh took after their father more than she did.

That he had a breaking point, and sometime over this thing with Heidi, he'd reached it. Her brother had broken; he'd become violent. He had escalated. And she hadn't even known.

BEING A DETECTIVE had its advantages. When you needed to find someone, you had avenues to do so. Officers were at Heidi's place within ten minutes of Greg's phone call. And in another five he knew that she'd been home all night. Heidi hadn't heard from either Josh or Jasmine Taylor and didn't expect to.

He ran a search on Jasmine's phone next. It wasn't pinging to any towers. Meaning she'd turned it off. He took heart from that. Assuming she'd done it herself.

His next phone call had another cruiser on its way to Josh's house.

In his car, racing toward The Lemonade Stand, praying that Jasmine was safely inside its walls, he put in a request to have Jasmine's phone dumped. He needed to know if she'd talked to anyone that afternoon.

He could be overreacting. Creating issues where there were none.

Creating drama.

He didn't give a damn if it meant that Jasmine and little Bella were safe.

He got Lila McDaniels Mantle on the phone before he reached the Stand. It wasn't like he could just go barging in there, anyway. He'd just wanted to be close, to be able to see Jasmine if she was there. And if not, he wanted to search the parking lot where her car had been.

See if it was still there.

Or if anything had been left behind.

Jasmine was a survivor. She'd taken multiple classes to teach her how to keep herself safe, and she always followed her rules.

"She left here right on time," Lila told him after putting him on hold long enough to check in with a few others on site. "She was fine when she picked up Bella. Maddie said she told her that she liked her shirt."

"And she didn't say anything to anyone about having any plans?"

"She passed Sara on the way out and just said that

she'd see her in the morning. Do I need to be concerned, Detective? Are Jasmine and Bella in some kind of trouble?"

"I hope not," he told her. And then added, "But you asked me once to be certain that the life I was saving was one I was meant to save, and I can assure you that Jasmine is on me. If she's in trouble, I'll find her."

"I'm going to call my husband and have him come in, then," the director said. "I had a session tonight, but was just getting ready to head home. We'll be here all night if you need anything. If there's anything we can do, even if you just have a question, you call. Doesn't matter what time it is."

"I'll call you as soon as I locate her," he told the woman, understanding that this was one person who wouldn't want to wait until morning to get news.

His phone buzzed as he was ringing off. Santa Barbara officers telling him that Josh wasn't home. Getting the man's phone number, Greg dialed it himself, praying that he was making a mistake. Making a big deal out of nothing.

That Josh would answer—even if just to curse him for doing such a thorough job with his investigation.

Josh Taylor didn't pick up.

Chapter Twenty-Three

"Get out of my way, Josh," Jasmine said for the third time, standing up to her brother as he continued to block her way to Bella.

"I'm going to take Bella home, put her to bed and then call you," she told him, meaning every word she said. She wasn't turning her back on him. But she had to get Bella out of there and home.

"I can't let you do that." He repeated words he'd been speaking to her for the past several minutes as they stood there, facing off.

"Yes, you can," she told him. "What's more, you know you have to." She was trying to find the reasonable man she knew him to be.

"You aren't understanding me," he said, calm, assured. "I'm going to take Bella out of the country. She's going to grow up happy and loved and as far away from Heidi as we can get."

"You're just going to walk away from your whole life…"

"Bella's all I need. We'll be fine, just the two of us."

Jasmine tried not to be hurt by the words. The obvious slam on her. He wasn't in his right mind. He'd apologize later.

They always did.

"Okay, well, I'm going to get her now," she said, turning toward the wall, giving her back to him, as she made to slide past. She got one step in, lifted her foot again, and the next thing she knew she was flat on the floor, her stomach pressed to the gleaming hardwood, ribs aching, gasping for air.

"Jasmine!" Josh's voice sounded above her. Concerned. She felt him lift her. Leaned into his familiar frame.

And noticed that the bedroom door was closed. He'd probably done it when he'd put Bella down, so she'd go to sleep.

And not hear them.

Knowing that she needed a minute to get her air back, she let Josh lead her over to the couch. It wasn't the first time she'd had the wind knocked out of her. She'd be fine.

"Are you okay?" Josh asked, taking her hand as he sat down beside her. Rubbing her back. "Does anything hurt?"

She shook her head. No, she wasn't okay. And nothing hurt. He could take his pick. One was true. One wasn't.

"What happened?" he asked. "One minute I was letting you by, and the next, you just went down. It's the floors. I had them polished. I knew they were too slick."

He knew what had happened. He'd tripped her. She could still feel the slide of his foot up her leg. Probably already had a bruise forming.

He'd become her father. Only worse. Because he'd hurt her right there in their safe house.

She was going to puke. For real. She was going to throw up all over those shiny wood floors.

Lurching, Jasmine made it to the kitchen sink and lost her dinner.

TIME PASSED SLOWLY. When Jasmine was docile, Josh was kind. Telling her again and again what he was going to do, what she was going to do and how the plan would work.

She tried to remain quiet until she could figure out what to do. Or he came to his senses. Praying that one or the other happened before morning, when Bella woke up.

When Josh had to go to the bathroom, he made her go ahead of him, tiptoe past the queen bed where the little girl lay all cuddled up in covers and stand, with her back to him, between the toilet and the tub.

She was his prisoner.

Josh's prisoner. Her cell phone was in her bag, which was still hanging off her arm. And if she reached her hand inside that bag, she knew Josh would hurt her again before she managed to do any good.

She was there. Watching. Feeling.

And yet she still couldn't believe it. Kept searching for some explanation. Waiting for something to happen that would make sense.

By two in morning, she was exhausted. Her ribs hurt. She was afraid at least one of them was cracked. And when she'd gone to the bathroom, a reverse of when he'd gone, with him standing guard with his back to her, she'd noticed a bruise on her chin, too. Probably where she'd hit the floor.

"You know I'm going to take her home," she finally said to him, too weary to play his game anymore. "There's no way I can just let you take her out of the country. This doesn't have to be a big deal, Josh. Whether you plead guilty or go to trial, the most you're going to get is mandatory counseling, and maybe supervised visitation for a while. You've got Play for the Win. And all of your other business interests. We'll all still be together. I love you so much, Josh. Please stop this before something really bad happens."

It had already happened. She knew it. And feared he did, too.

He'd exposed himself to her. The mean, angry, violent self. She'd never look at him the same way again.

Never trust him the same.

But she loved him the same.

"This is all your fault," he said, pacing behind her on the couch. His lack of fatigue worried her. He was on some kind of adrenaline high that could only be dangerous. "You and your need to screw cops!"

She felt his words as a physical blow to her heart. She couldn't believe he'd just said them.

"I notice you aren't denying it," he said.

Completely at a loss for words, she tried to find some truth to give him. Some way to reach him.

"You slept with him, didn't you? You bitch!" His hand at the back of her head almost knocked her unconscious. She saw stars. Watched them through the dizziness, determined to hang on. If she fell asleep, he'd take Bella and run.

It occurred to her then that he still loved her. He'd have just knocked her out and left her for dead if he didn't.

Why that should ease her pain, she didn't know.

But it did.

And she let it.

"How long have you been sleeping with him?" It was four in the morning, and Josh was still in a state. Jasmine's head hurt so bad she wasn't sure she could stand.

But knew that if she saw a chance to get Bella and go, she was going to have to take it.

She'd slept with Greg Johnson. She wasn't averse to lying to Josh about it at that point. Didn't feel there was enough to preserve to worry about upholding trust.

Wasn't even sure trust really existed. More like it was a phantom dream, like seeing Santa Claus. Or wishing on stars. None of it really worked.

And love wasn't beautiful, either. It tied you to people who hurt you.

No…she wasn't going there. Had chosen not to let bitterness take over her life. Right? Bloom's face showed clearly in her mind's eye. Her soft words started to slowly spread through her thoughts.

And Greg was there, too. Telling her he'd find the truth. Promising her.

He'd been on their side.

Shaking her head as she realized she'd been nodding off, she sat up. Her last thought still clearly in her mind. He'd promised her he'd find the truth. She'd known she could trust him to protect her.

He'd done the first.

And she'd bet her life that he'd die trying to do the second.

The man had agreed to be her forever friend with monogamous sex because he wanted her. The real her.

"I only slept with him once," she heard herself say. Finding strength in the memory. "He wanted to wait. Until after the trial. But… I seduced him."

She expected another blow to the head. Daddy style. She'd talked back to the old man, too. Her whole life she'd thought that she asked for the abuse by egging it on. Speaking out like that.

Truth was, it was the only way she knew to keep herself alive.

To speak her truth. To be heard.

"Look, sis." Josh was there, suddenly, taking her hand, looking at her with the familiar love in those brown eyes. The understanding. "I'm sorry about everything I said. I don't know…this past year…when Heidi started threatening me. I just… It was like she was never going to go away. Never let us just be happy. But you know this isn't me."

She couldn't. He wanted her to be who she was with him, and she couldn't.

He wasn't who she'd thought he was.

She understood. She loved him. But it wasn't the same.

"When you spoke just now… God, Jas, it was like the past coming up to hit me upside the head. It was hearing you with Dad. And knowing he was going to pound you for it. I just… This isn't me. You know it isn't. You have to believe me. It's Heidi, Jasmine. She put me up to this. Said that if I got you to bring Bella up here, she'd drop all charges. Leaving the country was her idea. You have to believe me," he said again. "You know this isn't me."

She didn't know. Not anymore.

And when he figured that out, he was going to hurt her.

Badly.

GREG SPENT THE night looking for her. He was fairly certain she was with Josh. Her brother had called her just before she'd left The Lemonade Stand the night before. And both of them were missing. He wanted to believe she'd left of her own accord. She'd gotten the call and had left the Stand—a place she knew she and Bella would be safe—anyway. She'd taken Bella with her.

No way would she knowingly put that child in danger. She'd have left the little girl with Lila and died first.

There'd been no sign of a struggle in the parking lot. No sign of another car by where hers had been parked, either. Sometime before dawn, Lila, who'd been in touch on and off all night, had pulled the security tapes for him. Two people had studied them. Seen Jasmine put Bella in her car seat as she did every afternoon. Watched as she kissed the little girl, gave her a snack pack and kissed her again before climbing into her own seat. She'd been smiling. A woman in danger didn't smile.

Not unless she was doing so in the direction of a security camera. Jasmine knew where the cameras at The Lemonade Stand were located. She hadn't glanced at any of them.

But he had a bad feeling.

A really bad feeling.

Using his clout, pulled strings and had APBs out on both her and Josh's cars. And had a missing person's report and an Amber alert out for Bella, as well. If he was wasting taxpayers' money, he'd pay back every dime. He didn't care if it took the rest of his life to do so.

He had to find her.

HE STILL HADN'T hurt her badly enough to take Bella and run. Forcing herself to find clarity through the pain, Jasmine wondered why Josh was just sitting there with her. Why didn't he just knock her out and go? Or take her with him, if he loved her so much?

For that matter, why hadn't he wanted to take her with

them to begin with? Why ask her to cover him while he left the country? Why hadn't the three of them just gone?

It wasn't like either of them had ties in California that couldn't be broken.

Especially now that he thought he'd turned her against Greg.

Whether he had or not, she didn't know. She was still thinking about that one, too.

The detective had done what he said he was going to do. He had said he was going to work so hard to find dirt on her brother.

But then, she wouldn't have expected any less of him. She'd asked him to find the truth.

The circle just continued. She'd get to that point and start over.

Same with Josh. Why? Why were they just sitting here?

"Do you really think, if you keep me here long enough, that I'm going to agree to cover for you while you leave with Bella? You think I won't call the cops the second I get a chance? Or were you thinking you'd make sure I didn't have the opportunity?"

She needed only one thing from at the moment. The thing she'd always counted on. His honesty.

"I hoped you'd love me enough to just leave Bella here with me," he said. Shaking his head. Giving her the first glimmer of hope she'd had all night.

"Then come with me, Josh. We'll forget this ungodly night ever happened. Go back. Face the charges and move on. You can leave the country later if you want, when you've gone through counseling and whatever else you have to do to win back full custody of Bella."

He shook his head. "Heidi's never going to stop."

That woman again.

"She will if you press charges against her for violating the new restraining order," she pointed out. "She'll go to jail for sure on a third count."

She heard a car then, almost fainted with relief. Somehow Greg must have found her.

Obviously hearing the car, too, Josh jumped up. Went to look through the blind into the darkness. And then over to the door.

Taking the key out of his pocket, he opened it and let their visitor inside.

"What's she still doing here?"

Heidi.

And her former sister-in-law was clearly not happy to see her.

Chapter Twenty-Four

"I thought you were going to get rid of her." Heidi walked into the room, in jeans and boots and a leather jacket with fur trim, as though she owned the place.

As far as Jasmine had known, no one but she and Josh had ever known about the cottage. He'd specifically told her he'd never informed Heidi about it. Because they'd made a pact to keep this one place sacred. They knew they could trust each other.

More of her world crumbled around her.

Not only did Heidi know about the cottage, she'd known they were there.

Josh had been expecting her.

"She's my sister," Josh said, as if that explained everything.

"Is Bella here?"

"Of course."

"I want to see her."

Bracing for Heidi's anger when Josh told his ex that he wasn't going to disturb the toddler, Jasmine sat, open-mouthed, while he moved toward the bedroom door instead. Just like that. He followed her orders.

And just like that, for the first time all night, he left Jasmine alone.

And in that second, she not only understood that she had to save her own life—and Bella's—she had to do it immediately. Shoving her hand into her purse—something she hadn't been able to do with Josh watching her all night—she quickly pushed and held the cell phone's power button.

Making a call was clearly out of the question. But if she knew Greg at all as well as she thought she did, he'd be looking for her.

And her phone would be on his radar.

"We've got to get going, Josh."

Heidi was whispering, but the sound held such fury, Jasmine could hear every word. They were still back at the bedroom door, but she could see half of Josh and knew he was watching her.

She could make a run for it. Could probably drive far enough to get help. Further if need be. She hurt like hell. She wasn't incapacitated.

But that would leave them with Bella, and she was certain that no matter how quickly the police got to the cottage, the baby wouldn't be there.

"We'll have to take her with us."

"No. This whole thing. You promised, Joshua. You said you'd put me first."

"You said you'd drop the charges if I got her to bring Bella up here."

"And then we'd leave the country. You promised. We're going to live someplace where our little issues aren't an issue. Where we can raise our daughter together."

Their voices were rising. If Bella wasn't waking, she would be soon.

"The charges have to be dropped first. You have to refuse to testify. Say you were lying or something."

"But you were going to get her to refuse to testify against me for that stupid hair-pulling thing. Who ever heard of going to jail for pulling someone's hair?"

As Jasmine listened, she felt sicker. And stronger, too.

"I can hear you two," she said. Her father's daughter again. The one who didn't just sit and take it without being heard.

"Yeah, well, you weren't supposed to still be here," Heidi said snottily, coming farther into the living space. "We're going to have to tie her up," Heidi added. "And leave her here. By the time someone finds her, we'll be long gone."

"Not until I have proof that you've said you won't testify."

She flashed her phone at him. "It's on airplane mode." She let him read what was there. "Sent an hour ago. My full confession that I was lying about all the things I said you did to me. My agreement to go back to counseling. And to pay all legal fees."

Because Josh was going to make certain that she got to live with Bella as her mother. In another country.

There was no reason for them to stick around then. Whether Josh was present or not, the case would go away.

"I have to be here until Thursday," he told Heidi, glancing toward Jasmine. "I have to appear or they're going to get suspicious. I'm not leaving this undone."

"The case will be dropped later today," Heidi told him.

Jasmine wasn't sure the other woman was wrong. It could happen that quickly.

"You should have waited another day to come up here,

love," Josh said, in a voice Jasmine had never heard before. "Like we planned."

"I couldn't be away from you any longer, sweet man. I waited all night…"

Heidi hadn't trusted Josh to turn on Jasmine. More clarity came. So much more. Her brother truly was a victim of his wife. He'd tried to fight it the right way, turning her in the first time. And even standing up to the charges when she came after him this last time.

Thinking he was going to win because he really was innocent.

And then he wasn't.

Heidi had screwed things up by coming after Jasmine. She'd needed more blame to put on Josh, so she'd brought up other times that Josh had been forced to protect their daughter against her and used them against him.

Josh really had been protecting Bella every time Heidi had been hurt. Which was why none of the injuries were serious. He wasn't their father.

He hadn't reached his breaking point as she thought. Not until that night.

He'd never purposefully hurt his wife.

But he'd hurt Jasmine. Just as he'd seen their father do. Not nearly as badly, though. He hadn't been trying to teach her a lesson, or make her afraid of him so he could control. He'd been desperate to have her leave his daughter at the cabin so that Heidi would set him free.

"We're going to have get rid of her," Heidi said. "Just until Thursday. We can say she took Bella away for a few days. The stress of the case was getting to her." Heidi had always been good at coming up with scenarios to fit whatever circumstances in which she'd found herself.

Came from a lifetime of lying to her mother to avoid further beatings, Jasmine guessed.

Maybe not. Maybe she was just a born liar.

"Josh," Jasmine said. "Think about what you're doing here."

Heidi didn't know Jasmine was hurt. Didn't know that in those hours alone in their safe place, Josh Taylor had become an abuser. The injuries didn't ever show, done Taylor style. Should have been a clue to her that Josh hadn't lost it and gone after Heidi. Her wrist injury was clearly visible.

"I love her, Jas," he said, sounding more helpless than she'd ever heard him.

"And I love you, too, sweet man," Heidi said, cuddling up to him.

Jasmine wondered how long it would take Greg to get up there. Didn't let herself consider the possibility that he wouldn't find her. When she'd turned the phone on, she'd turned the ringer off. If he was calling, she wouldn't know. But she pretended to herself that he was. That, right there in her purse, he was reaching out to her.

While he was on his way to find her.

And then she didn't pretend anything anymore as Heidi pulled out a gun and started toward her.

GREG HAD BEEN up most of the night. He'd gone home, lay down for a couple of hours, waiting for the phone to ring. Until he got more to go on, he had nowhere to go. Officers were stationed outside both Jasmine's and Josh's homes. Everyone was on alert. A tip line was active and getting calls. Uniforms were following up on them.

He didn't lie down until almost five. Slept restlessly

through his workout time. And was in the shower when he heard his line ring.

Dripping, he grabbed it up. Heard that Jasmine's phone had pinged and was out the door in jeans and the sweatshirt he'd had on the night before, unshaven and with his hair still wet, still asking questions and giving orders. Officers were already all over the area. Greg was to be called the second there was any sign of any of the three missing persons.

If they were too late…if Josh had hurt her…either of them…

Putting his bubble on his dash, he put his foot to the floor and drove toward his future. Whatever it turned out to be.

THEIR CARS HAD been located. He got the report while he was still twenty minutes from the remote cottage that wasn't even on any books. The land it sat on was registered as vacant.

And owned by a company that hadn't yet been linked to anything pertaining to Josh or Jasmine Taylor. It was close to the vacation home in which they'd spent so much of their time growing up. That couldn't be good.

Neither could the fact that there were three vehicles, not two, parked there. The third one being registered to Heidi Taylor.

Heart pounding, he asked the detective in charge, the one whose jurisdiction they were in, to please tread carefully. He didn't know about Josh, but he was certain that Heidi Taylor was unstable enough to do serious damage. Possibly even kill if she felt threatened. Detective Meridian told Greg he appreciated any help he could give him and said he'd keep in touch.

SHOTS HAD BEEN fired from inside the cottage. He got the call five minutes out. Detective Meridian believed they'd been warnings to him and his men. They'd counted three blasts, and there were three holes in the front window, which was covered by blinds.

No one knew for certain that little Bella was inside, but it was assumed that she was. Her empty car seat was in Jasmine's vehicle.

Jasmine would know what Greg had done by now, for sure. She'd know that he hadn't protected her brother as she'd assumed he'd been doing. He still didn't regret having done his job. She'd needed the truth. He'd gone after every piece of it he could find.

William's call the night before, Josh's continued refusal to take a plea deal that was sweeter than he could have hoped for…he didn't get that.

Meridian was waiting for him when he pulled up. He not only saw the man's badge clipped to his hip, but he also recognized the authority with which Meridian viewed the scene.

He filled Greg in on a few particulars. Movements they'd seen in the house. The fact that no one was answering their phones.

"Other than Jasmine's they seem to be turned off," he said. "They ring twice and go to voice mail."

He'd called her phone a couple of times since he'd heard it was back on. He'd had no response, either. "It's possible that she's got the volume down. That they don't know she has it on."

Jasmine was a smart woman. A true survivor. She knew what to do.

He had to believe that would be enough to get her and Bella out of this alive. Couldn't consider any other option.

A split second of panic hit as he glanced toward the house. A vision of his father slumped over the steering wheel the other night.

Same kind of stark, cold, horrifying fear. Like he was losing someone he…

He loved Jasmine. God in hell, what a time to figure that one out.

Didn't matter to him if they lived in separate countries for the rest of their lives, he loved her. Would always love her. She owned his heart, and he had to get her out of there alive.

"Let me go in," he said, removing his gun from his hip. "I know all three of them. Have had the trust of two of them at one time or another. It's a family thing," he said. Meridian already knew the basics.

"No way," the detective said. "I could be sending you into a massacre. I've called the negotiators. We've got a DV specialist on staff…"

"I'm a specialist," Greg said. He'd worked with the High-Risk Team. That made him special enough, as far as he was concerned. "I'm going in, Detective," he added, walking toward the door. "You can cover me or not."

His advance was slow, giving everyone notice that he was coming in. They could shoot him dead. Or they could talk to him. Either way, they weren't leaving on their own. And they weren't taking Bella with them.

As he walked, it occurred to him that Jasmine could have been in on it with her brother. That she and Josh were trying to take Bella and get away and that Heidi somehow found out. He wouldn't have put it past the other woman to have been having Josh watched.

They all had cause to hate him. He kept walking.

Thinking of Jasmine's cell phone going live. She had to have turned it on. A cry for help.

And help was there in the dozens.

"DETECTIVE JOHNSON'S HERE. He's walking toward the house."

Heidi, whose gun was held strategically behind her back, but pointing at Jasmine, made the statement in a happy-go-lucky voice.

"I do it!" Bella's equally happy voice rang out from the kitchen table, where Josh was feeding her breakfast and she wanted to hold her cereal spoon. Thank God for that baby. If she hadn't woken up at Josh's sharp rebuke of Heidi when she'd pulled the gun on Jasmine earlier, Jasmine would most probably be dead.

And the three of them would be on their way to Mexico. And beyond.

Greg was here. The knowledge gave her a sense of calm. It was all going to be over soon.

In the space of time since Heidi had first pulled the gun on her—a couple of hours, at least—Josh had tended to Bella, sat with her first and rocked her back to sleep for a bit, right there on the couch with Jasmine. Held his daughter while she slept. And then washing her up and getting her dressed—with clothes he'd brought for her from home, probably for a much longer trip—as was her usual routine.

Her "Hi, Mommy" when she walked out was as normal as could be. Bella was secure. Happy. With her family. But she didn't rush over to hug her mother. Didn't go to her at all.

The entourage outside had arrived while Josh had been

dressing Bella. Only God knew what would happen next. Would Heidi kill them all? And then shoot herself?

Like she'd shot off rounds when she'd first known cops were outside?

It happened. More often than a lot of people knew.

Jasmine had to pee, but there was no way she was going to get up off that couch, give Heidi a chance to accompany her through the bedroom and get her alone.

And yet…an idea occurred to her. They were all out there. If she got Heidi away from Bella, Greg would get the toddler and get her to safety…

Looking at Heidi by the door, she leaned forward, planning to stand, figuring she had to time things just right. A shard of pain hit her left side so sharply it took her breath away. She relaxed again, knowing that she'd have to factor the ribs into her plan.

"I'm coming in!" Greg's voice sounded in the distance. "I'm unarmed. Just want to talk."

"He's got his hands in the air," Heidi said, again in that singsong voice, as though giving good news to a child. At least the woman had learned enough to keep things light and easy around Bella. Josh had gotten through to her, at least a little bit. "I'm letting him in."

Tears sprang to Jasmine's eyes. Staring straight ahead when all she wanted to do was look at that door, to see Greg at least once more, she didn't move. Didn't dare give Heidi any indication that she cared one way or the other about the man. Josh knew she'd fallen for the detective. If Heidi didn't, they needed to keep it that way.

Not that she could count on her brother to be on her side anymore. He was so in love with his abusive wife, so controlled by her that…

The door opened.

Chapter Twenty-Five

"Detective, I'm so glad to see you." Heidi sounded like she was welcoming royalty. "I've been waiting for you."

What?

"I just knew, after you sent the officers to my place last night, that you'd have someone watching me," she continued, as though passing along an interesting piece of gossip. "I knew that I'd be followed up here. And we can end this once and for all. When I heard they were gone, I figured this was where they'd come and if I could get you all up here, you'd see what I've been saying all along. Jasmine and Josh…they're this impenetrable team. They were planning to run away together. To take all their money and my daughter and leave the country and I'd never see my sweet Bella again…"

What in the hell? What in the…

Her head screamed so loudly she couldn't find a clear thought. Heidi and *Greg* were in this together? But…

No, that didn't make sense. Why would Greg need to trap her and Josh? They already had their win. Whether Josh took the plea or not.

Obviously, someone had noticed her and Josh missing.

That had to mean Greg had been trying to contact her, right? Because they were…more than friends. He'd found out the truth like she'd asked. It would have been unethical for him to tell her. He'd wanted to wait to make love until after the trial.

She might not get out of there alive, but she could sit there thinking about Greg if she wanted to. Obviously distracting Heidi wasn't going to work now.

"Is everyone okay here?" Greg's voice, soft and sure... it was like warm blood in her frozen veins.

"We're all fine, but only because you got here," Heidi said, lowering her voice as well. "Josh had a gun. I had no idea."

"Shots were fired."

"That was Josh. Warning you all to back off."

Feeling like the statue she'd become, Jasmine didn't say a word. Wasn't sure how much Josh could hear. He'd taken Bella fully into the kitchen alcove and was talking to her loudly. About the difference between chocolate and regular milk and how chocolate had sugar and cereal had sugar and too much sugar in the morning...

"Ms. Taylor? You okay?" It took her a second to realize that Greg was talking to her. And had the inane realization that her ponytail had come loose. He could probably see her bald spot.

She made a half turn before her ribs screamed at her. "Yes. I'm fine," she said, knowing she didn't sound like herself at all. Hoping he'd hear the pain in her voice. Realize that she was injured. In case he was counting on her climbing mountains in the next minute or two. She'd do it, of course, but she couldn't guarantee how well.

Or how long she'd remain conscious.

"Okay, Heidi, what you did, bringing us here, helped a lot. Except, maybe, it would have been safer for you if you'd just told us where you thought they were."

"I could have been wrong," Heidi said, sounding completely rational now. "Besides, I had to see for myself," she told him. "I need to see them both taken away, and I knew if I asked if I could come along, you wouldn't let me."

The woman was diabolical. She truly did have an answer for everything.

"We'll get to that," Greg said. "But first, before anyone gets excited here, we need to get Bella out of here. Just let me take her out and then I'll bring officers in to arrest these two."

Greg was placating Heidi. He had to be. Surely he didn't believe her.

But Jasmine might have, given the same circumstance, if she didn't have years of living with Heidi's lies behind her. The other woman had twisted her and Josh up in knots for over a year before they'd come together, talked and figured out what was going on.

"Bella, look! It's a police car with bright lights! You want to go see it?" Josh's voice sounded behind Jasmine. She couldn't see him. Couldn't see her precious little baby girl. But she held her breath, waiting for Bella to get safely past her mother.

"Police car! Let's see! You want to see, Auntie JJ?"

"In a minute, sweet pea!" Jasmine called, wanting to turn but fearing the pain if she did so. She had to be ready and able to move. While Heidi's gun was no longer trained on her, she had no way of knowing whether or not Greg knew Heidi was the one armed.

"Detective Johnson's going to take you out to show you how the bright lights work," Josh said. "Daddy's going to put the milk away and be right out and then you can show me what you learned!"

Josh sounded as though they were going on a ride at the playground. A testament to how much he loved his daughter. And wanted her life free from witnessing violence. After all this, he was handing her over without a fight. Making it fun for her to go. Without even a kiss goodbye.

Jasmine wanted to be surprised by that. Strangely, she wasn't. Josh had always put Bella first.

Heidi locked the door again as soon as Greg was through it. Locking the three of them in. And that's what this was all about. Heidi was insanely jealous of Greg's relationship with Jasmine. And then, later, with Bella, but mostly it was Jasmine.

"Josh, come over here." Heidi was pointing her gun straight at Jasmine again. With Bella out of the way, there was nothing stopping her from shooting. Josh had already made his choice between the two of them clear.

She wasn't going to beg.

"Here's how this will work. You say Jasmine was the one with the gun. It's stolen, so there's no way to tell who really brought it up here. She knew you were up here. She purposely brought Bella to put you in a position where you'd be violating visitation if you were caught. She's here to force you into giving her custody of Bella, which is what she's been after all along. You and I, we love each other. We're just trying to get through our issues, get our counseling and be a family." She looked at Josh. "Right, sweet man?"

Josh just looked at her, standing there holding the gun trained on Jasmine. Heidi barely glanced in his direction. She was too busy doing what she did.

"Jasmine held you at gunpoint. Then I showed up unexpectedly, because she didn't know you'd told me about this place, and told me you were going to be up here, and I'd just managed to get the gun away from her before the cops got here and that's when you grabbed it and the gun accidently went off…"

Pounding came from the other side of the door. "It's Johnson. Let me in."

Heidi looked at Josh. "Got it, sweet man? We pin this on her. You go to your hearing on Thursday and take the plea—you're right about that. You need to have things all cleared up. And then we're through our counseling and put this mess behind us, we take Bella and go. Just like we planned…"

Josh looked at Jasmine. Greg pounded on the door a second time. Calling out for Heidi. Asking if she was okay.

"We didn't plan to leave the country, Heidi," Josh said, moving in slightly, closer to the couch. "I didn't tell you I was up here. You must've figured it out when the cops came to you last night, thinking you were involved in our disappearance. That's the first you knew of it, but you tried to reach me, you couldn't and so you came up here. Hoping they'd follow, just like you said."

Jasmine's eyes filled with tears, and this time, they spilled down her cheeks.

"I do love you," Josh continued. "I'd do almost anything for you. But I will not hurt Jasmine because of you or anything you do to me, to Bella, to anyone. I won't hurt her again. Not ever again."

She couldn't see through her tears, gave a single sob that rent through her upper body with blinding pain.

"Lower the gun, Heidi, please," Josh said. "Open the door. We can say whatever we need to say about what happened up here. We'll let the current charges play out against both of us and see where that leaves us. We can talk about the future. But right now, just put down the gun and open the door before you do something from which we can't recover."

She saw the look come over Heidi's face and knew that her brother had failed. Jasmine loved him so much for trying, though. He'd come through for her. Greg had, too. Bella was safe.

She could go.

"No!" Heidi screamed. "It's never going to end. You and her. Shutting me out. Treating me like I'm the crazy one. The *bad* one. It's all because of the two of you. You... No!" Jasmine saw her trigger finger move.

Was almost relieved to know it was over.

She saw flesh in front of her eyes. A body, flying through the air. Heard glass break.

The shot, when it hit her, wasn't nearly as painful as she'd expected. More like a heavy splash. On her face. Her neck. Maybe her hands.

Greg was there, by the window. She could see him. Was still sitting up, afraid to move in case she died.

"Josh, no!" She heard Heidi's scream. Saw her face, stricken and broken, as she rushed forward, only to be stopped by an armed officer.

Greg was on the floor, kneeling. At her brother's unconscious body.

It took her that long to figure it out.

She hadn't been shot. Josh had.

Her brother had jumped in front of the bullet meant for her.

GREG FELT A PULSE. Blood oozed into a pool on the floor beneath Josh Taylor, and Greg couldn't tell if it was coming from the man's neck, head or upper back. But he felt a pulse.

Officers swarmed the room now. Heidi was being handcuffed. Orders given. A paramedic came rushing in and Greg stood, only one thing in mind.

She was sitting on the couch, crying, holding her stomach, while she stared at her brother. Blood spatter dotted her forehead, cheek and neck.

"He's alive," Greg said to her, the rest of the cacophony in the room fading away as he sat down beside Jasmine, putting an arm around her. "He's losing a lot of blood. His pulse is a little weak but regular." He told her the truth.

"It was meant for me." Her lips mouthed the words more than she spoke them. "It was meant for me." She wasn't sobbing. The only real motions coming from her were the tears dripping down her face.

"He was protecting you," Greg said, trying to pull her more fully into his arms, to put himself in between her and the vision of her brother lying on the floor.

There was talk of blood pressure and other vitals behind him. Someone called for a stretcher, which was already coming in the door.

"Gunshot to the back," someone said.

"That's good news," Greg told Jasmine. It wasn't his head or neck. It still could have his heart.

Jasmine didn't respond to him. She'd slipped into a hell he couldn't penetrate. This wasn't the first time she'd witnessed violence. Or seen blood pooling from her brother's back. The fear Greg had felt after his father's accident, and again the night before, was back. He couldn't lose her now. Couldn't let her lose herself.

"Bella's out there. Are you going to be able to be there for her? Or do you want me to have someone take her?"

He had no idea where the words came from. Was shocked when he heard how heartless he sounded.

"No," Jasmine said, blinking, and looking away from the movement around Josh for the first time as she wiped away her tears. "No. She needs family. Stability. Now more than ever. I'll…um…am I free to go? I'm not under arrest or anything?"

"God, no, you're not under arrest." How could she think so? She was the victim here and…

Heidi's words came back to him. All lies. He'd known that immediately. Just known. And he suspected that Josh Taylor was the victim of an insidious woman, as well.

"Let's get you cleaned up a bit," he said, standing and reaching to support her under her arms as he helped her to stand. After the shock, she might be a bit weak-kneed. "You don't want Bella seeing you like…"

He stopped as Jasmine winced markedly as she stood.

"What's wrong?" he asked, heart pounding. Was the shot a through and through? Had she been hit after all and hadn't said anything? His gaze was poring over her. Looking for blood pools. Other than the spatter, and the tears, she looked unharmed.

"I just…fell," she said. "I actually tripped over Josh's foot on the way in to get Bella. Hurt my left rib."

He noticed a small redness on her chin, too, then. A little scrape. Had the feeling she was lying to him. And let it go. There would be time in the future to find out exactly what had gone on in that cabin.

At the moment, getting her out of there was more important.

JASMINE WATCHED THE paramedics load Josh onto a stretcher. Followed it to the door. Heidi had ben cuffed and lead away. She didn't watch that. Greg wanted Jasmine to ride in an ambulance to the hospital. When she wouldn't even consider doing so, he tried to get her to agree to an emergency room visit. She refused that, too. Her rib might be broken. It wouldn't be the first time.

There was nothing they'd do for it, except maybe wrap it. It was a rib. It hurt like hell. And then it wouldn't.

She didn't even tell him about the headache. One over-the-counter painkiller tablet and a good night's sleep would take care of that. She loved his concern and bit back telling him this wasn't her first rodeo.

It *was* the first time she'd ever had a gun pointed at her.

And the first time she'd seen her brother get shot.

She was shaken up. And was glad Greg was there.

Other than Bella, she couldn't think about the rest of it. Not then. Later. With Bloom. She'd figure it out. Mostly what stood out was that Josh hadn't purposely hurt Heidi. She'd been right about that all along. But Greg's evidence, all lies from Heidi that the prosecutor had believed, had panicked him to the point of doing what he felt he had to do to get Bella and run with her. To keep her safe from her mother.

Because he didn't believe in the system anymore. And he hadn't trusted Jasmine.

Because of her feelings for Greg.

She let the detective drive her and Bella back to Santa Raquel, to The Lemonade Stand. An officer following in Greg's car, with a third car behind that to bring the officer back. Feeling guilty for all the fuss, she just hadn't had the energy to argue about it.

Bella kept asking where Daddy was. She told her

he was busy with work. Told her it was a work and school day.

"I s'posed to show him the lights," she said.

"I know, and he wants to see them, too. You'll get a chance soon." She hoped to God she wasn't lying about that. Would deal with that obstacle when she had to do so.

The little girl, kicking her feet lightly in her car seat as she often did, seemed satisfied with the answer. She never asked about her mother.

Leaving her niece at daycare, where she knew she'd be safe and loved, she had Greg take her home, where their entourage left them.

And then, there they were. Alone. In her house. She couldn't stay, of course. She had to get to the hospital. To Josh.

But for just that one second, she wished that Greg would always be there with her. In her home. In her heart…forever.

Chapter Twenty-Six

Josh was going to be fine. Sore. He'd need therapy to get back full use of his shoulder, but by the next afternoon he'd been released from the hospital. As there were no longer any charges against him, he was free to see Bella. Jasmine knew that if he'd intended to seriously hurt her in the cabin, he'd have succeeded. After speaking to her counselor and Josh's, with his permission, she agreed to bring Bella and stay the first couple of nights with him after his release. He had some real issues to work through; he'd purposely put his foot up to slow Jasmine down, though he hadn't meant her to fall flat on the ground. And he'd backhanded her—though not with full force as their father had done. It was nothing that would hold weight in court in terms of charges. And after the hell Heidi had put him through over the past year, Jasmine wasn't pressing any. Josh had just risked his life to save hers. He deserved a second chance. And he'd already met extensively with his therapist. After visiting her own doctor to make certain that she was fine, and hearing that her ribs were only bruised, Jasmine took Bella to pick her father up from the hospital and then back to her own home for the first time in a while. She didn't see Greg at all.

He called, though. Each night.

And they texted, too, after each of them got in their respective beds. They didn't talk about what had happened, other than Greg asking how Josh was doing. And she asked how his father was getting along.

They didn't talk about cases. Or Heidi.

Or them, either. They just...talked.

Something was different with him. He seemed warmer and yet more distant, too. Maybe he'd had second thoughts about their friendship arrangement.

She wasn't ready to hear about it if he had. She just needed another few days. Long enough to be able to sit up without holding her breath.

"We have to talk," Josh said to her on the second night at his house. Bella was in bed, and she and Josh were in his living room—him lying back in his recliner, where he'd determined he could sleep more comfortably. She'd just come out to check on him before turning in herself.

She shook her head. "Not now, Josh. Someday, maybe. Not now." She was leaving in the morning to head back home, back to work. And taking Bella with her. For the time being.

"Now," he said, pushing the foot of the recliner down as he sat up straight. His movements were slow, controlled. The tears in his eyes weren't.

"Josh." She was on the floor at his feet, kneeling there. Not in submission. Or fear. Nothing but love emanated from her. *Healthy* love. "Don't do this...you saved my life. You were going to die for me. That trumps any and everything else." She'd already come to that conclusion. What had happened in their cottage that night...it was their secret. Two kids who'd grown up in hell and somehow managed to save each other from it, too.

"It's not okay, Jas." Reaching out, he smoothed the hair off her forehead, her cheek. "Hurting you is not okay," he said softly. "Throwing myself in front of that bullet... I'd rather be dead than hurt you."

She covered his hand on her face with her own. "I know." She got it. "I hurt you once, too, Josh," she reminded him. "The important thing is that it never happened again. And it won't with you, either."

She'd worked it all out... He'd been absolutely certain that the only chance of saving Bella from Heidi had been to get her away from Jasmine and out of the country. With Heidi's last lies being believed, Josh had lost all trust in the system.

"You pushed me in desperation, not anger," he said, a look in his eye she'd never seen before. Resolution. Acceptance.

"And that's exactly why you lifted your foot when I was about to take Bella and go. You knew if I did, Heidi would get her."

"I was just in a bad place. Feeling completely trapped. I hadn't done anything wrong, but right wasn't going to win."

"I know." She was glad to know that he knew, too.

"I want to go forward with the custody thing, Jas. Just for now. I want to give you guardianship of Bella." With Heidi in jail, where she would most likely be for the next couple of decades, he could proceed more easily.

"Josh, please. You're such a great dad. And she needs you."

"She needs me healthy, sis. And I'm not. All of these years with Heidi..." The charges against him had been dropped. He'd been telling the truth all along, as Heidi had finally corroborated. Each time she'd been hurt, she'd been egging him on and had worked it so that she got hurt. Even the foot in the door. She'd deliberately put her foot in the way of the door closing. She was hoping, by confessing, to win back Josh's love and support.

"I need some time. Counseling. I need to learn how to trust myself again." He looked at her. "And to forgive myself. And..."

He looked away, and then back again. "I need you to press charges against me, Jasmine."

She stared at him, mouth open. Was he insane? Had he... What on...

"Hear me out," he said when she started to shake her head. Vigorously. "I need you to do it for me. I have to be held accountable. To pay for what I did. Or I'm never going to be able to get past it. It will always be there with me. Unfinished business. But more, I need it for you, Jas. I can't look at you, love you, knowing that I hurt you and you just took it. It's eating me alive inside that I'm that guy." He started to cry. "Please, sis. If you do nothing else for me, please, go to the police. Tell them what happened that night at the cabin."

But Josh...he was a victim who'd made a horrendous mistake and was holding himself accountable to it. He was giving up his daughter until he knew he was well. Pressing charges...the court wasn't going to do anything but recommend counseling.

"I'll tell you what," she offered. "I'll tell Greg. He's an officer of the law. If he thinks we should take it further, we will."

Josh studied her, his bottom lip jutted out. And then he nodded.

"And if he agrees with me, that there's good reason,

for anyone, to not let this go—with the understanding that you complete counseling—then we let it go."

"Let's see what he has to say," Josh told her. But he gave her a sad smile. "I love you so much, Jasmine. I can't believe I let her get to me to the point that I betrayed your trust. Even for a second."

"Yeah. You want to know something I've figured out through all of this?"

He nodded again.

"Trust doesn't die because the human holding it, or giving it, makes one mistake. Trust dies when the same mistakes are repeated multiple times." She was never going to forget that horrible night, or the pain he'd caused her, emotionally and physically. What he'd done wasn't okay. But she'd already forgiven him for it. More, she trusted him not to do it again.

Just as she'd always known Wynne's lack of verbal control that one time had been a momentary overload, not an underlying illness. Or a personality factor.

Josh reached for with his good arm, gave her a gentle hug, about the shoulders, careful of her ribs. "I love you, Jasmine. In so many ways, you are my salvation."

"And you are mine," she told him with complete honesty.

GREG HAD NO idea what to expect when he showed up at Jasmine's house Friday night—her first night home from Josh's. He called just outside the gate to let her know he was there. He'd leave if she asked him to do so.

It was eight thirty. Long since dark. Bella would be in bed. And Jasmine might be lying in bed already, after the week she'd had.

Bella…if things worked out with Jasmine, and he had

to believe they would…he'd have a child in his life full time. Not his biologically, but he wasn't his parents' biological child, either. It didn't take biology to be a good protector and teacher. All it took was love.

And he wanted it.

All of it. The good, the not so good. He wanted what his parents had made with him. A family of his own.

She answered on the first ring, as though she'd been waiting for his call. Sounded excited when he told her he was outside.

If she wanted him over that badly, she could have invited him.

He'd debated what to wear—such a dramatic thing for a guy who lived life on the sidelines—but he was getting more used to the other man who'd been lurking in his skin all these years. Guiding his life.

In black jeans, a button-up shirt and leather slip-ons, he knocked on her door. He wasn't sure about spending the rest of his life living alone. But knew that, for her, he had to try.

Drama had a way of showing you the truth. About yourself. About life—and about those in it.

He didn't get a chance to knock. She was there, pressing her lips against his, her hands on his hips, as though steadying herself. He ached to pull her against him, beneath him, on top, next to him, just to have all of her touching all of him.

And didn't want to hurt her. Those ribs. They were going to have to talk about them.

"You smell so good," she told him. "So…*you*."

So did she. Smell good. He wanted to take her to bed, even just to lie next to her, and smell that scent all night.

Kissing her back, hard and wanting her, he thought about ways they could have sex without hurting her.

Her on top, for sure. Naked. His hands on her hips. Or her nipples. Nipples were good. Not attached to ribs...

He broke the kiss.

They had some details to get through first. Because he was, after all, the guy who took care of things...

Taking his hand, she led him back toward her bedroom. He knew he should stop her. That there was serious business ahead. But watching her move in those leggings, the long shirt hiding most of what he knew was beneath it...wanting to be in bed with her won out.

Wanting to be in *her* bed.

"I've never had a relationship with a child in the house," she was saying. "I told Bella that if she ever wakes up in the night and Auntie JJ's door is closed, then she should just knock and Auntie JJ will answer right away. We practiced and made a game of it. She waited until I opened the door and then laughed and squealed when I made a big deal of her being there."

She was speaking softly as they made their way down the hall. And shut her bedroom door behind them as they arrived.

The suite was opulent. Off-whites. Some gold. Roses. Maroon and darker green pillows propped up against an entire wall of pillows, some with shams that matched the comforter. Off-white with rose prints. He could see into the bathroom from two steps into the room. Could see the garden tub, at least. He knew she had a walk-in tiled shower from a conversation they'd had late one night. And double sinks.

She always only used one—the same one.

"And there's the monitor," she said now, pointing to

the speaker on one of the two nightstands. The right one. She'd said she slept on the right side of the bed. He was a middle, take-up-the-whole-thing guy. When he slept alone.

"Can you stay?" she asked him, reaching for the top button on her blouse. And it occurred to him that she was trying too hard.

Talking too much, but not about anything they needed to discuss.

Walking toward her on the thick carpet, thinking he should have removed his shoes, praying they didn't leave marks, he took both her hands. Sat on the end of the bed with her.

"We need to talk."

Everything about her stilled. Her energy. Her breathing. The way she'd been looking all over the place. Head bowed, she nodded.

"I expect you're going to tell me that you've had a change of heart…"

"I have."

"I don't blame you. At all. My family… Josh and I, we're messy. That whole thing with Heidi. I know it was over-the-top out there. Who does that? What kind of family continues to care about a person like that? How can I understand Josh still loving her? It's just…until you've lived it…"

He listened. It was what he did. He was good at it.

When it seemed like her pause was more than just that, he said, "My change of heart has nothing to do with your family. Or what happened." He thought for a second. "Or rather, it does have some to do with what happened. But then, I realized that as much as I want to be married, to have a traditional home and family life, I want, no… I *need* you more."

Not looking at her, he pulled an envelope out of his back pocket. "I just need you to know, before I say any more, that I will agree to whatever relationship constraints you need. I just have to try…"

He handed her the envelope. All sealed, with the contents notarized.

"What's this?"

"I know it's way too soon to discuss marriage between us," he said. "But I'd like it to be on the table. For the future. I'd like it to be where we're headed. To that end, I've drafted up a pre-confession and had it notarized." He nodded toward the envelope. "It's yours, to keep someplace safe. Someplace I can't get to. In it I admit to being fully at fault for the demise of our relationship."

She sucked in a breath. Dropped the envelope like it burned her. "Is this some kind of joke?" He supposed, from the outside looking in, he was out on a serious limb here. But he knew her. He trusted her.

"I agree to give you our home. To take only my personal possessions when I leave. And to split with you whatever we've earned together. The rest of your money is your own. And… Bella, even if I were to adopt her, too, you'd get full custody."

Jumping up, hands on her hips, she stared at him. "Have you lost your mind? I don't get it. What on earth are you doing here? Because if you think…"

He took one of her hands. As gently as he could with her all het up. Held it between both of hers. "I'm a big man," he started.

She pulled her hand away. Kicked at the envelope with her foot. "I'm not the least bit bothered by your size. I don't really even notice. It's just you." The kick might have been more effective if the envelope had actually moved.

Taking her hand again, he looked her in the eye long enough for her to take a deep breath. She was still blinking more than normal. Something he'd noticed she did when she was pissed. "Hear me out, please?" he asked.

She nodded. Kept looking him in the eye.

"I know you aren't ever going to have cause to use the contents of that envelope, Jasmine. And I trust you so completely I can give it to you knowing that you would never use it without cause. But I also know that it's the only way I can make you feel safe about contemplating a live-in relationship with me. The very first time you feel in danger of being abused, you pull out that envelope. It's your get-out-of-jail-free card."

"Oh God, Greg…" She picked up the envelope, taking a bit of extra time standing back up with it. And then ripped it. Again and again and again. "I don't need this," she told him. "I don't even want it. I want a healthy relationship, not one with escape cards."

Watching the pieces of paper fall to the floor, he was a bit irritated. His plan had been a good one. The only one he could come up with…

Moving her legs around his, she slid onto his lap, facing him. Her hands on his shoulders.

"I want you to have the envelope," he told her, not one to give up easily. "I'll make another copy."

"Make a hundred of them," she said. "A thousand. I don't care. Paper the entire house with them. I'm telling you, I don't need it."

She was looking him right in the eye. Paper the house? As in one? Hers? Or his? Or…just one house?

"I love you, Greg Johnson. So much I can hardly believe it's possible. This is all I've ever wanted. To love and be loved. In my home. Or yours. Or wherever we end up. The others... I was so anxious to have that home I wanted that I jumped too soon. Yeah, I've got a pattern. I am attracted to a certain type of person. And some of it might have to do with my growing up. But that's true for pretty much everyone. What I know now is that I'm a survivor of domestic violence, but not a victim of it. I'm not that person. For whatever reason, I get myself out. I survive. And if I ever find myself in danger again, I'd get myself out again. Or die trying. There are no guarantees in life, but I know myself. I trust me, Greg. Which allows me to trust my feelings for you. And to believe in the trust I feel for you."

That was a whole lot of stuff in a very short time. While the woman of his dreams was straddling his thighs.

Greg wanted to sit right there and savor every bit of it.

"You're saying that you want to move toward..."

"Everything. All of it. One house. One family. Hopefully more than one child."

Well, that pretty much said it all. His heart pounded. His penis shot up beneath his fly in celebration.

"There are some other things we need to talk about," he remembered before he did something foolish, like throw caution to the wind and just...

"I know. Josh, for one. And the whole rib thing. It's been taken care of, but I promised him I'd run it by you..."

"Promised him?"

"Yeah. He wants me to press charges, but I'm not going to. Assuming you agree, of course."

Just damn it to hell. He and his big mouth. His *de-*

tails. Afraid she was going to slide right off his lap and maybe even out of his life, he said, "He did do it, then? Your brother physically abused you?" His voice rose. He tried to temper it. To remain calm. But...

"Yes," she said, putting a finger to his lips. "But hear me out. Please?" She mimicked his earlier request.

And so he did. He sat there and listened to her far into that night. On his lap. And as the conversation continued, propped up on pillows in the dark. He asked questions. Hard questions. She had answers. Some that made him sick to hear.

Sometime in the small morning hours, they both fell silent.

"So... Detective, what do you think about pressing charges?"

He was tired. And yet not exhausted. Sleepy, and so alive. And thinking clearly. "I think I want you to write down everything about that cabin night. Then we have Josh sign it..."

"And have it notarized," she said, a glint in her eye as she turned to him in the darkness.

"Just to be safe."

"Okay."

"Okay?"

"Yeah."

"So, can we lie down and let me hold you for a bit?" He'd prefer sex, but he understood about her ribs.

"This is as lying down as I'm getting right now," she told him. "But I'd love to sit up a while. If you can think of anything I can sit on..."

The woman was going to keep him on his toes. And on his knees. But he knew she'd be right there, kneeling beside him.

He'd been left as trash on a bathroom floor, but he'd been picked up by angels and was destined to spend the rest of his life with one.

"I love you, Jasmine Taylor."

"Not as much as I love you, Detective Johnson."

For once, he knew she was wrong.

* * * * *

COMING SOON!

We really hope you enjoyed reading this book.
If you're looking for more romance, be sure to
head to the shops when new books are
available on

Thursday 8th
July

To see which titles are coming soon, please visit
millsandboon.co.uk/nextmonth

MILLS & BOON

THE HEART OF ROMANCE

A ROMANCE FOR EVERY READER

MODERN

Prepare to be swept off your feet by sophisticated, sexy and seductive heroes, in some of the world's most glamourous and romantic locations, where power and passion collide.

HISTORICAL

Escape with historical heroes from time gone by. Whether your passion is for wicked Regency Rakes, muscled Vikings or rugged Highlanders, awaken the romance of the past.

MEDICAL

Set your pulse racing with dedicated, delectable doctors in the high-pressure world of medicine, where emotions run high and passion, comfort and love are the best medicine.

True Love

Celebrate true love with tender stories of heartfelt romance, from the rush of falling in love to the joy a new baby can bring, and a focus on the emotional heart of a relationship.

Desire

Indulge in secrets and scandal, intense drama and plenty of sizzling hot action with powerful and passionate heroes who have it all: wealth, status, good looks…everything but the right woman.

HEROES

Experience all the excitement of a gripping thriller, with an intense romance at its heart. Resourceful, true-to-life women and strong, fearless men face danger and desire - a killer combination!

To see which titles are coming soon, please visit

millsandboon.co.uk/nextmonth

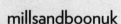